TEEN DOG ™

CREATED, ILLUSTRATED, AND WRITTEN BY
JAKE LAWRENCE

BOOM! BOX ™

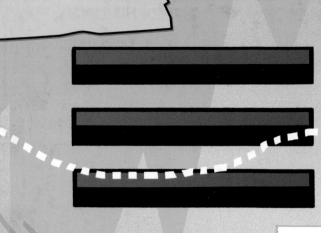

ROSS RICHIE *CEO & Founder*
MATT GAGNON *Editor-in-Chief*
FILIP SABLIK *President of Publishing & Marketing*
STEPHEN CHRISTY *President of Development*
LANCE KREITER *VP of Licensing & Merchandising*
PHIL BARBARO *VP of Finance*
BRYCE CARLSON *Managing Editor*
MEL CAYLO *Marketing Manager*
SCOTT NEWMAN *Production Design Manager*
IRENE BRADISH *Operations Manager*
CHRISTINE DINH *Brand Communications Manager*
SIERRA HAHN *Senior Editor*
DAFNA PLEBAN *Editor*
SHANNON WATTERS *Editor*
ERIC HARBURN *Editor*
IAN BRILL *Editor*
WHITNEY LEOPARD *Associate Editor*
JASMINE AMIRI *Associate Editor*
CHRIS ROSA *Associate Editor*
ALEX GALER *Assistant Editor*
CAMERON CHITTOCK *Assistant Editor*
MARY GUMPORT *Assistant Editor*
KELSEY DIETERICH *Production Designer*
JILLIAN CRAB *Production Designer*
KARA LEOPARD *Production Designer*
MICHELLE ANKLEY *Production Designer*
DEVIN FUNCHES *E-Commerce & Inventory Coordinator*
AARON FERRARA *Operations Coordinator*
JOSÉ MEZA *Sales Assistant*
JAMES ARRIOLA *Mailroom Assistant*
ELIZABETH LOUGHRIDGE *Accounting Coordinator*
STEPHANIE HOCUTT *Marketing Assistant*
SAM KUSEK *Direct Market Representative*
HILLARY LEVI *Executive Assistant*
KATE ALBIN *Associate Assistant*

TEEN DOG, December 2015. Published by BOOM! Box, a division of Boom Entertainment,
Inc. Teen Dog is ™ & © 2015 Jake Lawrence. Originally published in single magazine form as
TEEN DOG No. 1-8. ™ & © 2014, 2015 Jake Lawrence. All rights reserved. BOOM! Box™
and the BOOM! Box logo are trademarks of Boom Entertainment, Inc., registered in various
countries and categories. All characters, events, and institutions depicted herein are fictional.
Any similarity between any of the names, characters, persons, events, and/or institutions
in this publication to actual names, characters, and persons, whether living or dead, events,
and/or institutions is unintended and purely coincidental. BOOM! Box does not read or accept
unsolicited submissions of ideas, stories, or artwork.

A catalog record of this book is available from OCLC and from the BOOM! Studios website,
www.boom-studios.com, on the Librarians page.

BOOM! Studios, 5670 Wilshire Boulevard, Suite 450, Los Angeles, CA 90036-5679.
Printed in China. First Printing.

ISBN: 978-1-60886-729-5, eISBN: 978-1-61398-400-0

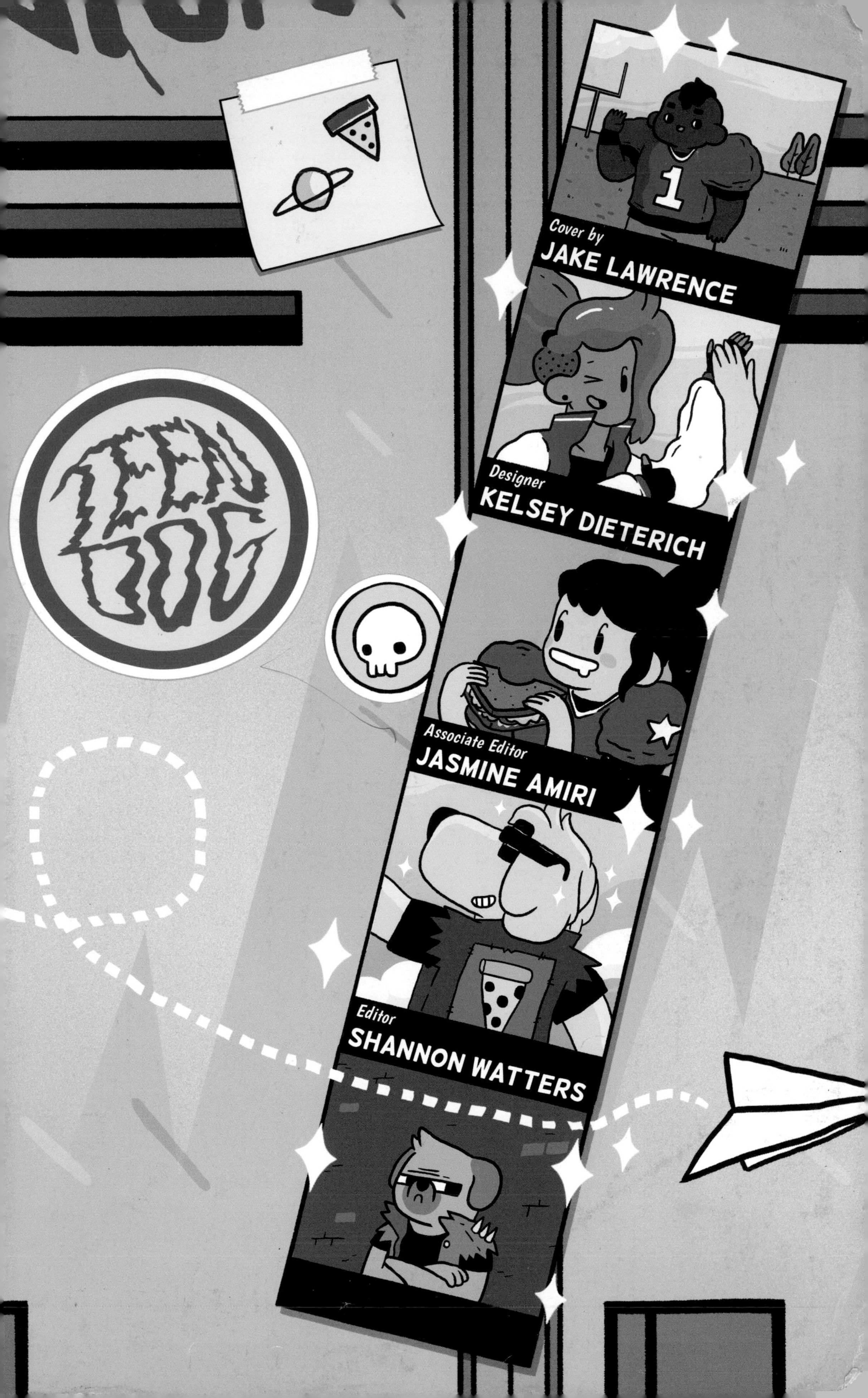

Cover by
JAKE LAWRENCE
Designer
KELSEY DIETERICH
Associate Editor
JASMINE AMIRI
Editor
SHANNON WATTERS

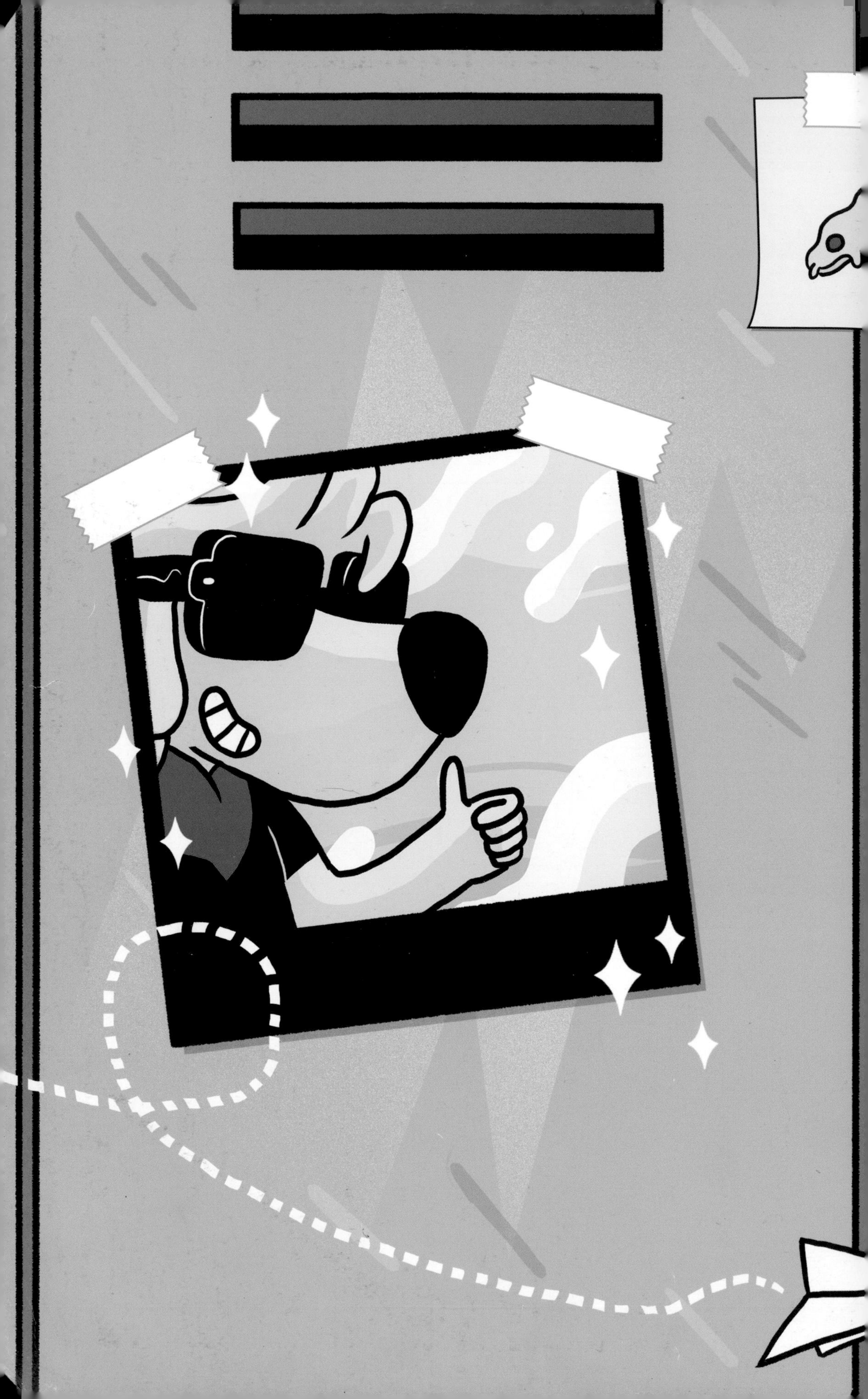

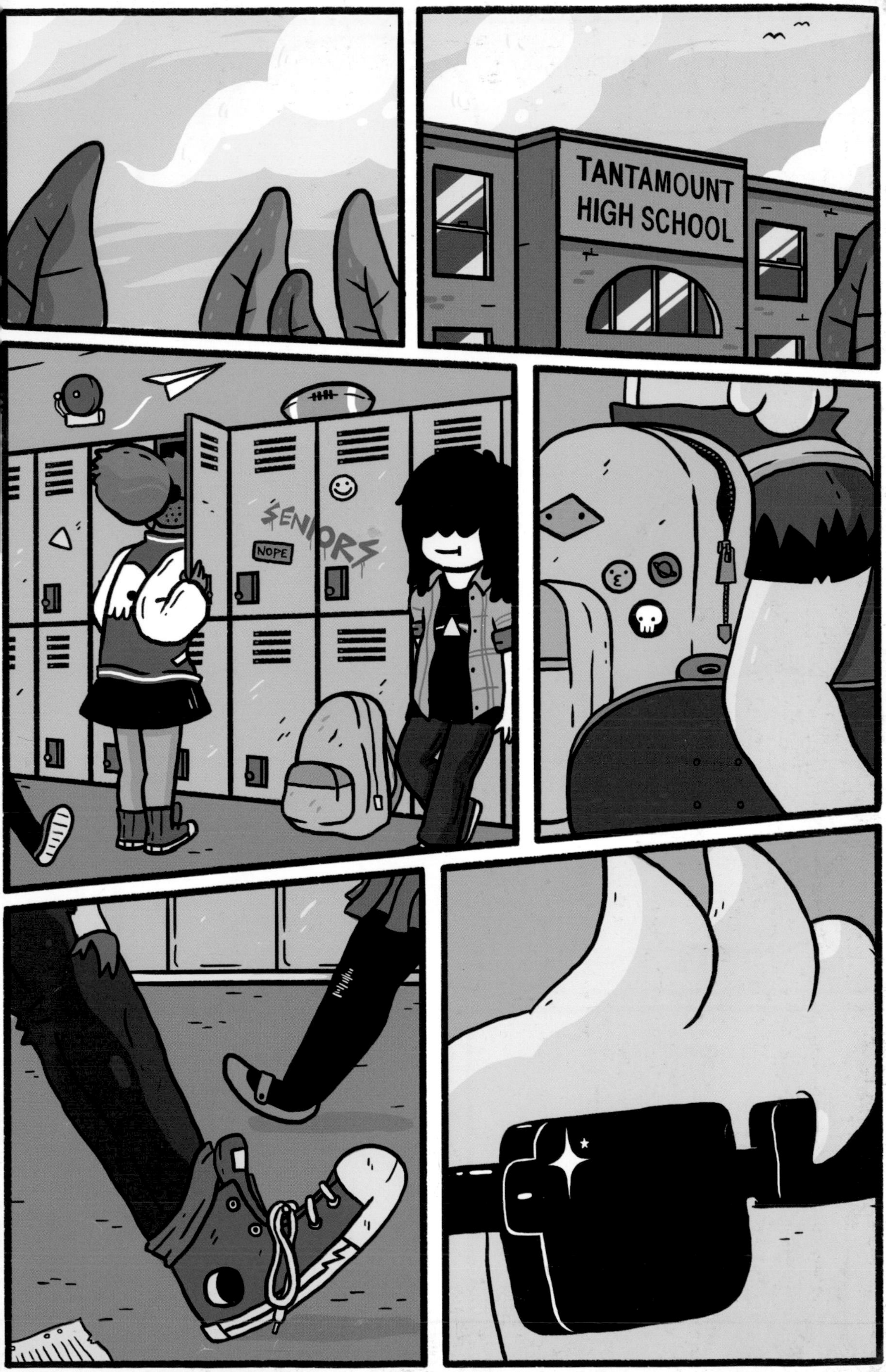
TANTAMOUNT
HIGH SCHOOL
SENIORS
NOPE

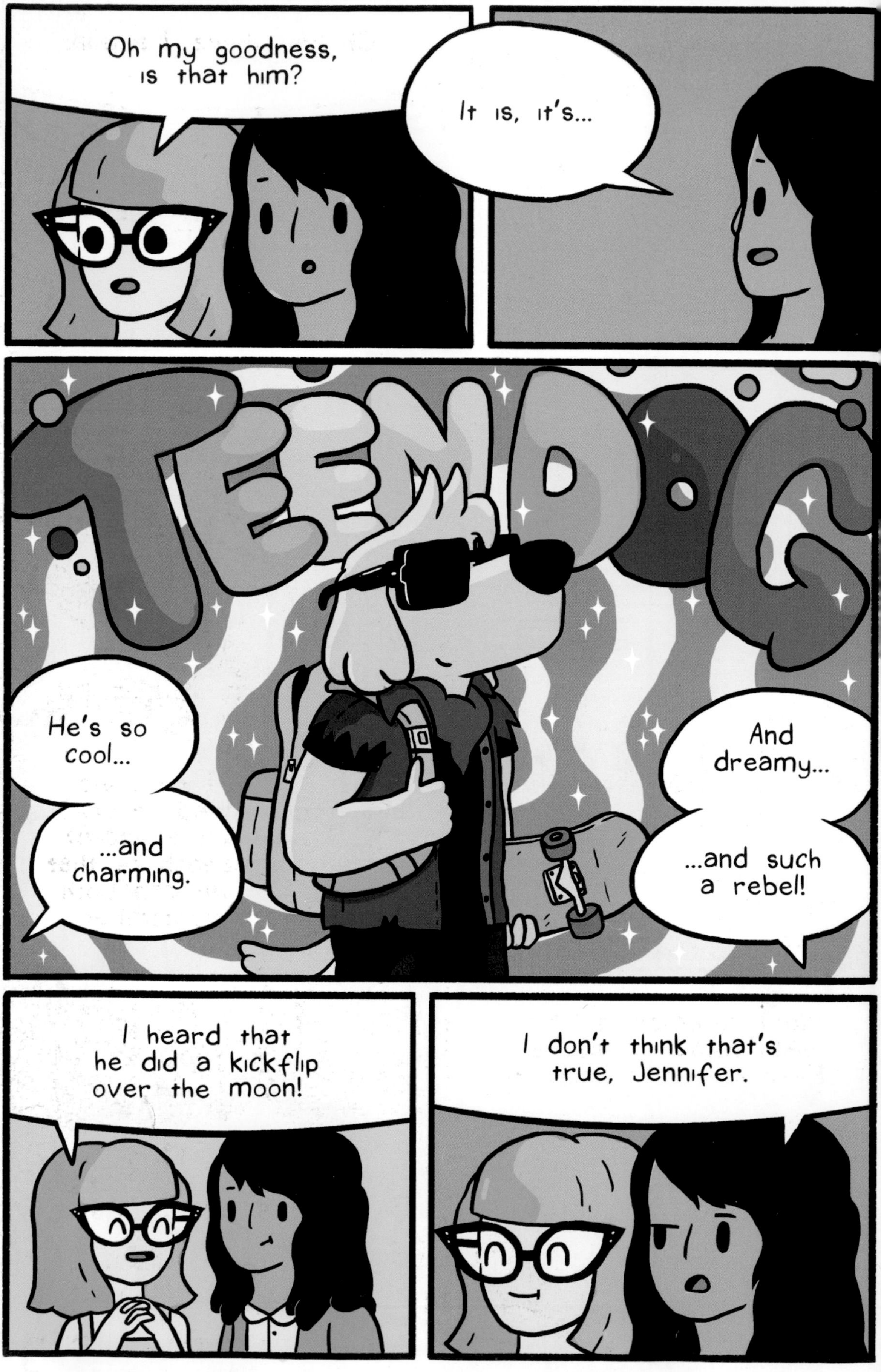
Oh my goodness, is that him?
It is, it's...
TEEN DOG
He's so cool...
...and charming.
And dreamy...
...and such a rebel!
I heard that he did a kickflip over the moon!
I don't think that's true, Jennifer.

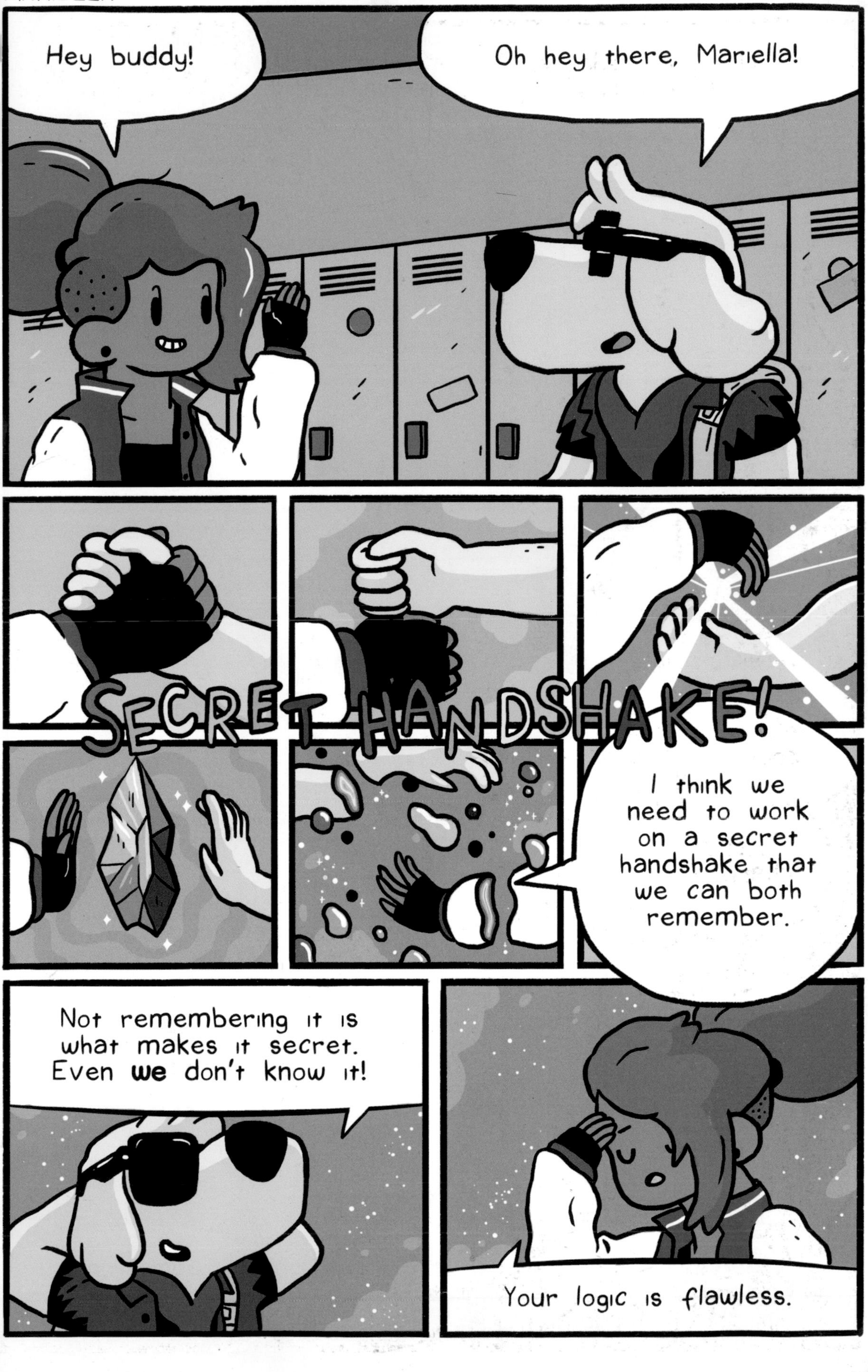
Hey buddy!
Oh hey there, Mariella!
SECRET HANDSHAKE!
I think we need to work on a secret handshake that we can both remember.
Not remembering it is what makes it secret. Even **we** don't know it!
Your logic is flawless.

FOOL PROOF

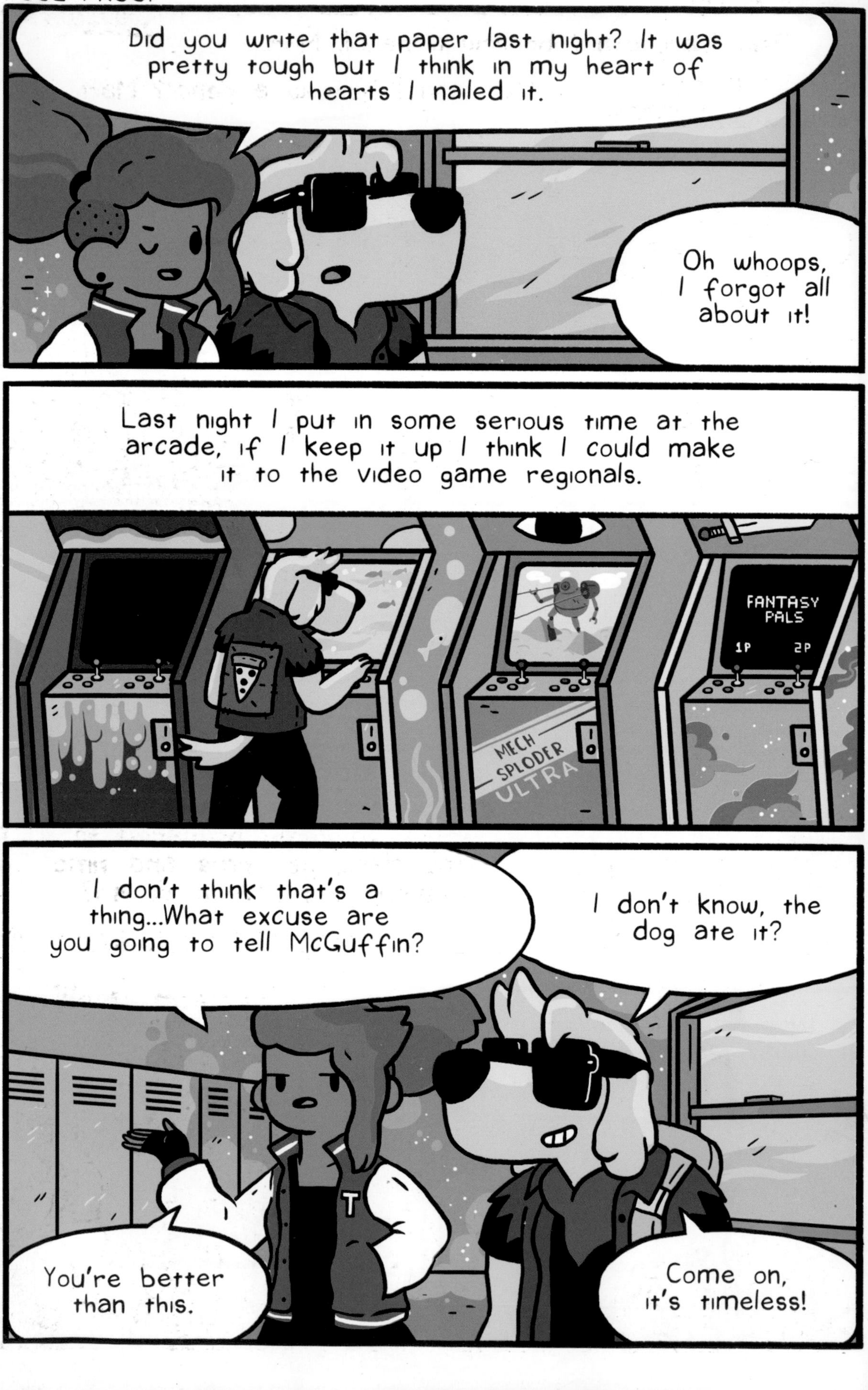
Did you write that paper last night? It was pretty tough but I think in my heart of hearts I nailed it.
Oh whoops, I forgot all about it!
Last night I put in some serious time at the arcade, if I keep it up I think I could make it to the video game regionals.
FANTASY PALS
1P
2P
MECH SPLODER ULTRA
I don't think that's a thing...What excuse are you going to tell McGuffin?
I don't know, the dog ate it?
You're better than this.
Come on, it's timeless!

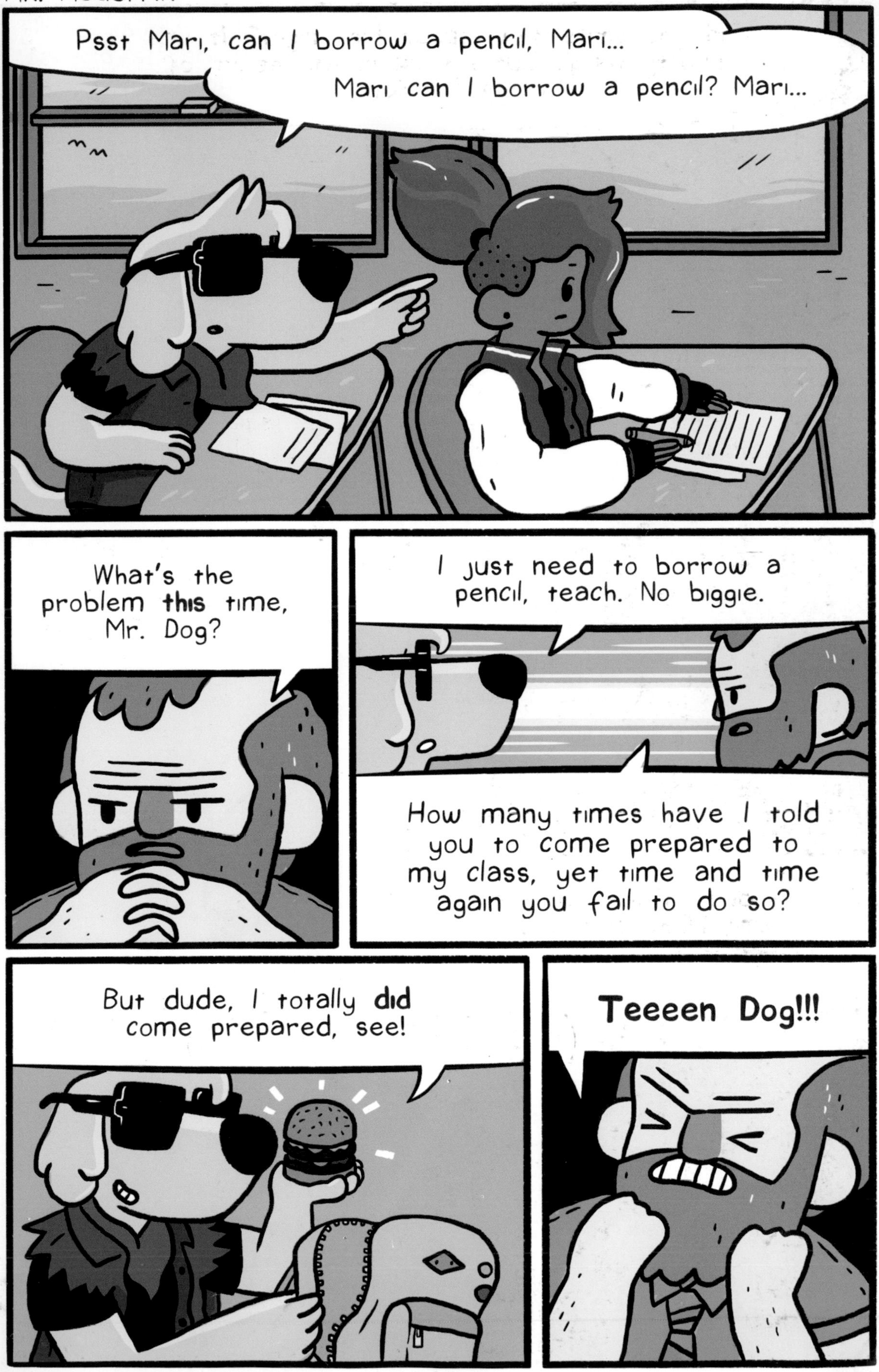
Psst Mari, can I borrow a pencil, Mari...
Mari can I borrow a pencil? Mari...
What's the problem **this** time, Mr. Dog?
I just need to borrow a pencil, teach. No biggie.
How many times have I told you to come prepared to my class, yet time and time again you fail to do so?
But dude, I totally **did** come prepared, see!
Teeeen Dog!!!

THE TEEN DOG TOUCH

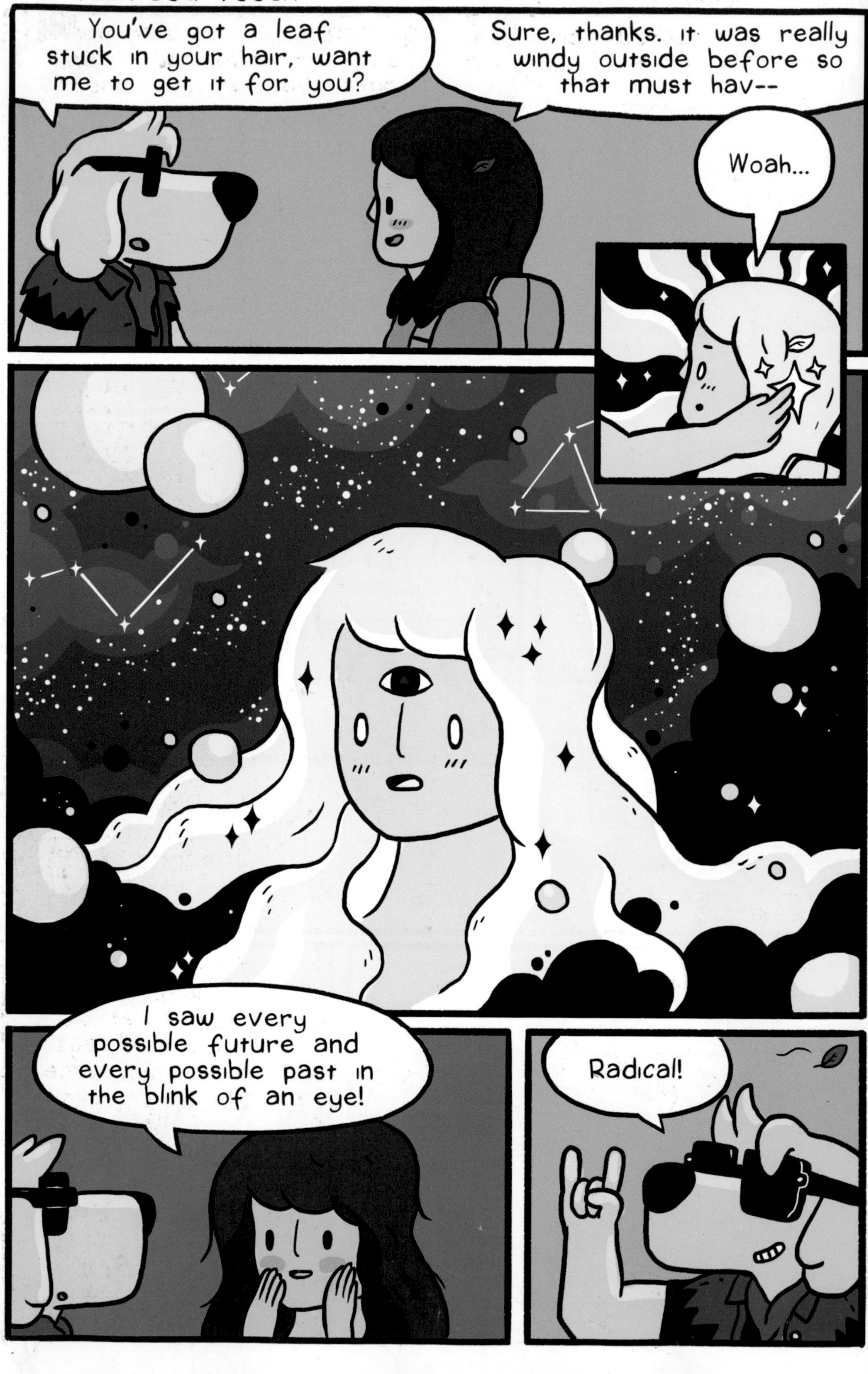

CHAPTER ONE

You've got a leaf stuck in your hair, want me to get it for you?
Sure, thanks. It was really windy outside before so that must hav--
Woah...
I saw every possible future and every possible past in the blink of an eye!
Radical!

ALRIGHT ALRIGHT ALRIGHT

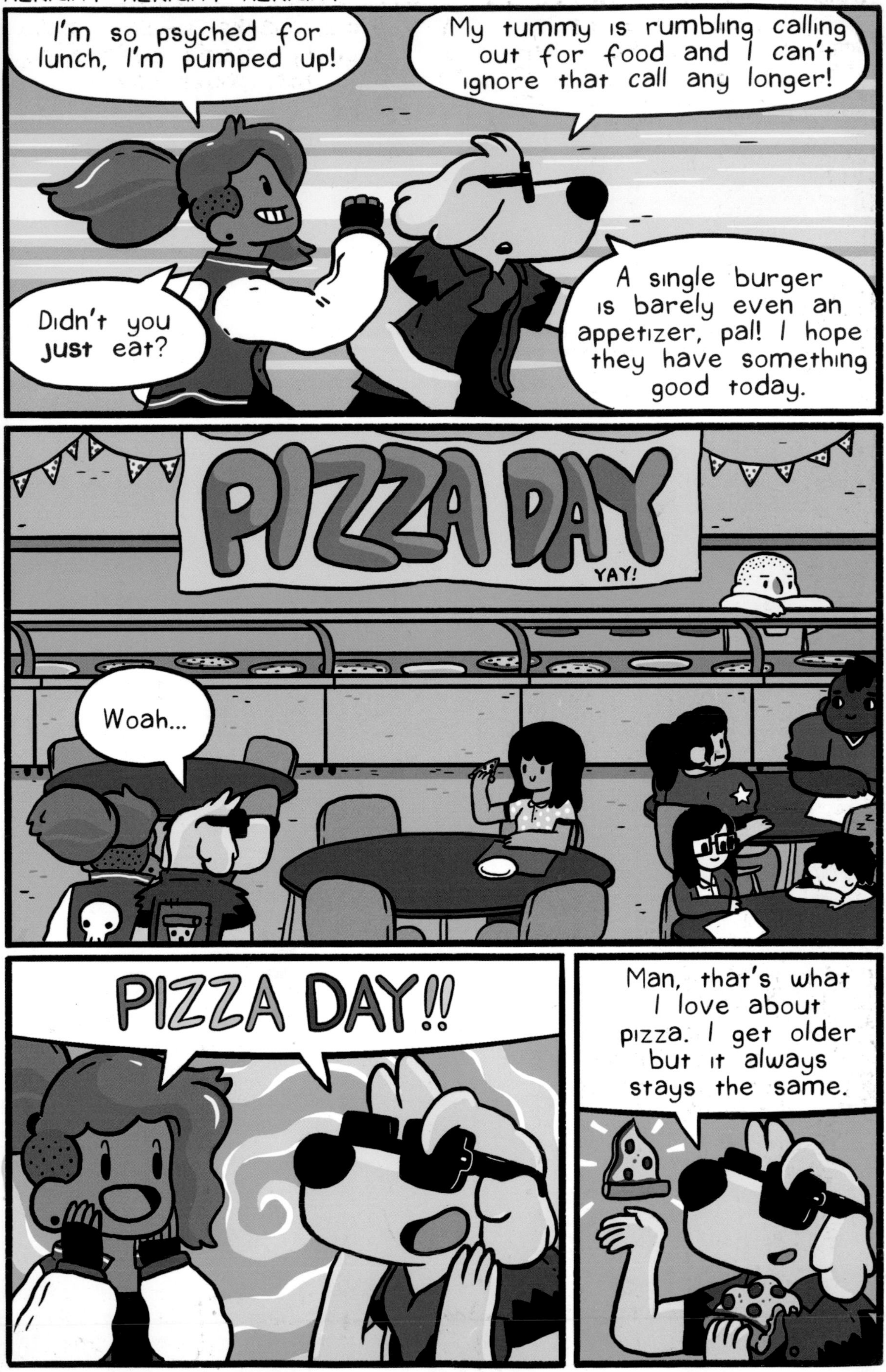
I'm so psyched for lunch, I'm pumped up!
My tummy is rumbling calling out for food and I can't ignore that call any longer!
Didn't you **just** eat?
A single burger is barely even an appetizer, pal! I hope they have something good today.
PIZZA DAY
YAY!
Woah...
PIZZA DAY!!
Man, that's what I love about pizza. I get older but it always stays the same.

FACTIONS

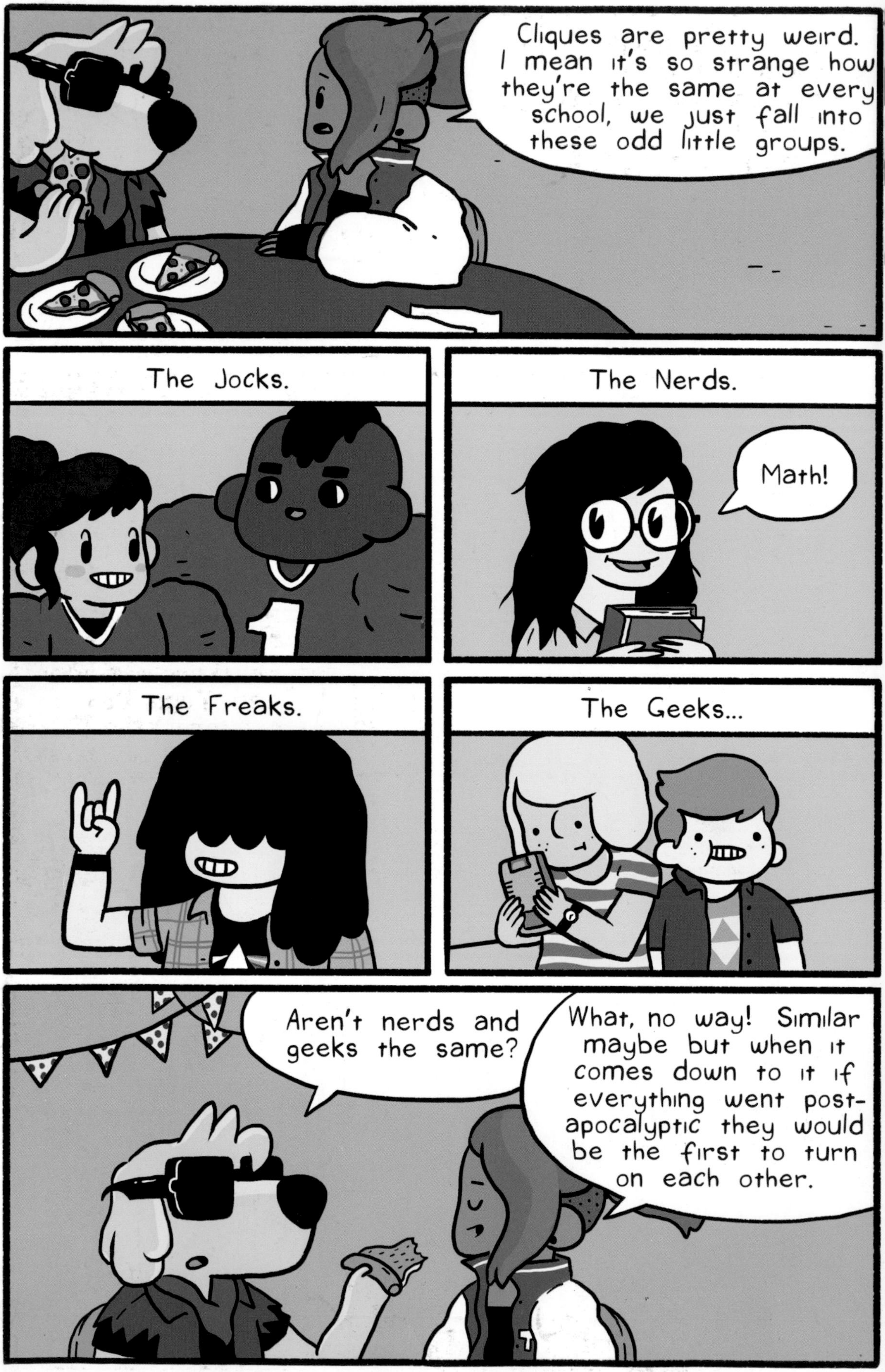
Cliques are pretty weird. I mean it's so strange how they're the same at every school, we just fall into these odd little groups.
The Jocks.
The Nerds.
Math!
The Freaks.
The Geeks...
Aren't nerds and geeks the same?
What, no way! Similar maybe but when it comes down to it if everything went post-apocalyptic they would be the first to turn on each other.

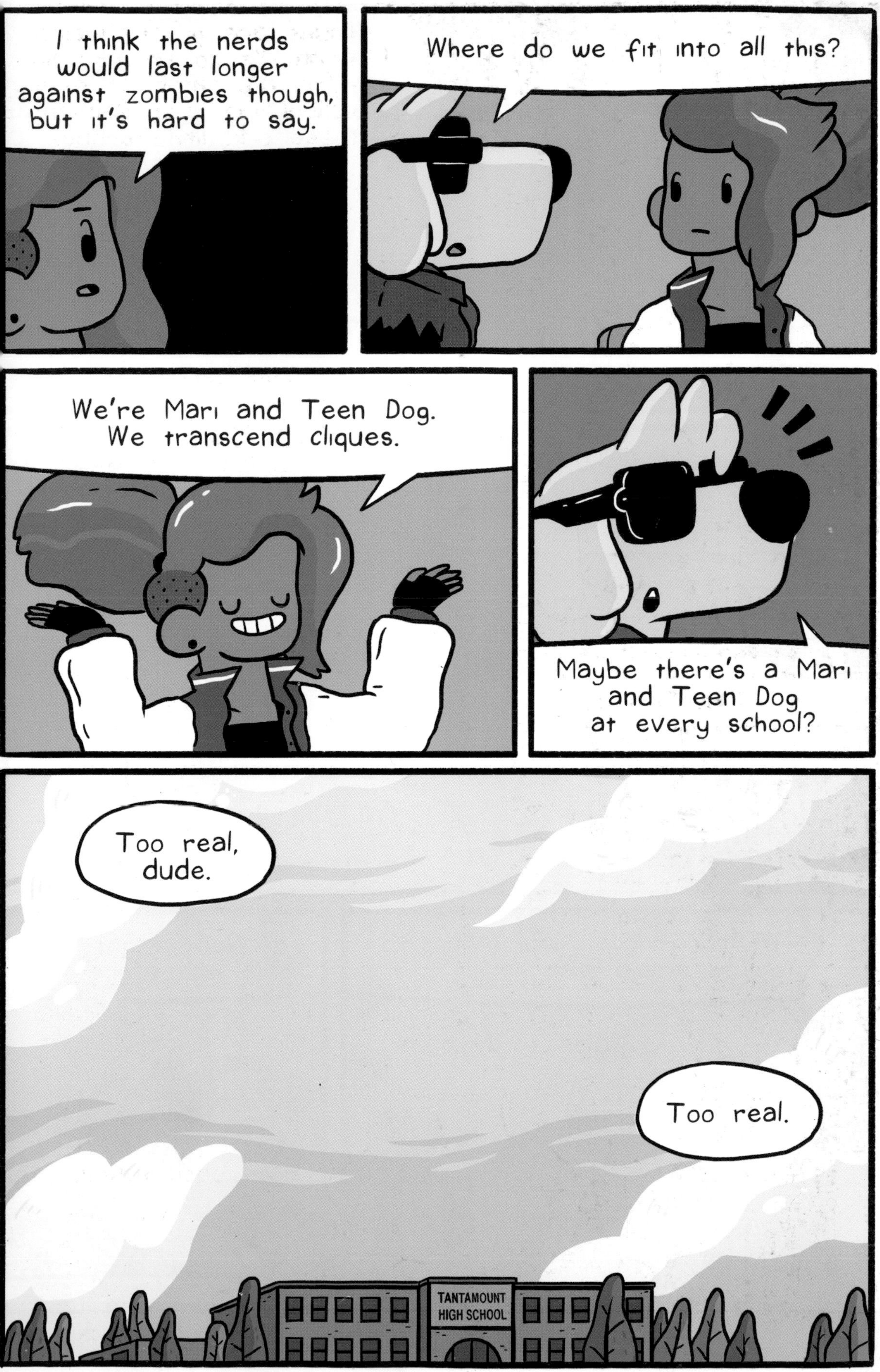
I think the nerds would last longer against zombies though, but it's hard to say.
Where do we fit into all this?
We're Mari and Teen Dog. We transcend cliques.
Maybe there's a Mari and Teen Dog at every school?
Too real, dude.
Too real.
TANTAMOUNT HIGH SCHOOL

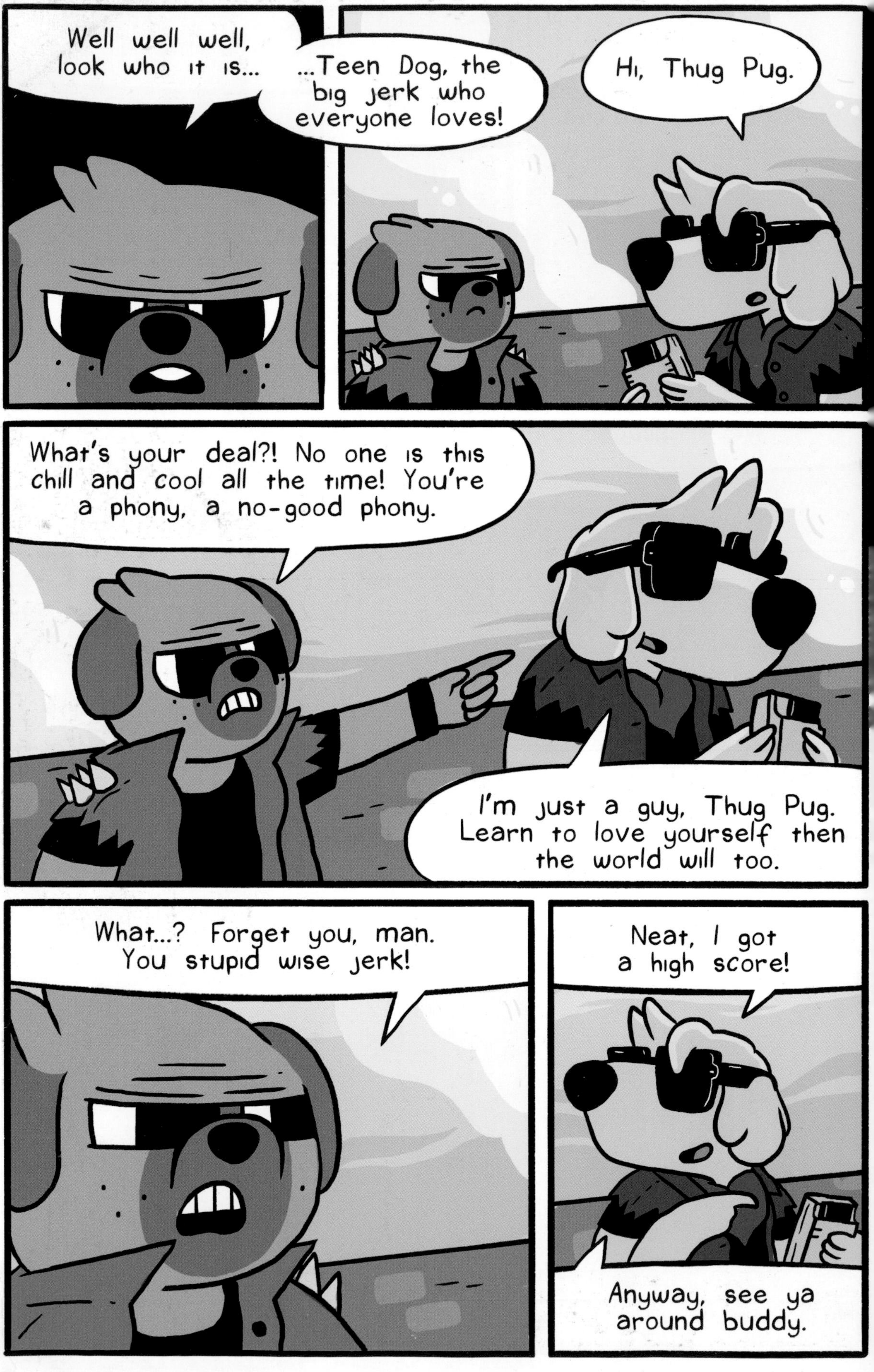
Well well well, look who it is...
...Teen Dog, the big jerk who everyone loves!
Hi, Thug Pug.
What's your deal?! No one is this chill and cool all the time! You're a phony, a no-good phony.
I'm just a guy, Thug Pug. Learn to love yourself then the world will too.
What...? Forget you, man. You stupid wise jerk!
Neat, I got a high score!
Anyway, see ya around buddy.

DEEP THOUGHTS

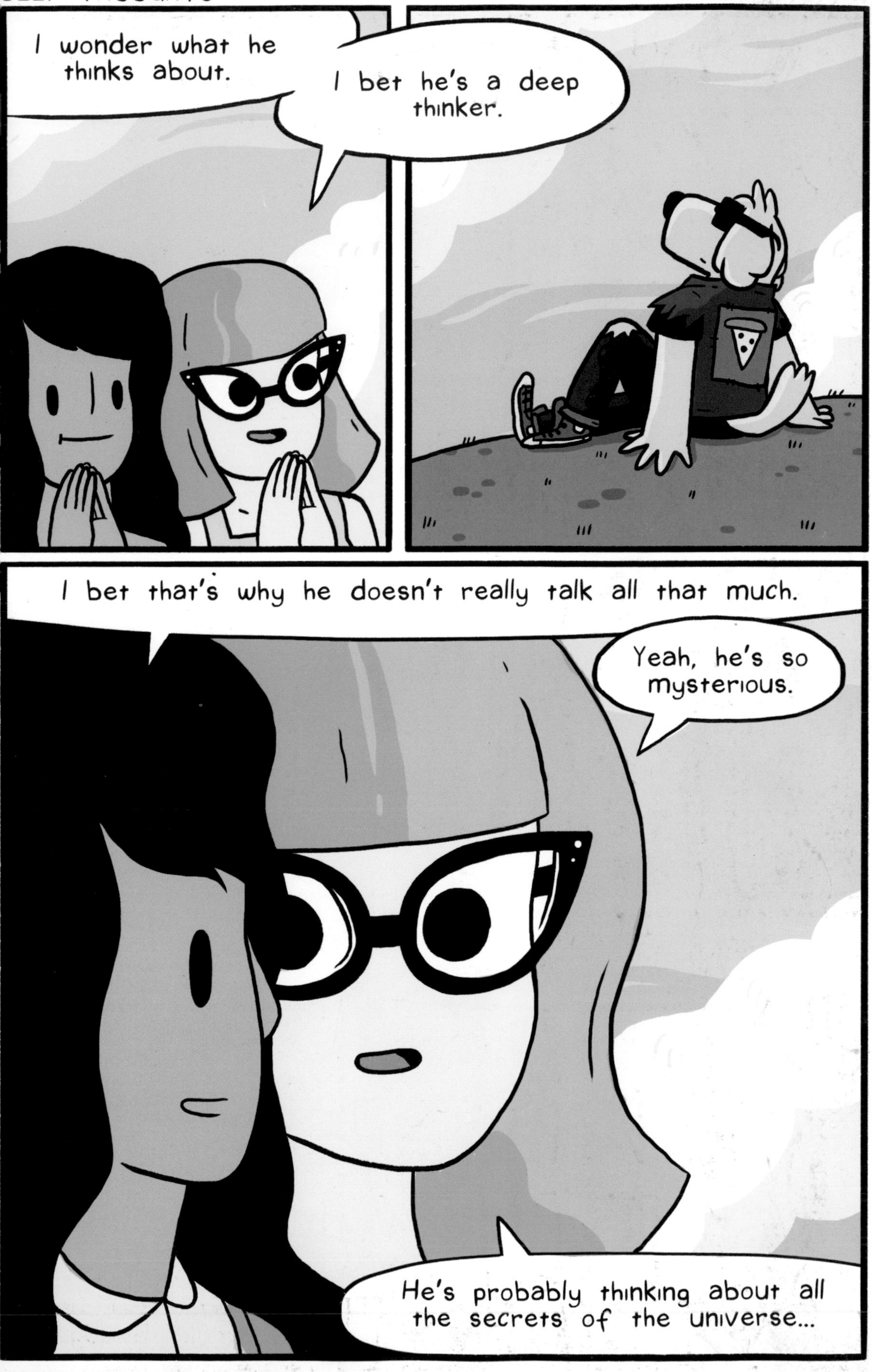
I wonder what he thinks about.
I bet he's a deep thinker.
I bet that's why he doesn't really talk all that much.
Yeah, he's so mysterious.
He's probably thinking about all the secrets of the universe...

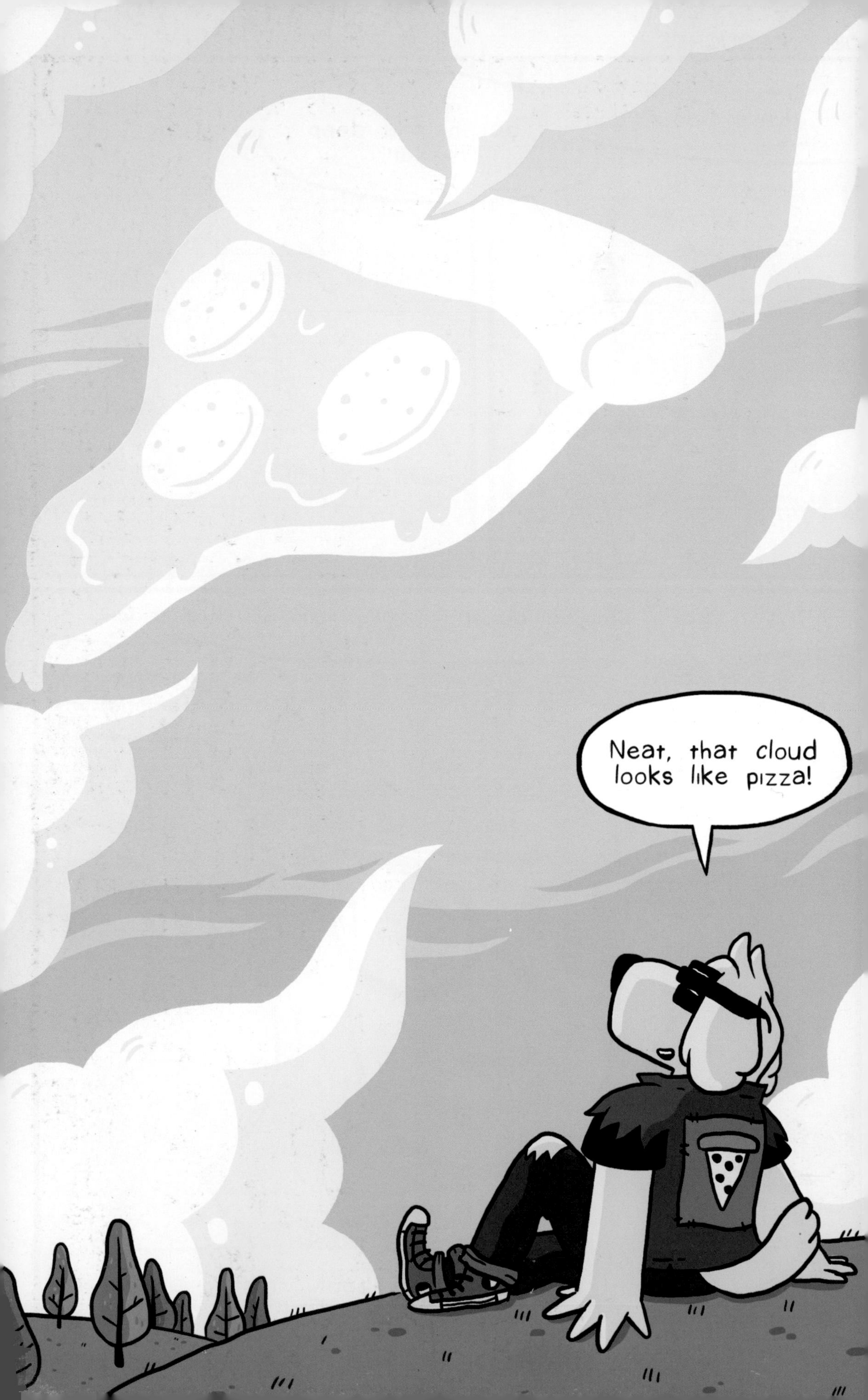
Neat, that cloud looks like pizza!

THE TEST

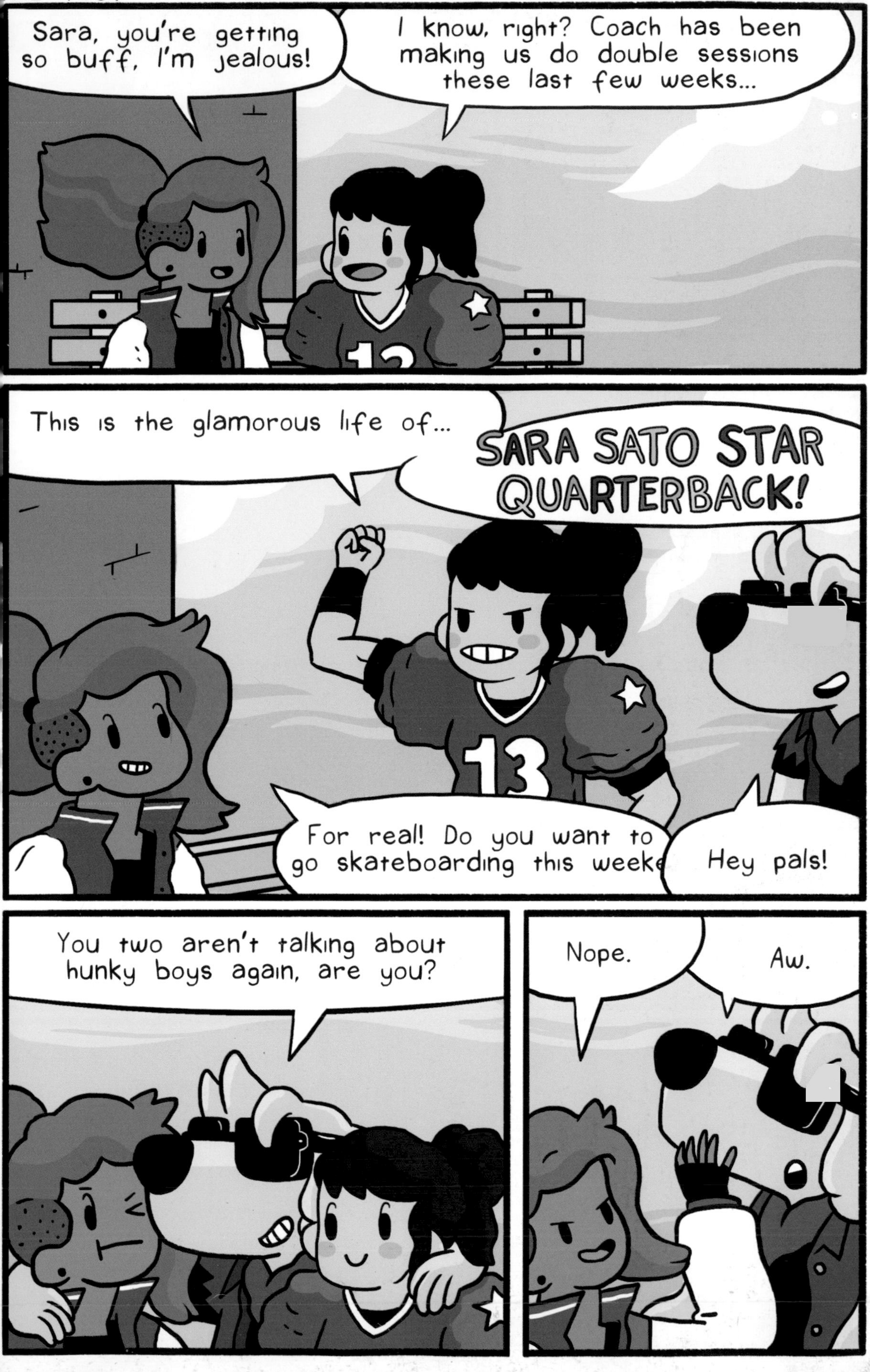

Sara, you're getting so buff, I'm jealous!
I know, right? Coach has been making us do double sessions these last few weeks...
This is the glamorous life of...
SARA SATO STAR QUARTERBACK!
For real! Do you want to go skateboarding this weeke
Hey pals!
You two aren't talking about hunky boys again, are you?
Nope.
Aw.

MYSTERY LURKS WITHIN

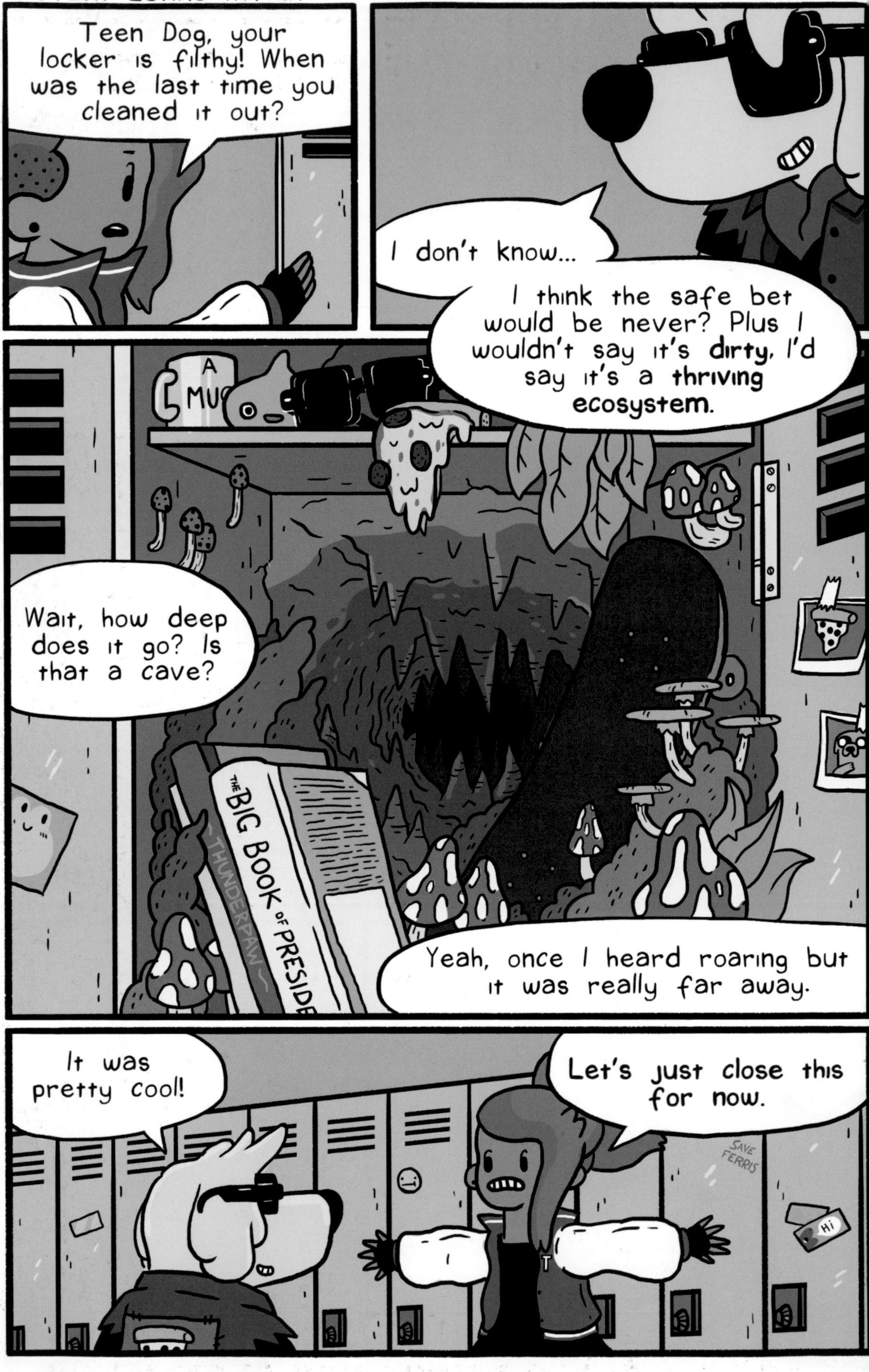

Teen Dog, your locker is filthy! When was the last time you cleaned it out?
I don't know...
I think the safe bet would be never? Plus I wouldn't say it's **dirty**, I'd say it's a **thriving ecosystem**.
A MUG
Wait, how deep does it go? Is that a cave?
THE BIG BOOK OF PRESIDE
THUNDERPAW
Yeah, once I heard roaring but it was really far away.
It was pretty cool!
Let's just close this for now.
SAVE FERRIS
HI

Listen Teen Dog, we need to talk about this test.

You answered every single question with "Teen Dog".

You were not on the Mayflower, nor are you the capital of Texas...

...and you're certainly not the 34th president!

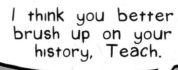

CATS

I think you better brush up on your history, Teach.

THE BIG BOOK of PRESIDENTS

What did you **do** with Eisenhower?!

34th PRE

TEEN DOG

PARTY: YES

35th PRESIDENT

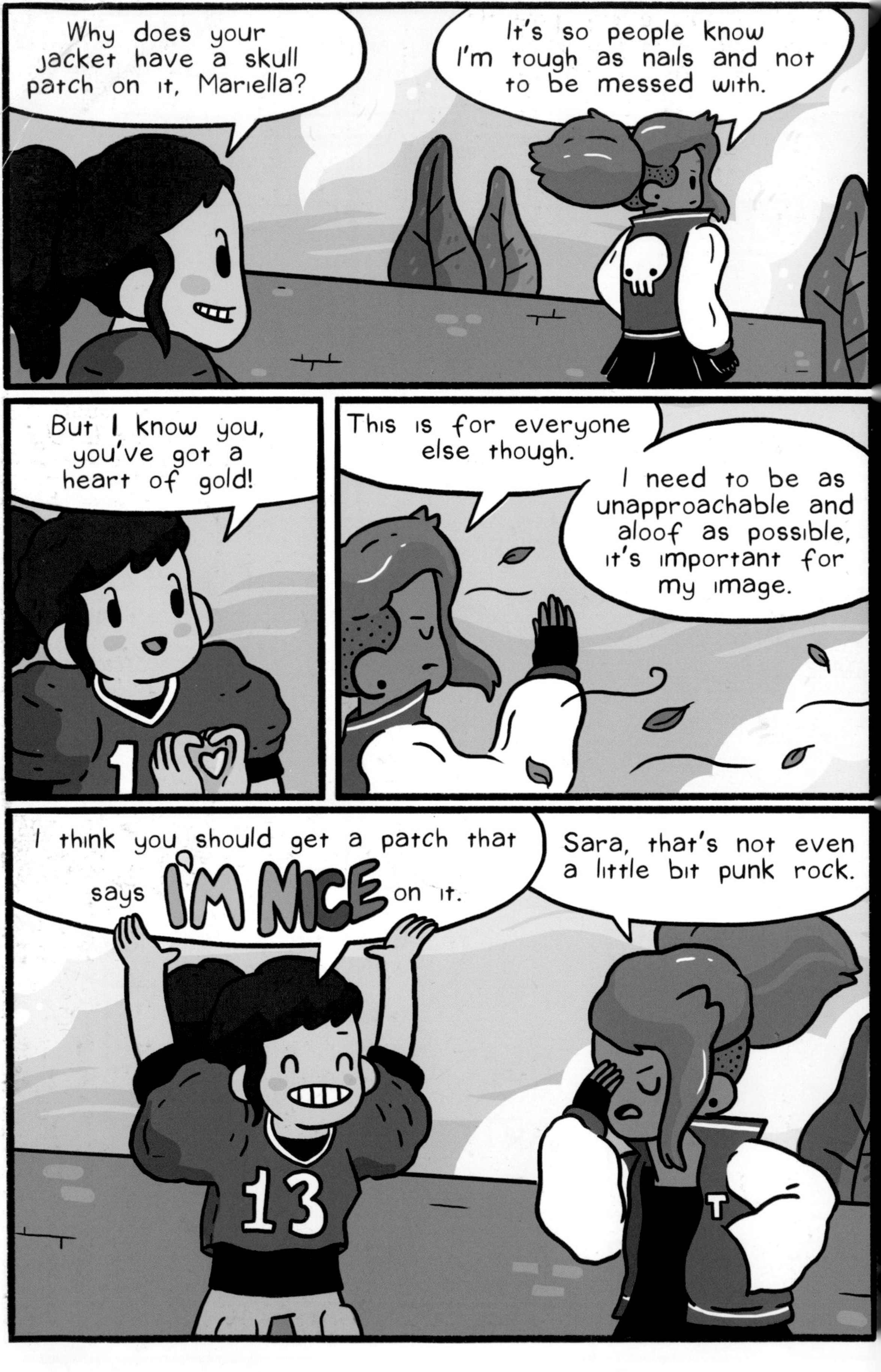
Why does your jacket have a skull patch on it, Mariella?
It's so people know I'm tough as nails and not to be messed with.
But I know you, you've got a heart of gold!
1
This is for everyone else though.
I need to be as unapproachable and aloof as possible, it's important for my image.
I think you should get a patch that says I'M NICE on it.
Sara, that's not even a little bit punk rock.
13
T

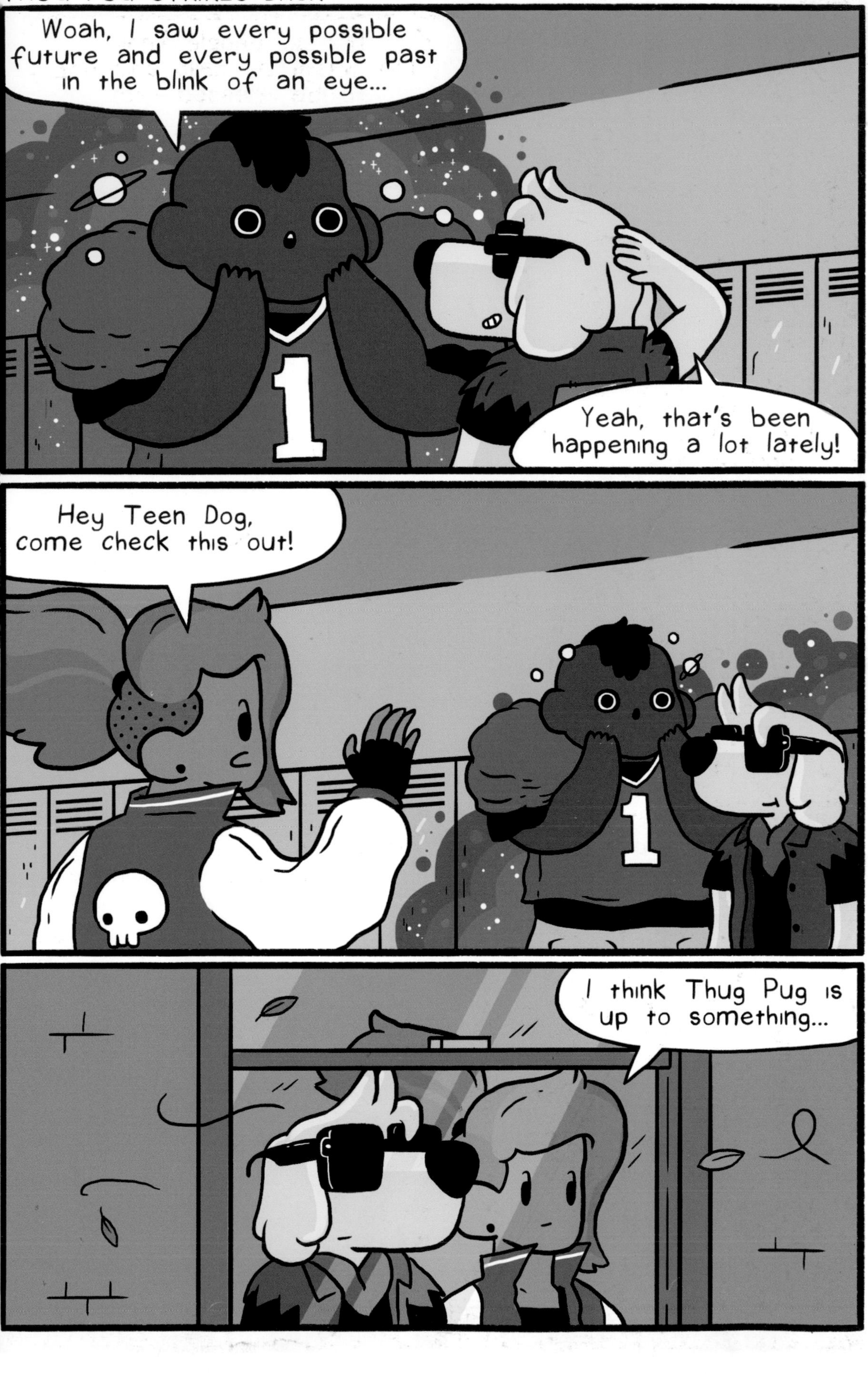
Woah, I saw every possible future and every possible past in the blink of an eye...
Yeah, that's been happening a lot lately!
Hey Teen Dog, come check this out!
I think Thug Pug is up to something...

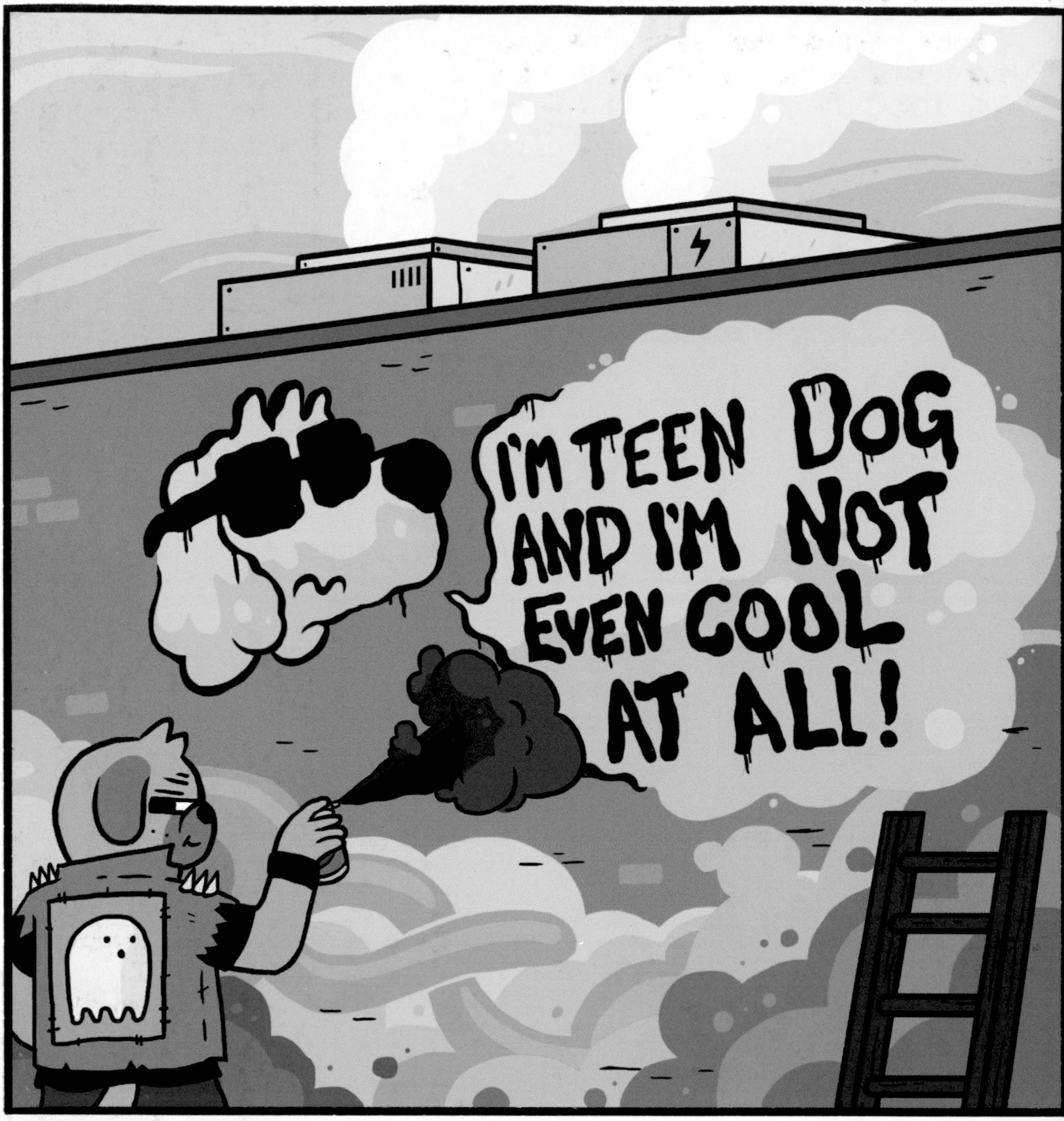
I'M TEEN DOG AND I'M NOT EVEN COOL AT ALL!
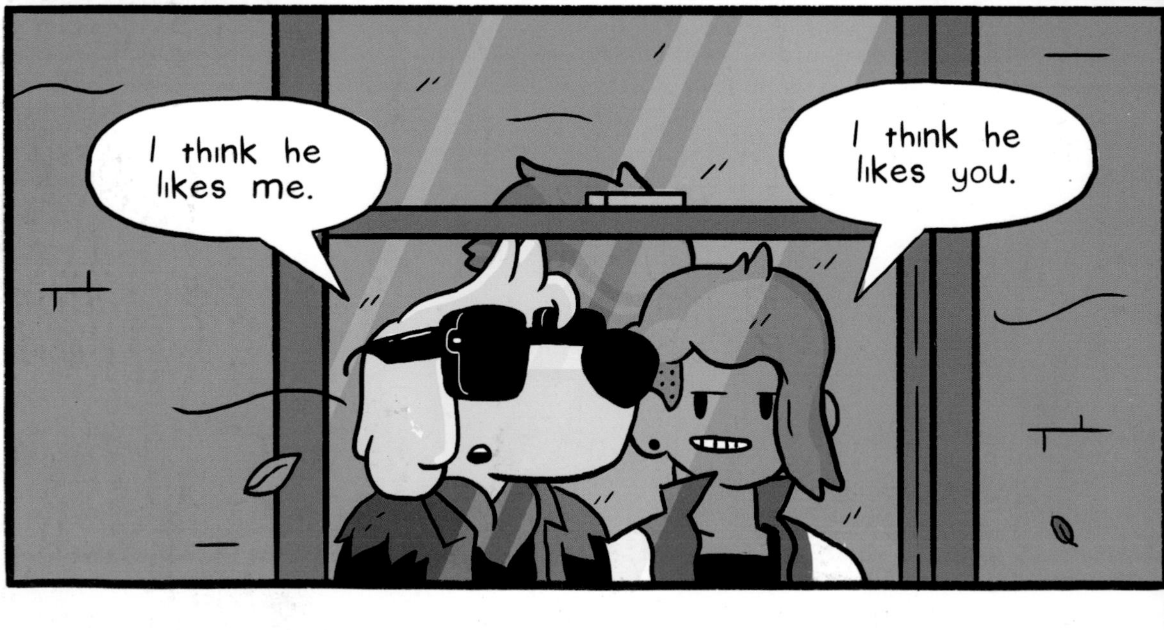
I think he likes me.
I think he likes you.

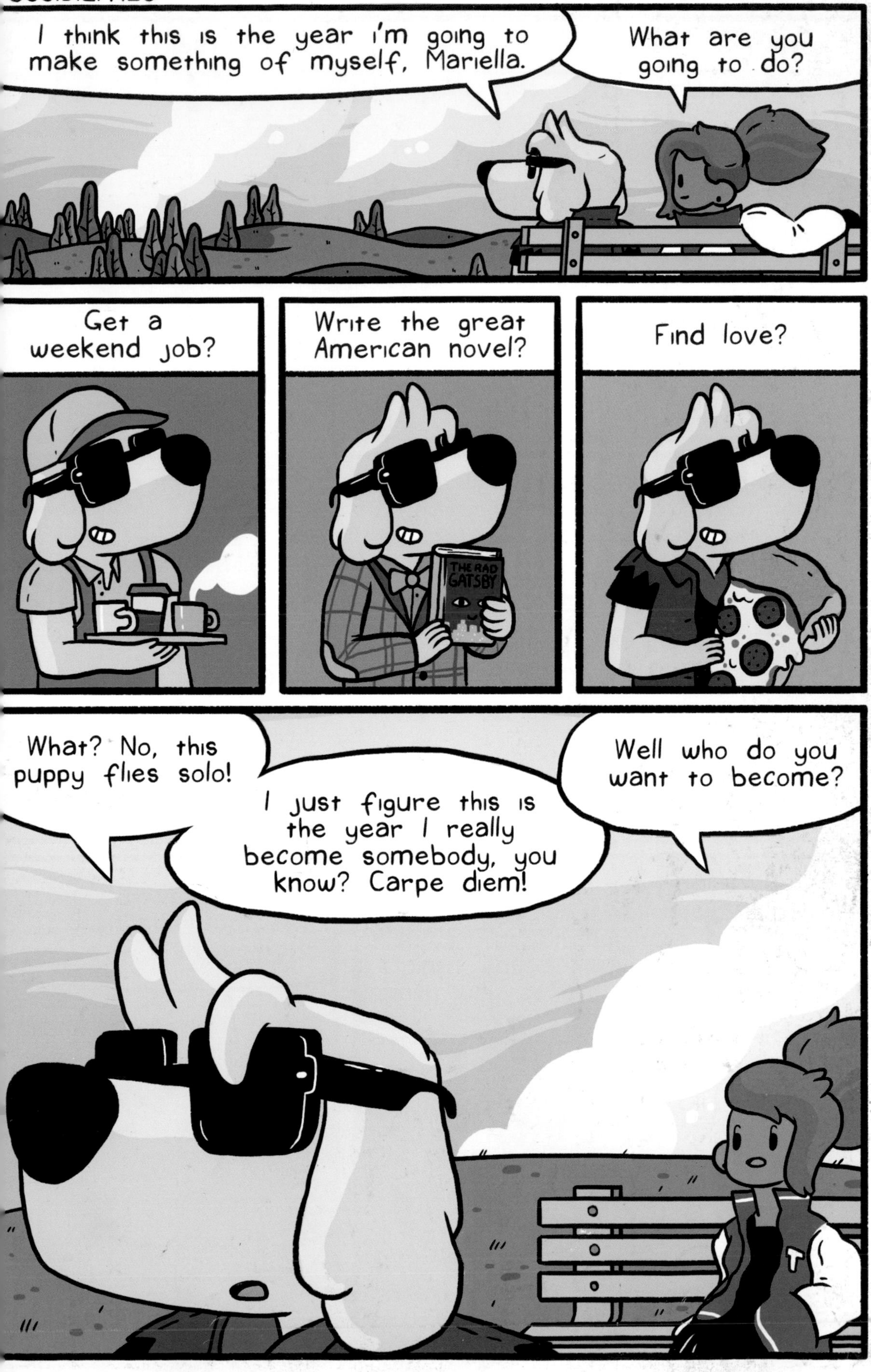
I think this is the year i'm going to make something of myself, Mariella.
What are you going to do?
Get a weekend job?
Write the great American novel?
THE RAD GATSBY
Find love?
What? No, this puppy flies solo!
I just figure this is the year I really become somebody, you know? Carpe diem!
Well who do you want to become?

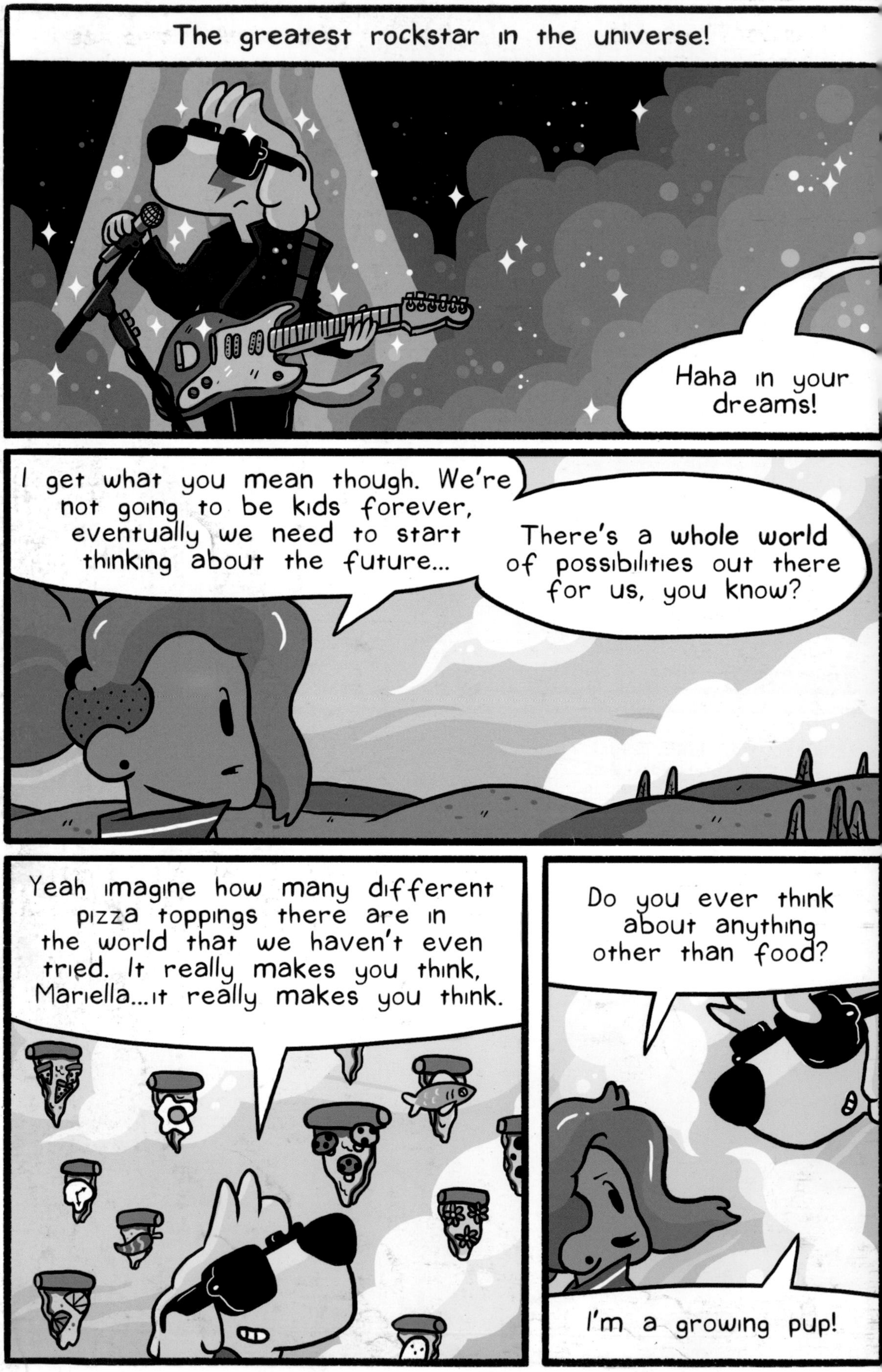
The greatest rockstar in the universe!
Haha in your dreams!
I get what you mean though. We're not going to be kids forever, eventually we need to start thinking about the future...
There's a **whole world** of possibilities out there for us, you know?
Yeah imagine how many different pizza toppings there are in the world that we haven't even tried. It really makes you think, Mariella...it really makes you think.
Do you ever think about anything other than food?
I'm a growing pup!

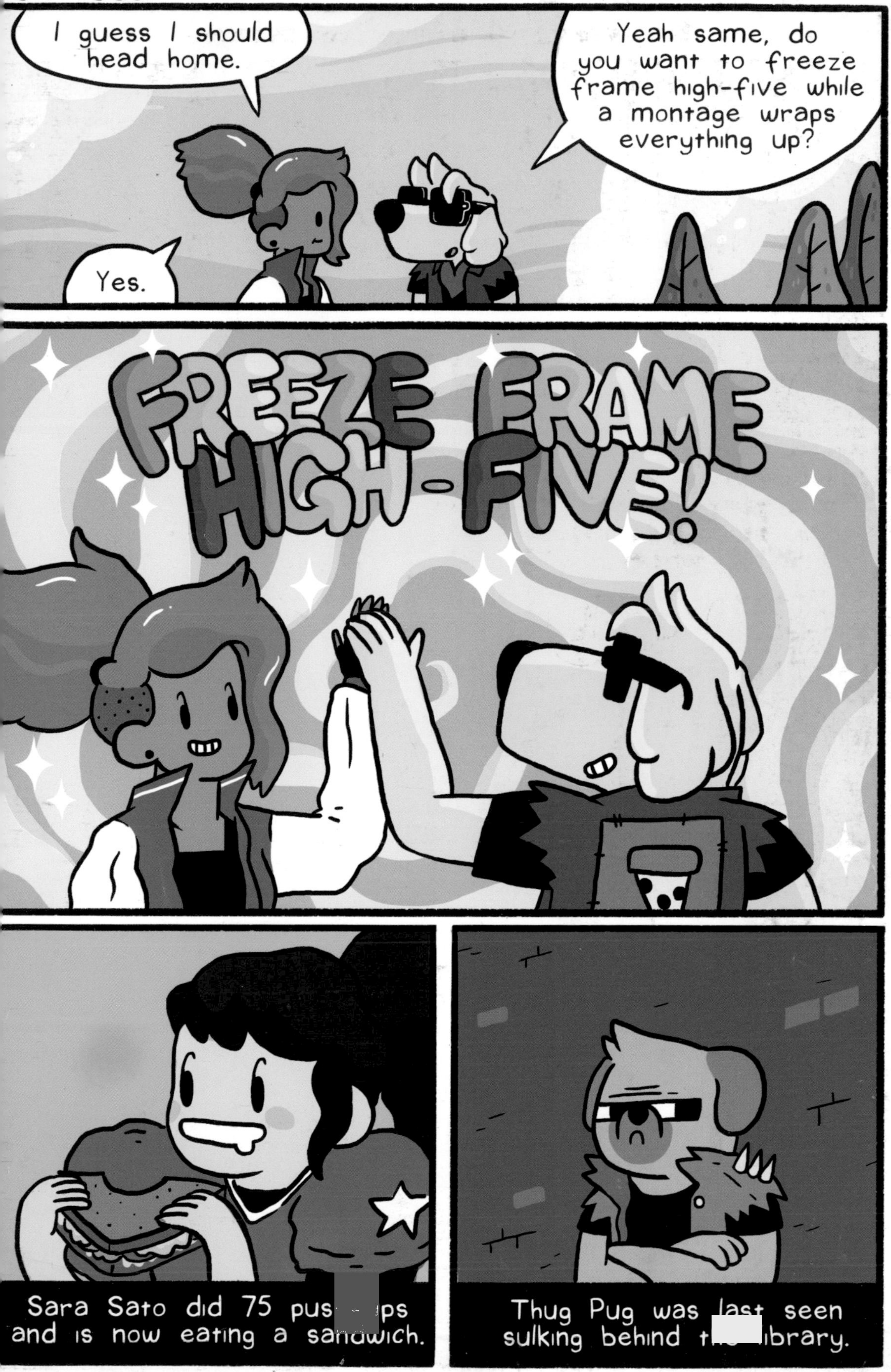
I guess I should head home.
Yeah same, do you want to freeze frame high-five while a montage wraps everything up?
Yes.
FREEZE FRAME HIGH-FIVE!
Sara Sato did 75 pus ps and is now eating a sandwich.
Thug Pug was last seen sulking behind t ibrary.

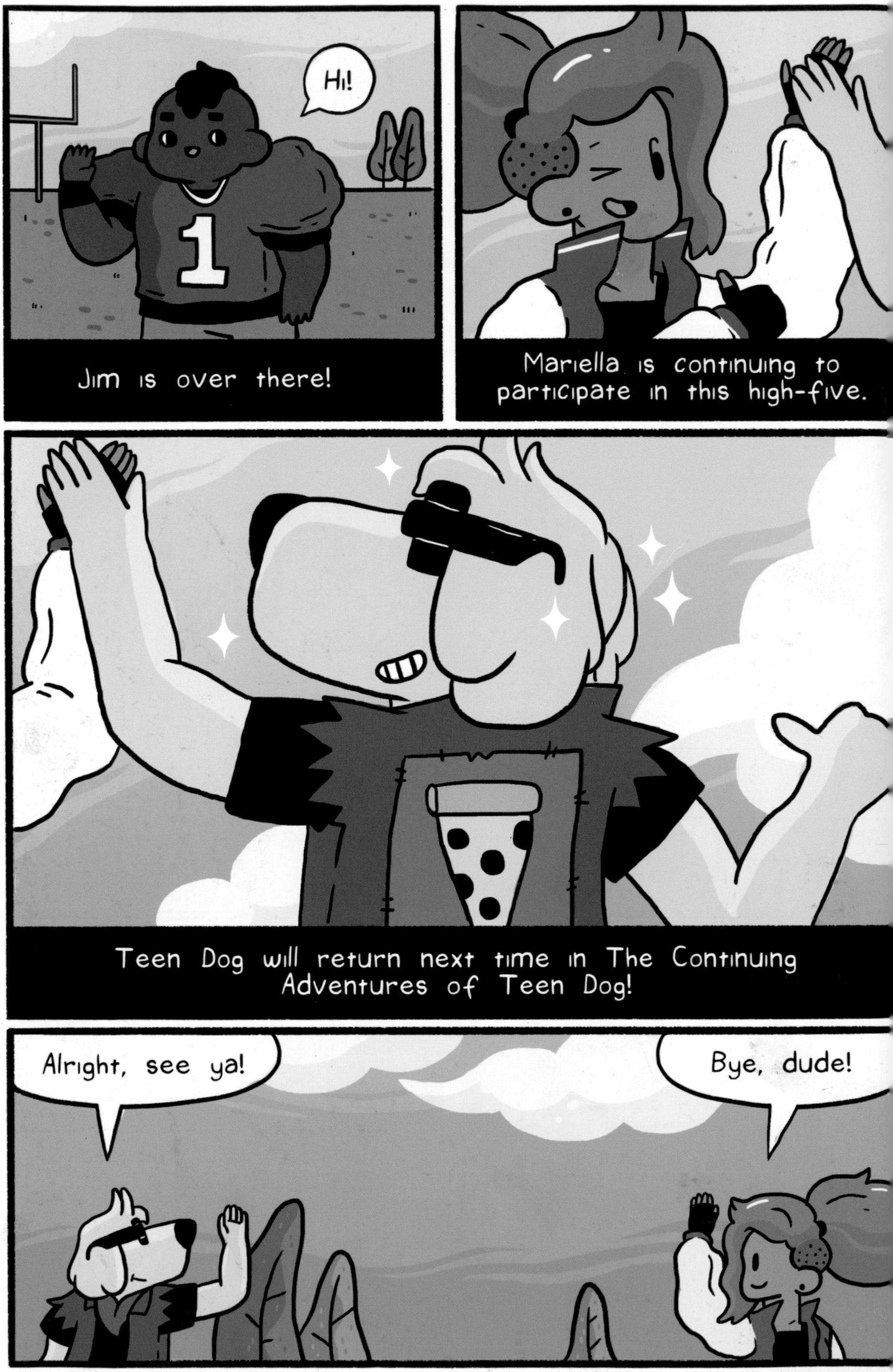
Hi!
Jim is over there!
Mariella is continuing to participate in this high-five.
Teen Dog will return next time in The Continuing Adventures of Teen Dog!
Alright, see ya!
Bye, dude!

CHAPTER ENDS

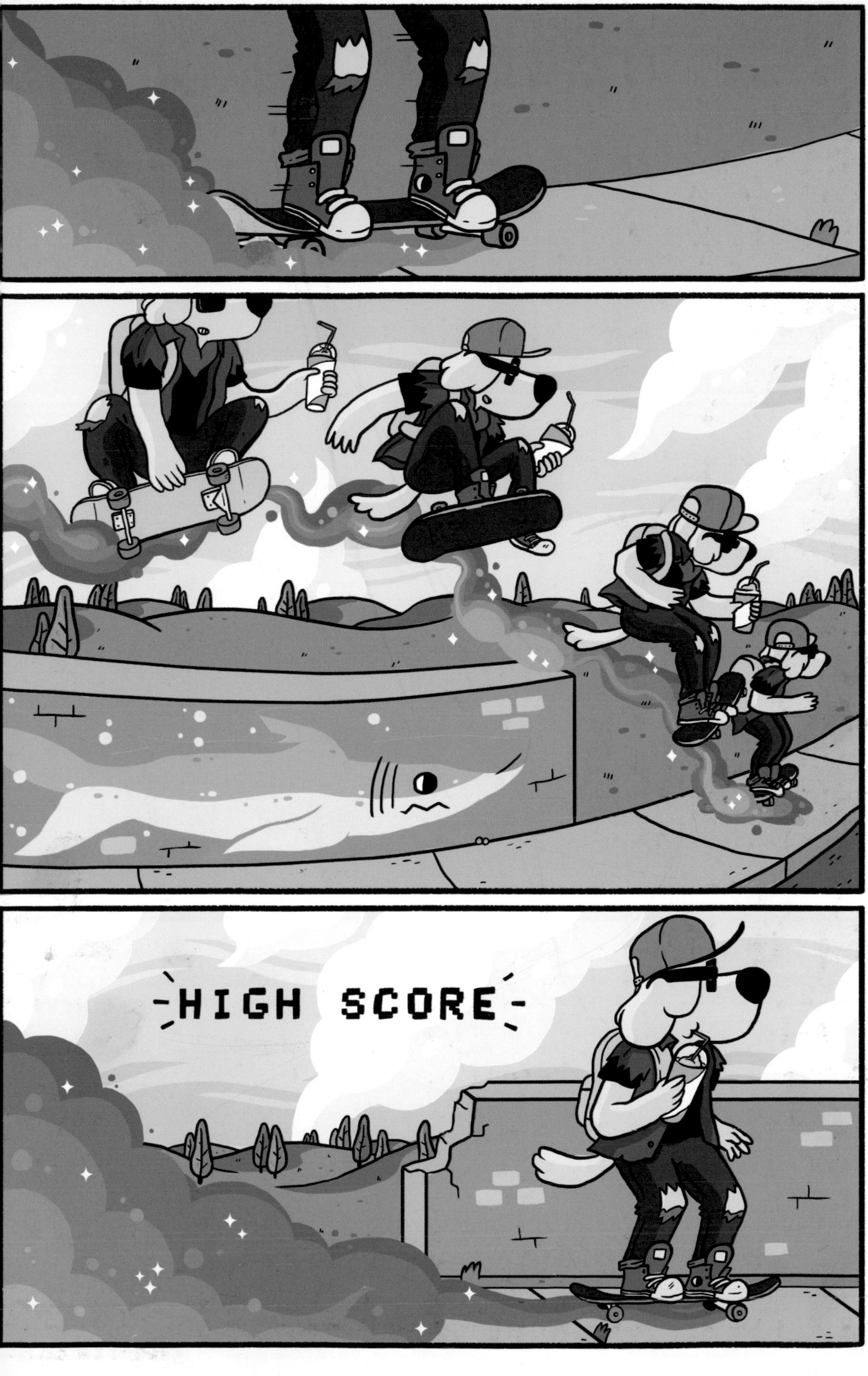
HIGH SCORE

THE CONTINUING ADVENTURES OF TEEN DOG

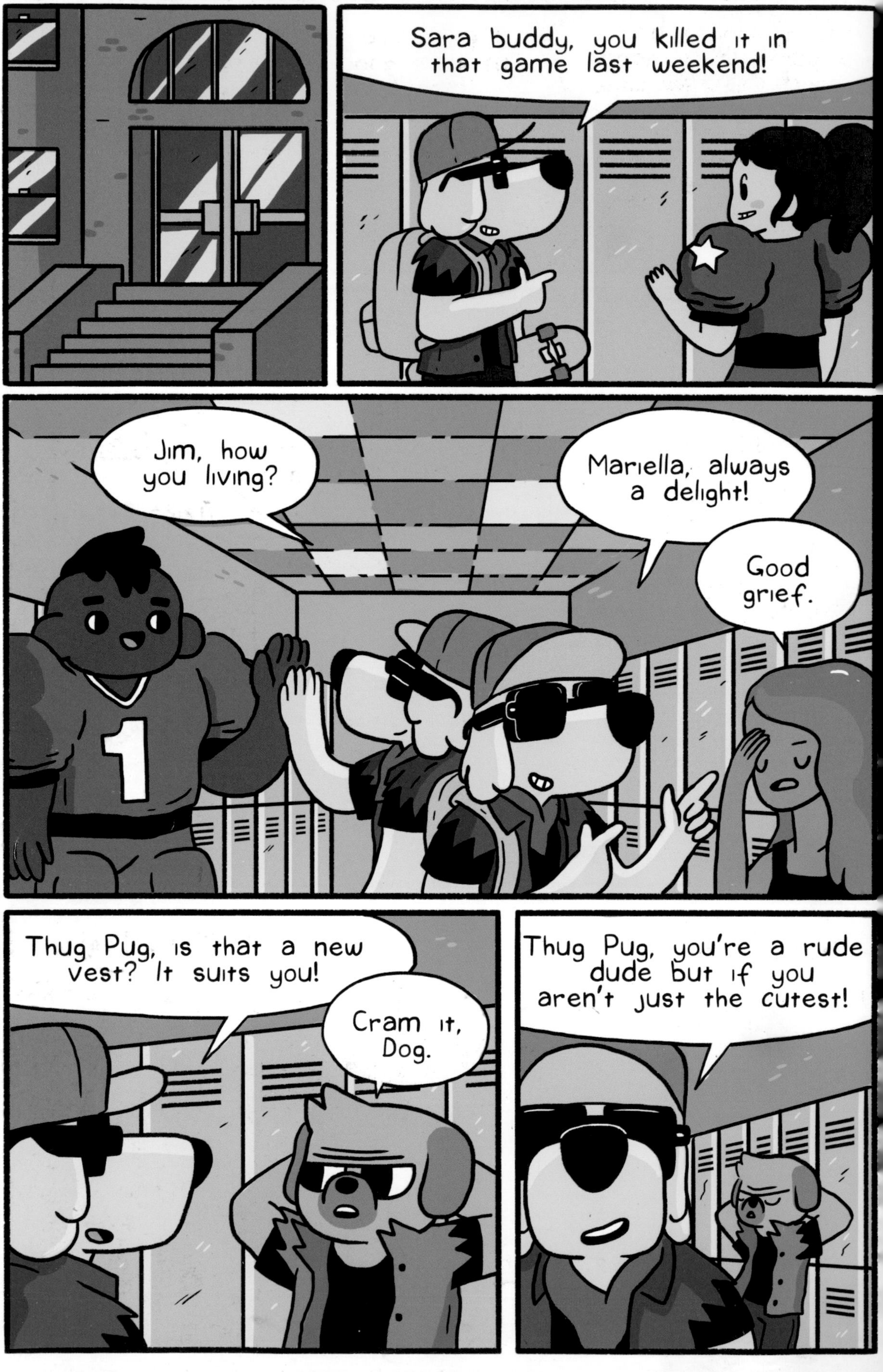

CHAPTER TWO

Sara buddy, you killed it in that game last weekend!
Jim, how you living?
Mariella, always a delight!
Good grief.
Thug Pug, is that a new vest? It suits you!
Cram it, Dog.
Thug Pug, you're a rude dude but if you aren't just the cutest!

BEST FRIENDS FOREVER

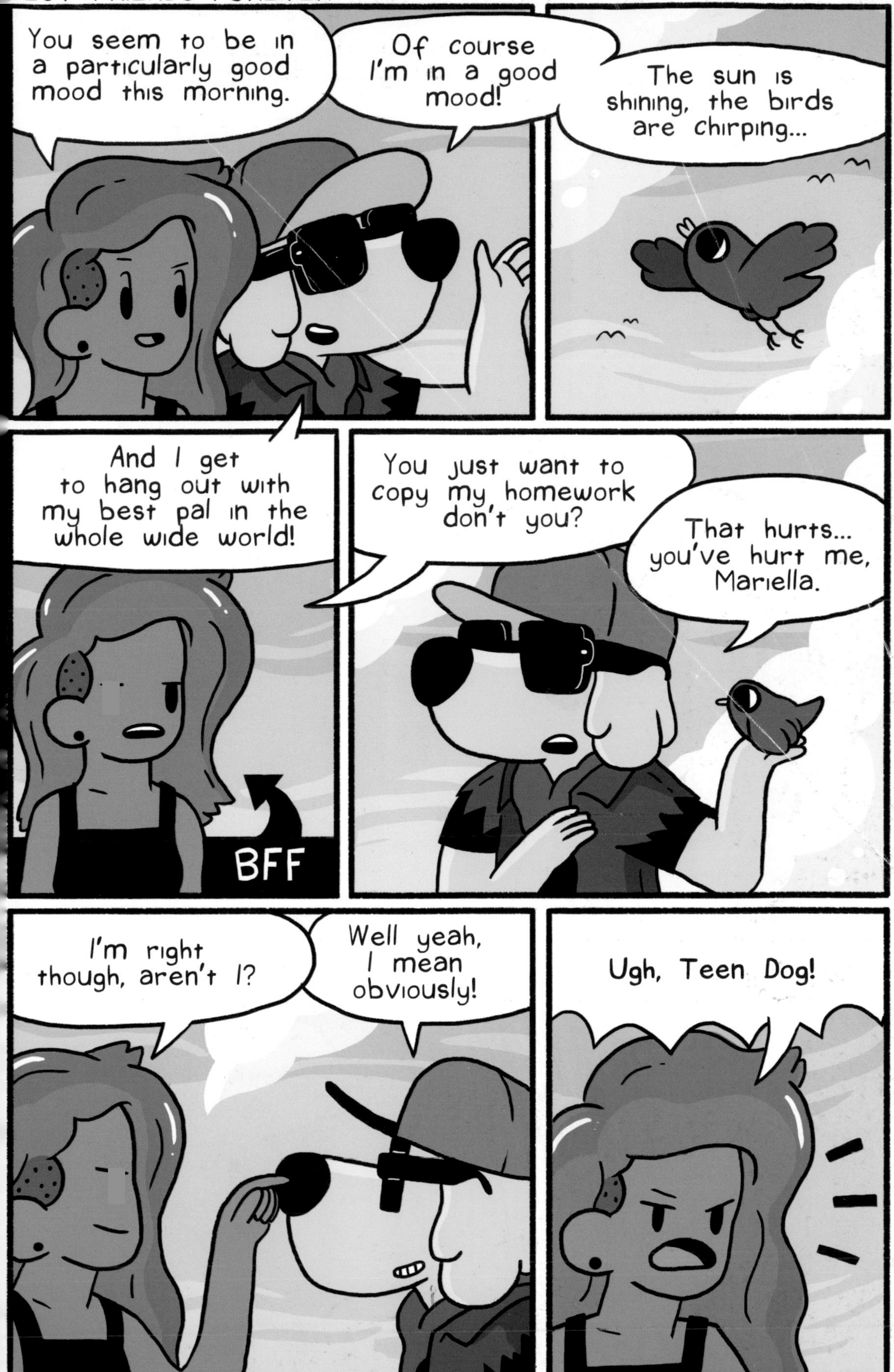
You seem to be in a particularly good mood this morning.
Of course I'm in a good mood!
The sun is shining, the birds are chirping...
And I get to hang out with my best pal in the whole wide world!
BFF
You just want to copy my homework don't you?
That hurts... you've hurt me, Mariella.
I'm right though, aren't I?
Well yeah, I mean obviously!
Ugh, Teen Dog!

ENTER THE VOID

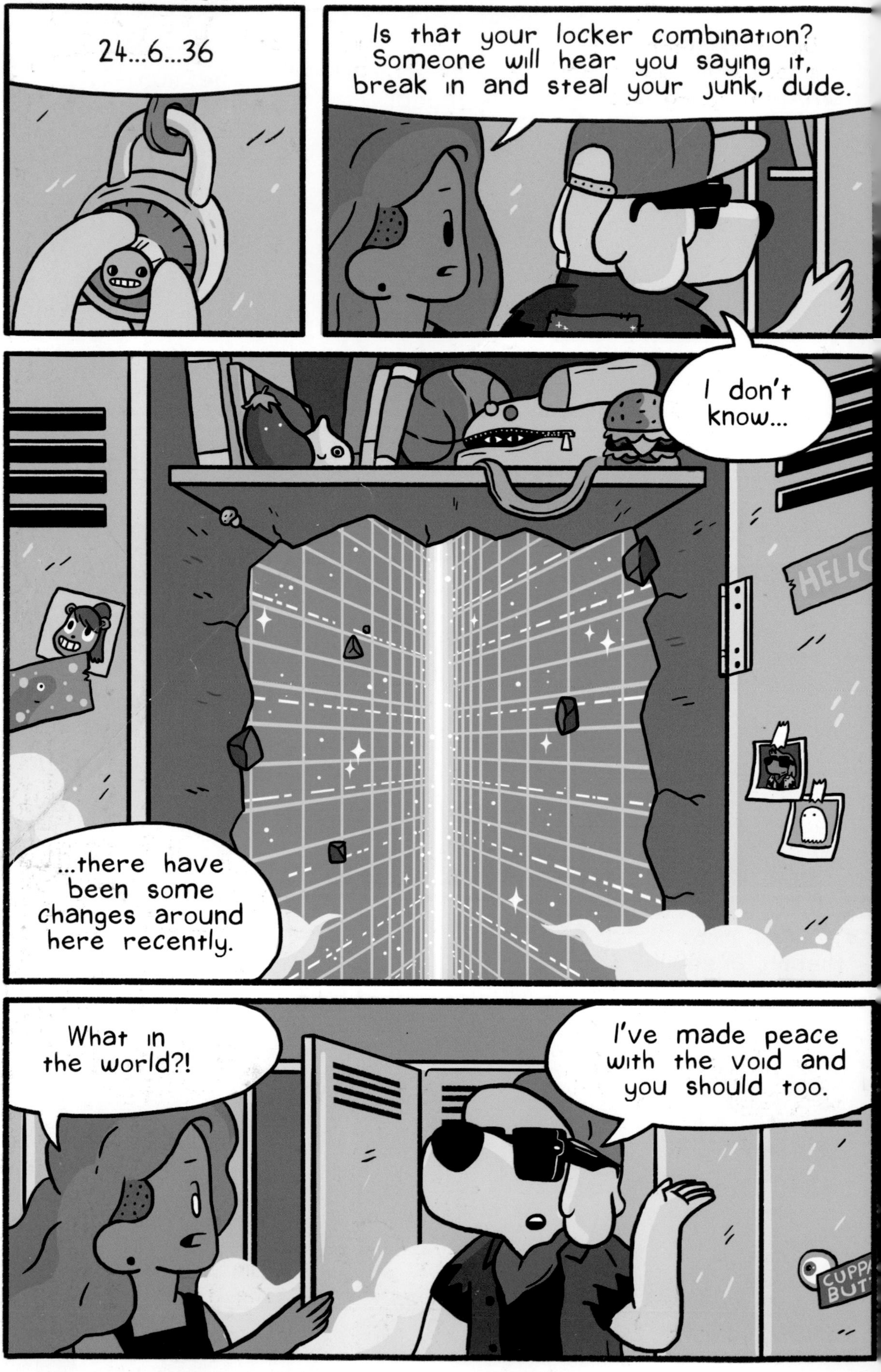

24...6...36
Is that your locker combination? Someone will hear you saying it, break in and steal your junk, dude.
I don't know...
...there have been some changes around here recently.
What in the world?!
I've made peace with the void and you should too.

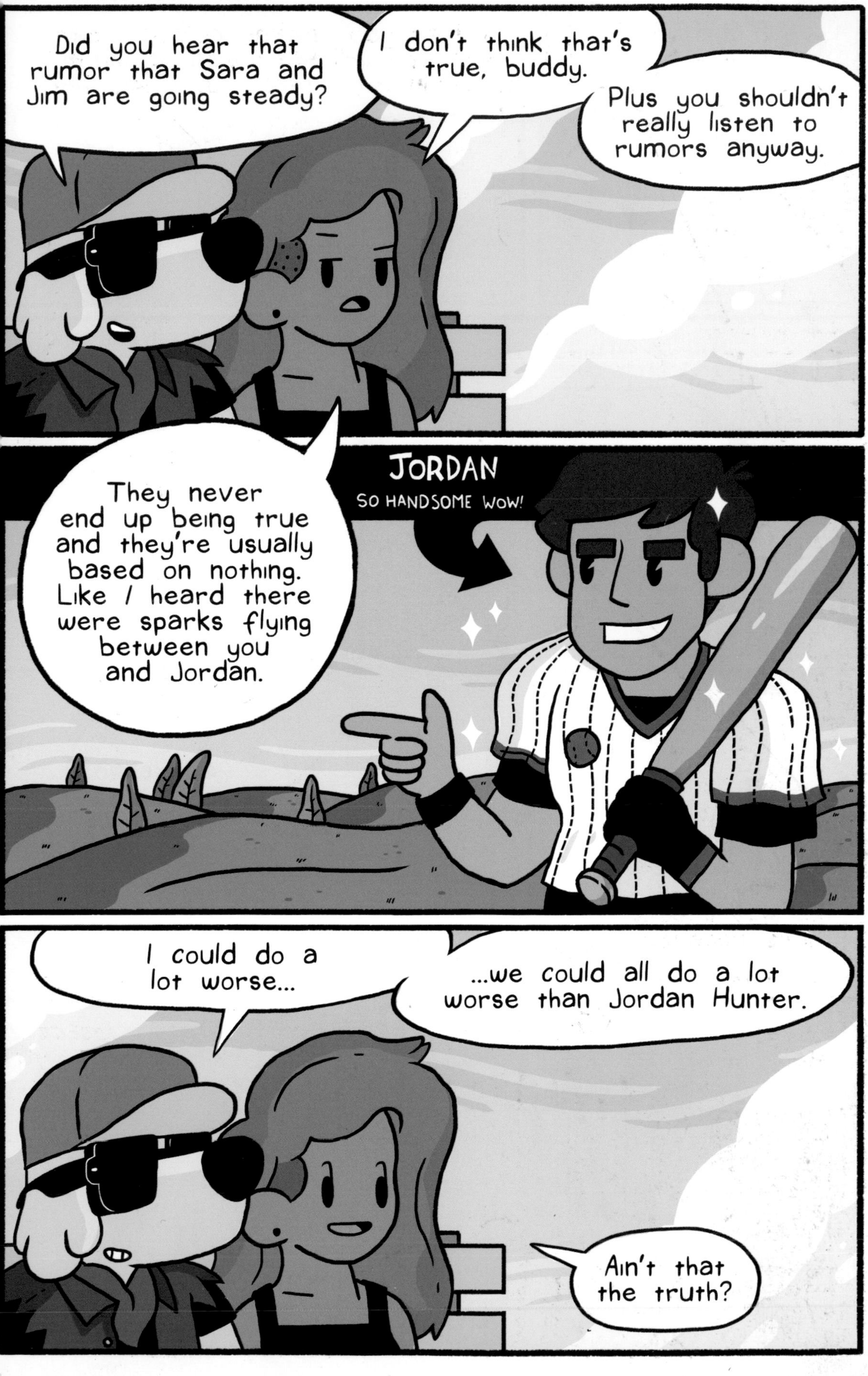
Did you hear that rumor that Sara and Jim are going steady?
I don't think that's true, buddy.
Plus you shouldn't really listen to rumors anyway.
They never end up being true and they're usually based on nothing. Like I heard there were sparks flying between you and Jordan.
JORDAN
SO HANDSOME WOW!
I could do a lot worse...
...we could all do a lot worse than Jordan Hunter.
Ain't that the truth?

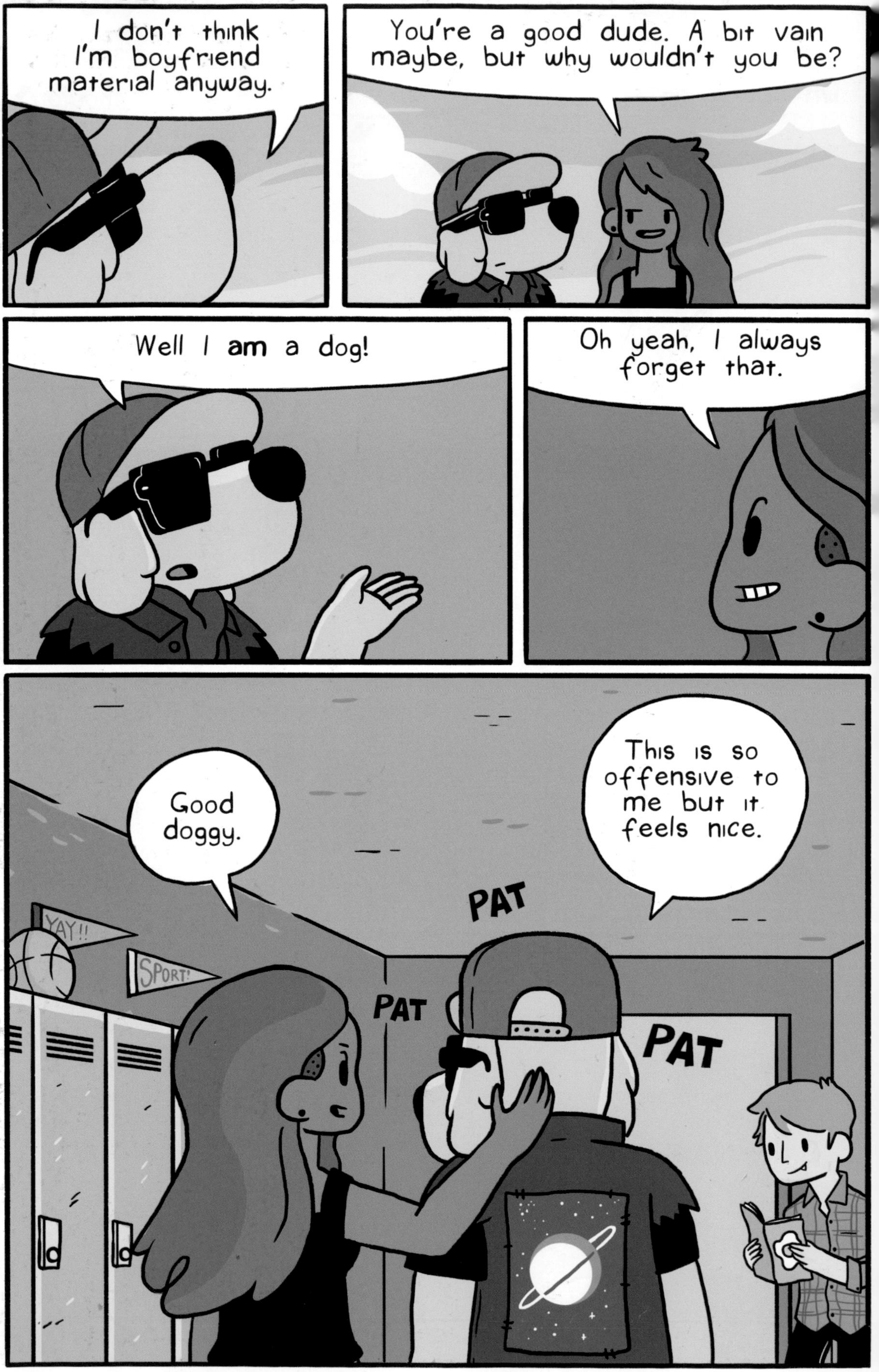
I don't think I'm boyfriend material anyway.
You're a good dude. A bit vain maybe, but why wouldn't you be?
Well I **am** a dog!
Oh yeah, I always forget that.
Good doggy.
This is so offensive to me but it feels nice.
PAT
PAT
PAT
YAY!!
SPORT!

SCIENCE!

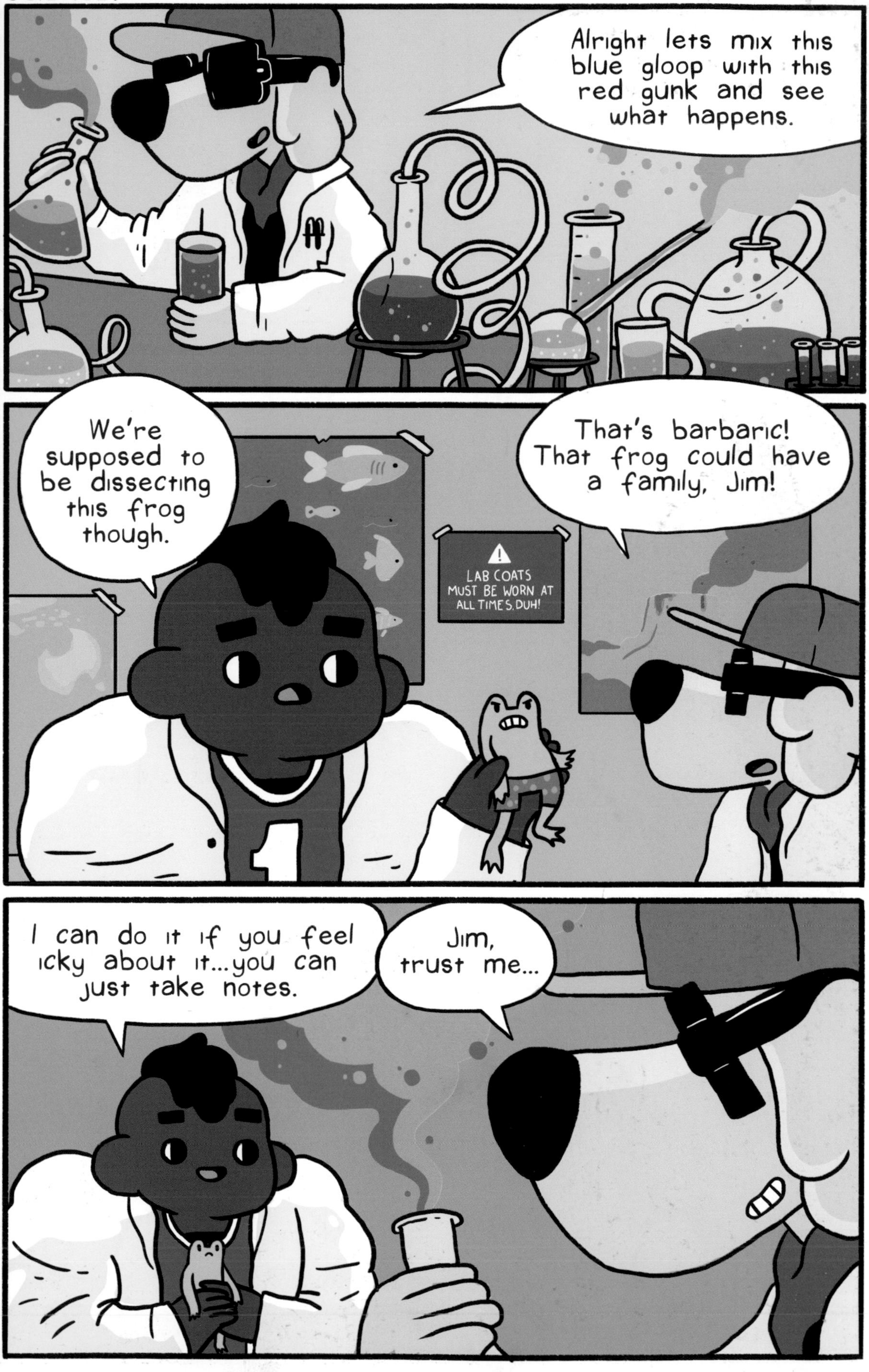
Alright lets mix this blue gloop with this red gunk and see what happens.
We're supposed to be dissecting this frog though.
That's barbaric! That frog could have a family, Jim!
LAB COATS MUST BE WORN AT ALL TIMES, DUH!
I can do it if you feel icky about it...you can just take notes.
Jim, trust me...

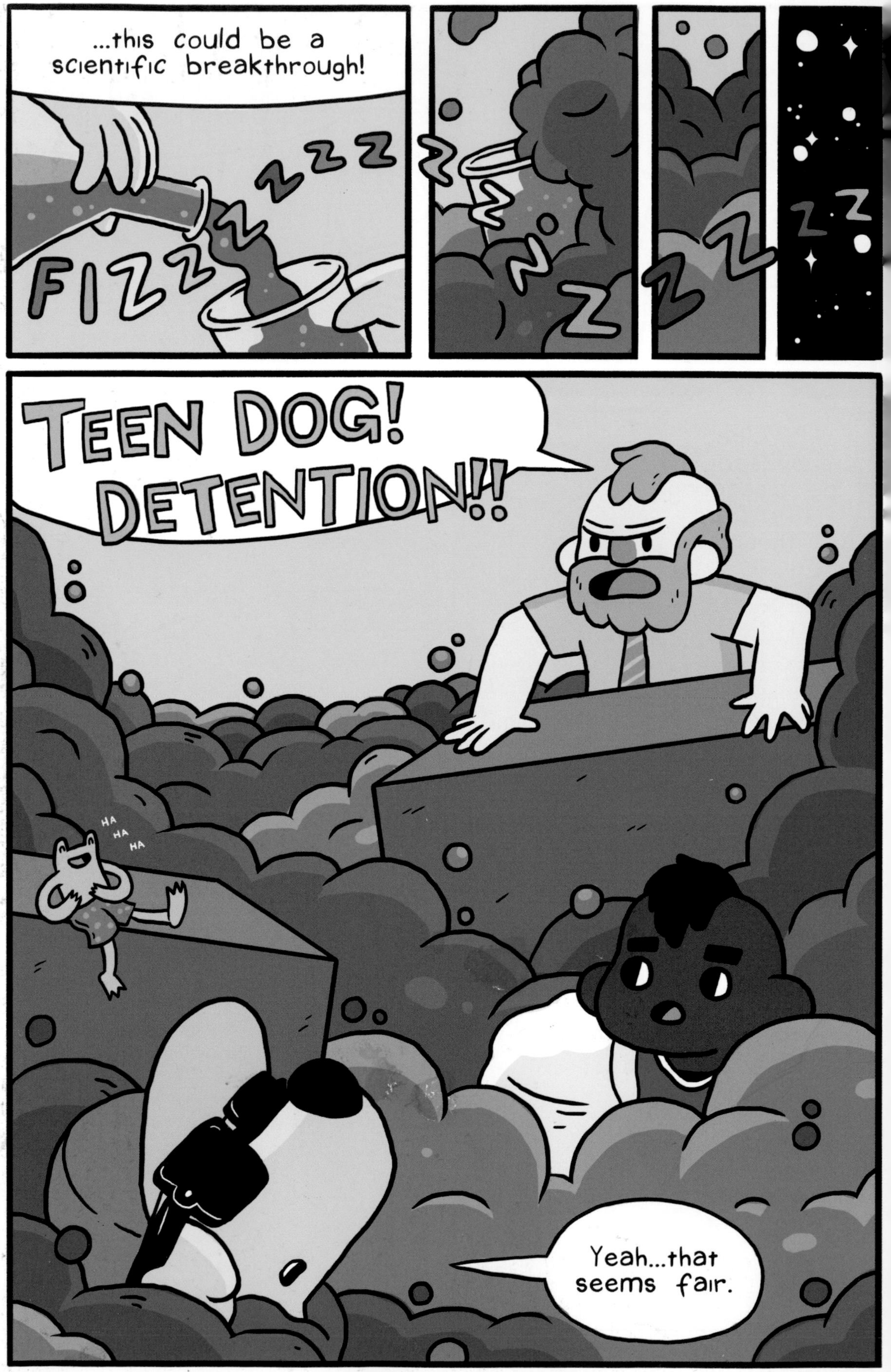
...this could be a scientific breakthrough!
FIZZZZZZZZ
ZZZ
ZZZZ
ZZ
TEEN DOG! DETENTION!!
HA HA HA
Yeah...that seems fair.

CHECK

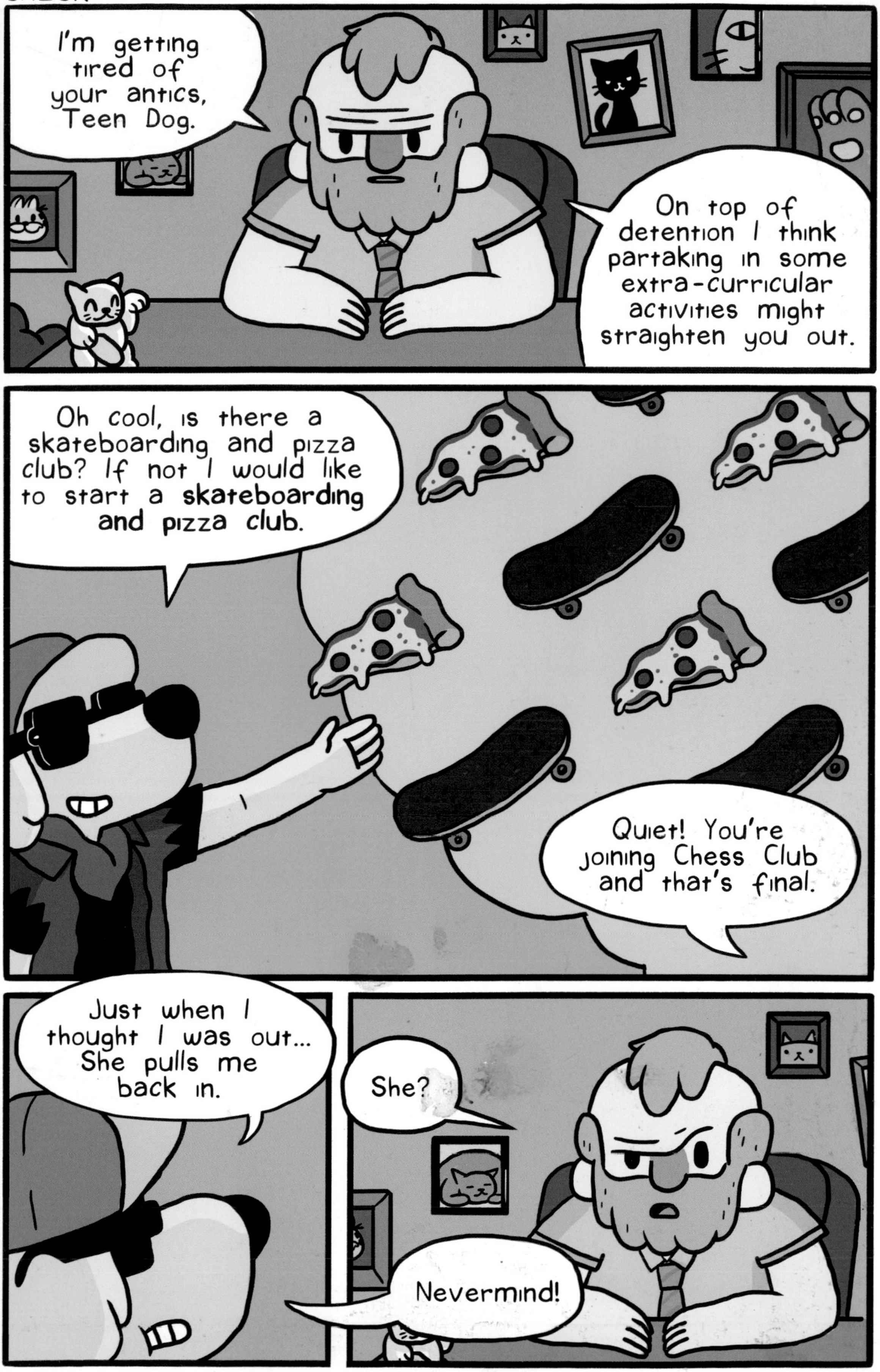
I'm getting tired of your antics, Teen Dog.
On top of detention I think partaking in some extra-curricular activities might straighten you out.
Oh cool, is there a skateboarding and pizza club? If not I would like to start a **skateboarding and pizza club.**
Quiet! You're joining Chess Club and that's final.
Just when I thought I was out... She pulls me back in.
She?
Nevermind!

FEUDALISM AND THE FRONTIER

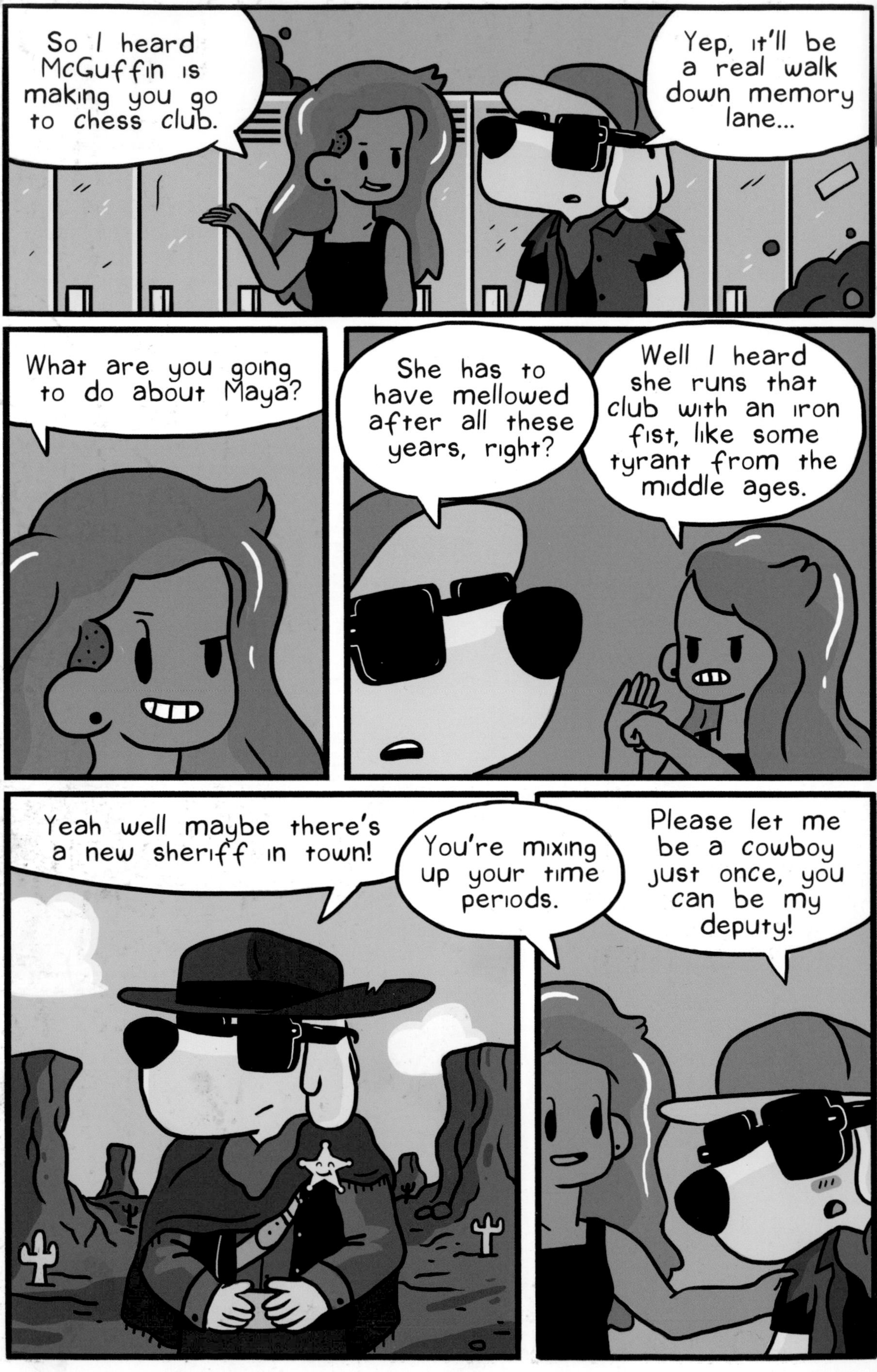
So I heard McGuffin is making you go to chess club.
Yep, it'll be a real walk down memory lane...
What are you going to do about Maya?
She has to have mellowed after all these years, right?
Well I heard she runs that club with an iron fist, like some tyrant from the middle ages.
Yeah well maybe there's a new sheriff in town!
You're mixing up your time periods.
Please let me be a cowboy just once, you can be my deputy!

IT'S DANGEROUS TO GO ALONE

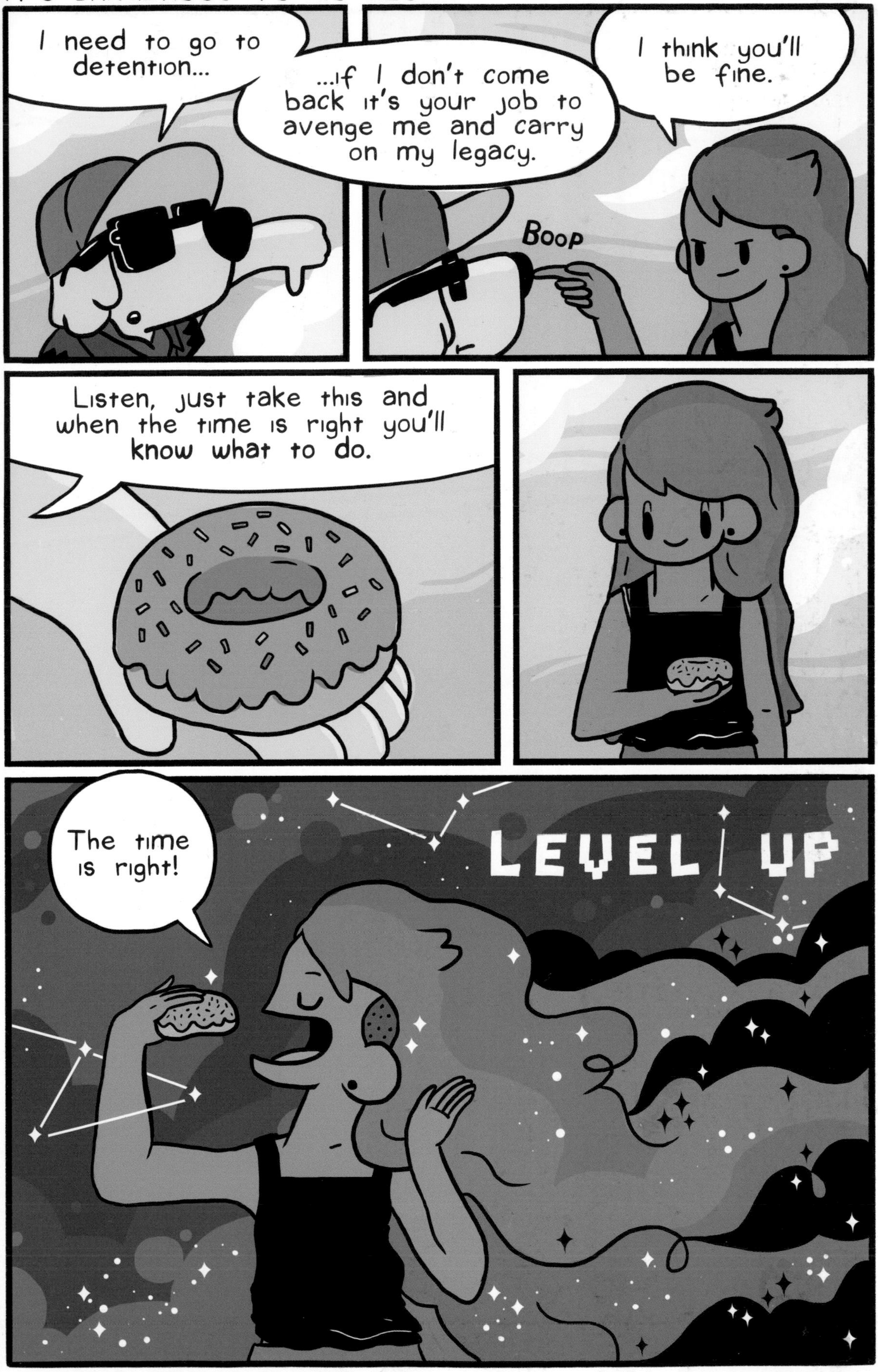
I need to go to detention...
...if I don't come back it's your job to avenge me and carry on my legacy.
I think you'll be fine.
BOOP
Listen, just take this and when the time is right you'll know what to do.
The time is right!
LEVEL UP

TOO COOL

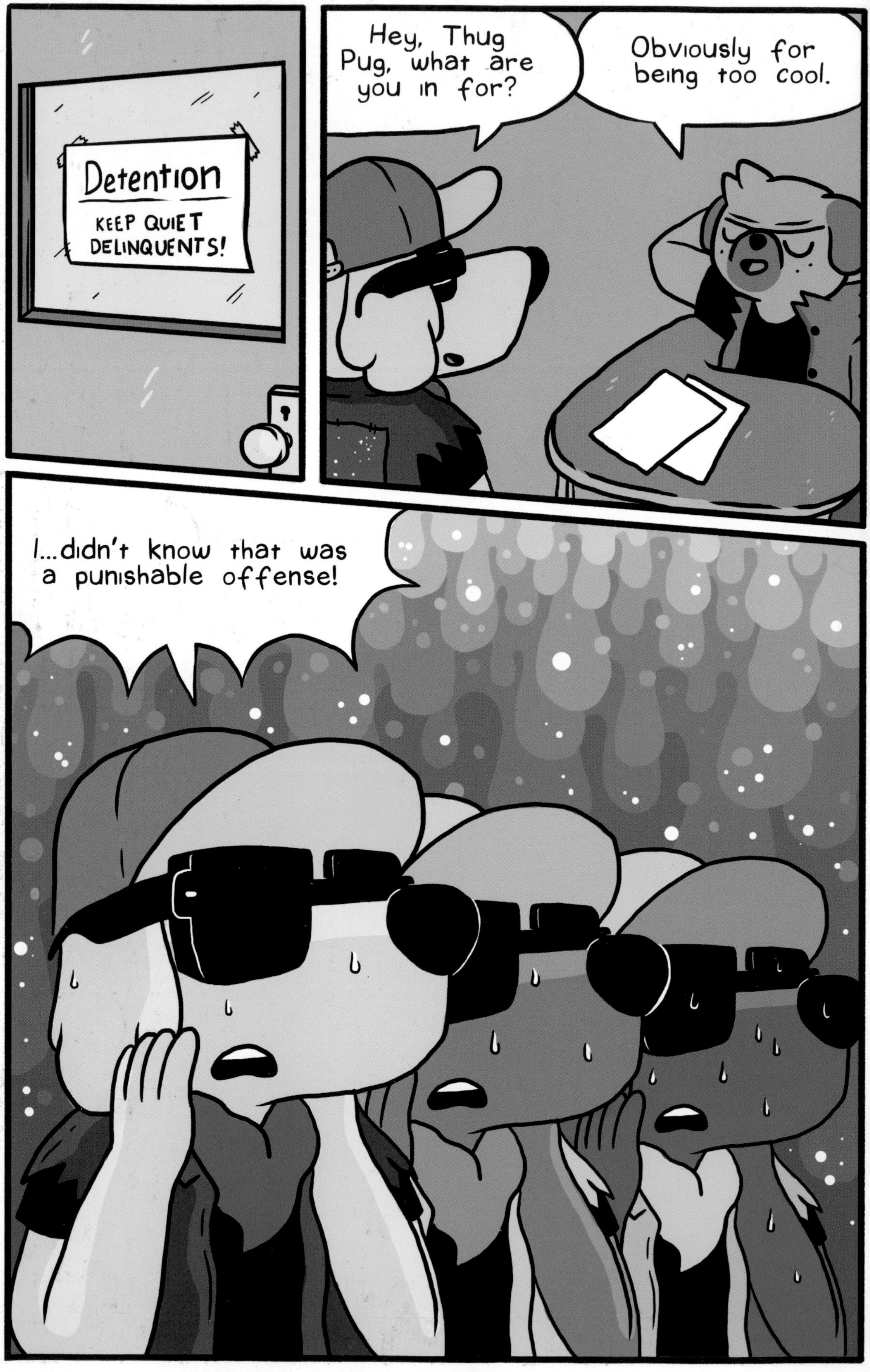
Detention
KEEP QUIET DELINQUENTS!
Hey, Thug Pug, what are you in for?
Obviously for being too cool.
I...didn't know that was a punishable offense!

SINCERELY YOURS...

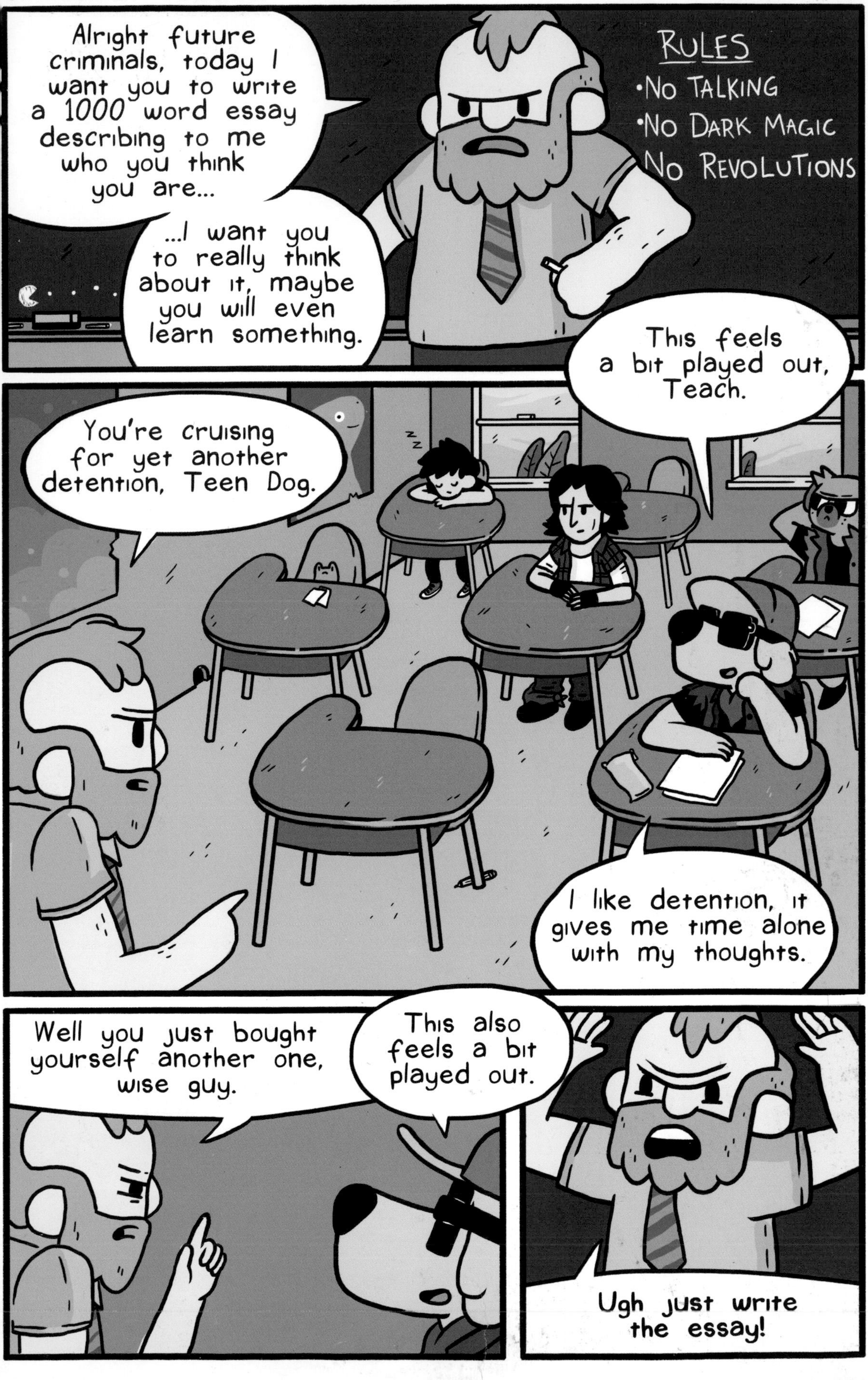
Alright future criminals, today I want you to write a 1000 word essay describing to me who you think you are...
RULES
•No Talking
•No Dark Magic
•No Revolutions
...I want you to really think about it, maybe you will even learn something.
This feels a bit played out, Teach.
You're cruising for yet another detention, Teen Dog.
I like detention, it gives me time alone with my thoughts.
Well you just bought yourself another one, wise guy.
This also feels a bit played out.
Ugh just write the essay!

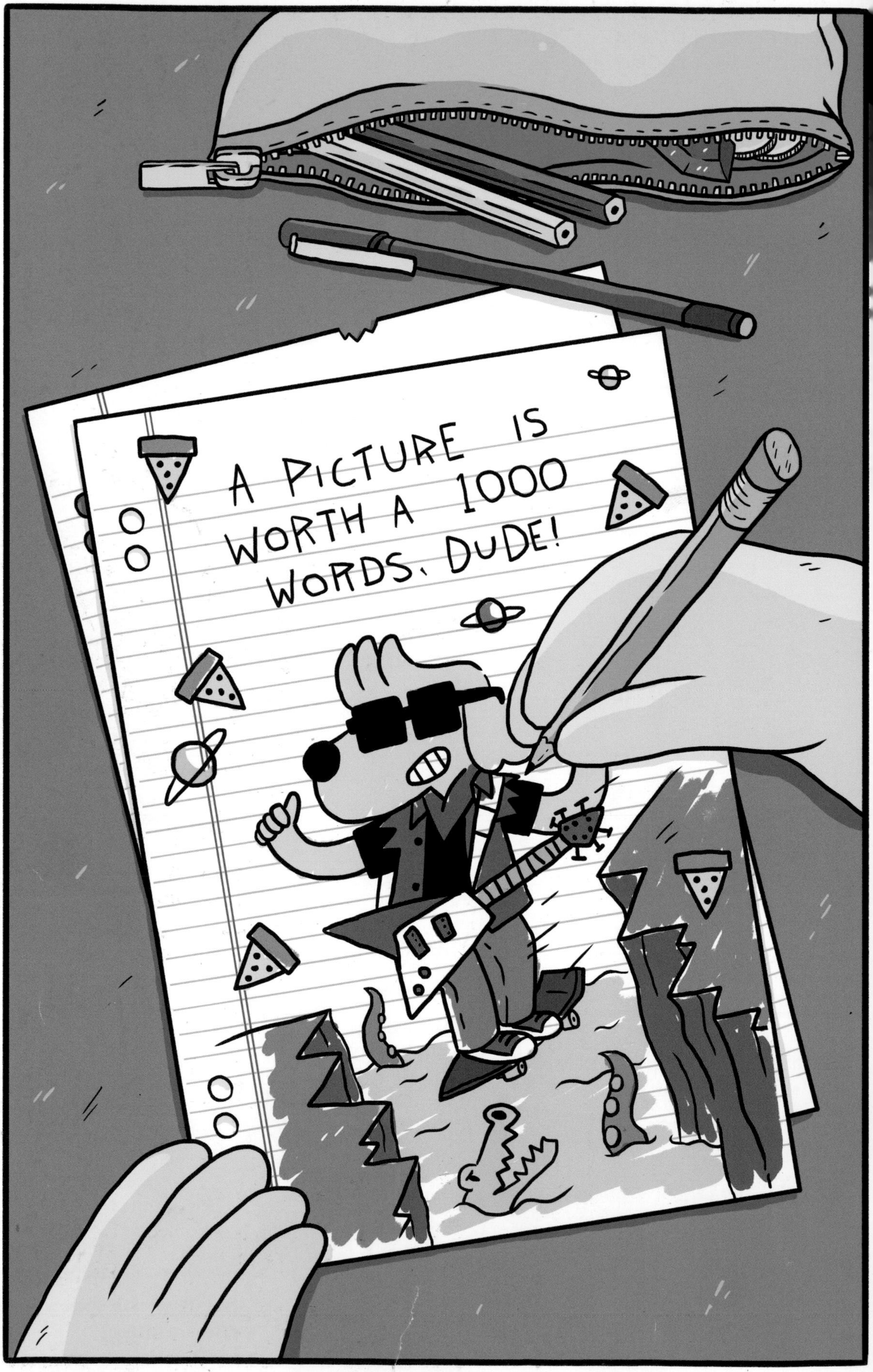
A PICTURE IS WORTH A 1000 WORDS, DUDE!

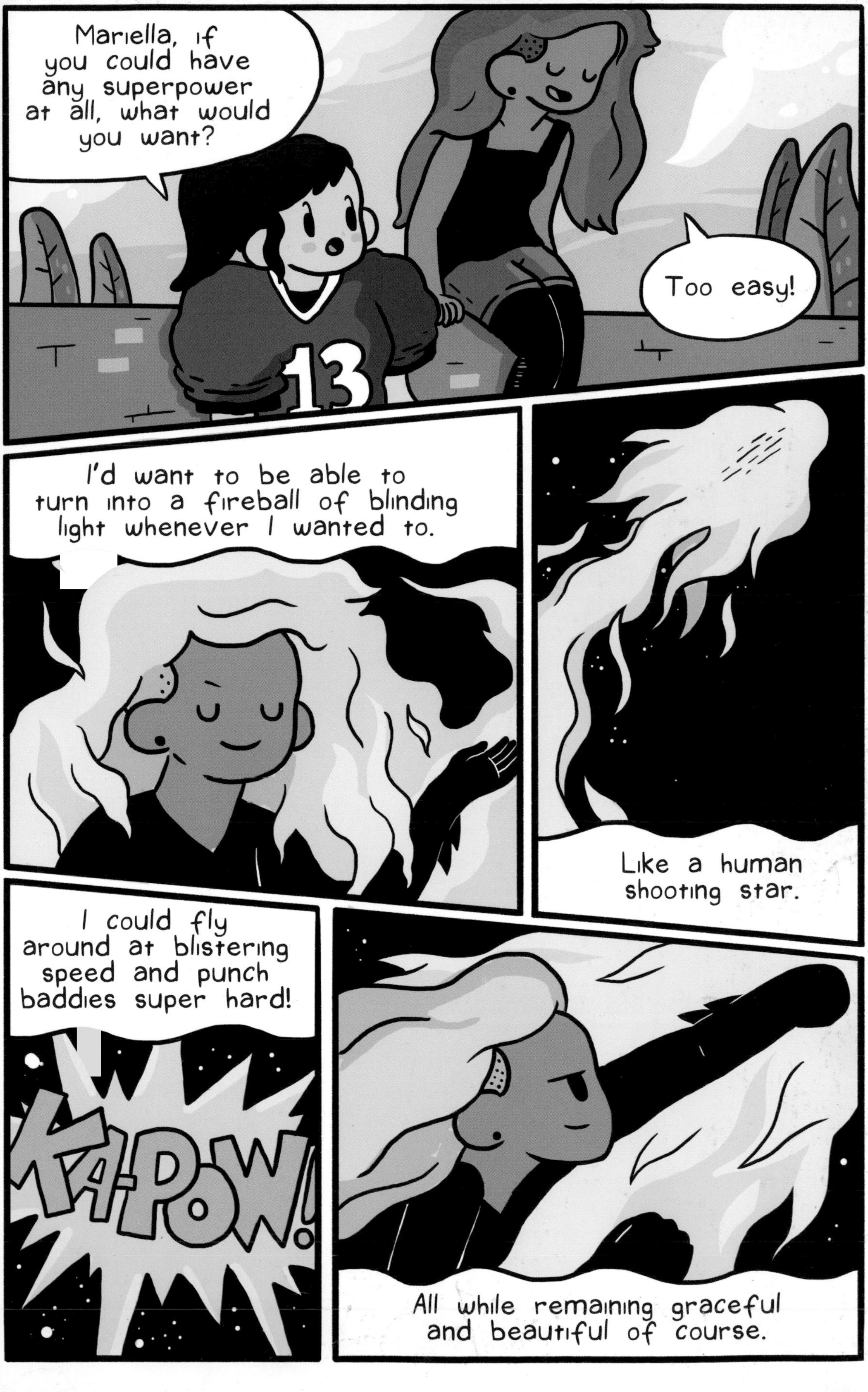
Mariella, if you could have any superpower at all, what would you want?
Too easy!
13
I'd want to be able to turn into a fireball of blinding light whenever I wanted to.
Like a human shooting star.
I could fly around at blistering speed and punch baddies super hard!
KA-POW!
All while remaining graceful and beautiful of course.

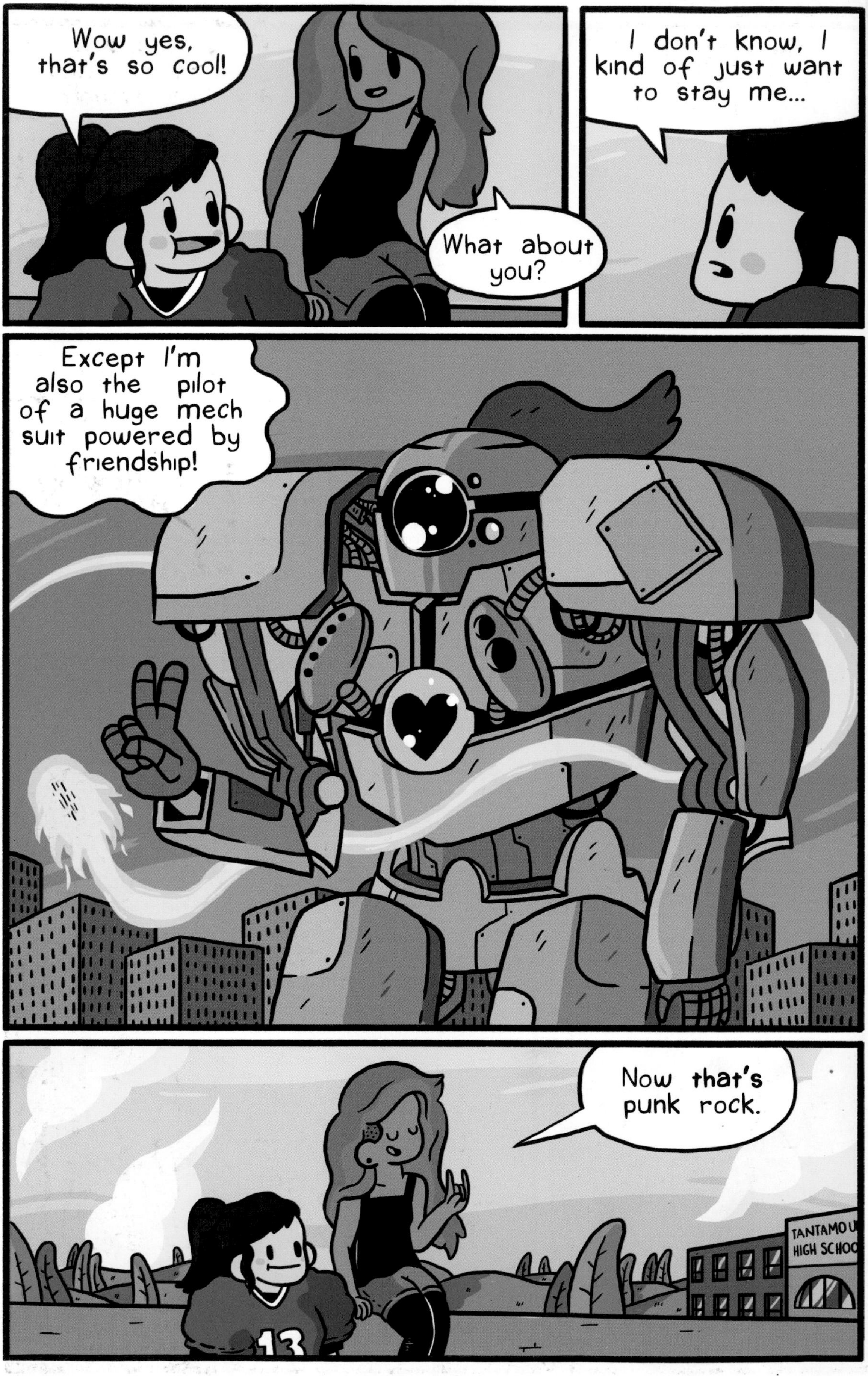
Wow yes, that's so cool!
What about you?
I don't know, I kind of just want to stay me...
Except I'm also the pilot of a huge mech suit powered by friendship!
Now that's punk rock.
TANTAMOU HIGH SCHOO
13

FONZARELLI

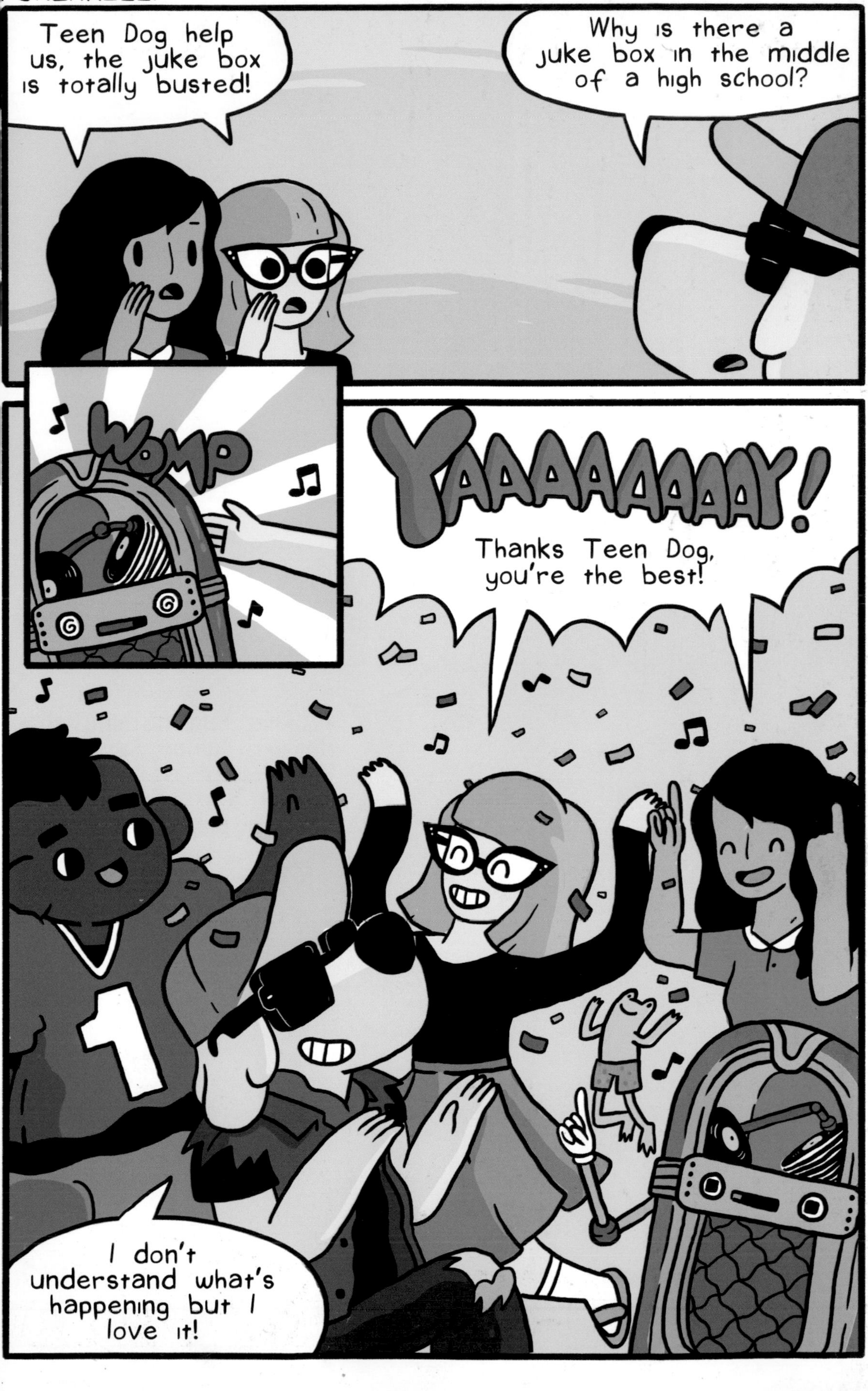

Teen Dog help us, the juke box is totally busted!
Why is there a juke box in the middle of a high school?
WOMP
YAAAAAAAAY!
Thanks Teen Dog, you're the best!
1
I don't understand what's happening but I love it!

MAYA AND THE CHESS CLUB GANG

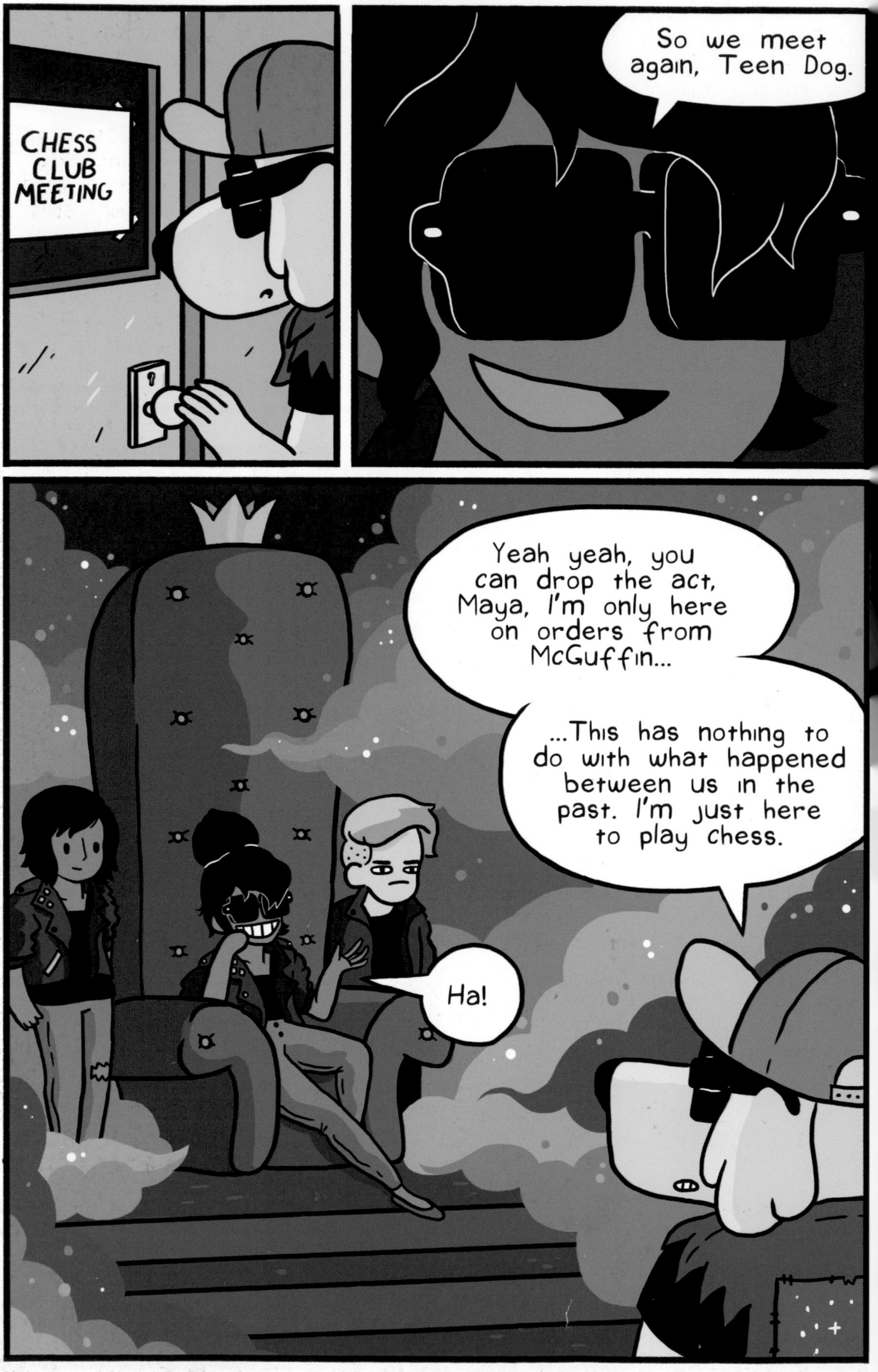
CHESS CLUB MEETING
So we meet again, Teen Dog.
Yeah yeah, you can drop the act, Maya, I'm only here on orders from McGuffin...
...This has nothing to do with what happened between us in the past. I'm just here to play chess.
Ha!

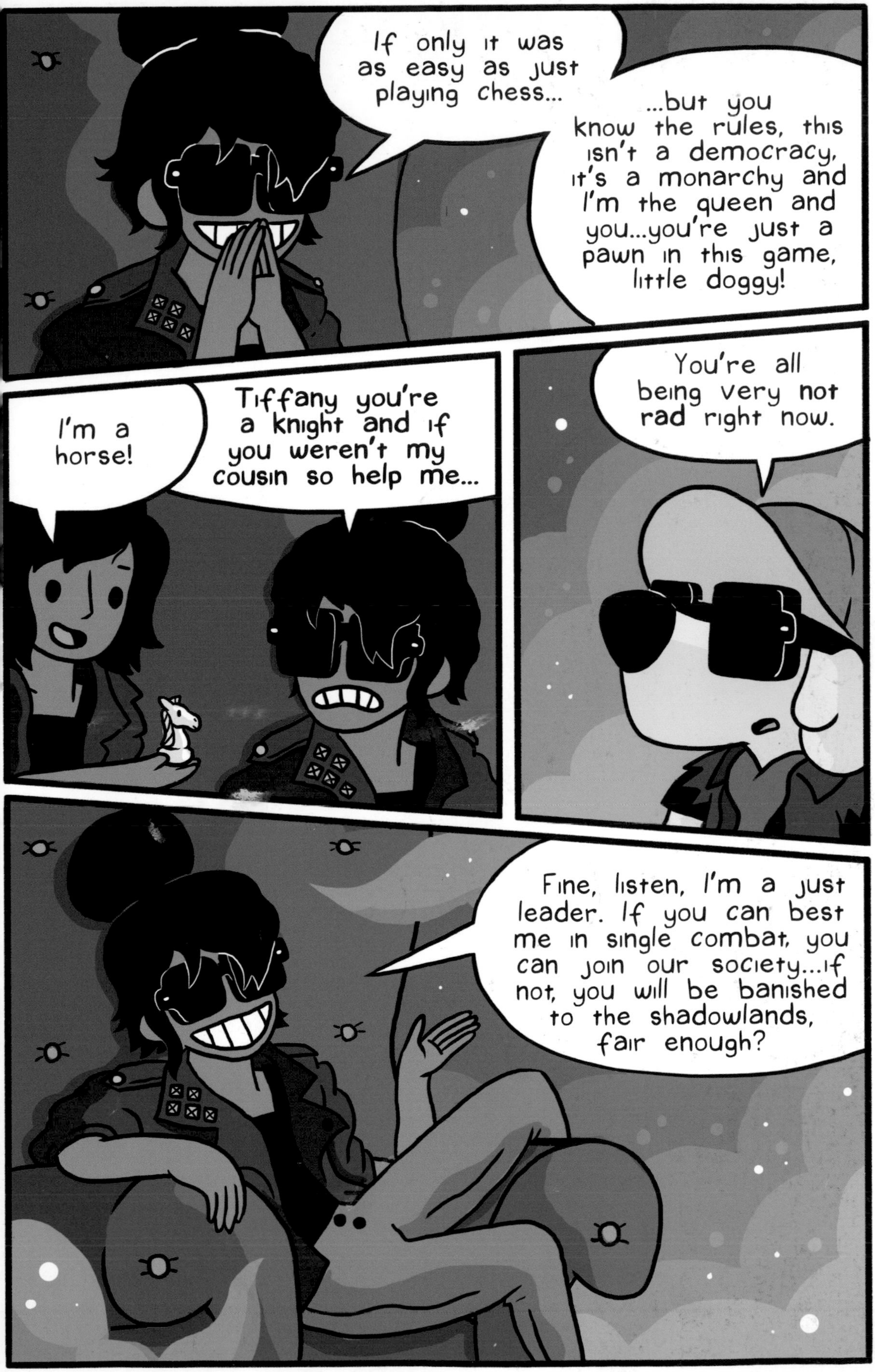
If only it was as easy as just playing chess...
...but you know the rules, this isn't a democracy, it's a monarchy and I'm the queen and you...you're just a pawn in this game, little doggy!
Tiffany you're a knight and if you weren't my cousin so help me...
I'm a horse!
You're all being very not rad right now.
Fine, listen, I'm a just leader. If you can best me in single combat, you can join our society...if not, you will be banished to the shadowlands, fair enough?

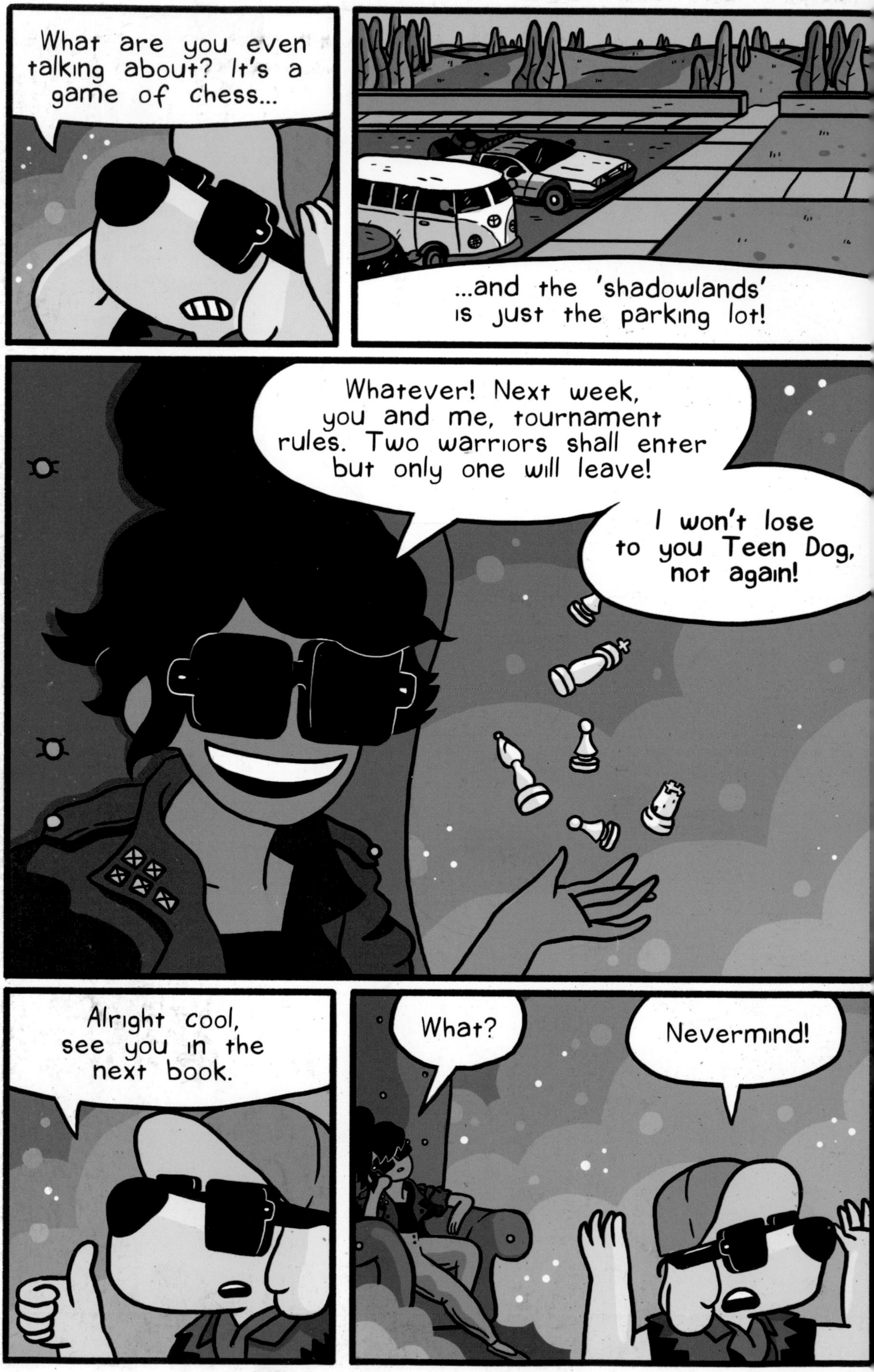
What are you even talking about? It's a game of chess...
...and the 'shadowlands' is just the parking lot!
Whatever! Next week, you and me, tournament rules. Two warriors shall enter but only one will leave!
I won't lose to you Teen Dog, not again!
Alright cool, see you in the next book.
What?
Nevermind!

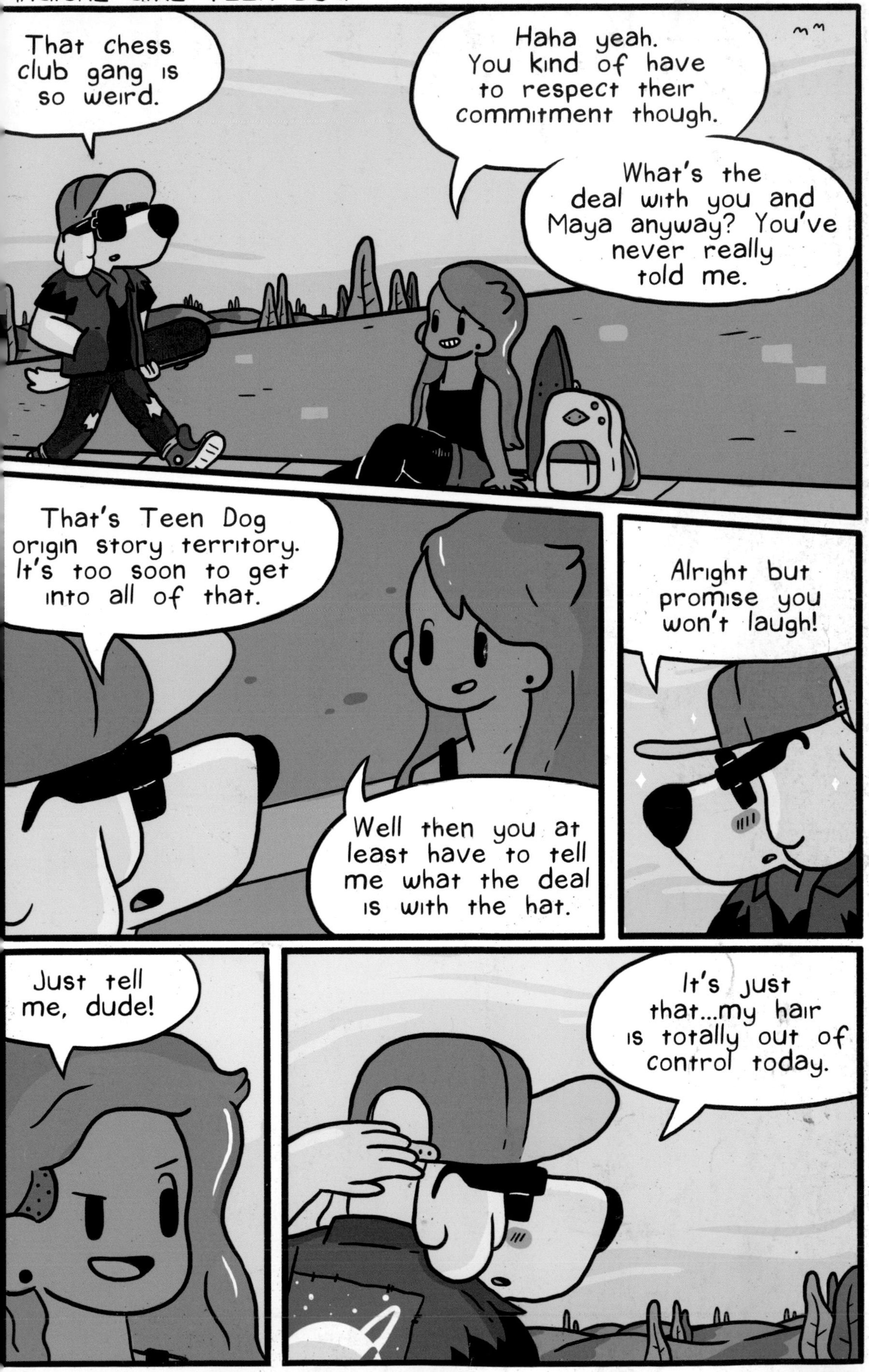
That chess club gang is so weird.
Haha yeah. You kind of have to respect their commitment though.
What's the deal with you and Maya anyway? You've never really told me.
That's Teen Dog origin story territory. It's too soon to get into all of that.
Well then you at least have to tell me what the deal is with the hat.
Alright but promise you won't laugh!
Just tell me, dude!
It's just that...my hair is totally out of control today.

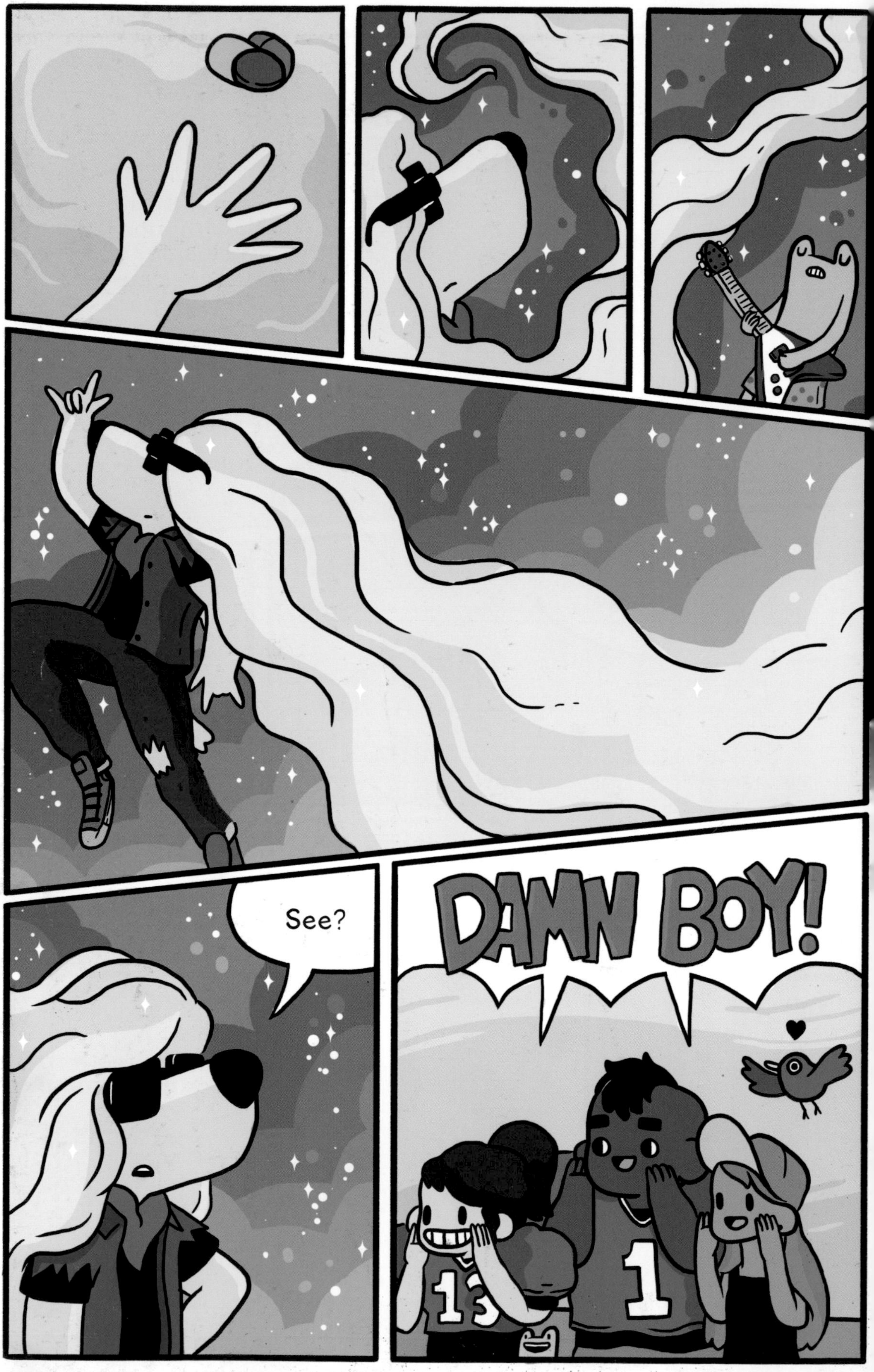
See?
DAMN BOY!
13
1

CHAPTER ENDS

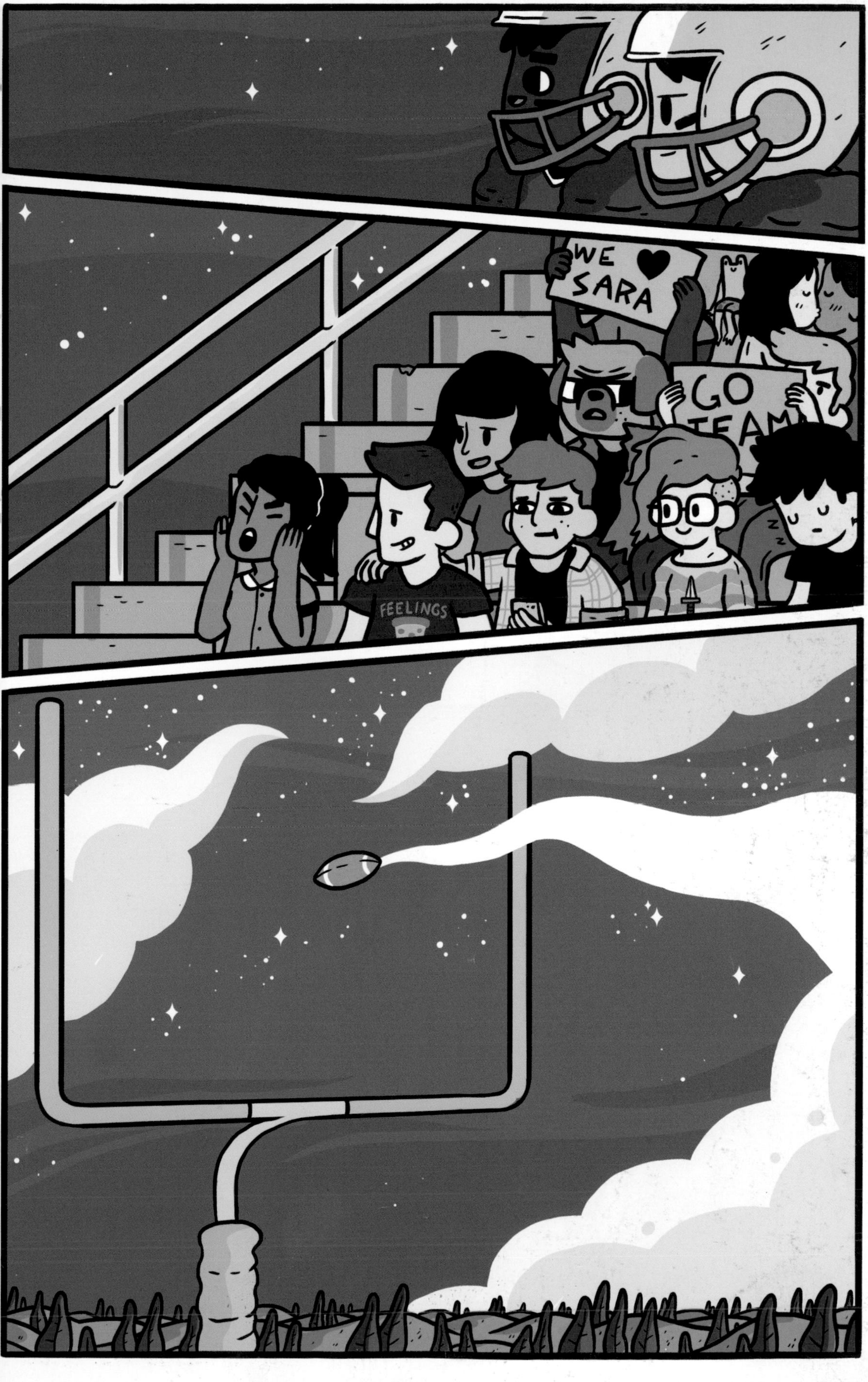
WE ♥ SARA
GO TEAM
FEELINGS

WELCOME BACK SPORTS FANS

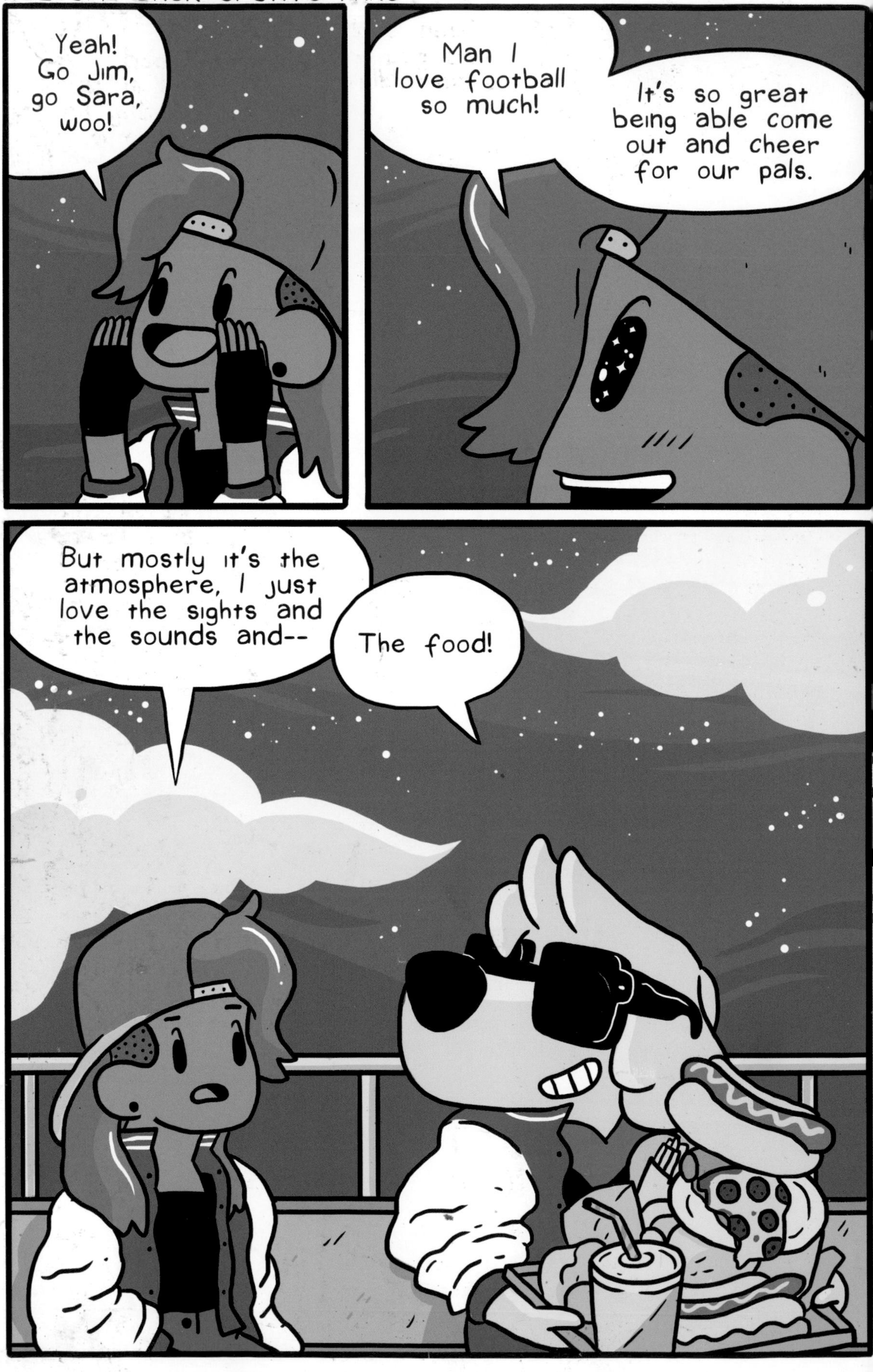

CHAPTER THREE

Yeah! Go Jim, go Sara, woo!
Man I love football so much!
It's so great being able come out and cheer for our pals.
But mostly it's the atmosphere, I just love the sights and the sounds and--
The food!

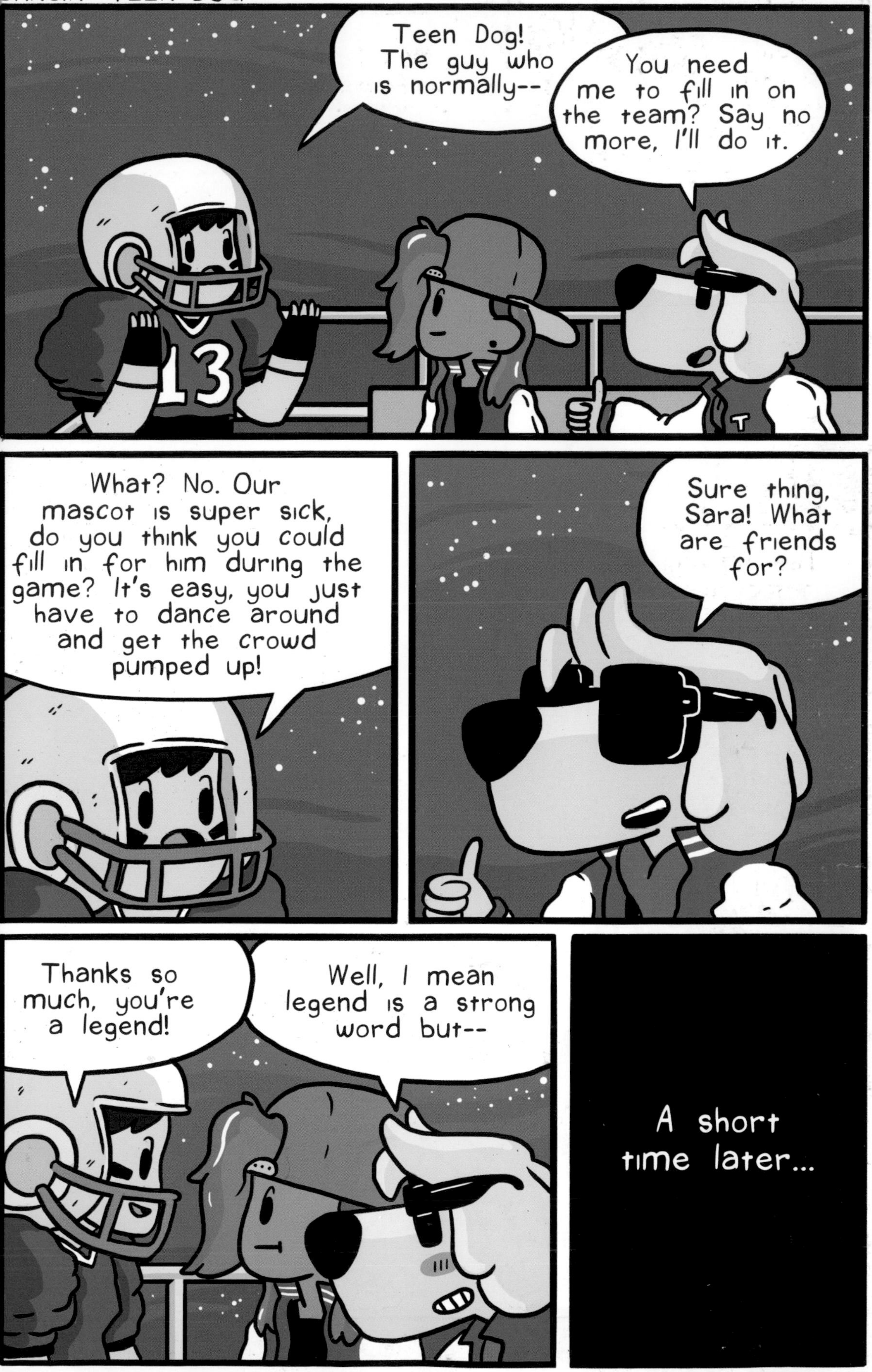
Teen Dog! The guy who is normally--
You need me to fill in on the team? Say no more, I'll do it.
13
T
What? No. Our mascot is super sick, do you think you could fill in for him during the game? It's easy, you just have to dance around and get the crowd pumped up!
Sure thing, Sara! What are friends for?
Thanks so much, you're a legend!
Well, I mean legend is a strong word but--
A short time later...

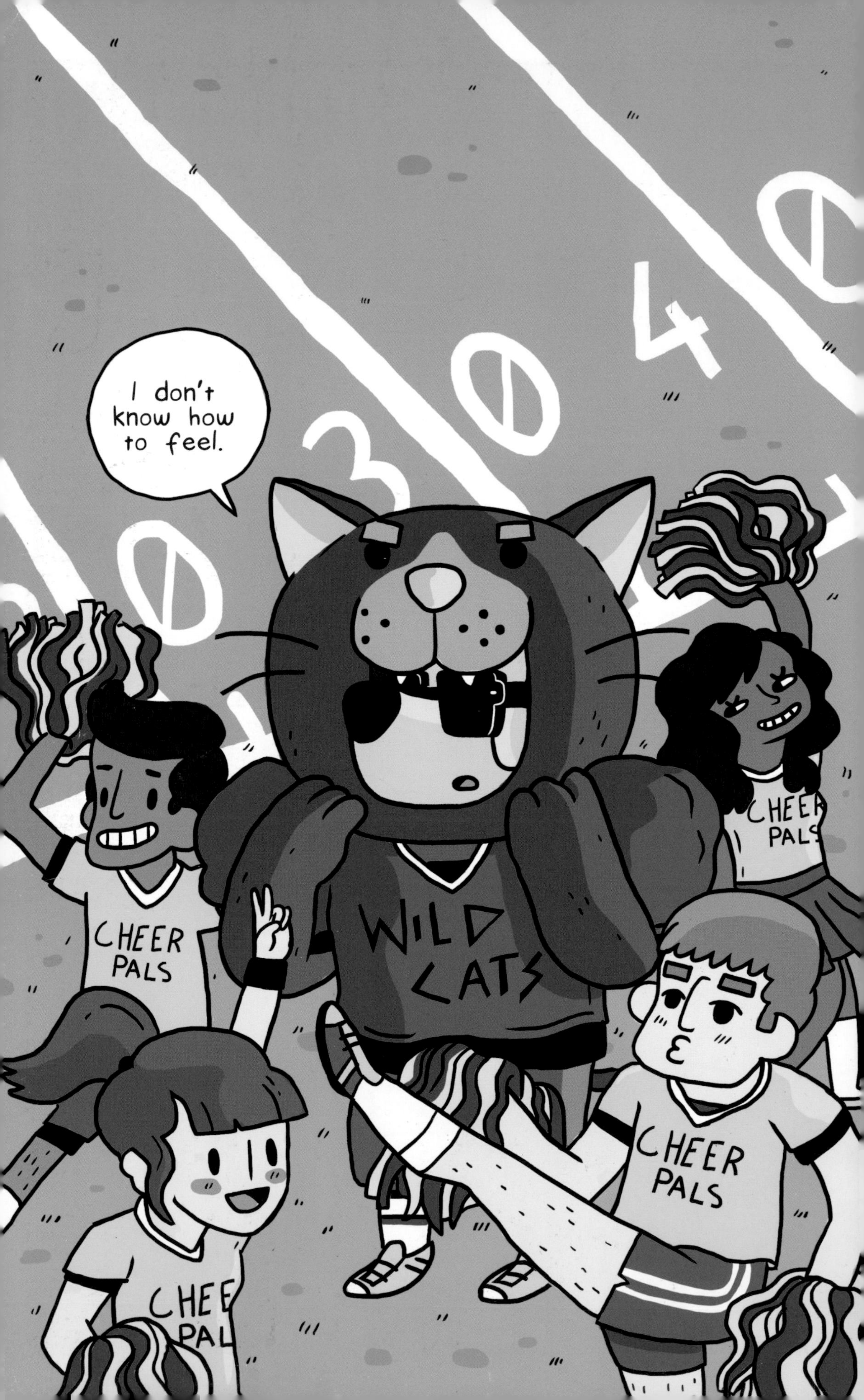
I don't know how to feel.
30
40
WILD CATS
CHEER PALS
CHEER PALS
CHEER PALS
CHEER PALS
CHEE PAL

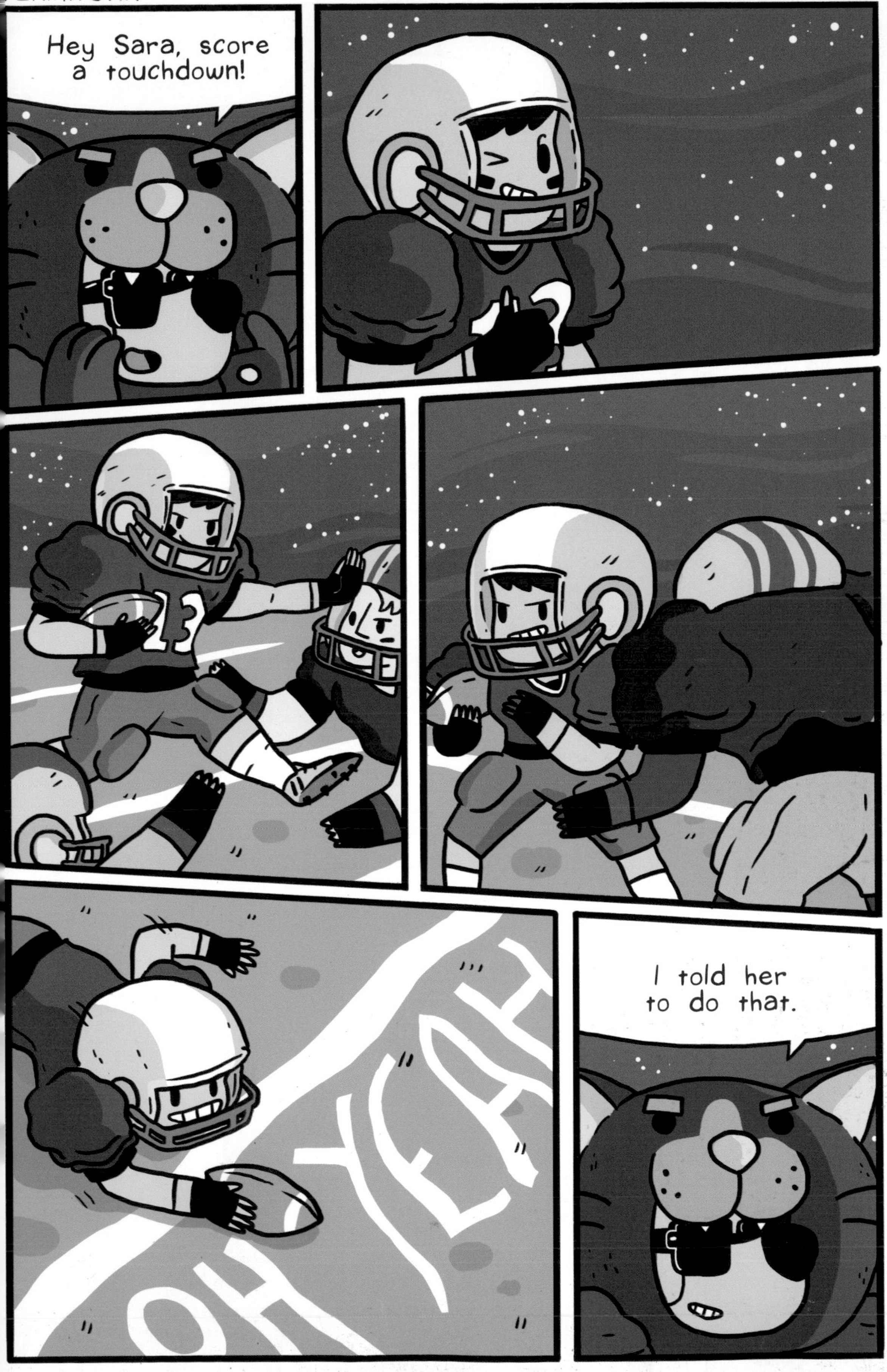
Hey Sara, score a touchdown!
OH YEAH
I told her to do that.

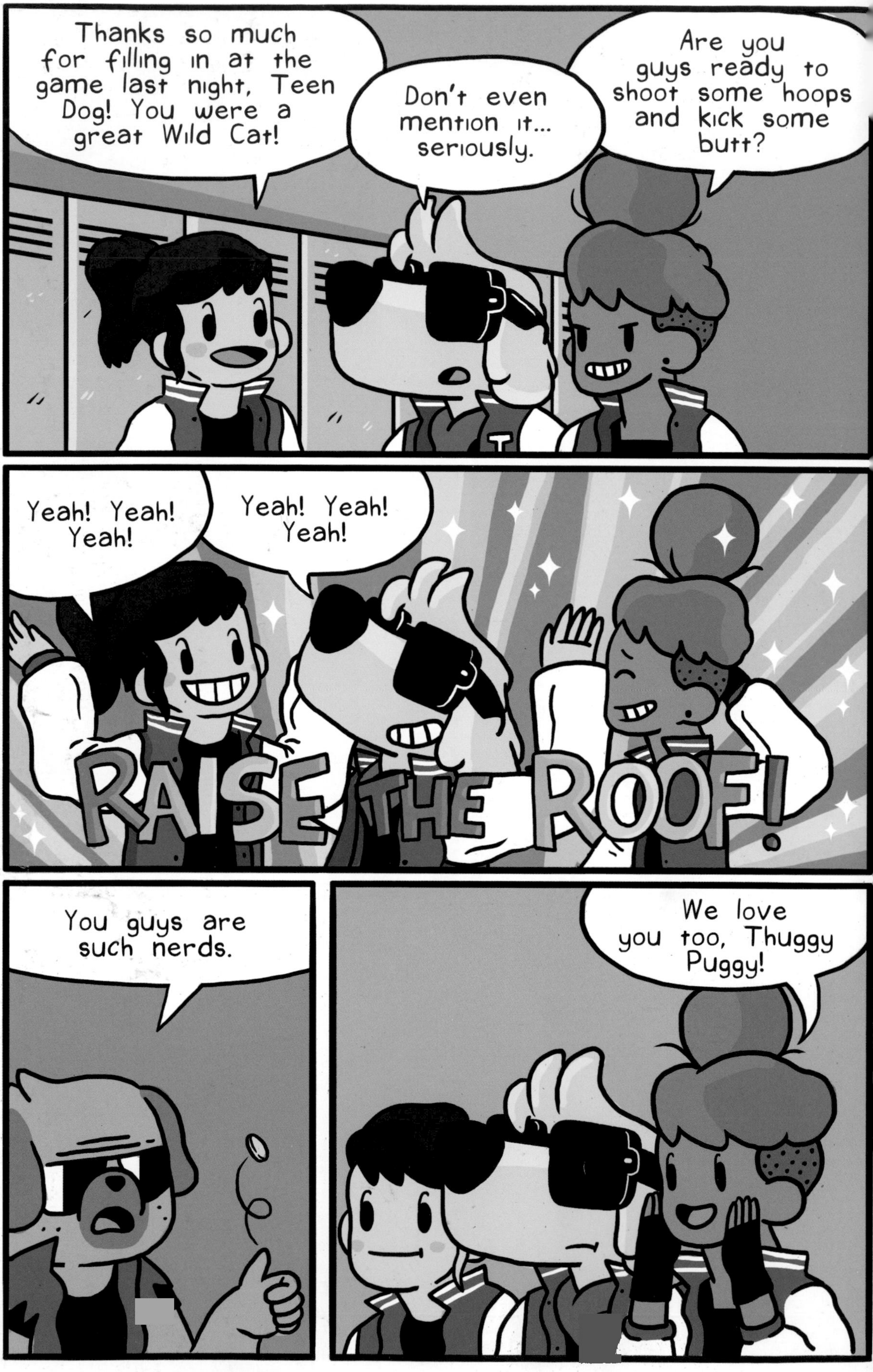
Thanks so much for filling in at the game last night, Teen Dog! You were a great Wild Cat!
Don't even mention it... seriously.
Are you guys ready to shoot some hoops and kick some butt?
Yeah! Yeah! Yeah!
Yeah! Yeah! Yeah!
RAISE THE ROOF!
You guys are such nerds.
We love you too, Thuggy Puggy!

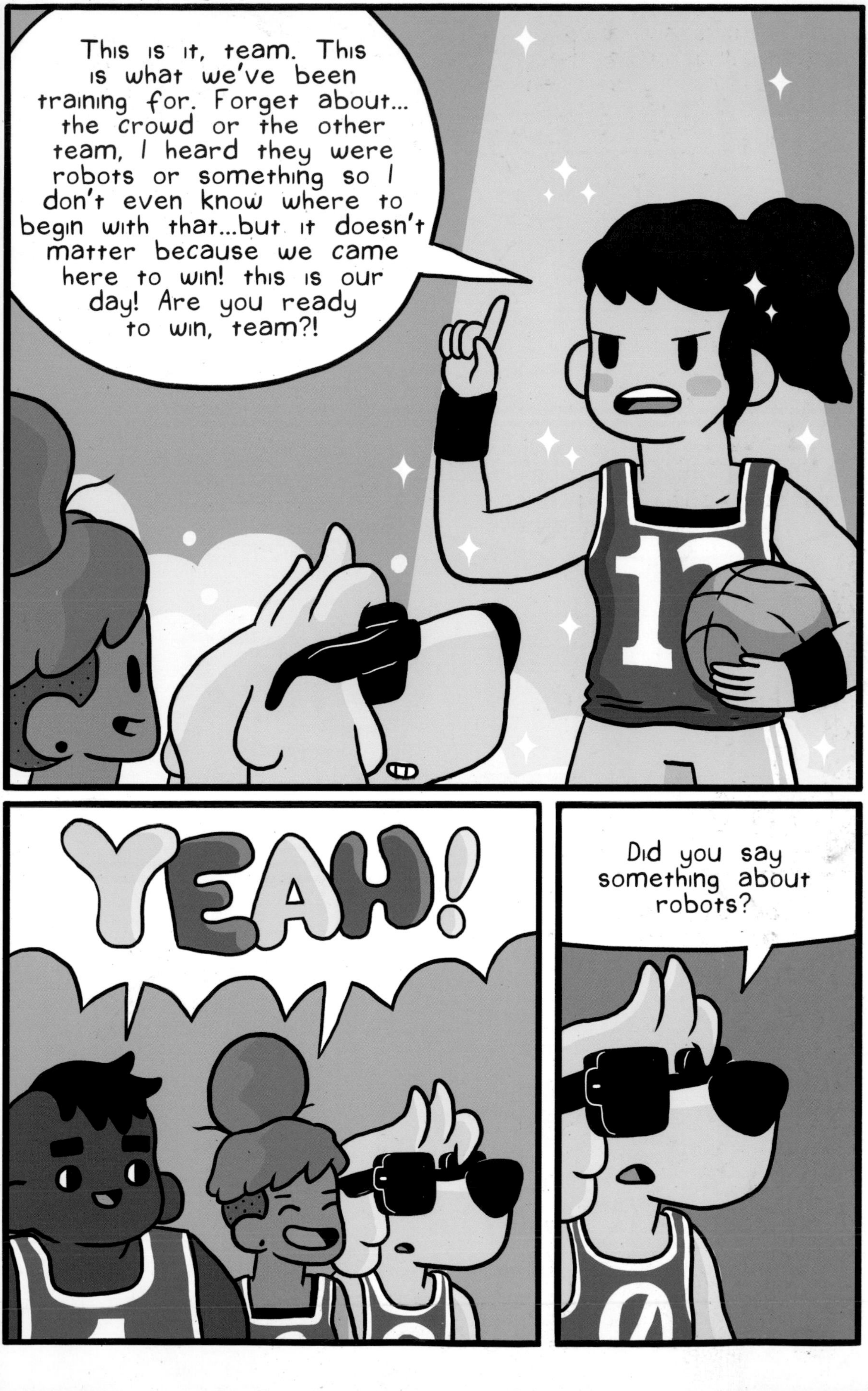
This is it, team. This is what we've been training for. Forget about... the crowd or the other team, I heard they were robots or something so I don't even know where to begin with that...but it doesn't matter because we came here to win! this is our day! Are you ready to win, team?!
YEAH!
Did you say something about robots?

AIR BUDS

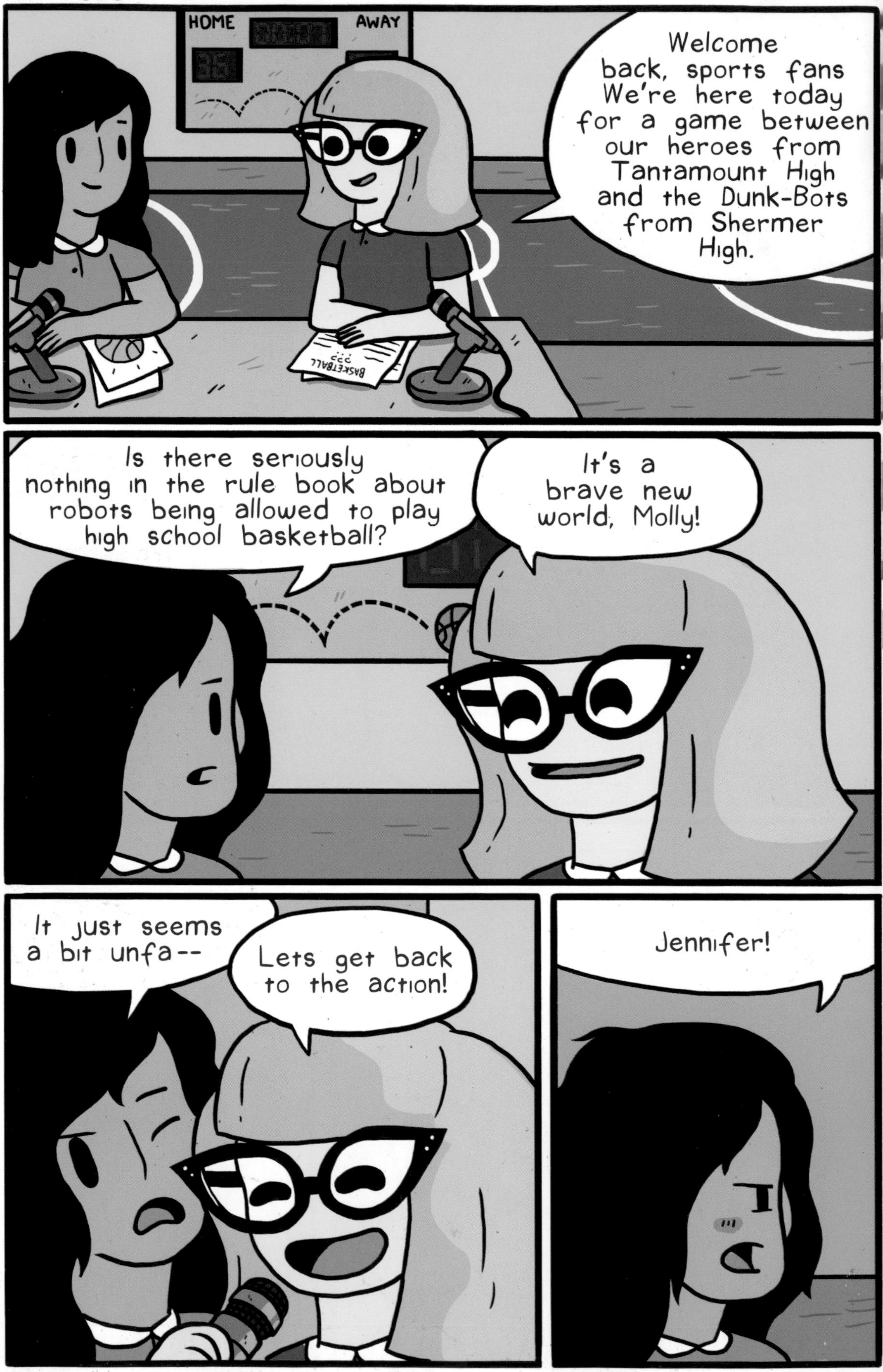
HOME
AWAY
Welcome back, sports fans We're here today for a game between our heroes from Tantamount High and the Dunk-Bots from Shermer High.
Is there seriously nothing in the rule book about robots being allowed to play high school basketball?
It's a brave new world, Molly!
It just seems a bit unfa--
Lets get back to the action!
Jennifer!

OUR HEROES VERSUS THE DUNK-BOTS

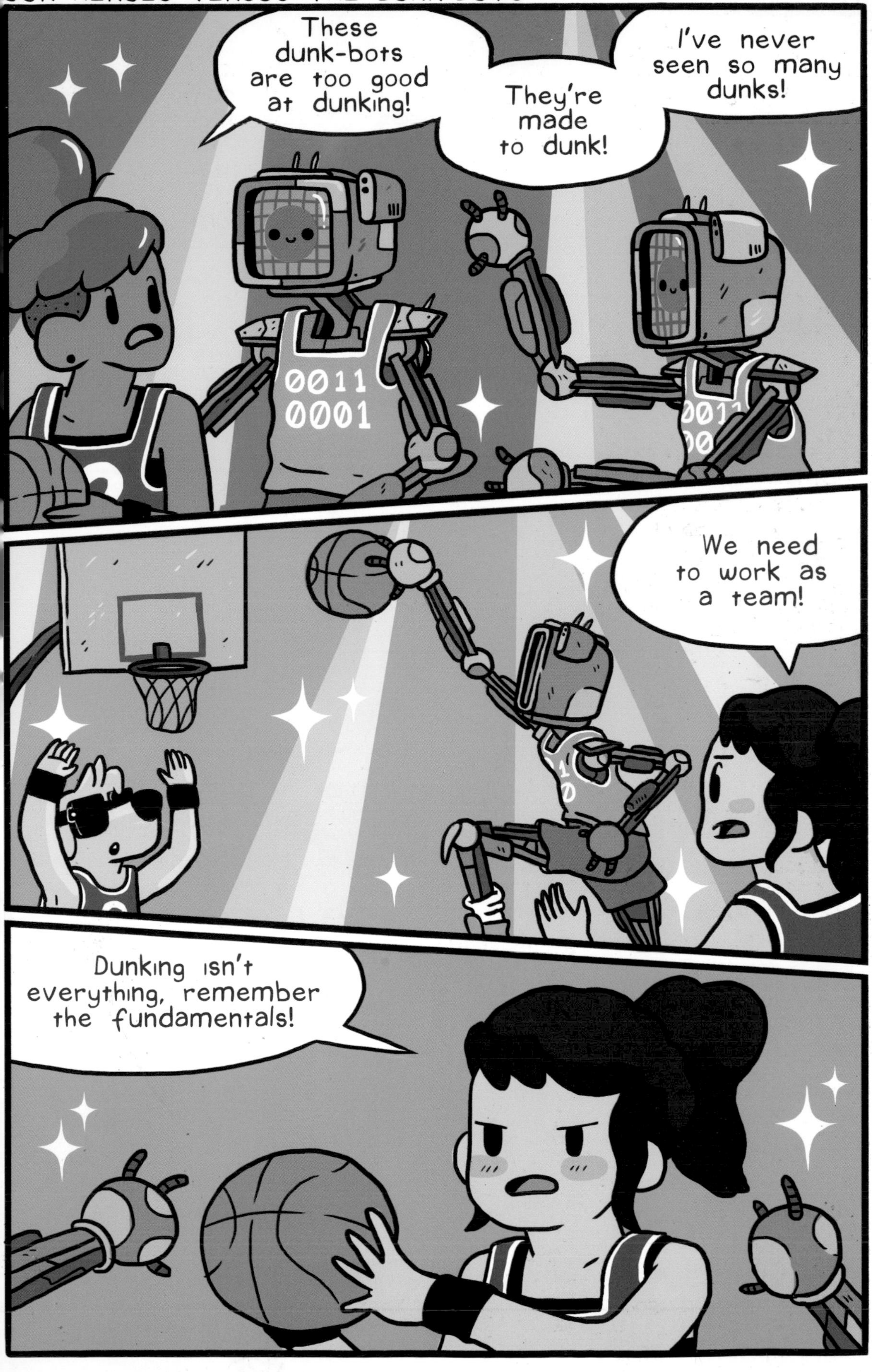
These dunk-bots are too good at dunking!
They're made to dunk!
I've never seen so many dunks!
0011 0001
We need to work as a team!
Dunking isn't everything, remember the fundamentals!

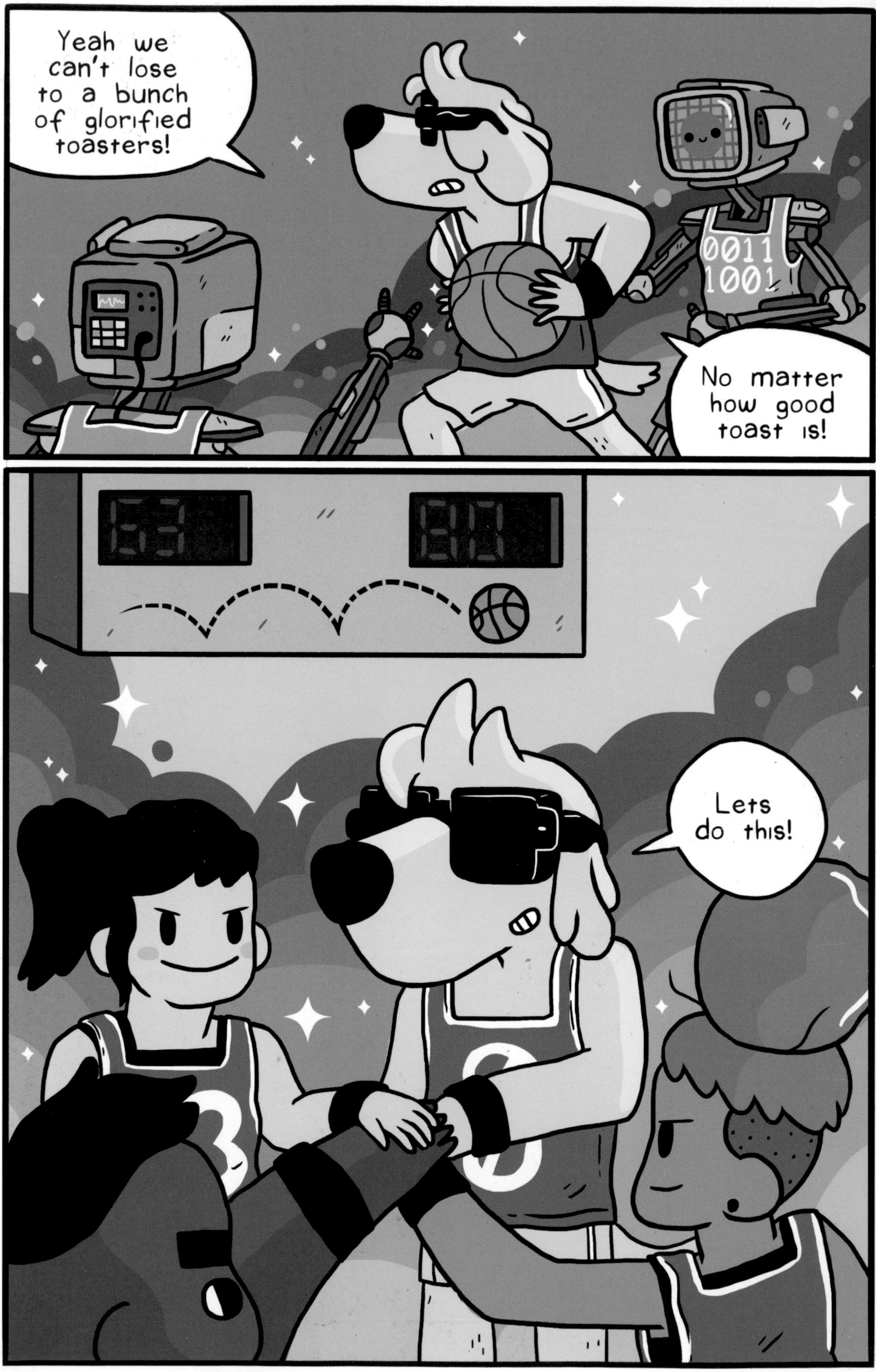
Yeah we can't lose to a bunch of glorified toasters!
No matter how good toast is!
Lets do this!

TERMINATED

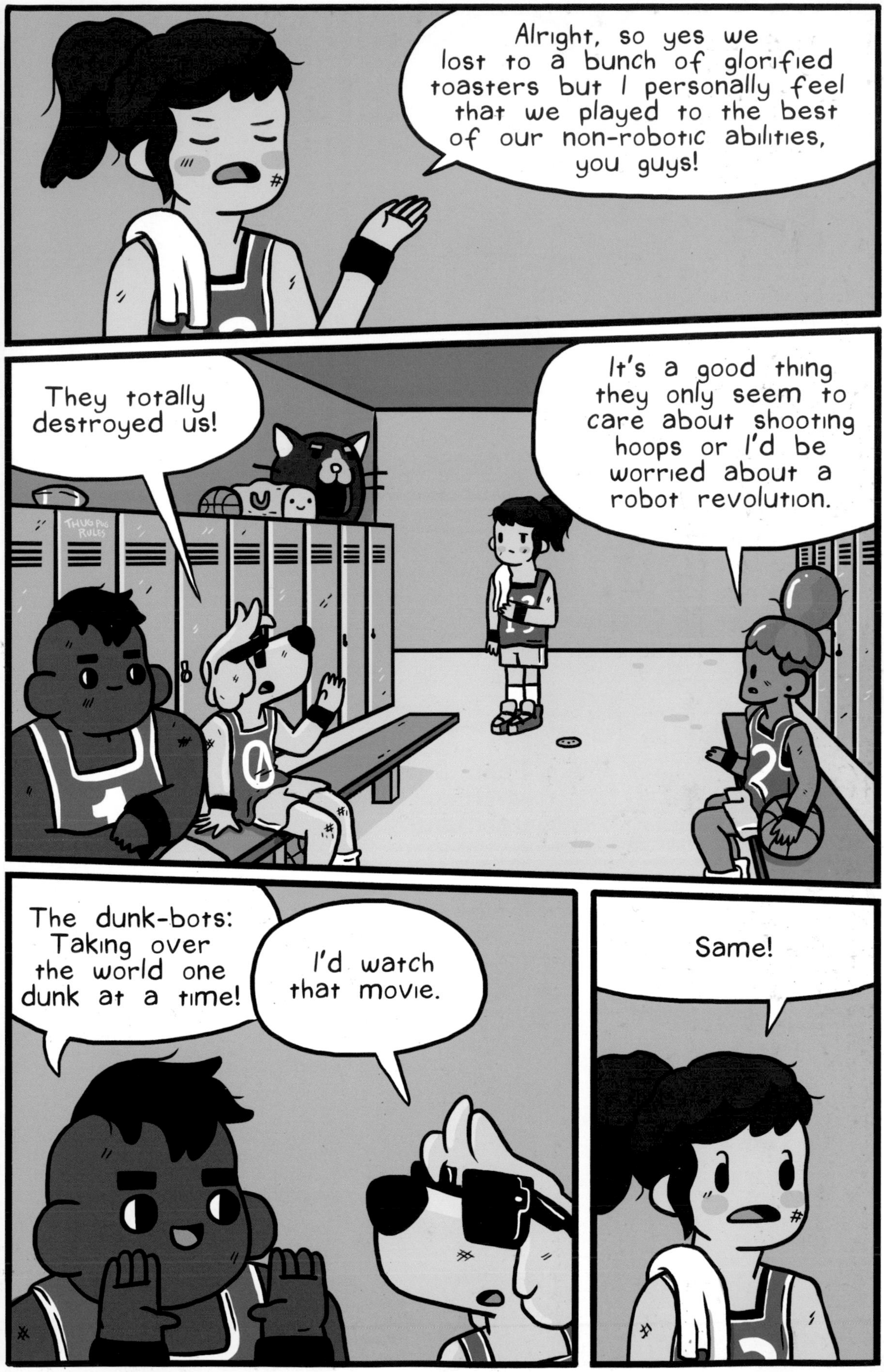

Alright, so yes we lost to a bunch of glorified toasters but I personally feel that we played to the best of our non-robotic abilities, you guys!
They totally destroyed us!
It's a good thing they only seem to care about shooting hoops or I'd be worried about a robot revolution.
THUG PUG RULES
The dunk-bots: Taking over the world one dunk at a time!
I'd watch that movie.
Same!

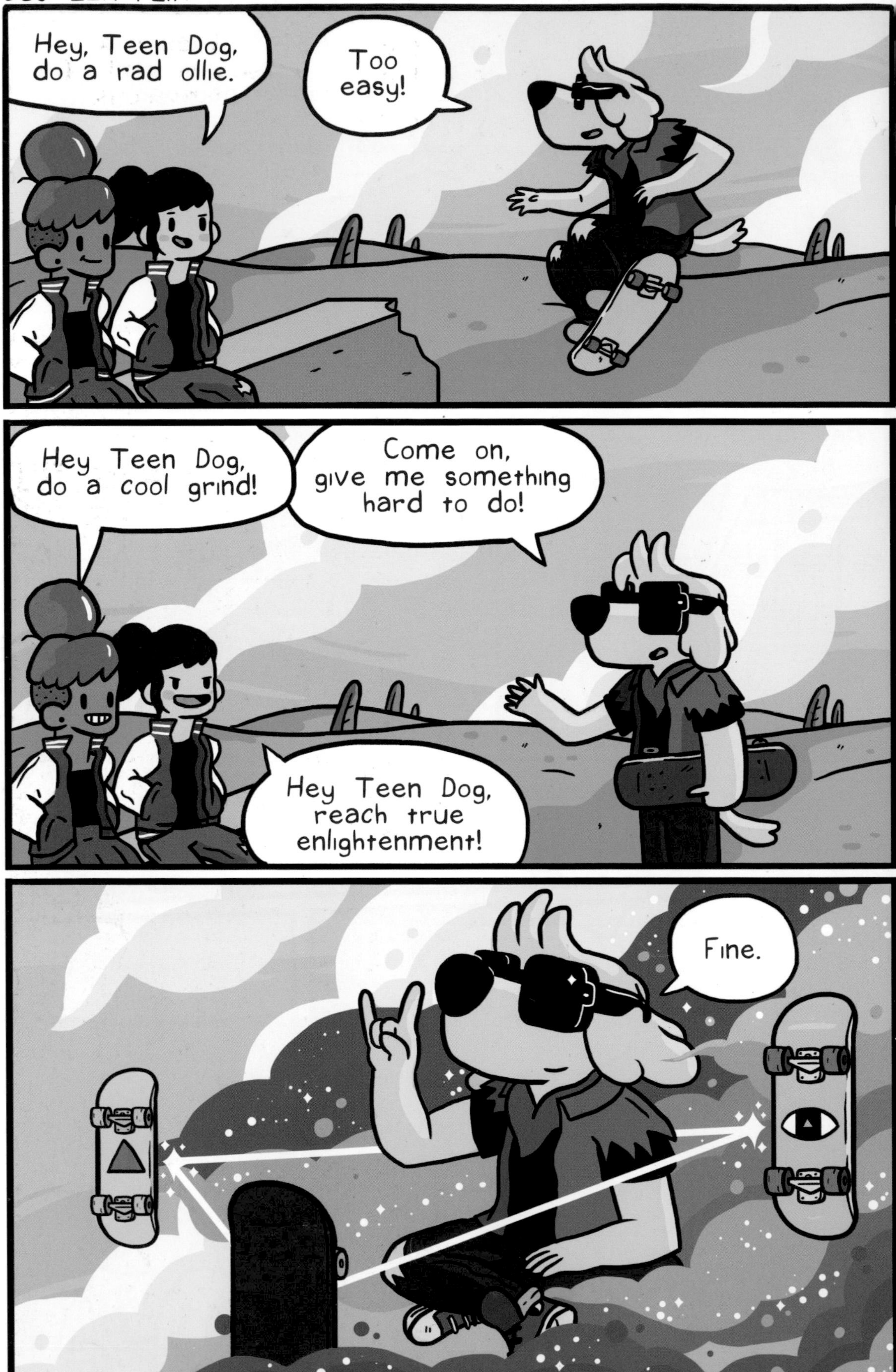
Hey, Teen Dog, do a rad ollie.
Too easy!
Hey Teen Dog, do a cool grind!
Come on, give me something hard to do!
Hey Teen Dog, reach true enlightenment!
Fine.

WHERE WE'RE GOING, WE DON'T NEED SKATEBOARDS

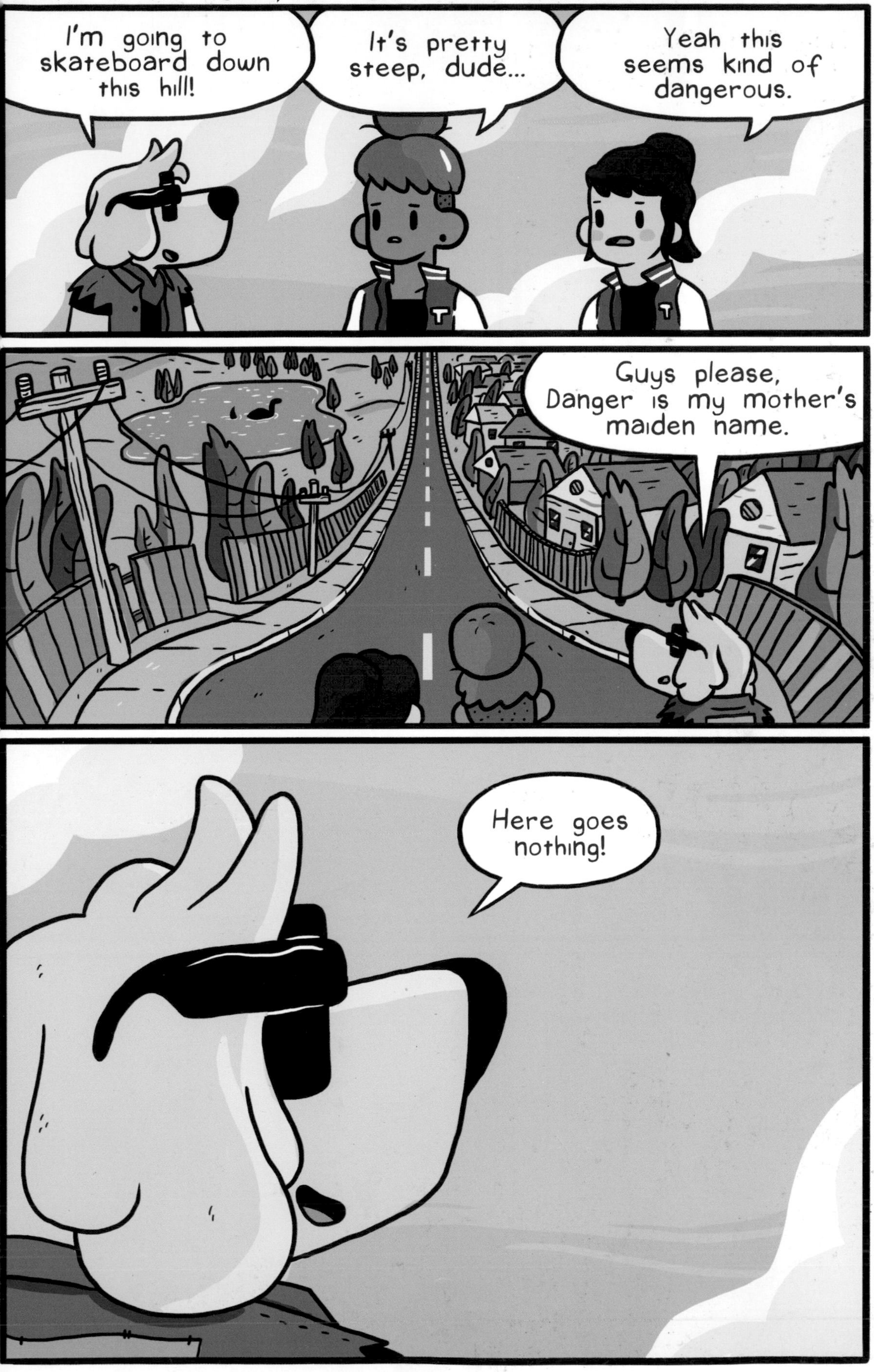

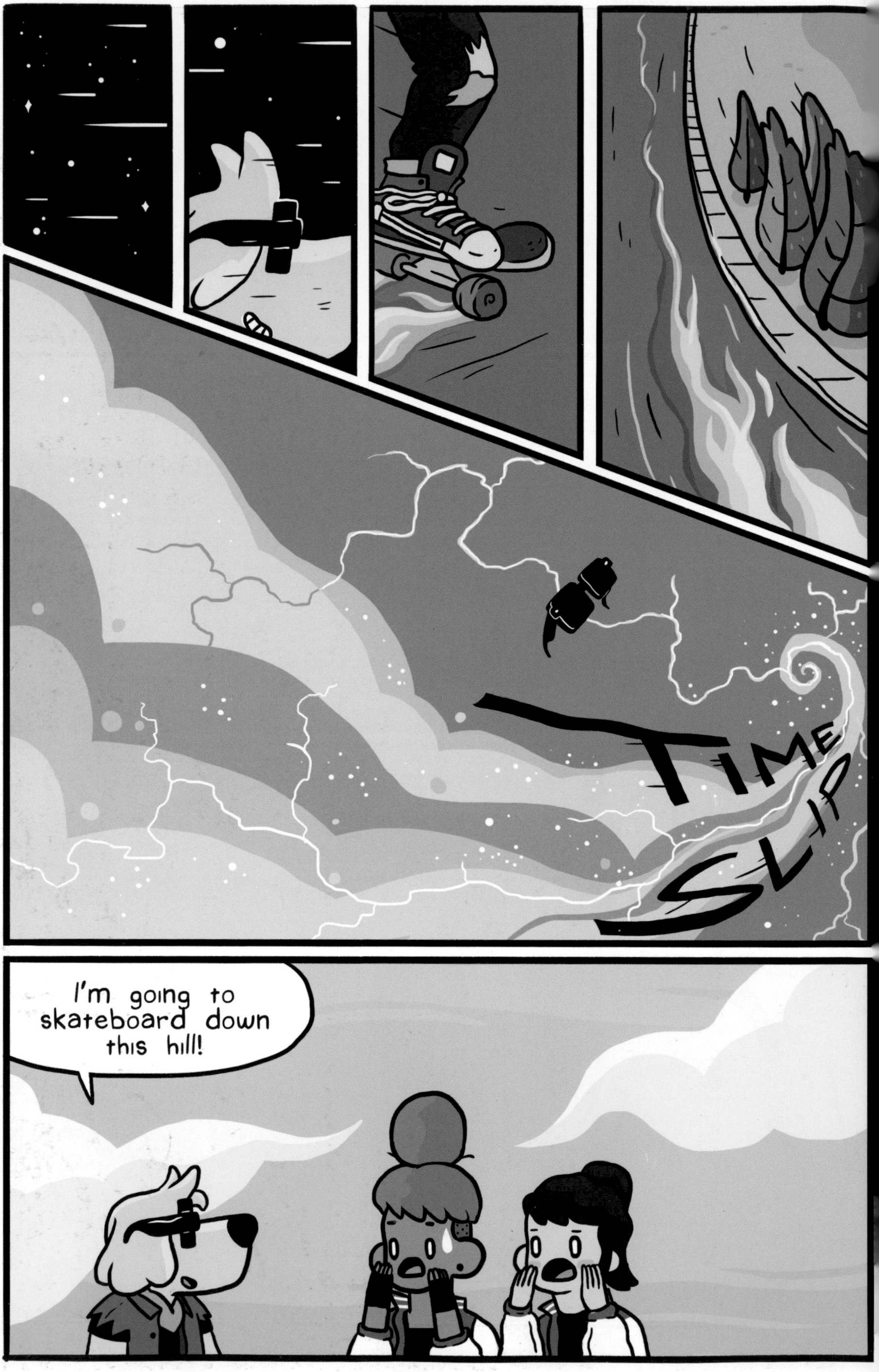
TIME SLIP
I'm going to skateboard down this hill!

HURL SCOUTS, EAT YOUR HEART OUT

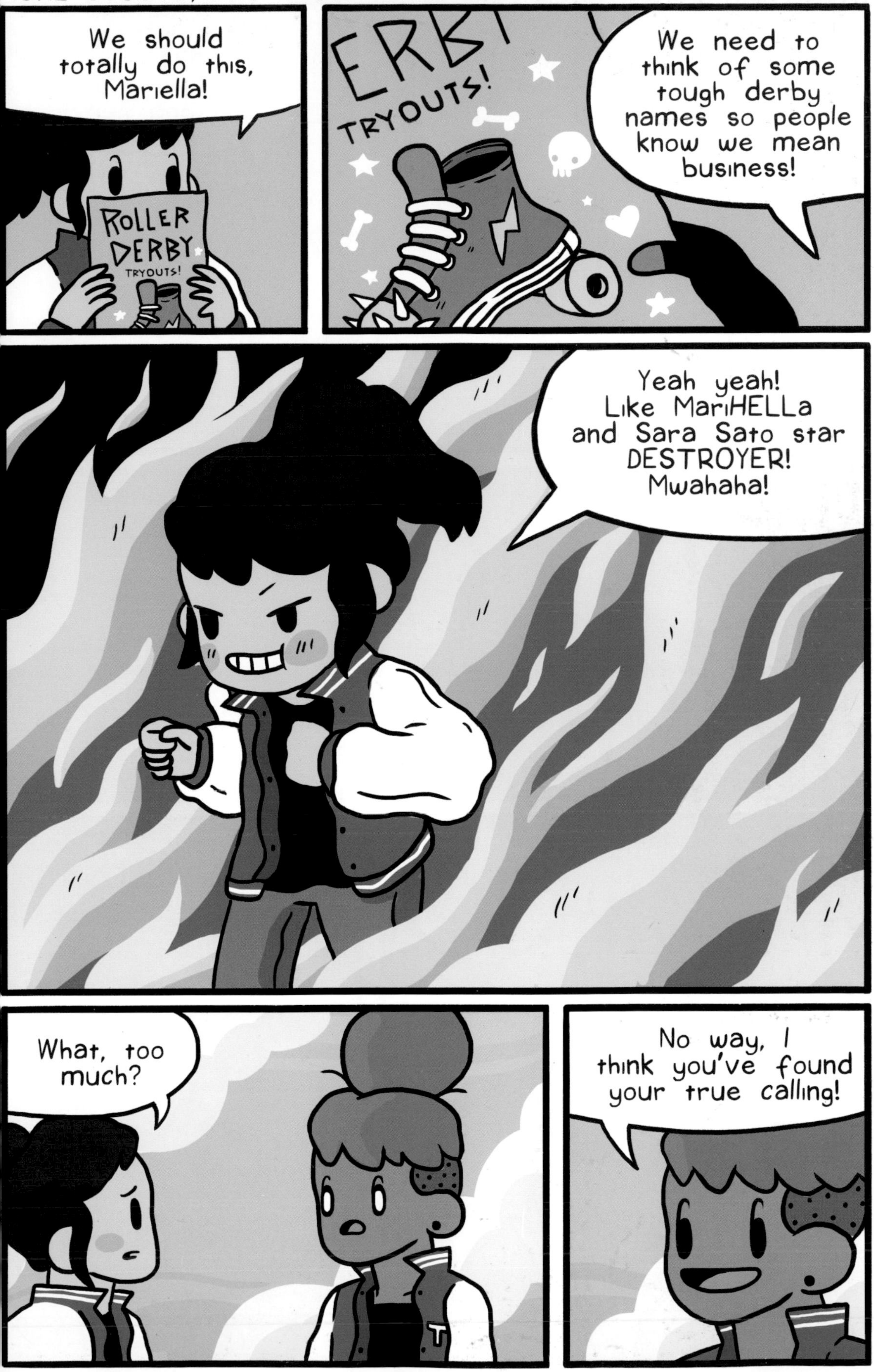

We should totally do this, Mariella!
ROLLER DERBY TRYOUTS!
ERBY TRYOUTS!
We need to think of some tough derby names so people know we mean business!
Yeah yeah! Like MariHELLa and Sara Sato star DESTROYER! Mwahaha!
What, too much?
No way, I think you've found your true calling!

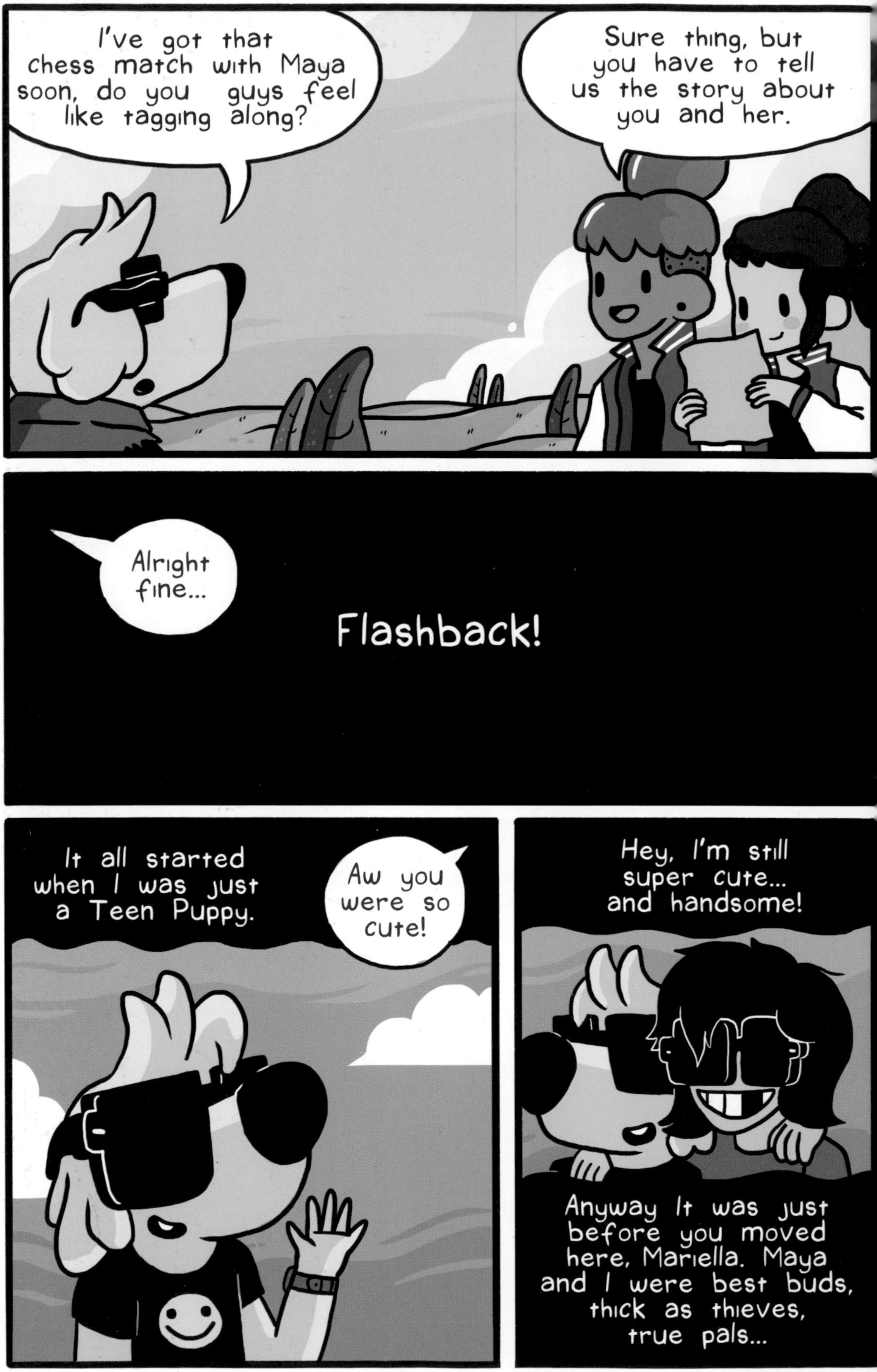
I've got that chess match with Maya soon, do you guys feel like tagging along?
Sure thing, but you have to tell us the story about you and her.
Alright fine...
Flashback!
It all started when I was just a Teen Puppy.
Aw you were so cute!
Hey, I'm still super cute... and handsome!
Anyway It was just before you moved here, Mariella. Maya and I were best buds, thick as thieves, true pals...

We hung out all the time, skipping stones...

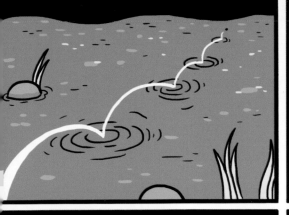

Catching frogs, you know regular kid stuff?

Then one rainy day we were stuck inside so we played chess like we always did on rainy days.

I won one match against her and she just flipped out! After that we just kind of stopped hanging out all the time.

Wait, does she have latent psychic powers?

Yeah something like that.

That's so punk!

THE SHOWDOWN

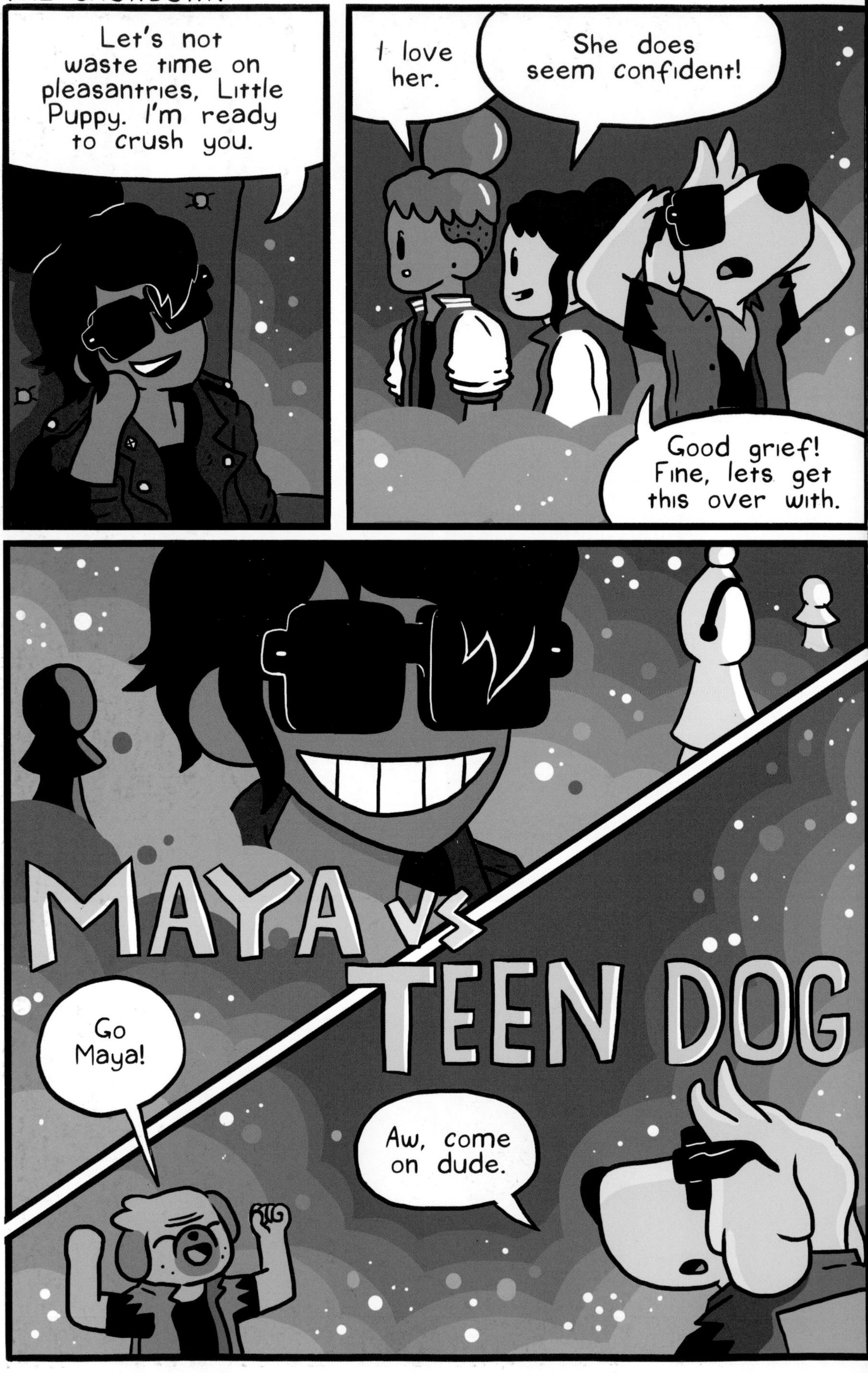
Let's not waste time on pleasantries, Little Puppy. I'm ready to crush you.
I love her.
She does seem confident!
Good grief! Fine, lets get this over with.
MAYA VS TEEN DOG
Go Maya!
Aw, come on dude.

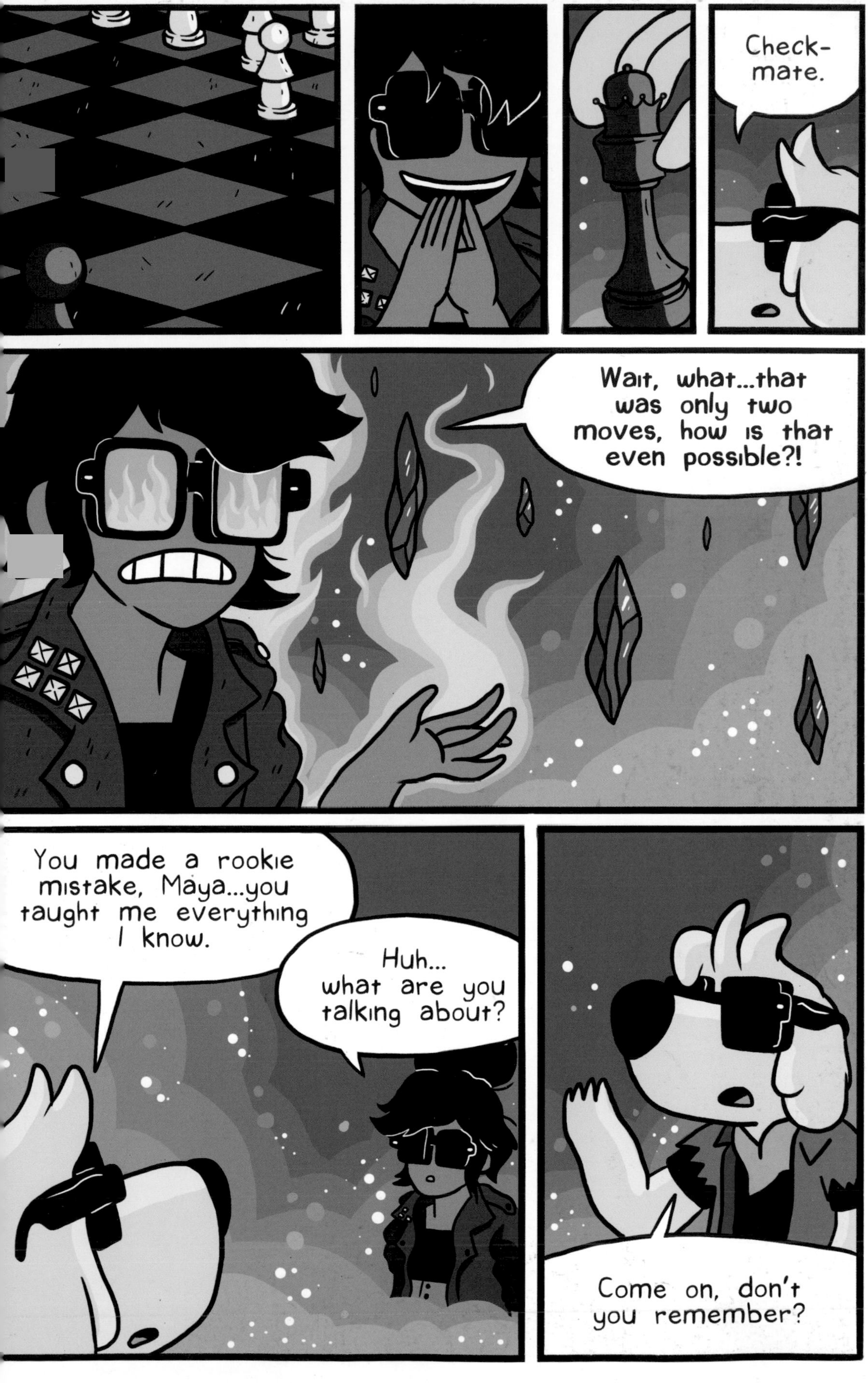
Check-
mate.
Wait, what...that was only two moves, how is that even possible?!
You made a rookie mistake, Maya...you taught me everything I know.
Huh... what are you talking about?
Come on, don't you remember?

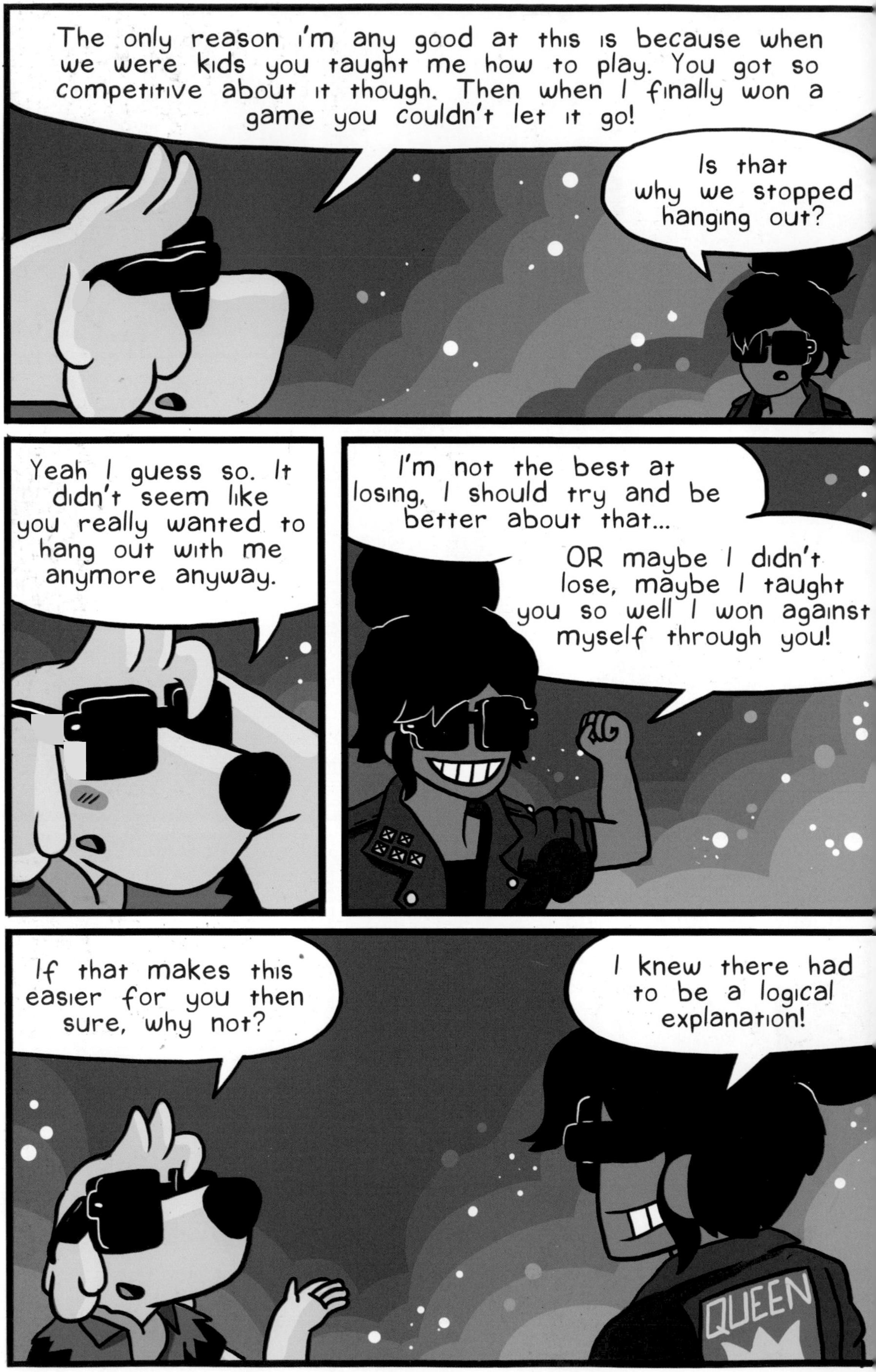
The only reason i'm any good at this is because when we were kids you taught me how to play. You got so competitive about it though. Then when I finally won a game you couldn't let it go!
Is that why we stopped hanging out?
Yeah I guess so. It didn't seem like you really wanted to hang out with me anymore anyway.
I'm not the best at losing, I should try and be better about that...
OR maybe I didn't lose, maybe I taught you so well I won against myself through you!
If that makes this easier for you then sure, why not?
I knew there had to be a logical explanation!
QUEEN

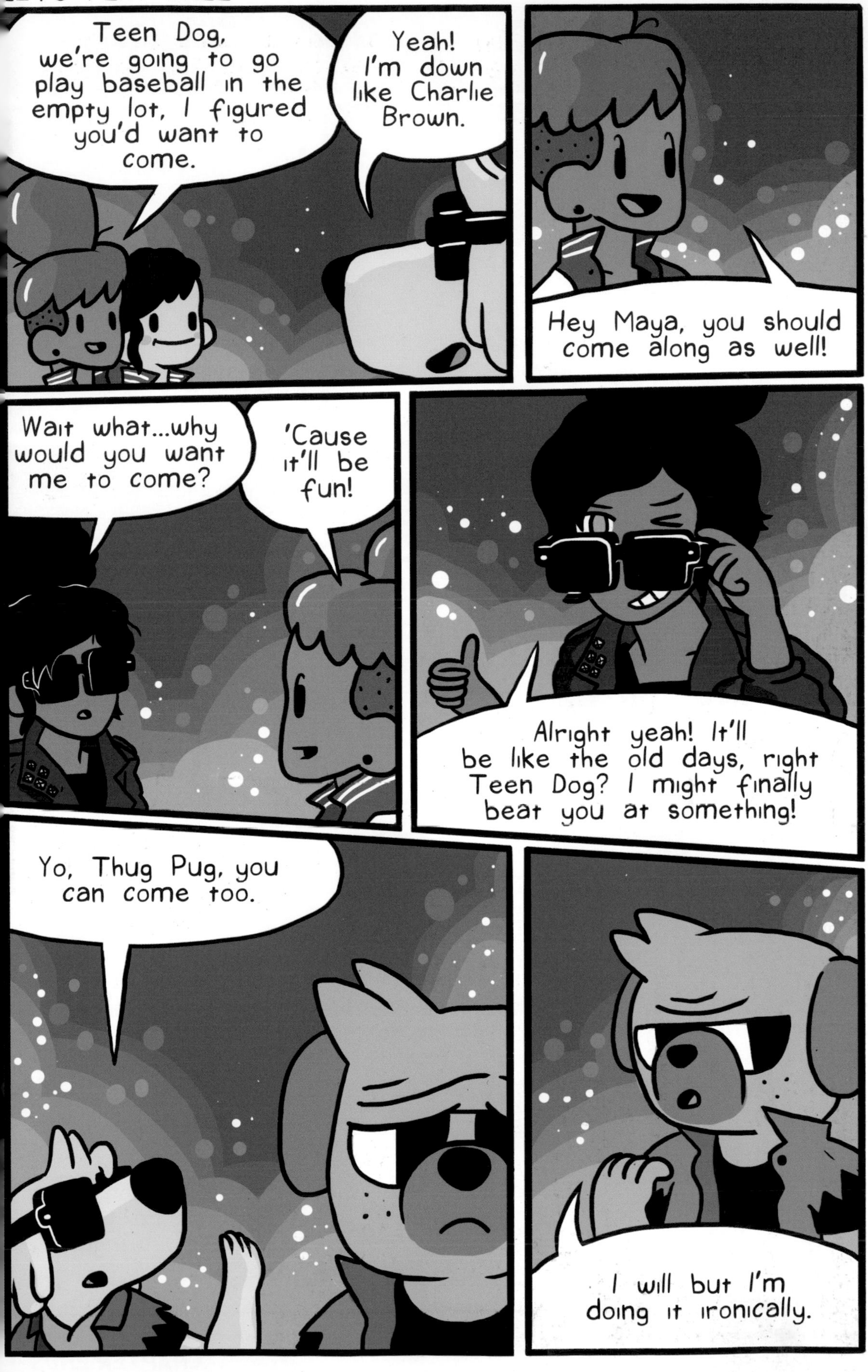
Teen Dog, we're going to go play baseball in the empty lot, I figured you'd want to come.
Yeah! I'm down like Charlie Brown.
Hey Maya, you should come along as well!
Wait what...why would you want me to come?
'Cause it'll be fun!
Alright yeah! It'll be like the old days, right Teen Dog? I might finally beat you at something!
Yo, Thug Pug, you can come too.
I will but I'm doing it ironically.

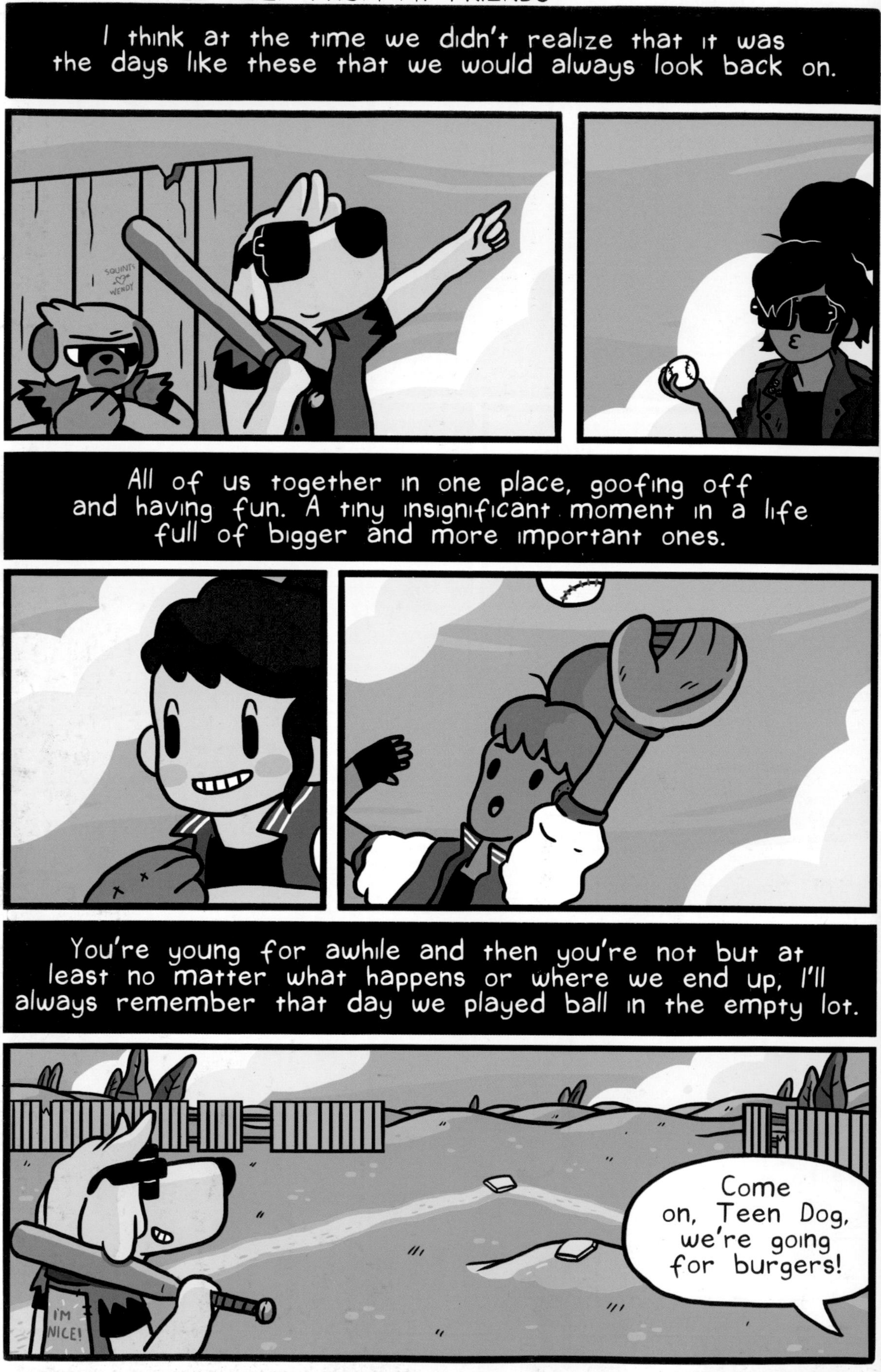
I think at the time we didn't realize that it was the days like these that we would always look back on.
SQUINTS ♡ WENDY
All of us together in one place, goofing off and having fun. A tiny insignificant moment in a life full of bigger and more important ones.
You're young for awhile and then you're not but at least no matter what happens or where we end up, I'll always remember that day we played ball in the empty lot.
I'M NICE!
Come on, Teen Dog, we're going for burgers!

CHAPTER ENDS

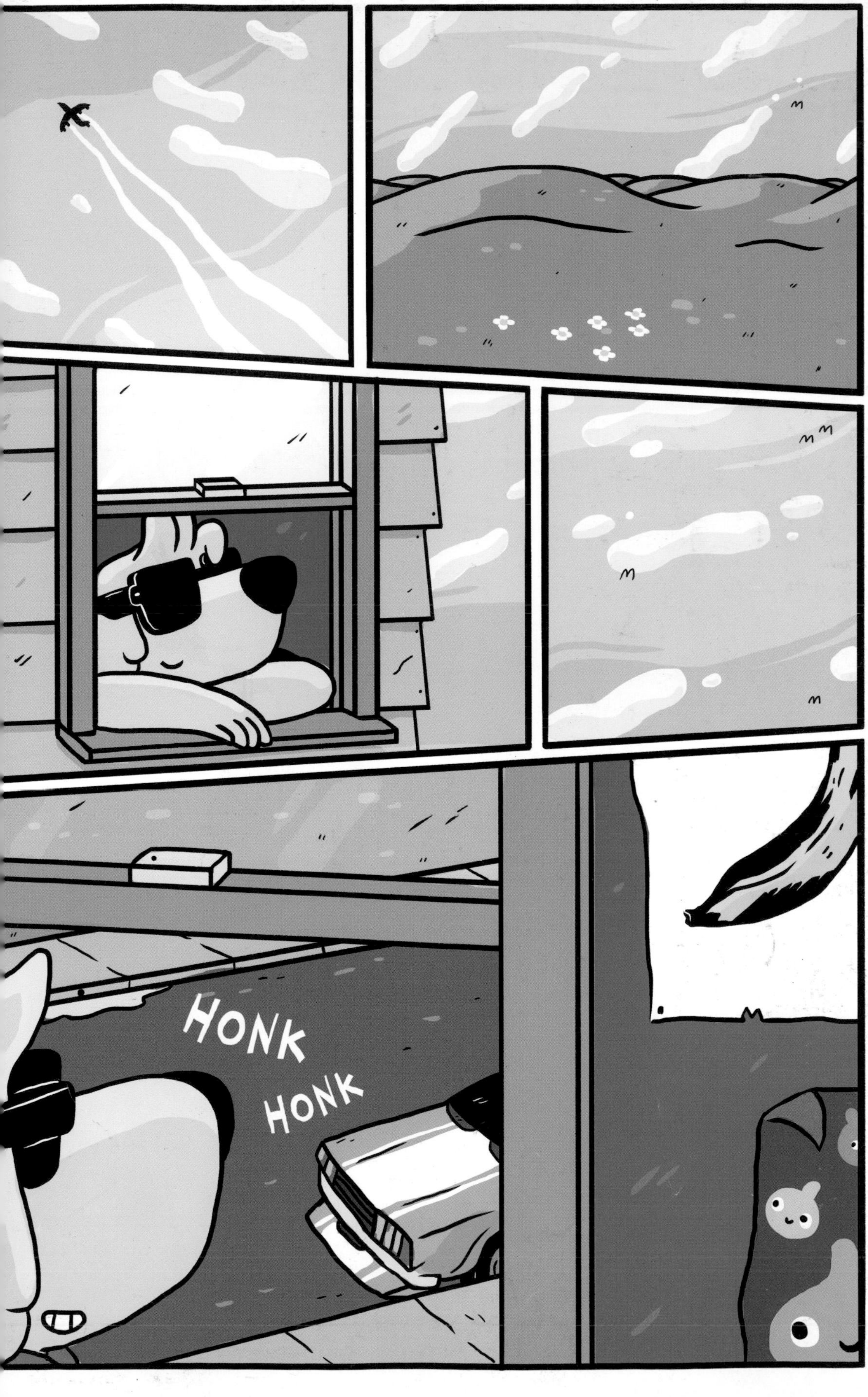
HONK
HONK

SPRINGTIME FOR TEEN DOG

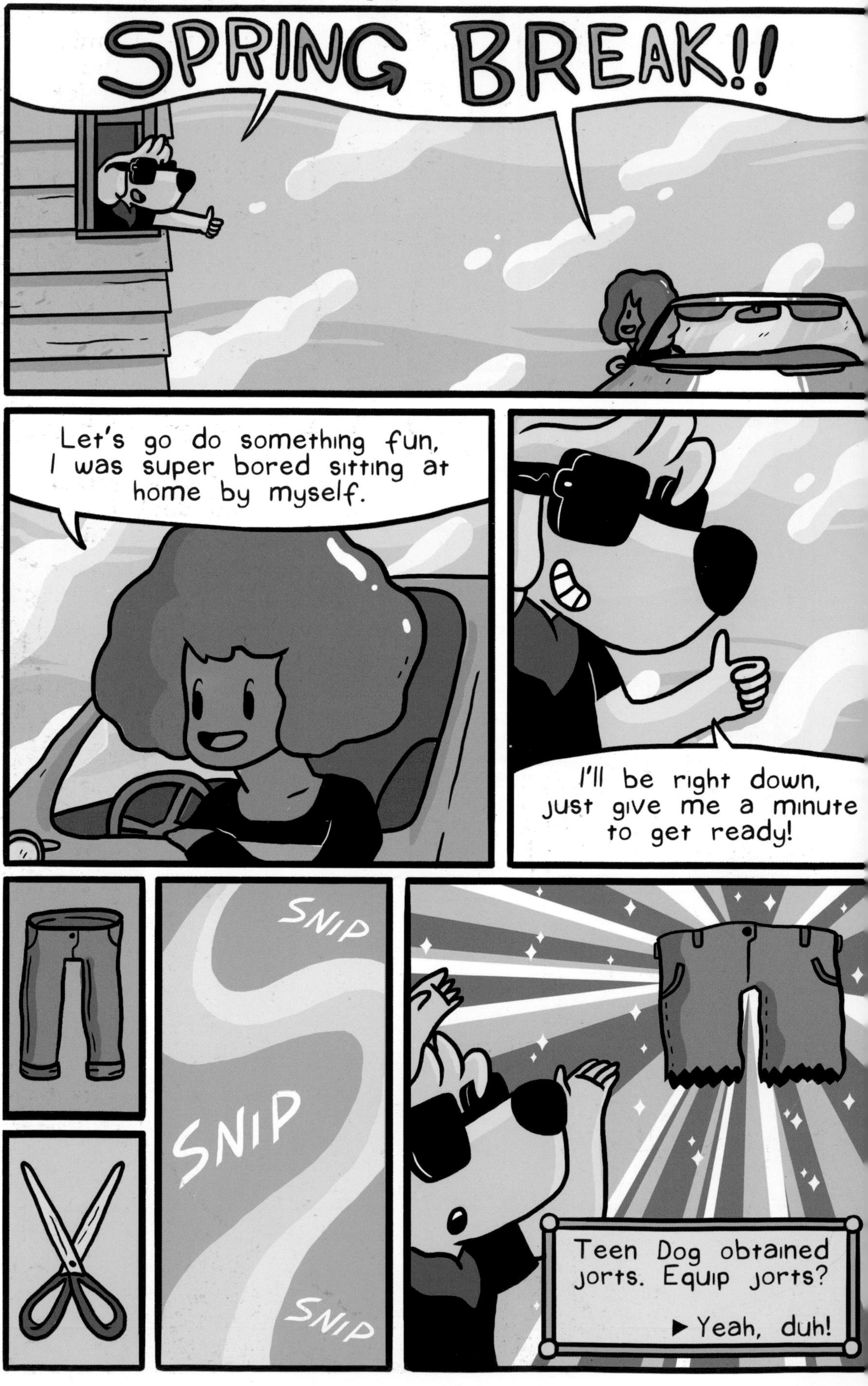
SPRING BREAK!!
Let's go do something fun, I was super bored sitting at home by myself.
I'll be right down, just give me a minute to get ready!
SNIP
SNIP
SNIP
Teen Dog obtained jorts. Equip jorts?
▶ Yeah, duh!

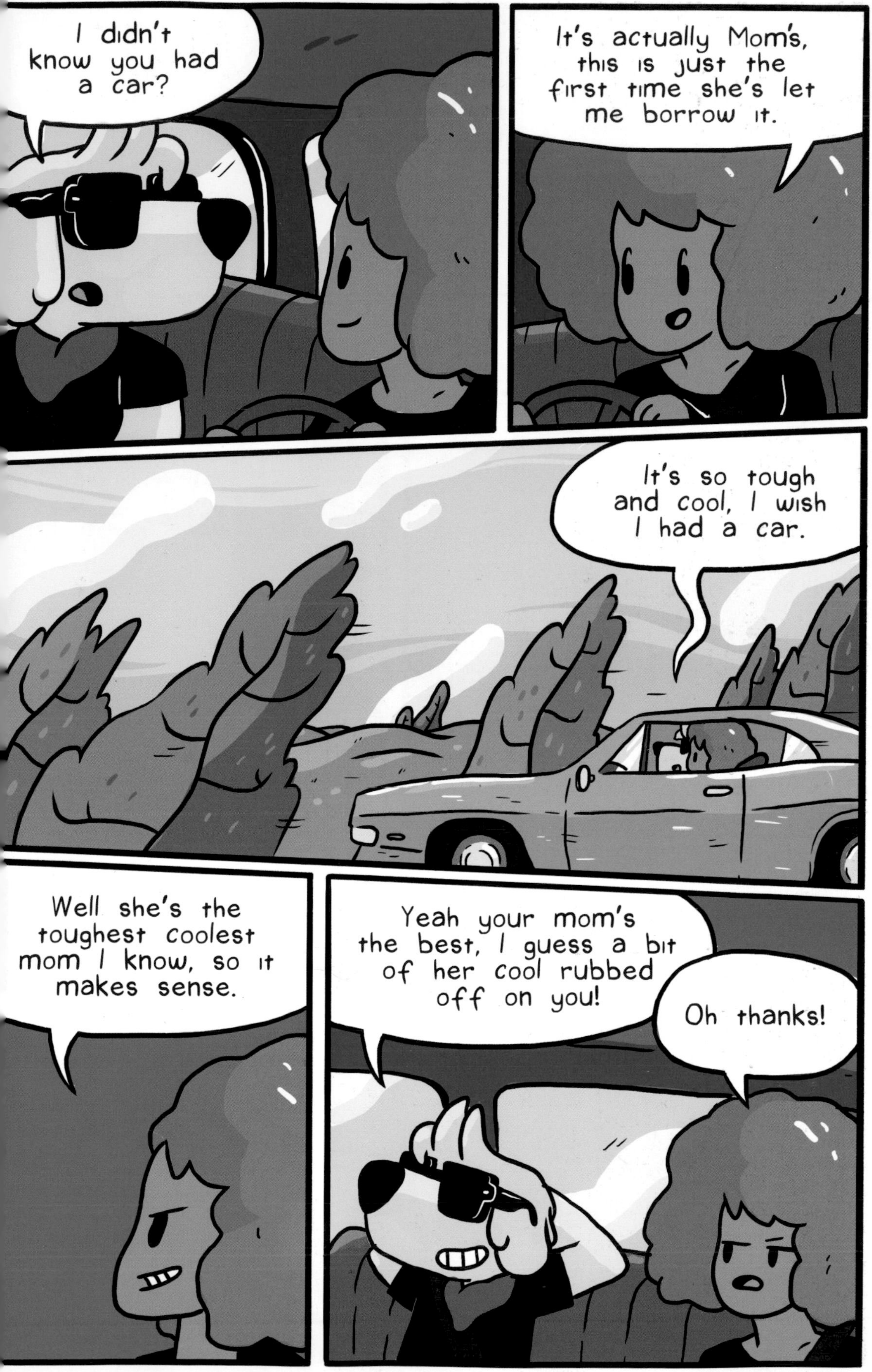
I didn't know you had a car?
It's actually Mom's, this is just the first time she's let me borrow it.
It's so tough and cool, I wish I had a car.
Well she's the toughest coolest mom I know, so it makes sense.
Yeah your mom's the best, I guess a bit of her cool rubbed off on you!
Oh thanks!

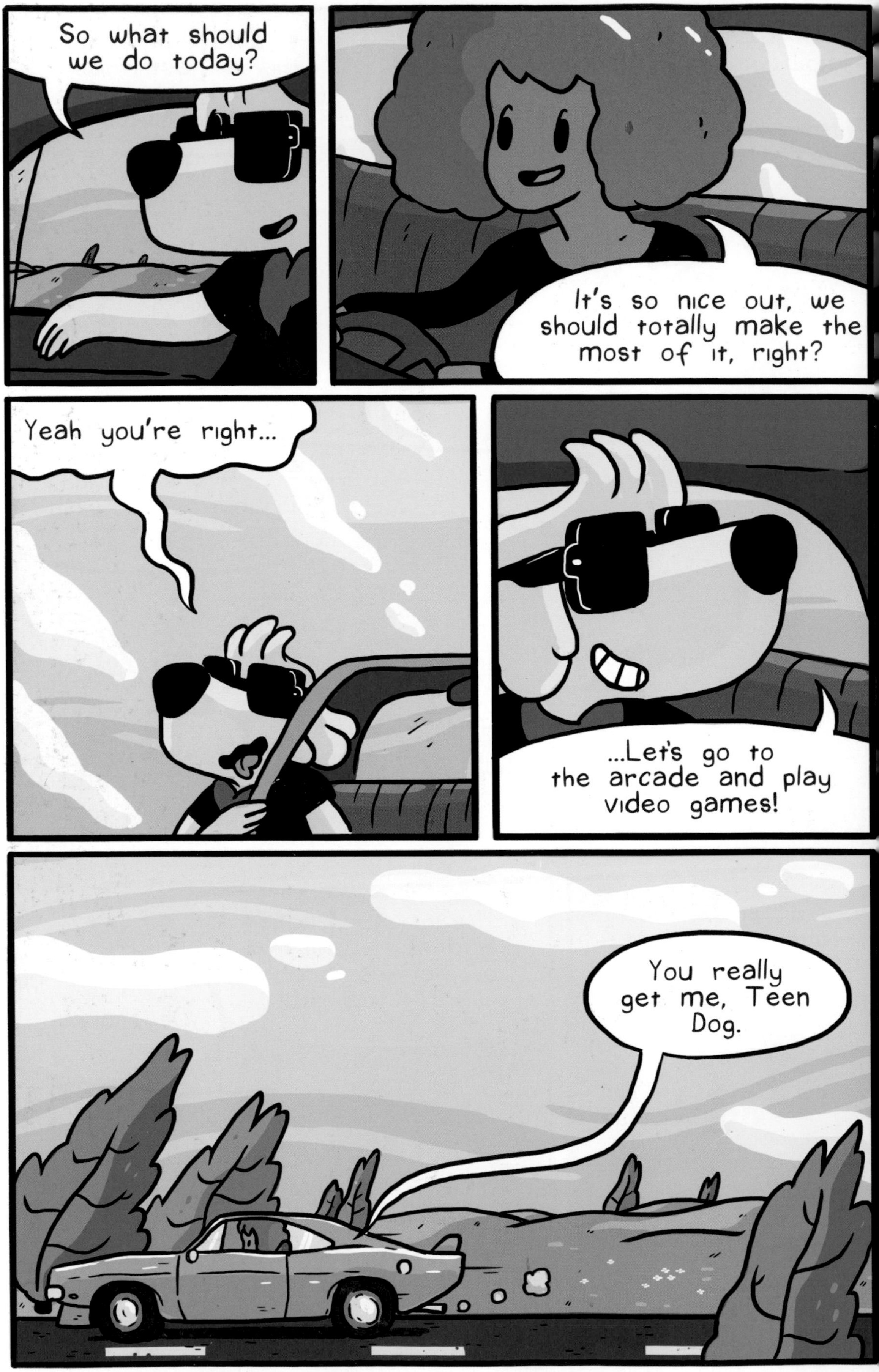
So what should we do today?
It's so nice out, we should totally make the most of it, right?
Yeah you're right...
...Let's go to the arcade and play video games!
You really get me, Teen Dog.

THE BIRTHDAY PUG

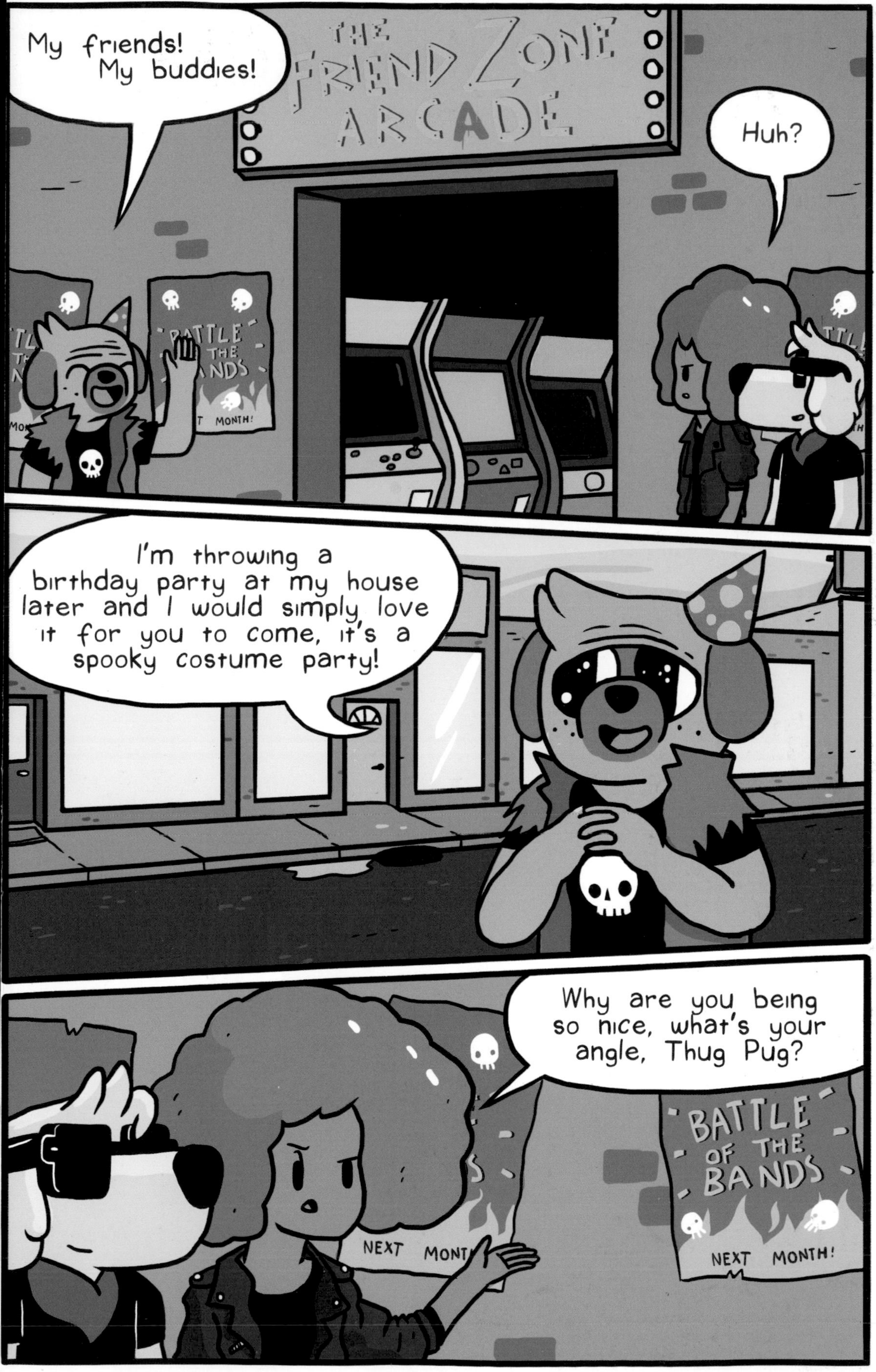
THE FRIEND ZONE ARCADE
My friends! My buddies!
Huh?
I'm throwing a birthday party at my house later and I would simply love it for you to come, it's a spooky costume party!
Why are you being so nice, what's your angle, Thug Pug?
BATTLE OF THE BANDS
NEXT MONTH!

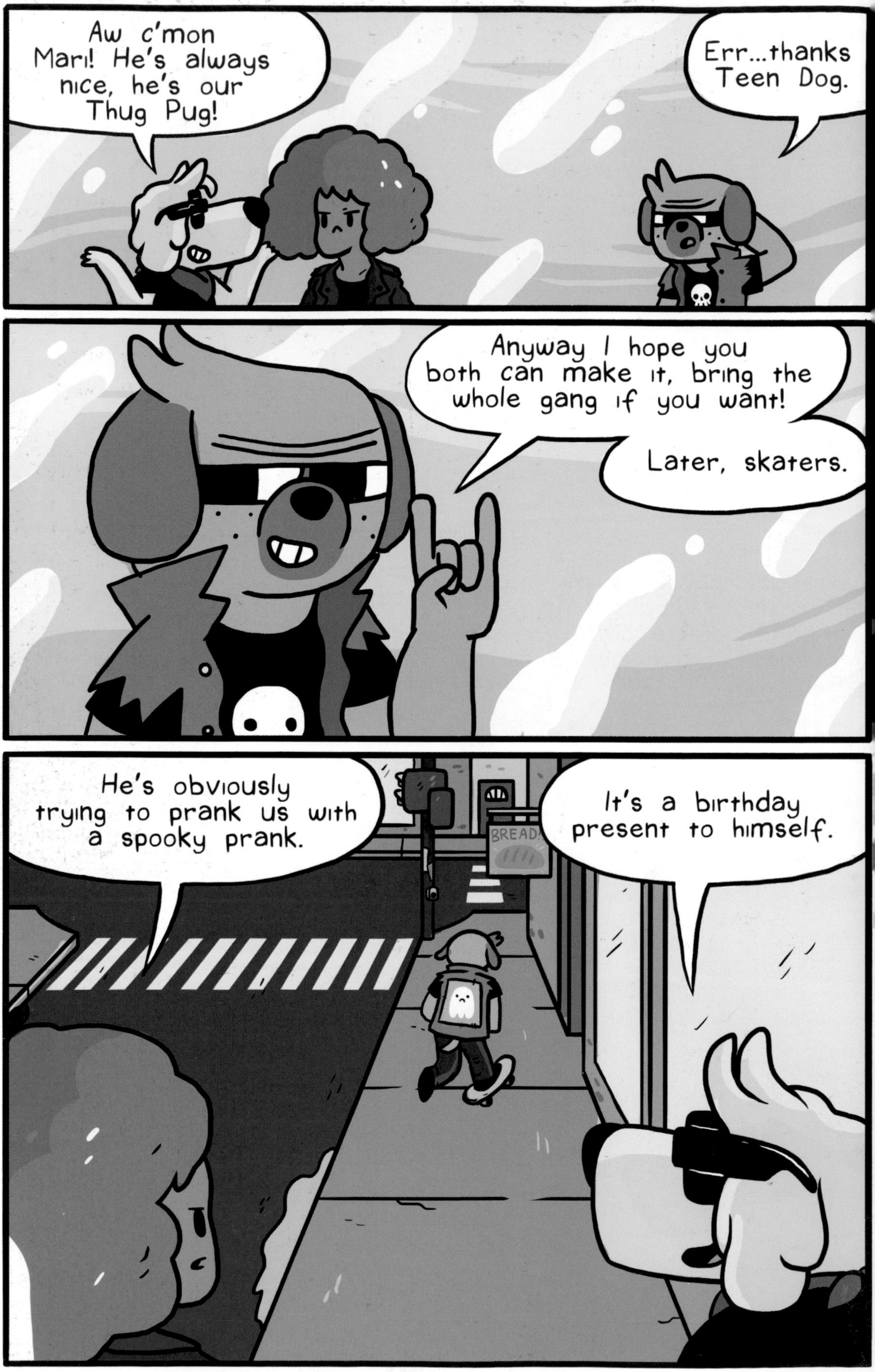
Aw c'mon Mari! He's always nice, he's our Thug Pug!
Err...thanks Teen Dog.
Anyway I hope you both can make it, bring the whole gang if you want!
Later, skaters.
He's obviously trying to prank us with a spooky prank.
It's a birthday present to himself.
BREAD!

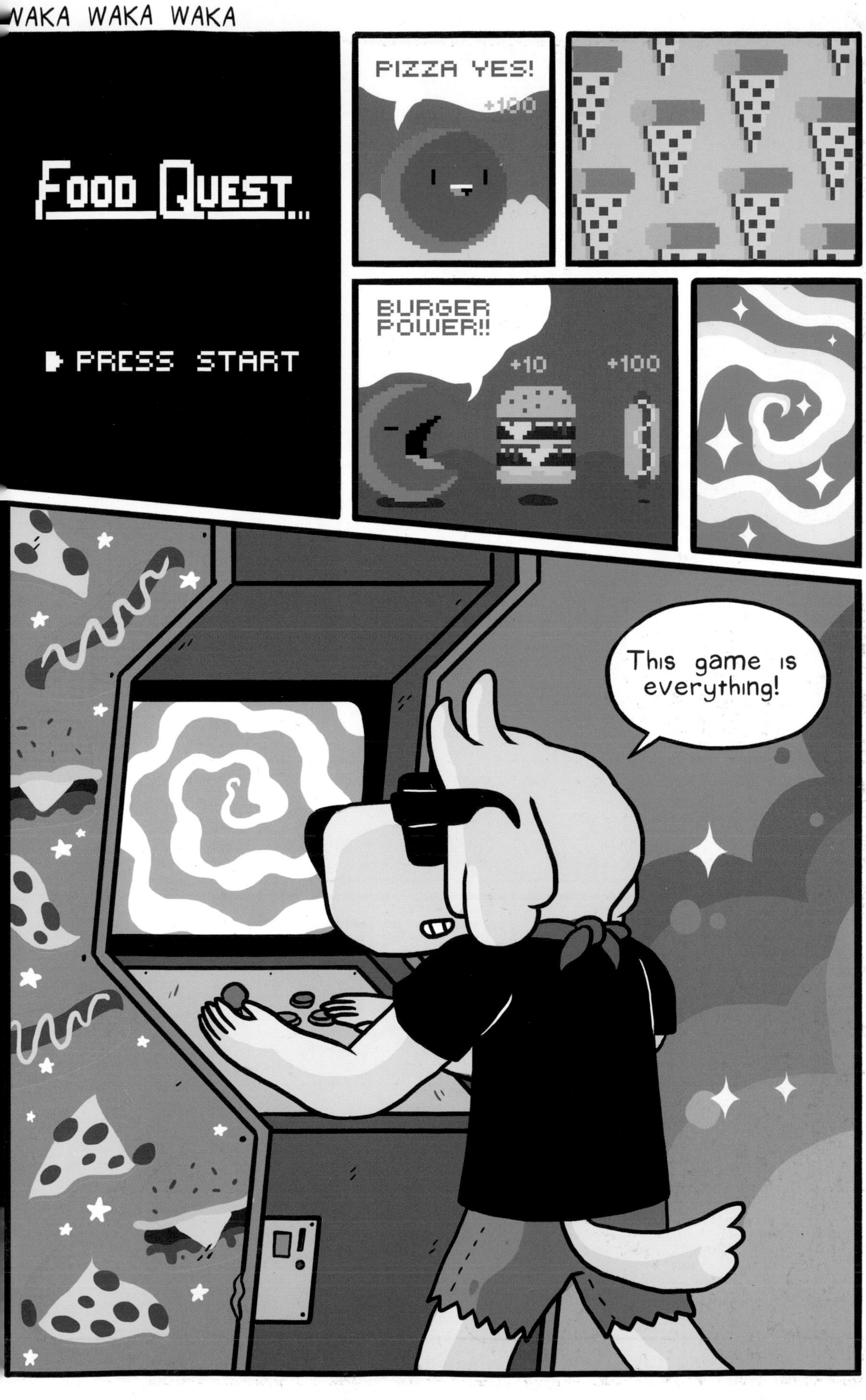
WAKA WAKA WAKA
FOOD QUEST...
PRESS START
PIZZA YES!
+100
BURGER POWER!!
+10
+100
This game is everything!

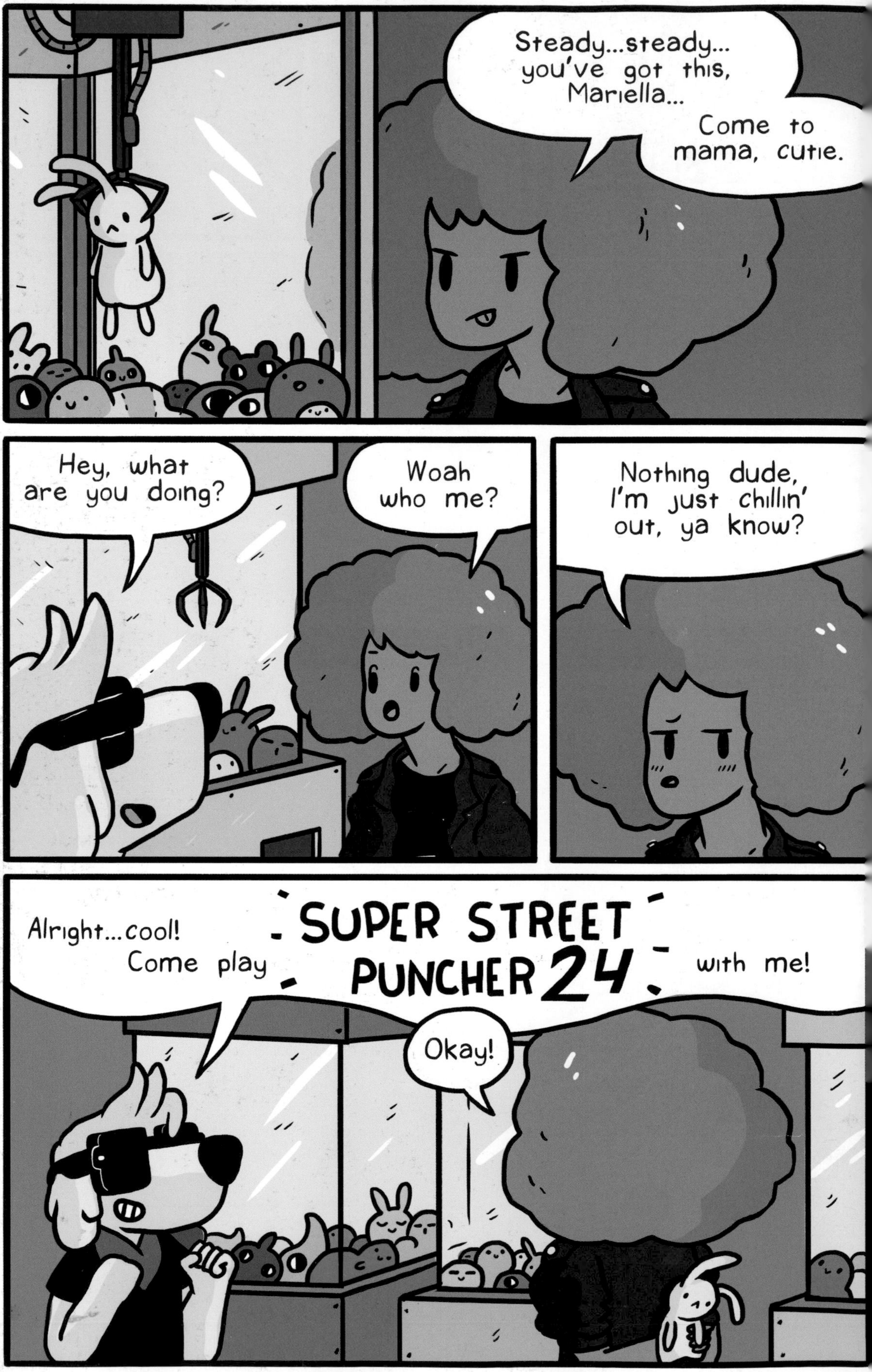
Steady...steady... you've got this, Mariella...
Come to mama, cutie.
Hey, what are you doing?
Woah who me?
Nothing dude, I'm just chillin' out, ya know?
Alright...cool! Come play SUPER STREET PUNCHER 24 with me!
Okay!

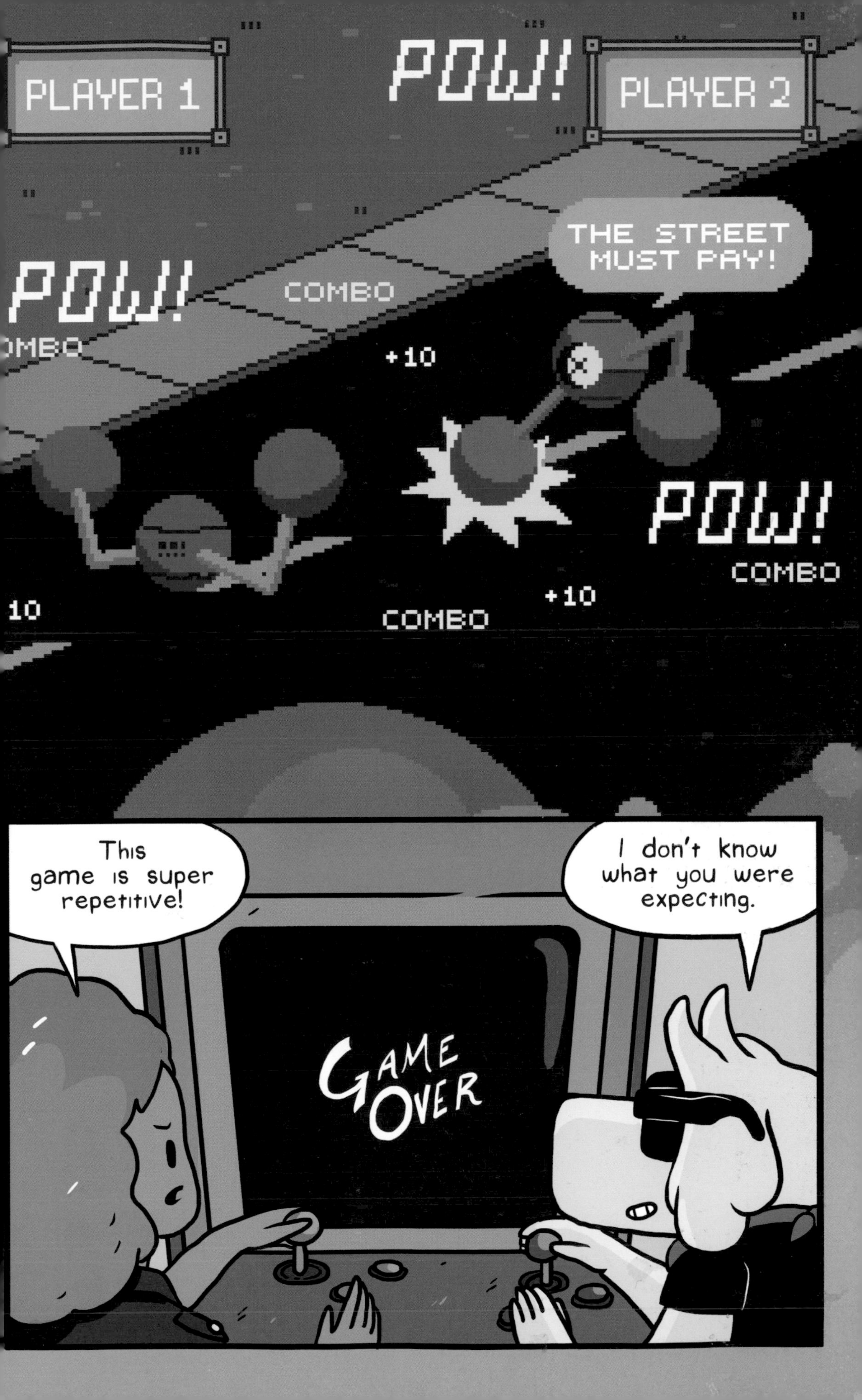
PLAYER 1
POW!
PLAYER 2
THE STREET MUST PAY!
POW!
COMBO
OMBO
+10
POW!
COMBO
10
COMBO
+10
This game is super repetitive!
I don't know what you were expecting.
GAME OVER

THE FUTURE

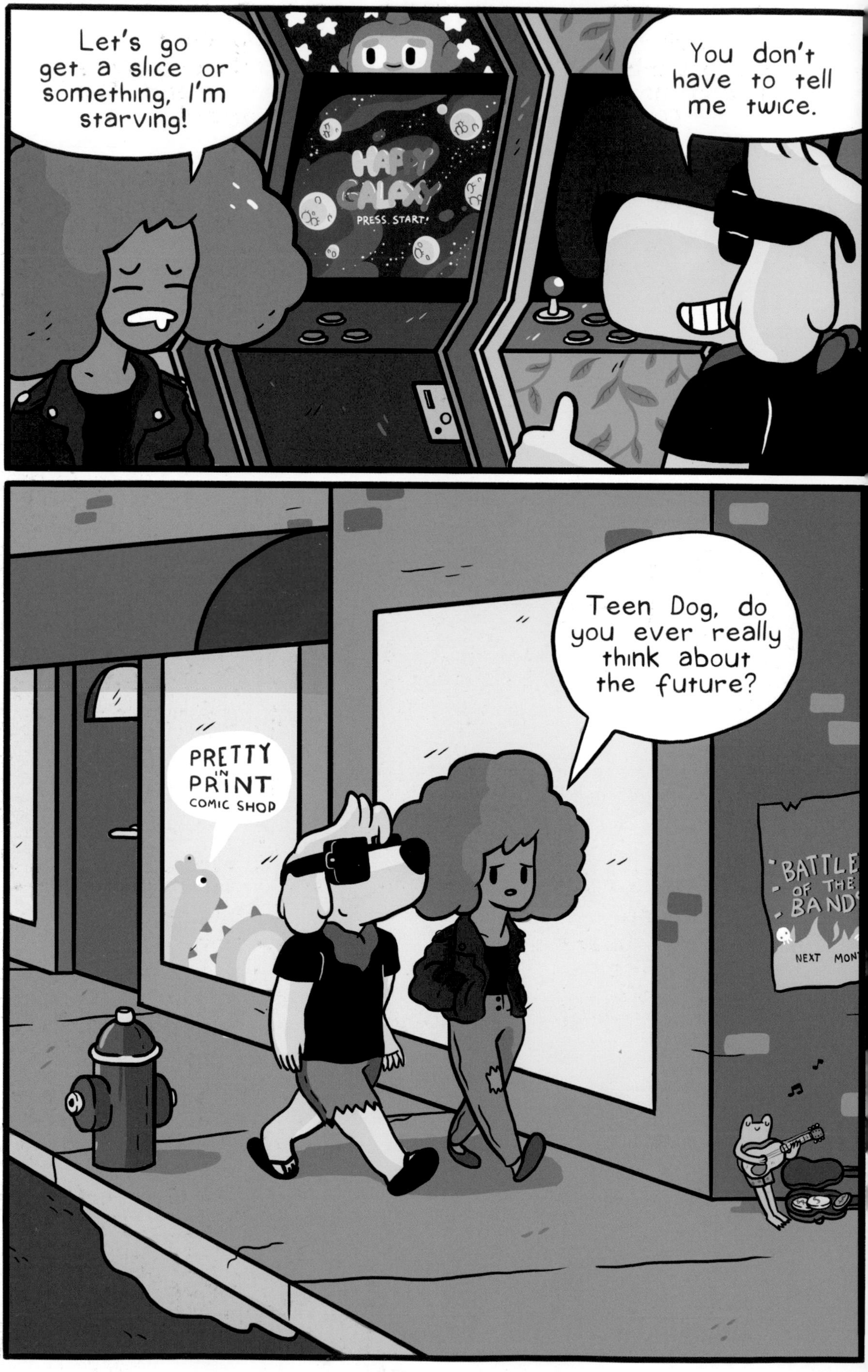
Let's go get a slice or something, I'm starving!
GALAXY
PRESS. START!
You don't have to tell me twice.
PRETTY IN PRINT COMIC SHOP
Teen Dog, do you ever really think about the future?
NEXT

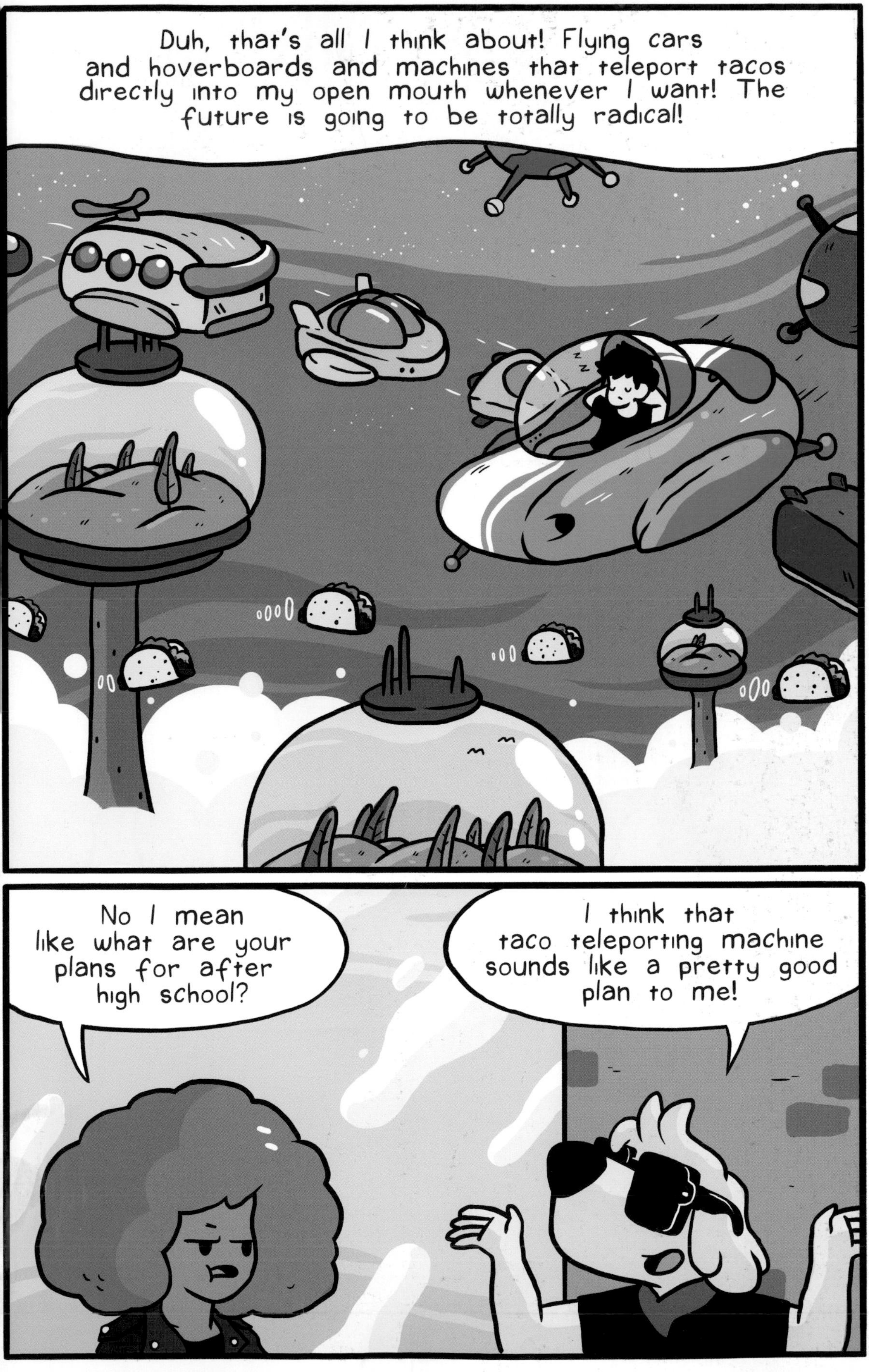
Duh, that's all I think about! Flying cars and hoverboards and machines that teleport tacos directly into my open mouth whenever I want! The future is going to be totally radical!
No I mean like what are your plans for after high school?
I think that taco teleporting machine sounds like a pretty good plan to me!

Hey, It's Sara!

Hey you two! I heard there was going to be a big party over at Thug Pug's house.

Yeah, I'm pretty sure he's trying to prank us.

That guy's trouble...he's trouble, right?

He's okay, he just needs a big hug.

You should totally come though, you never know it might be fun! Oh and you have to dress spooky!

Doesn't he know Halloween is ages away?

Halloween is the most goth day of the year, so aside from Thug Pug's obvious sinister motives, I'm all for a spooky party!

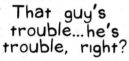

EXISTENCE

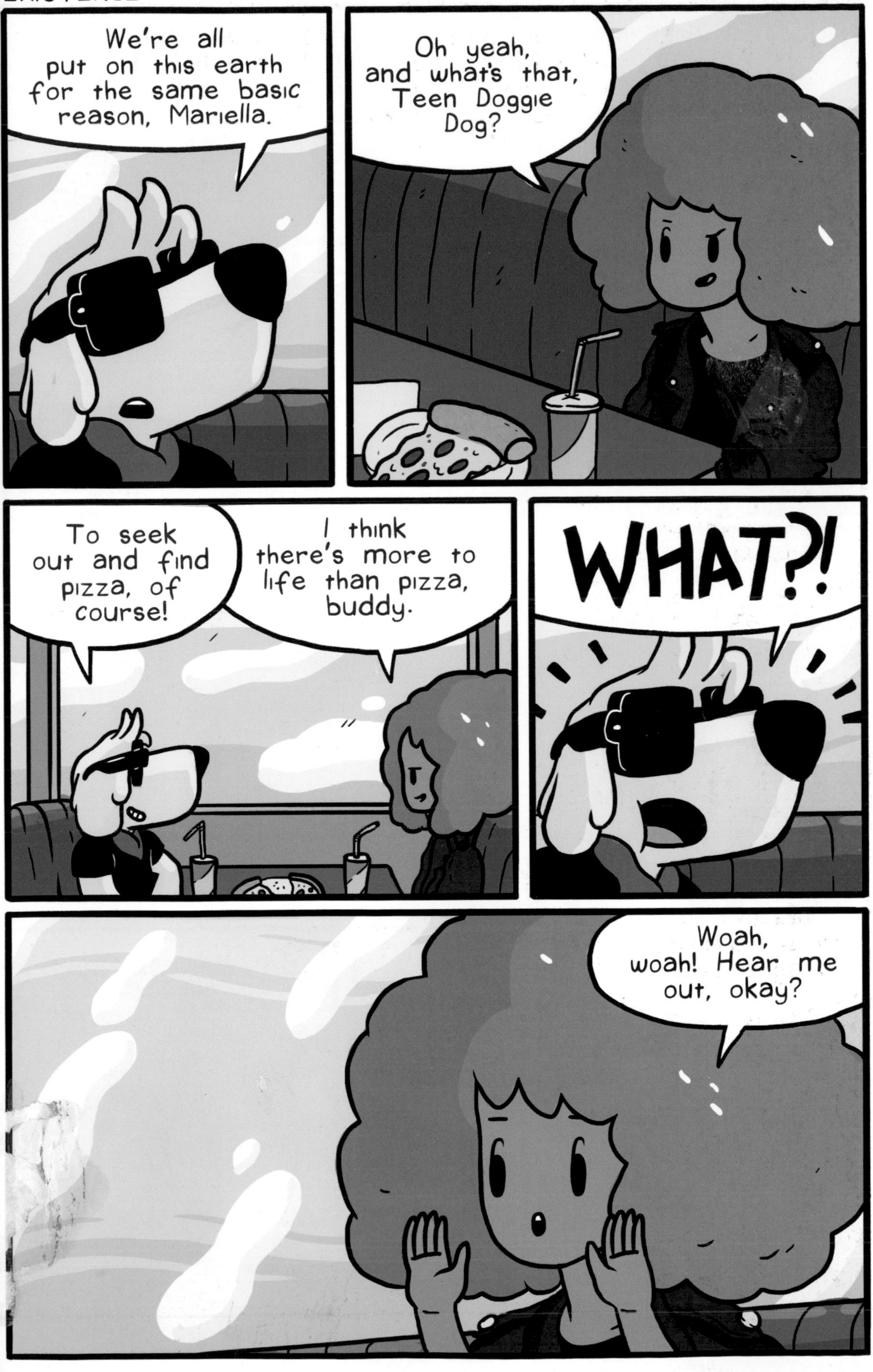
We're all put on this earth for the same basic reason, Mariella.
Oh yeah, and what's that, Teen Doggie Dog?
To seek out and find pizza, of course!
I think there's more to life than pizza, buddy.
WHAT?!
Woah, woah! Hear me out, okay?

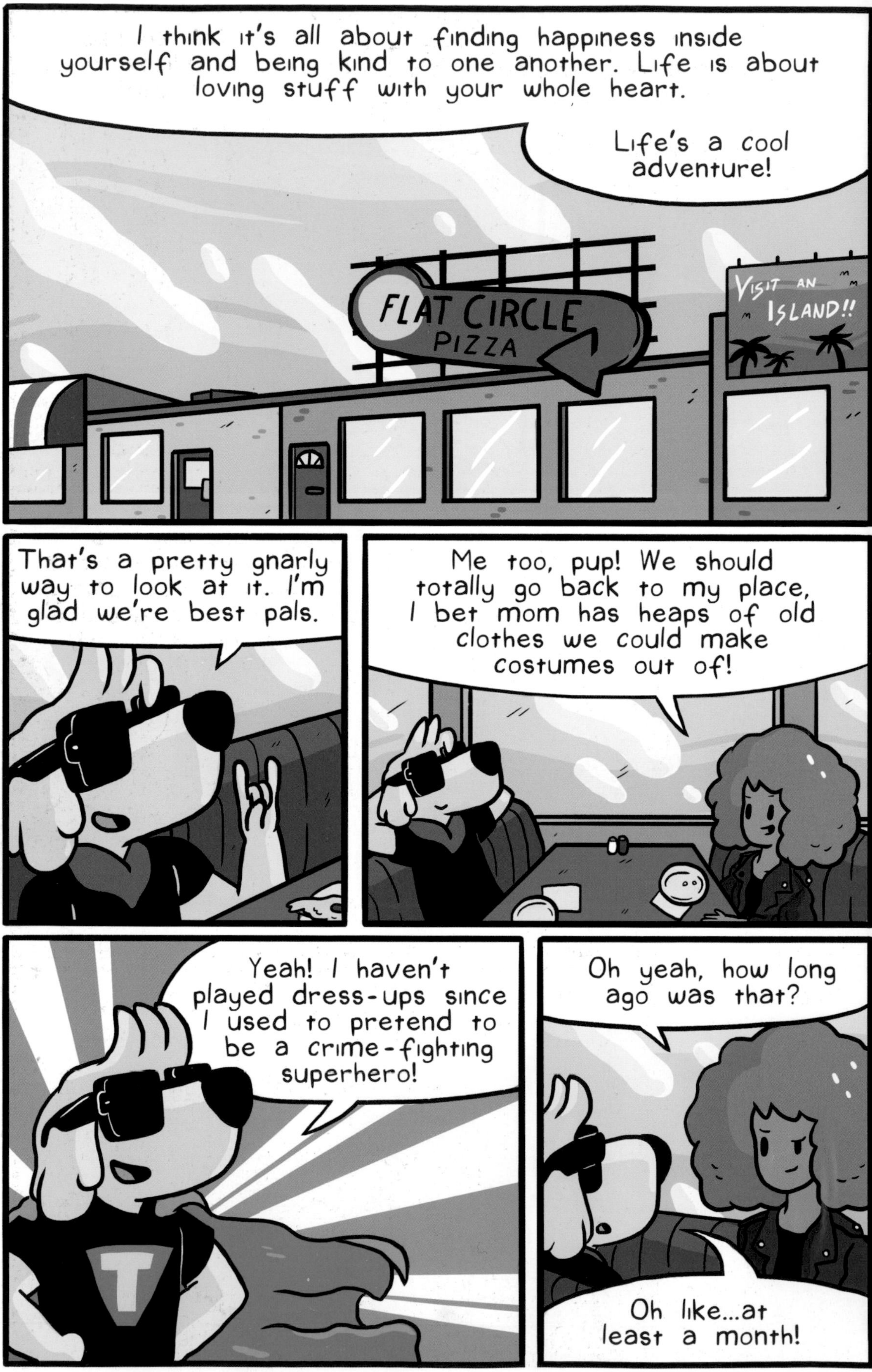
I think it's all about finding happiness inside yourself and being kind to one another. Life is about loving stuff with your whole heart.
Life's a cool adventure!
FLAT CIRCLE PIZZA
VISIT AN ISLAND!!
That's a pretty gnarly way to look at it. I'm glad we're best pals.
Me too, pup! We should totally go back to my place, I bet mom has heaps of old clothes we could make costumes out of!
Yeah! I haven't played dress-ups since I used to pretend to be a crime-fighting superhero!
T
Oh yeah, how long ago was that?
Oh like...at least a month!

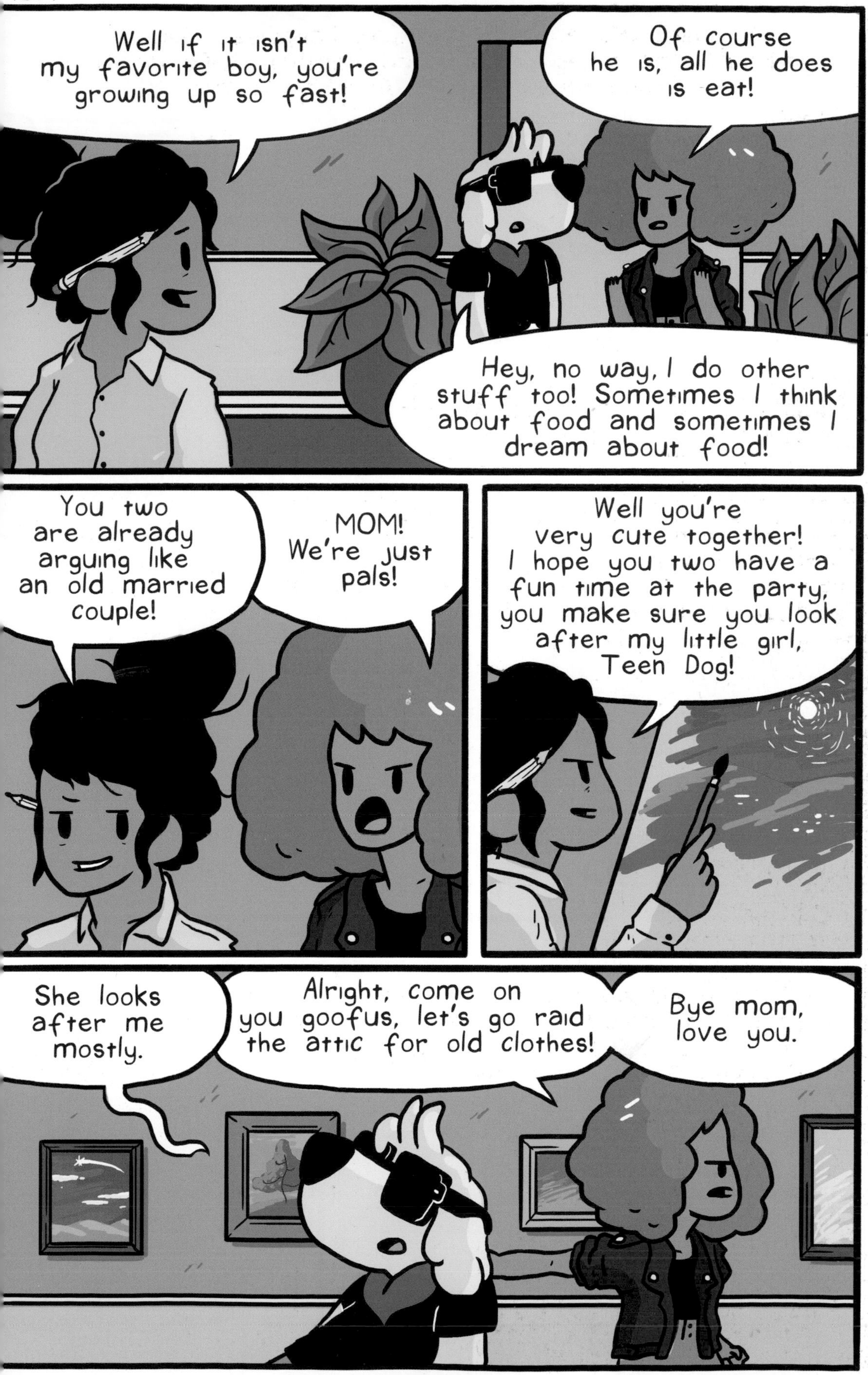
Well if it isn't my favorite boy, you're growing up so fast!
Of course he is, all he does is eat!
Hey, no way, I do other stuff too! Sometimes I think about food and sometimes I dream about food!
You two are already arguing like an old married couple!
MOM! We're just pals!
Well you're very cute together! I hope you two have a fun time at the party, you make sure you look after my little girl, Teen Dog!
She looks after me mostly.
Alright, come on you goofus, let's go raid the attic for old clothes!
Bye mom, love you.

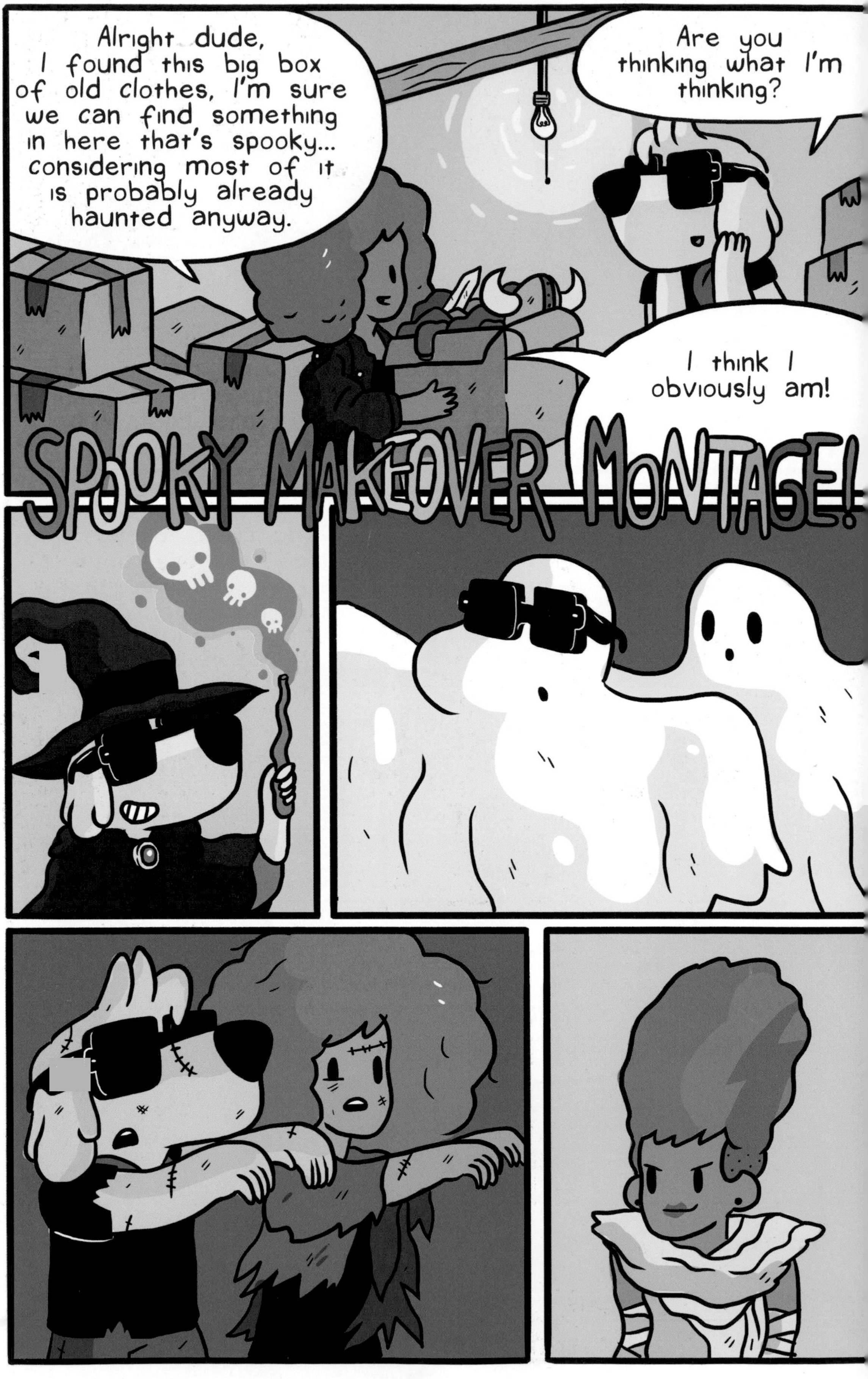
Alright dude, I found this big box of old clothes, I'm sure we can find something in here that's spooky... considering most of it is probably already haunted anyway.
Are you thinking what I'm thinking?
I think I obviously am!
SPOOKY MAKEOVER MONTAGE!

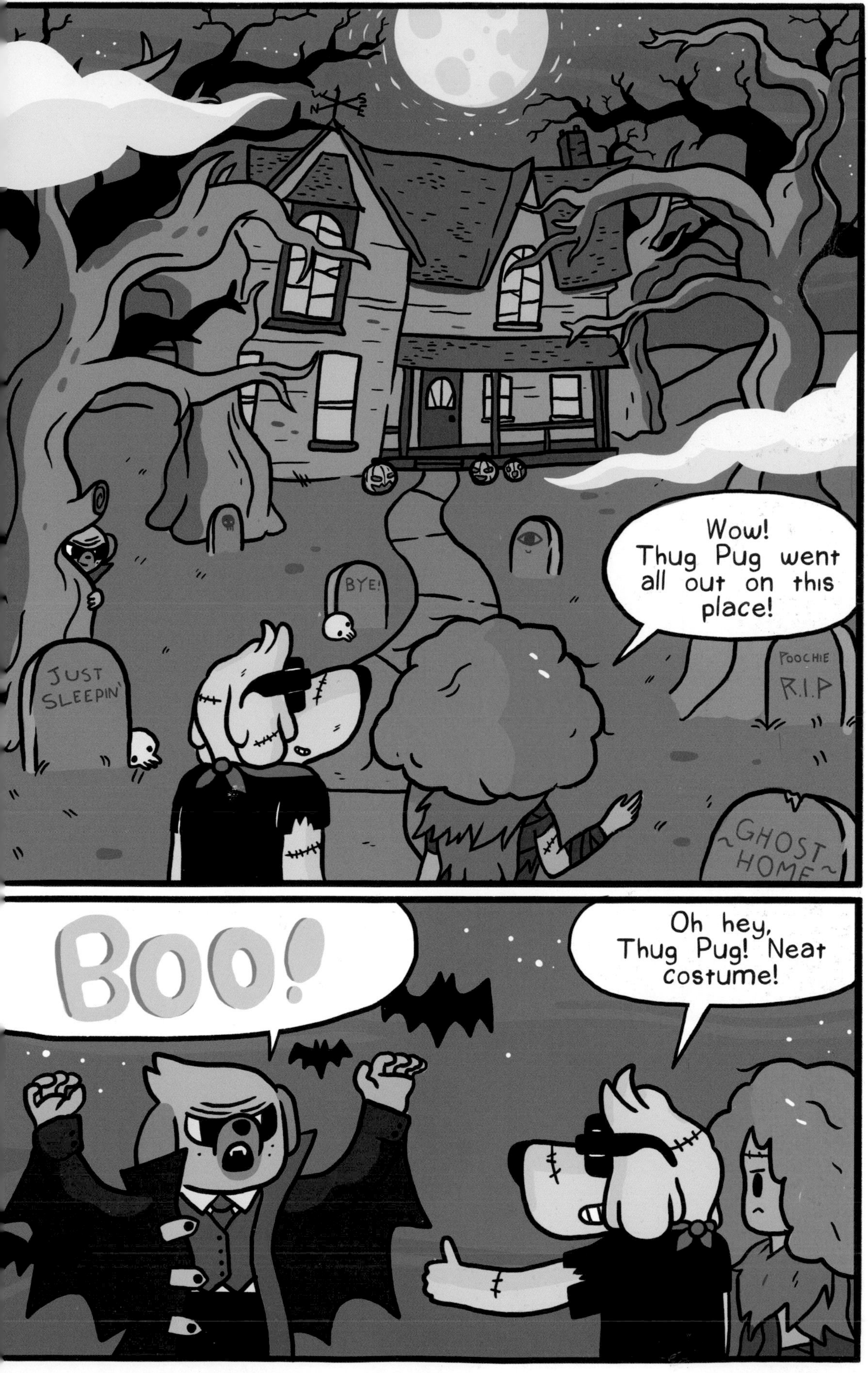
JUST SLEEPIN'
BYE!
Wow! Thug Pug went all out on this place!
POOCHIE R.I.P
~GHOST HOME~
BOO!
Oh hey, Thug Pug! Neat costume!

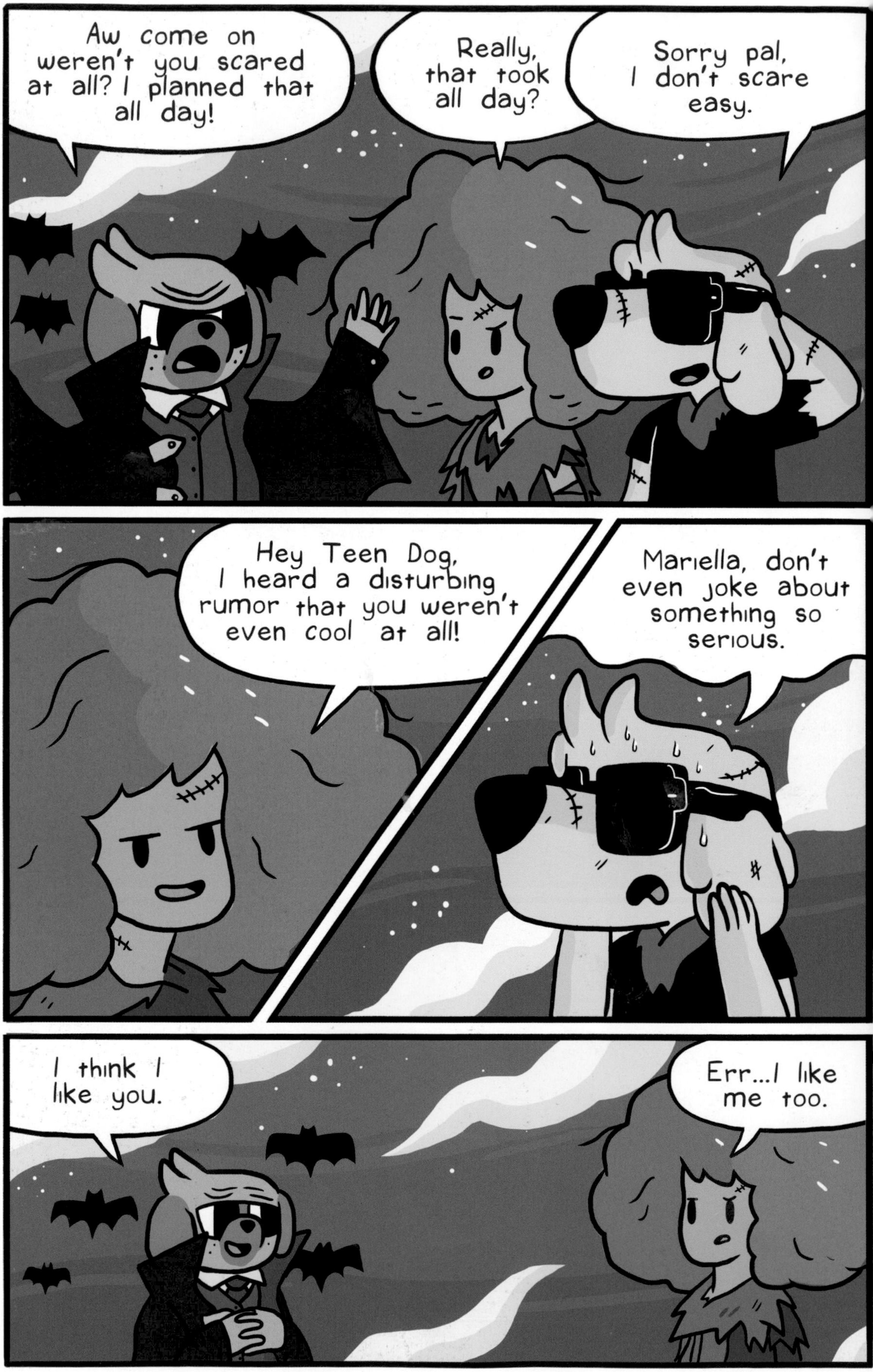
Aw come on weren't you scared at all? I planned that all day!
Really, that took all day?
Sorry pal, I don't scare easy.
Hey Teen Dog, I heard a disturbing rumor that you weren't even cool at all!
Mariella, don't even joke about something so serious.
I think I like you.
Err...I like me too.

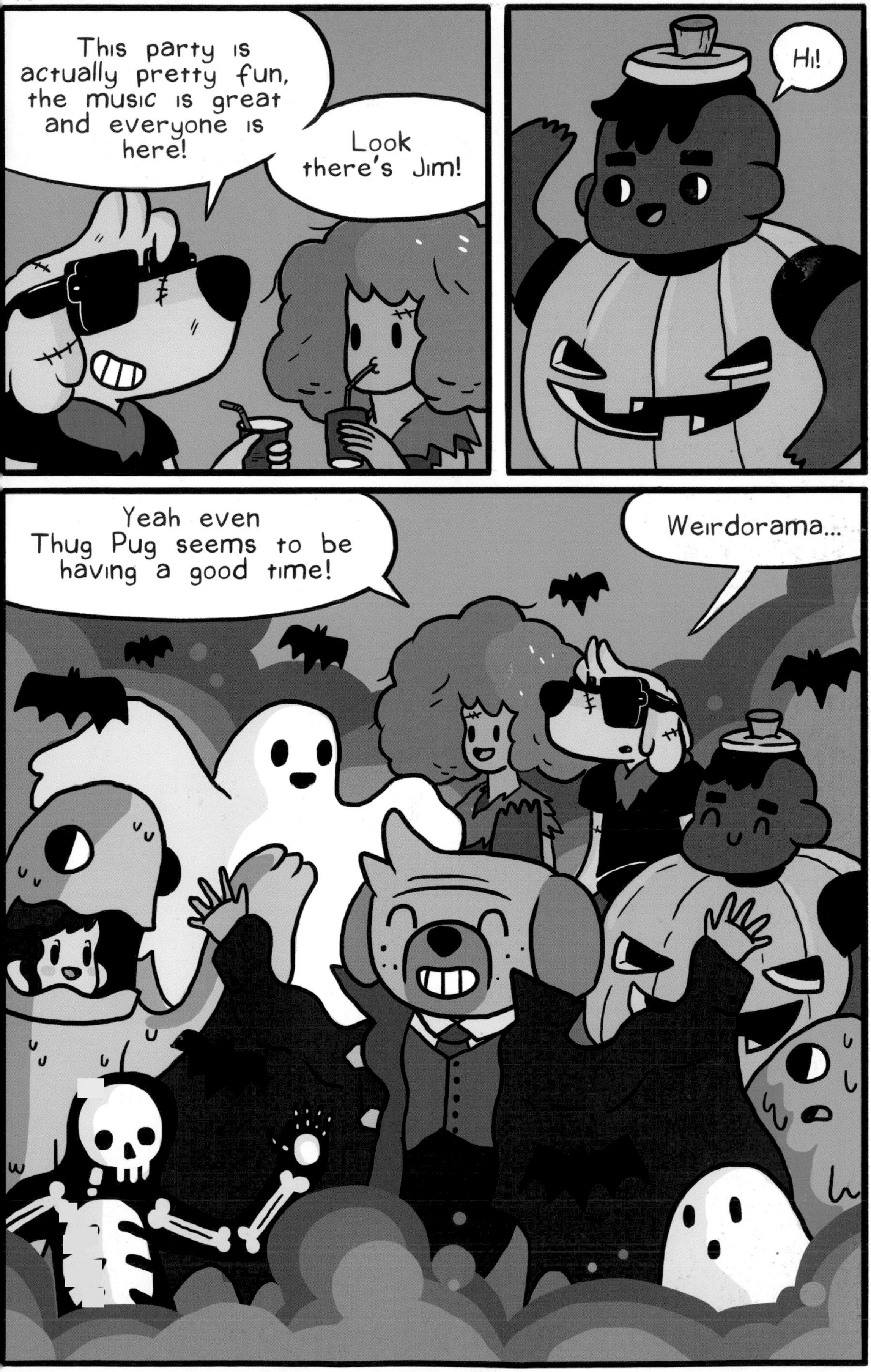
This party is actually pretty fun, the music is great and everyone is here!
Look there's Jim!
Hi!
Yeah even Thug Pug seems to be having a good time!
Weirdorama...

DARK PAST

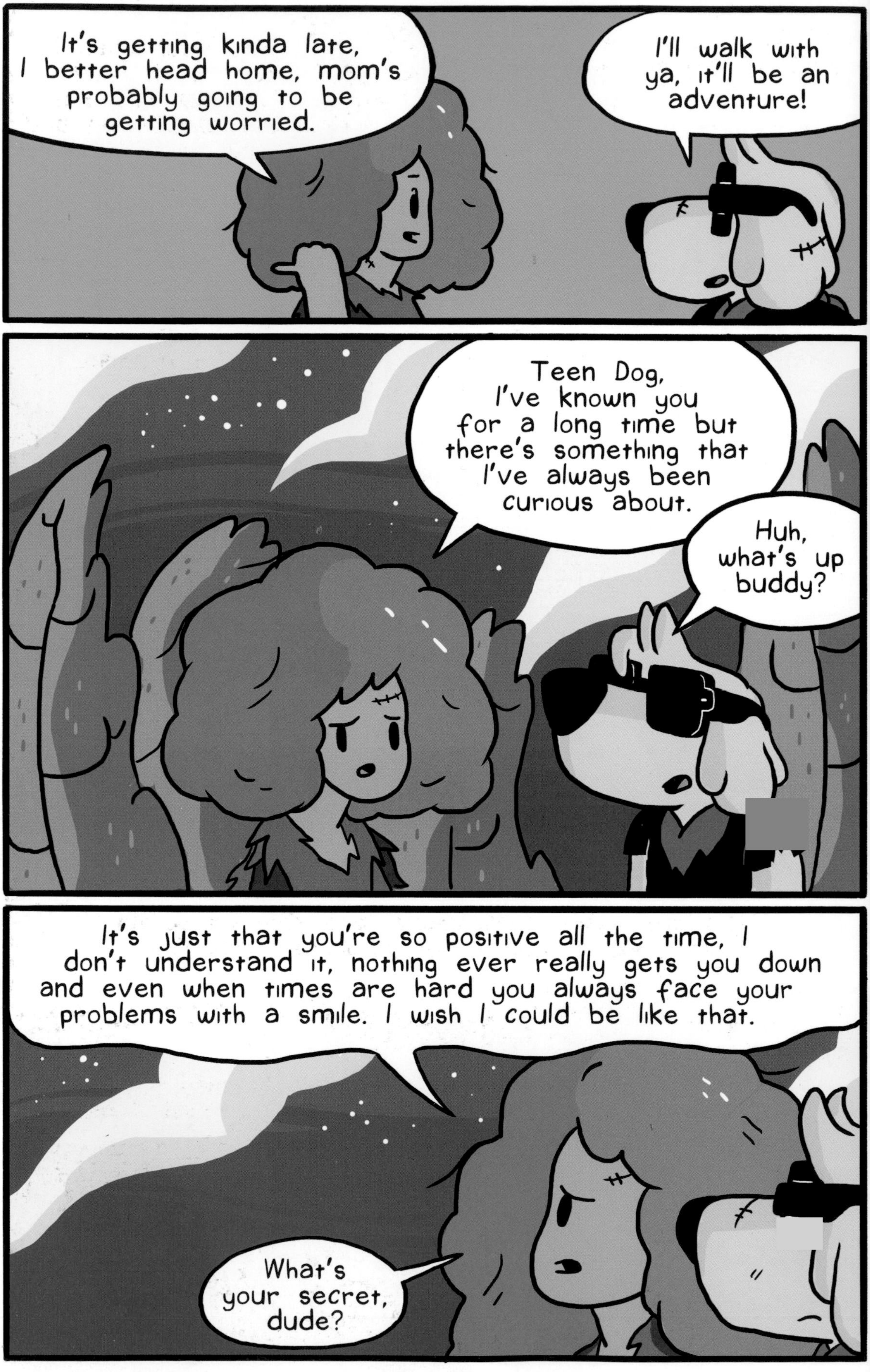
It's getting kinda late, I better head home, mom's probably going to be getting worried.
I'll walk with ya, it'll be an adventure!
Teen Dog, I've known you for a long time but there's something that I've always been curious about.
Huh, what's up buddy?
It's just that you're so positive all the time, I don't understand it, nothing ever really gets you down and even when times are hard you always face your problems with a smile. I wish I could be like that.
What's your secret, dude?

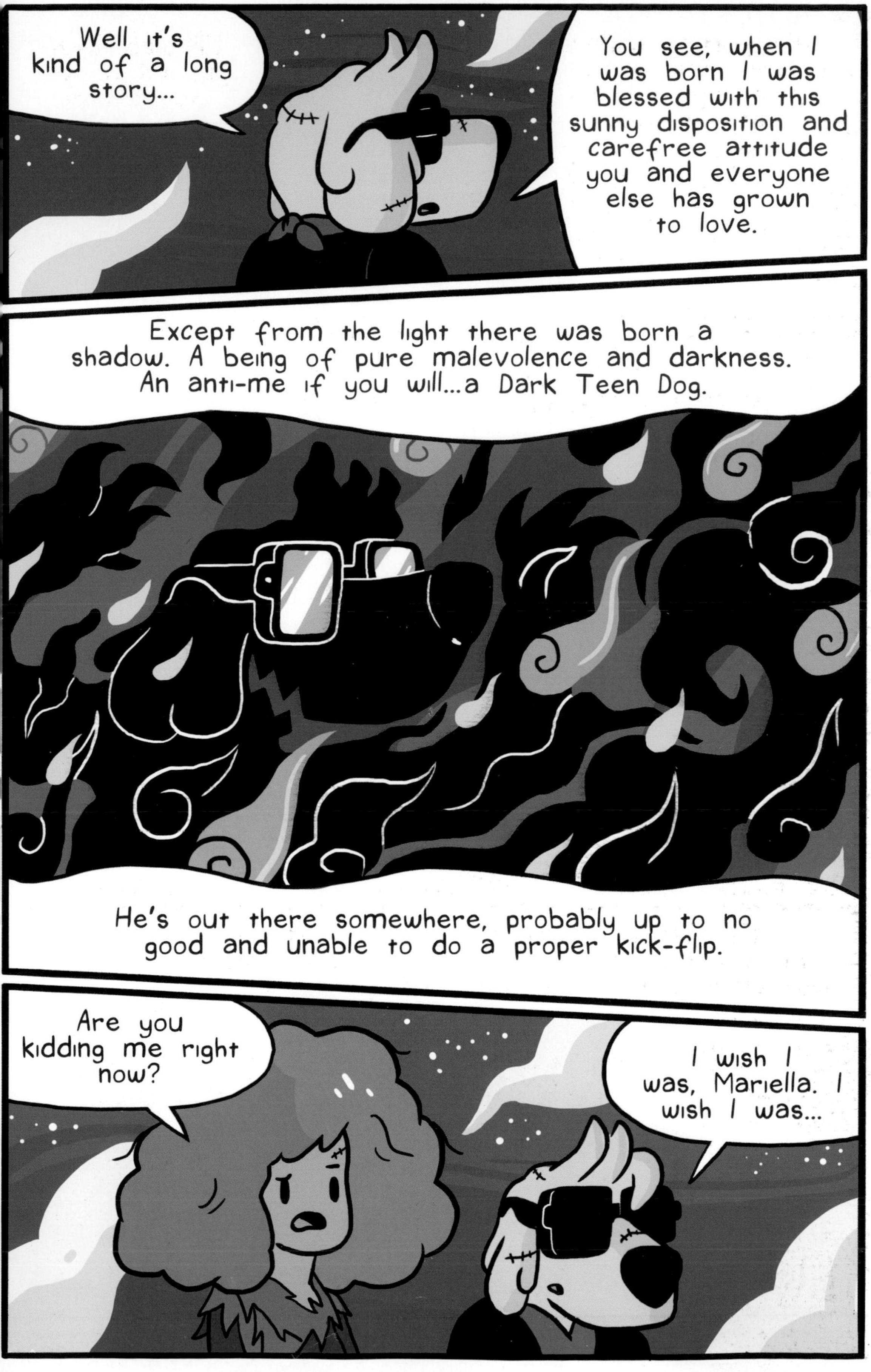
Well it's kind of a long story...
You see, when I was born I was blessed with this sunny disposition and carefree attitude you and everyone else has grown to love.
Except from the light there was born a shadow. A being of pure malevolence and darkness. An anti-me if you will...a Dark Teen Dog.
He's out there somewhere, probably up to no good and unable to do a proper kick-flip.
Are you kidding me right now?
I wish I was, Mariella. I wish I was...

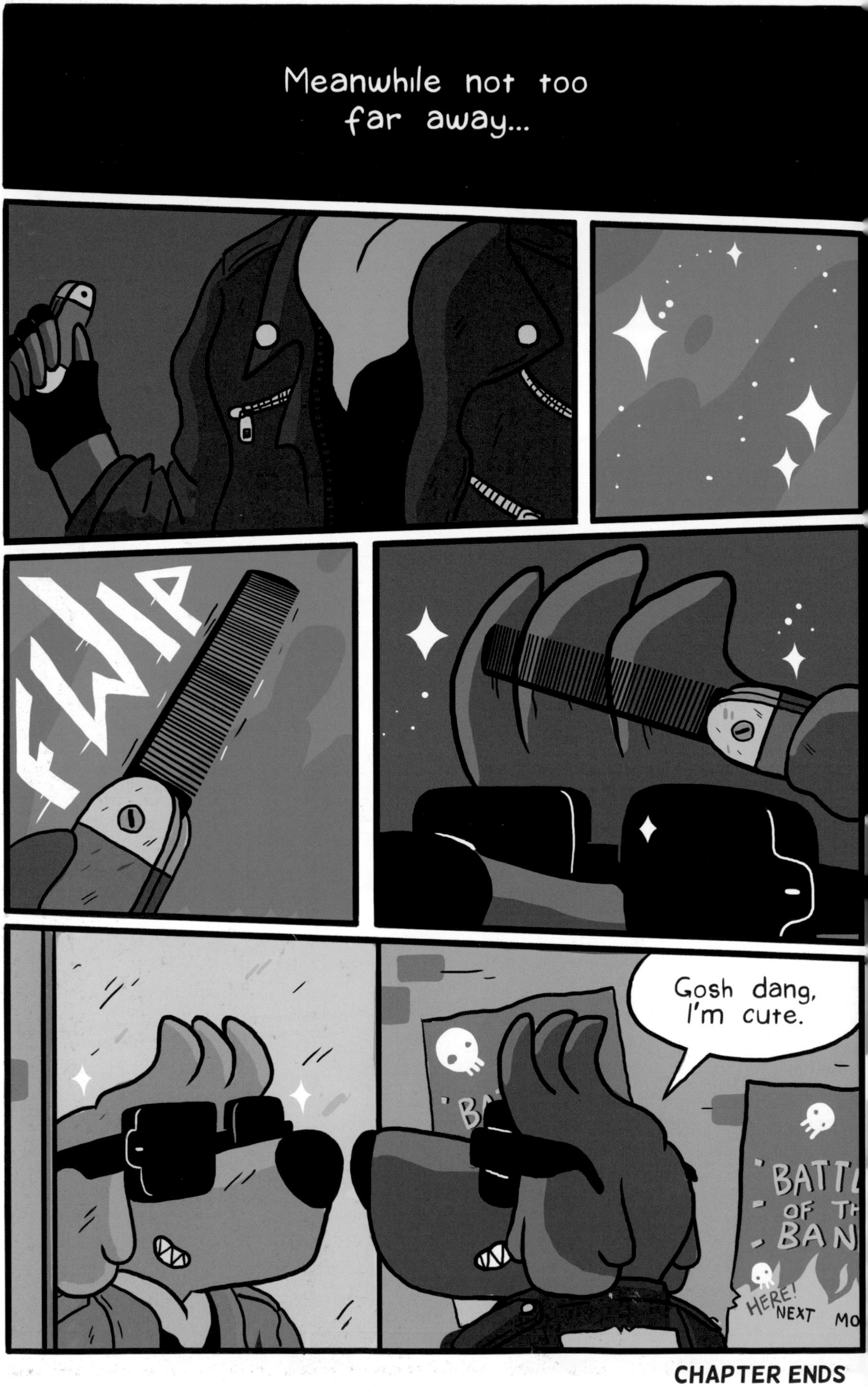
Meanwhile not too far away...
FWIP
Gosh dang, I'm cute.
HERE!
NEXT

CHAPTER ENDS

CHAPTER FIVE

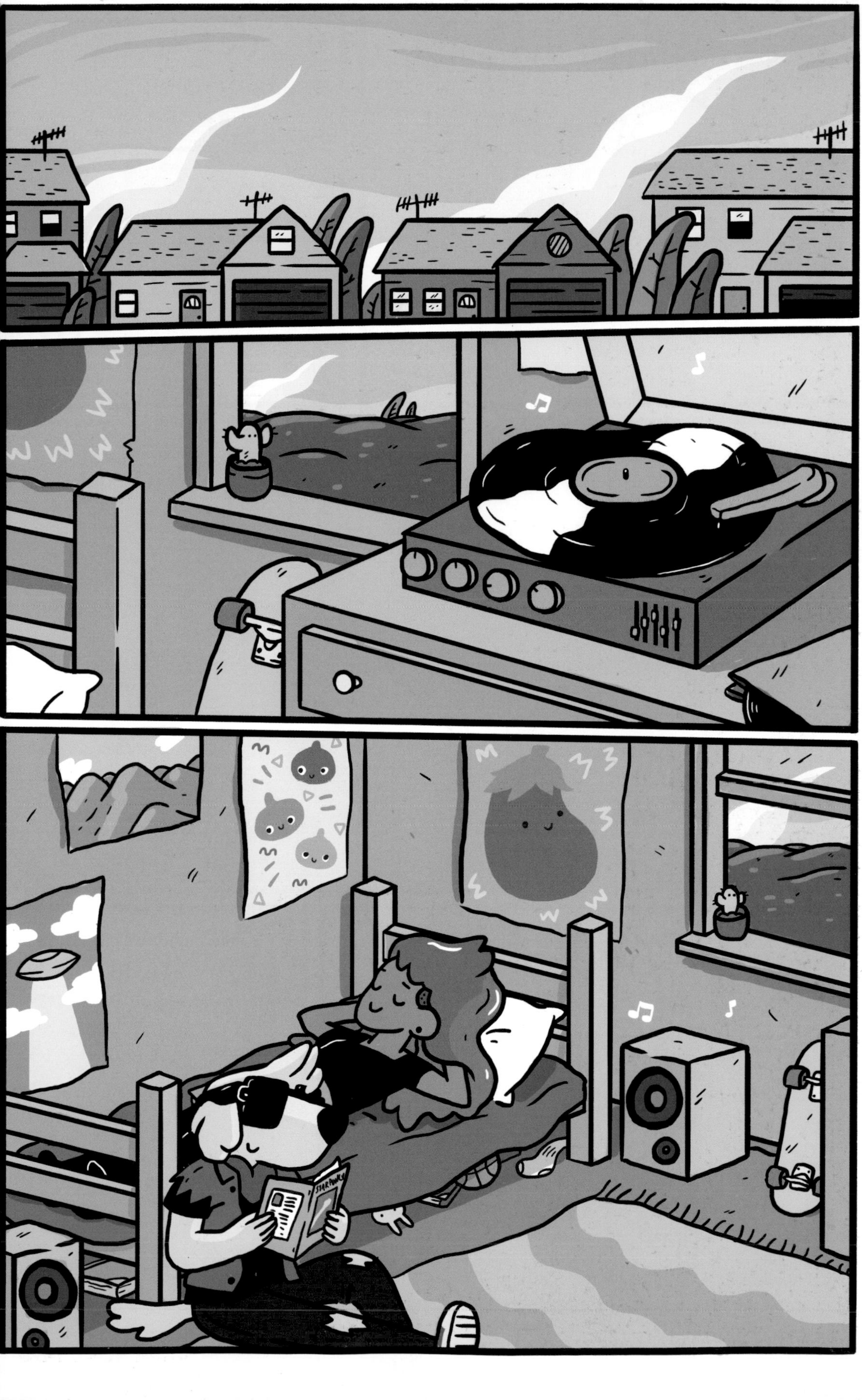

SPACE ODDITY

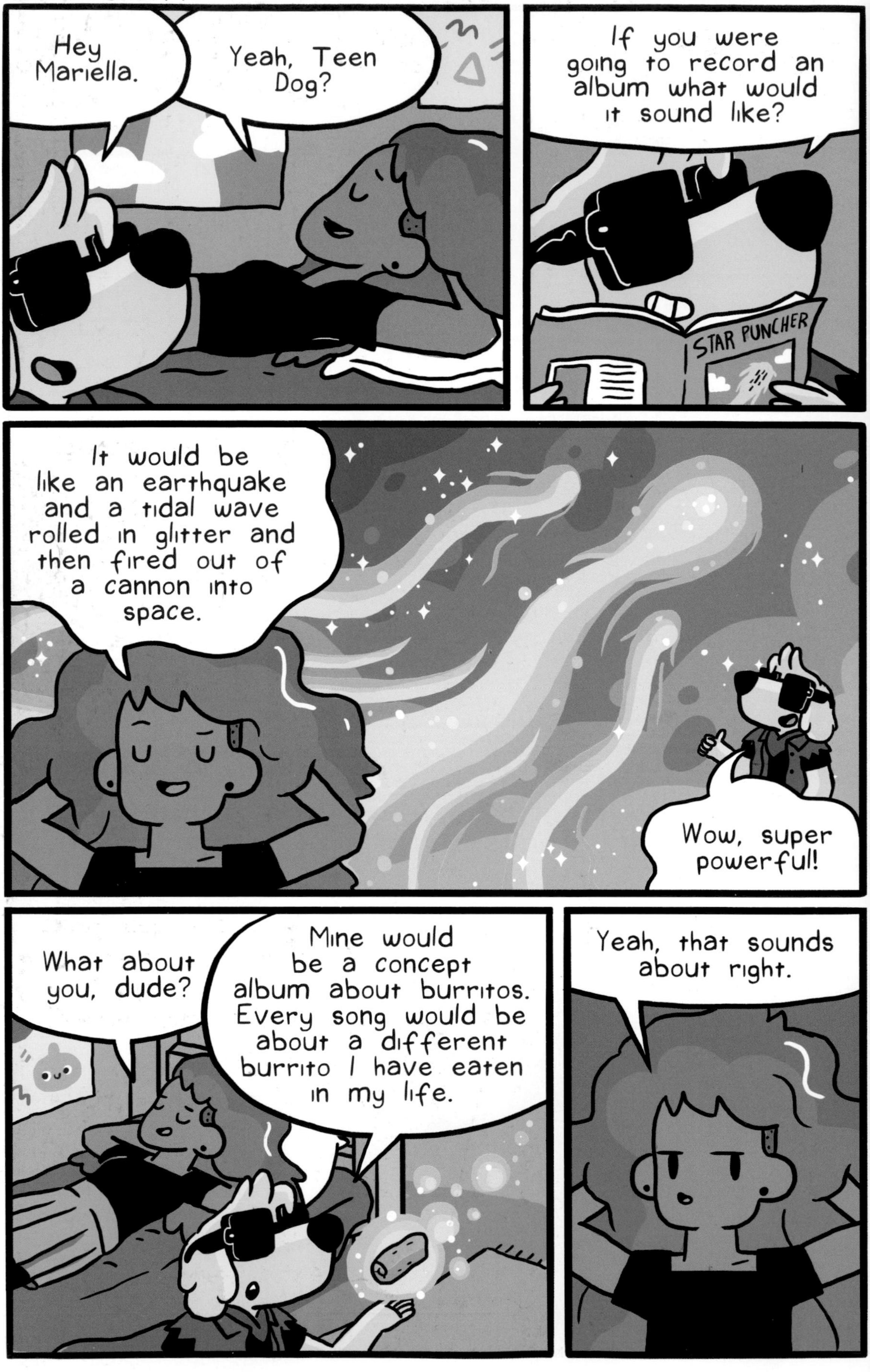

Hey Mariella.
Yeah, Teen Dog?
If you were going to record an album what would it sound like?
STAR PUNCHER
It would be like an earthquake and a tidal wave rolled in glitter and then fired out of a cannon into space.
Wow, super powerful!
What about you, dude?
Mine would be a concept album about burritos. Every song would be about a different burrito I have eaten in my life.
Yeah, that sounds about right.

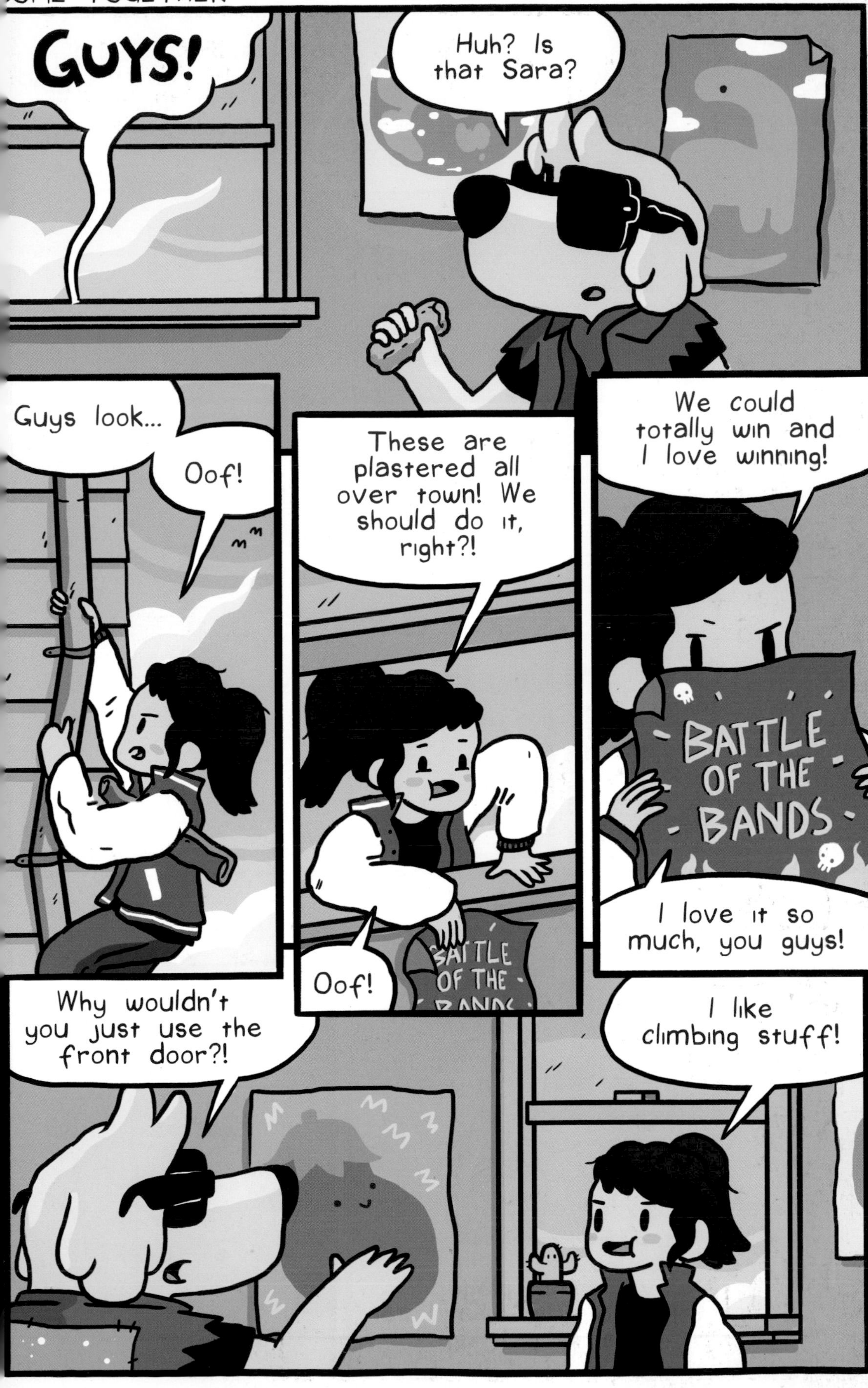
GUYS!
Huh? Is that Sara?
Guys look...
Oof!
These are plastered all over town! We should do it, right?!
Oof!
BATTLE OF THE BANDS
We could totally win and I love winning!
BATTLE OF THE BANDS
I love it so much, you guys!
Why wouldn't you just use the front door?!
I like climbing stuff!

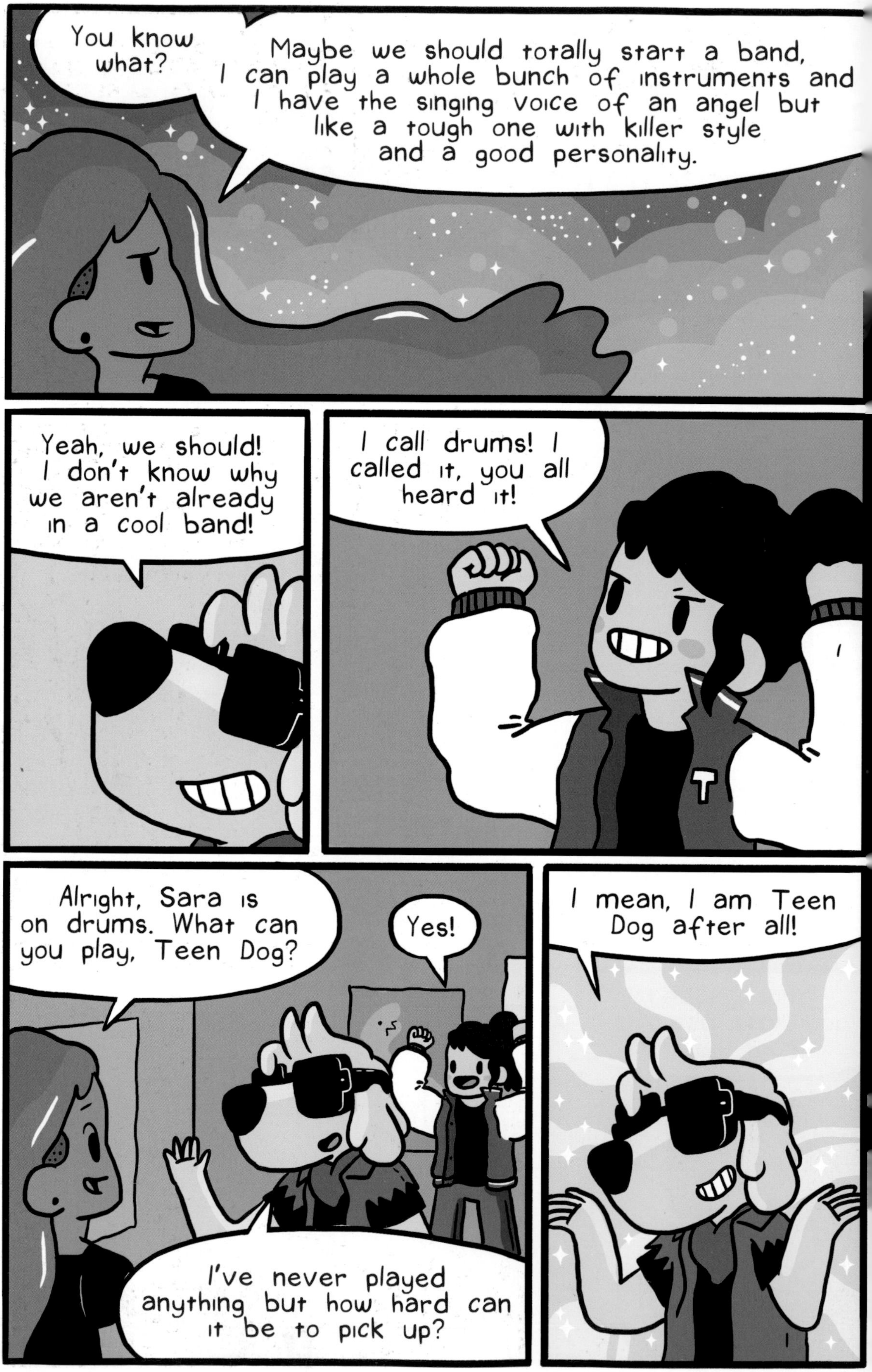
You know what?
Maybe we should totally start a band, I can play a whole bunch of instruments and I have the singing voice of an angel but like a tough one with killer style and a good personality.
Yeah, we should! I don't know why we aren't already in a cool band!
I call drums! I called it, you all heard it!
Alright, Sara is on drums. What can you play, Teen Dog?
Yes!
I've never played anything but how hard can it be to pick up?
I mean, I am Teen Dog after all!

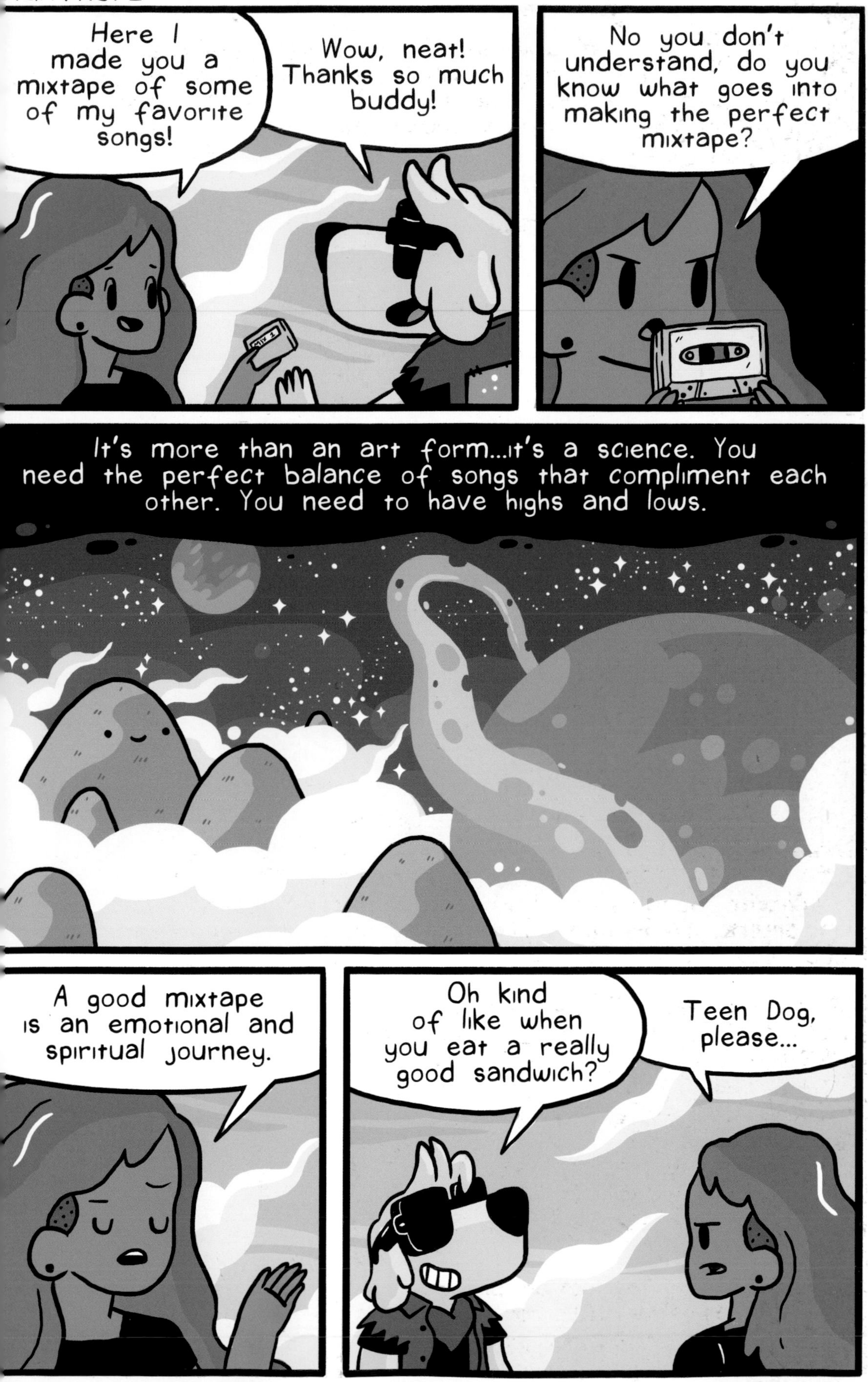
Here I made you a mixtape of some of my favorite songs!
Wow, neat! Thanks so much buddy!
No you don't understand, do you know what goes into making the perfect mixtape?
It's more than an art form...it's a science. You need the perfect balance of songs that compliment each other. You need to have highs and lows.
A good mixtape is an emotional and spiritual journey.
Oh kind of like when you eat a really good sandwich?
Teen Dog, please...

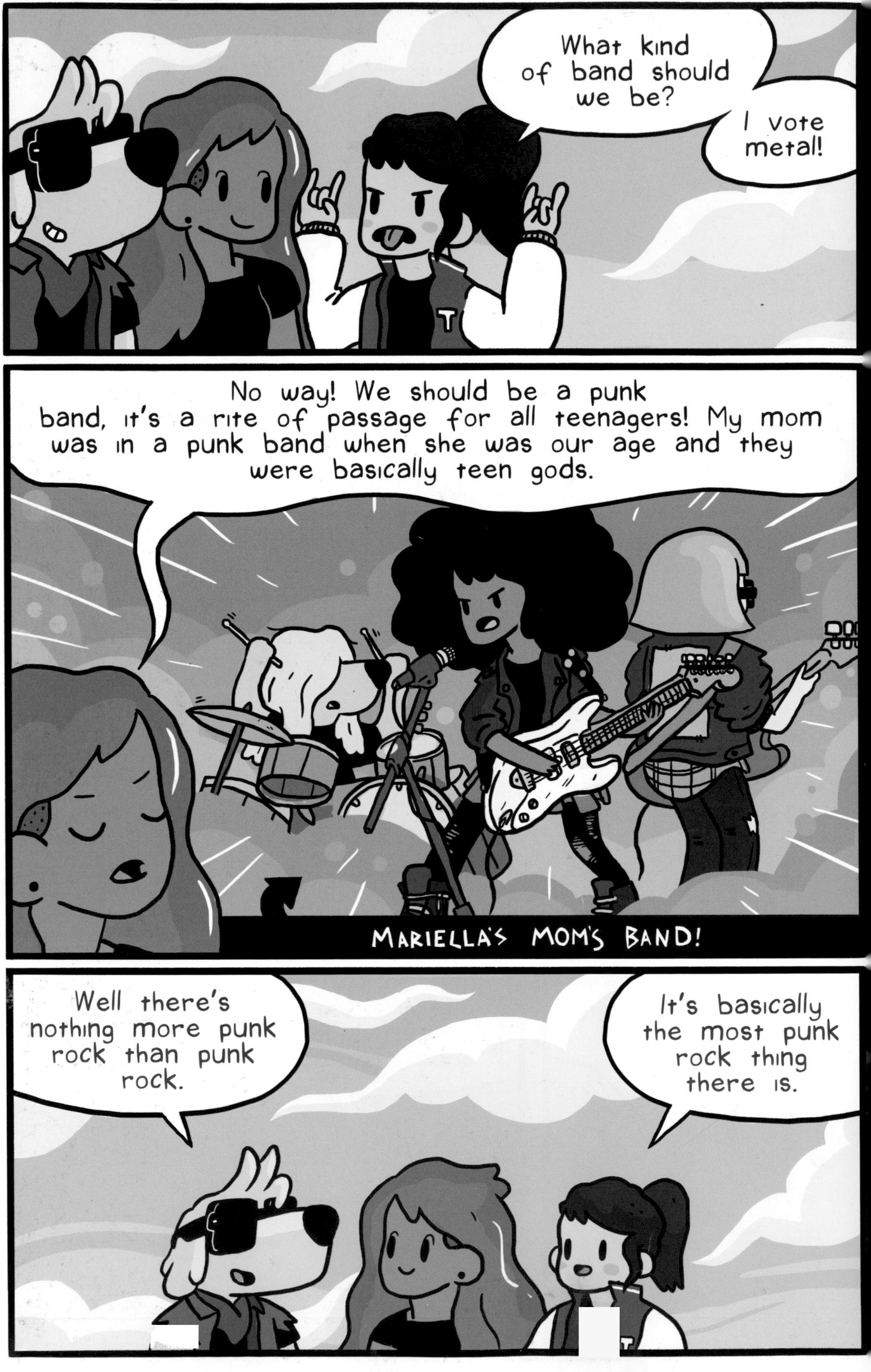
What kind of band should we be?
I vote metal!
No way! We should be a punk band, it's a rite of passage for all teenagers! My mom was in a punk band when she was our age and they were basically teen gods.
MARIELLA'S MOM'S BAND!
Well there's nothing more punk rock than punk rock.
It's basically the most punk rock thing there is.

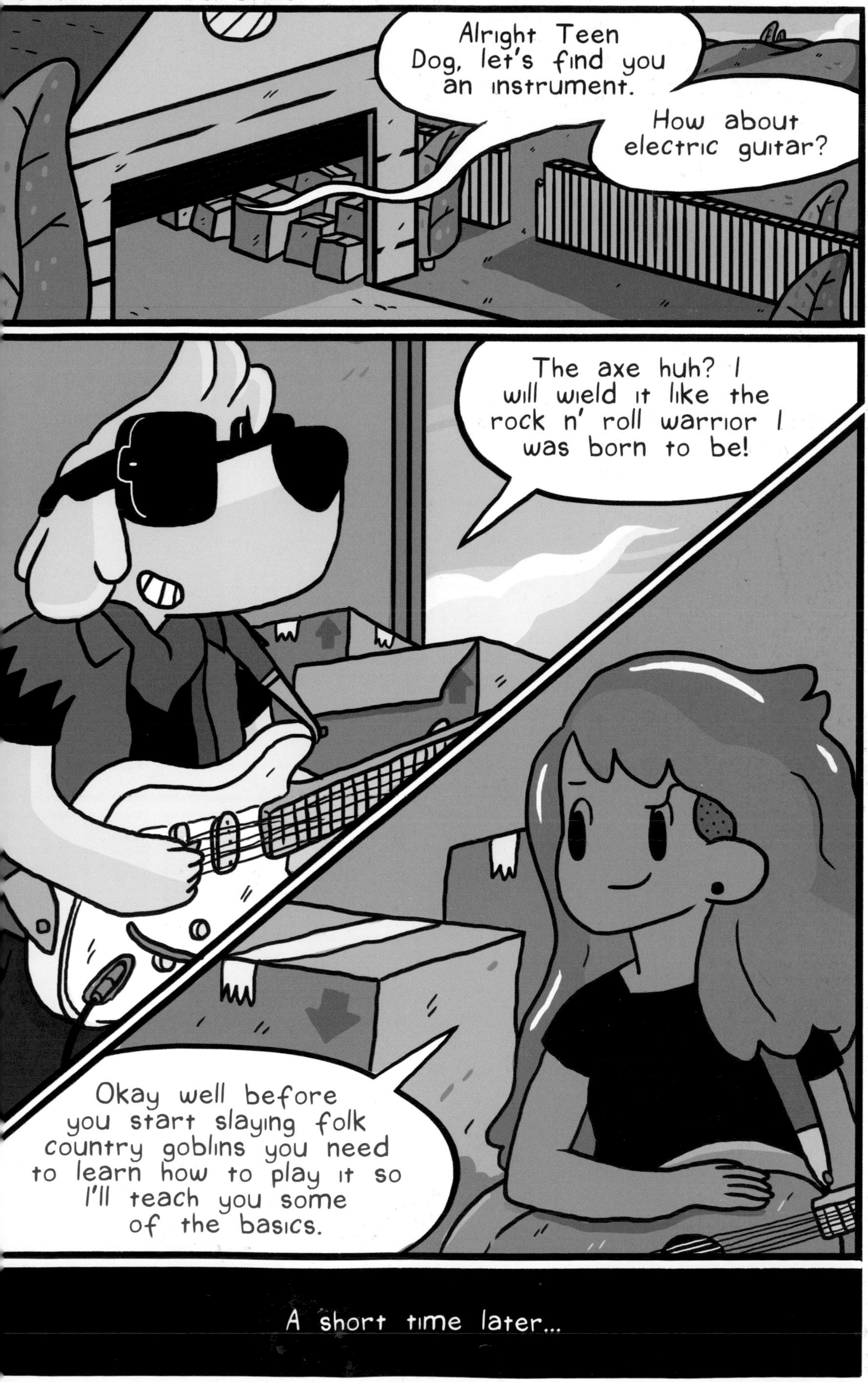
Alright Teen Dog, let's find you an instrument.
How about electric guitar?
The axe huh? I will wield it like the rock n' roll warrior I was born to be!
Okay well before you start slaying folk country goblins you need to learn how to play it so I'll teach you some of the basics.
A short time later...

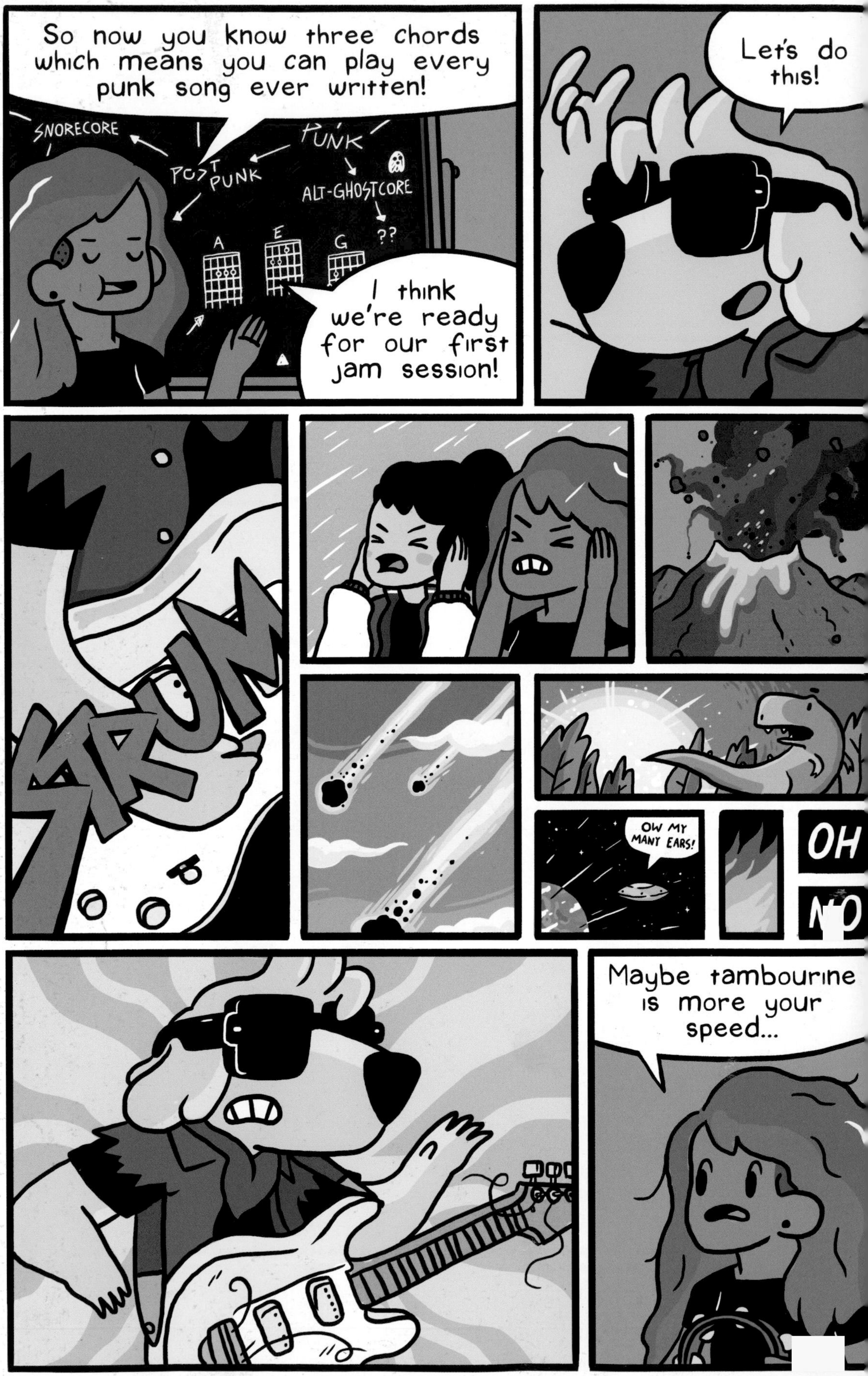
So now you know three chords which means you can play every punk song ever written!
SNORECORE
PUNK
POST PUNK
ALT-GHOSTCORE
??
A
E
G
I think we're ready for our first jam session!
Let's do this!
SKRUM
OW MY MANY EARS!
OH
NO
Maybe tambourine is more your speed...

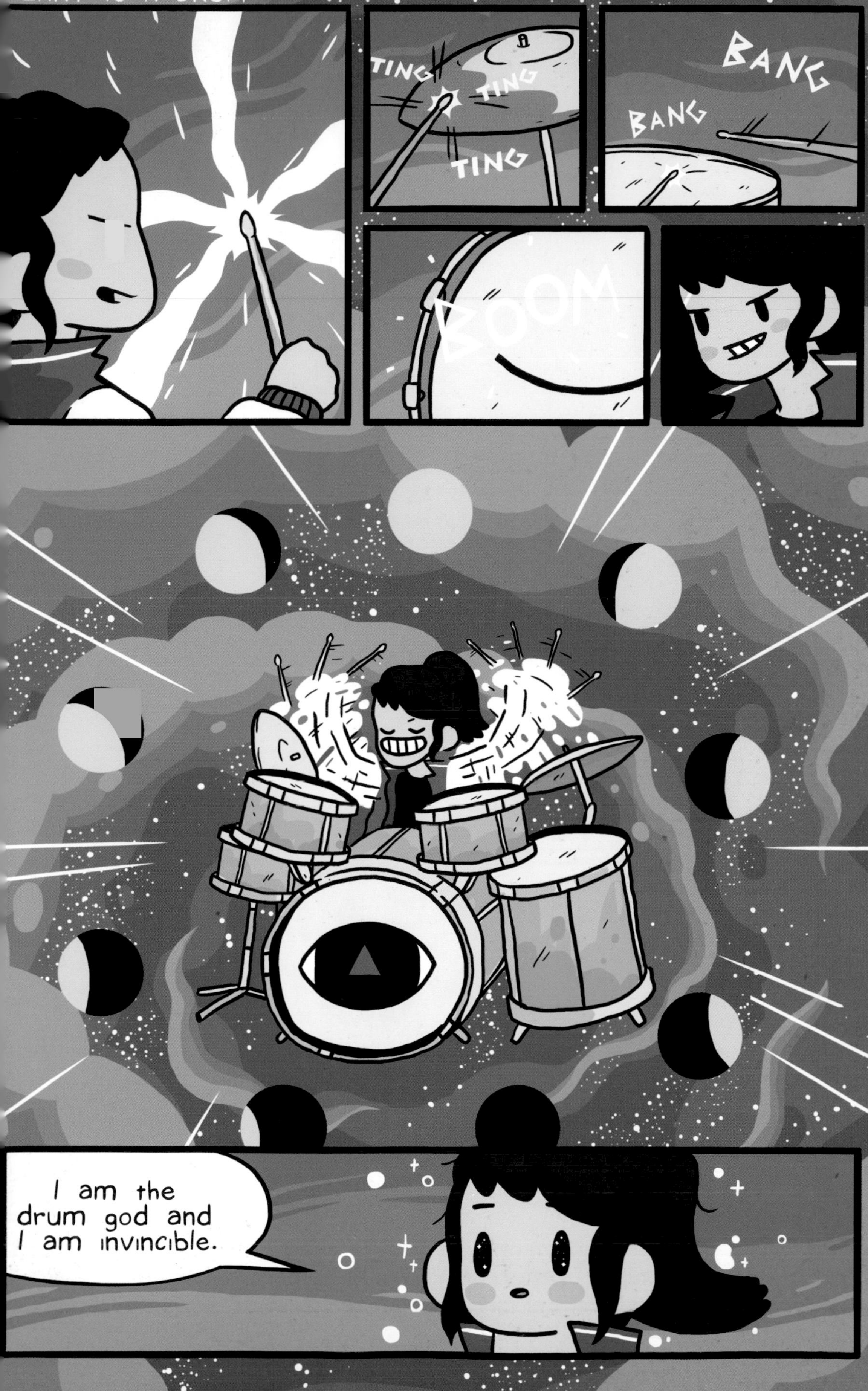
TING
TING
TING
BANG
BANG
BOOM
I am the drum god and I am invincible.

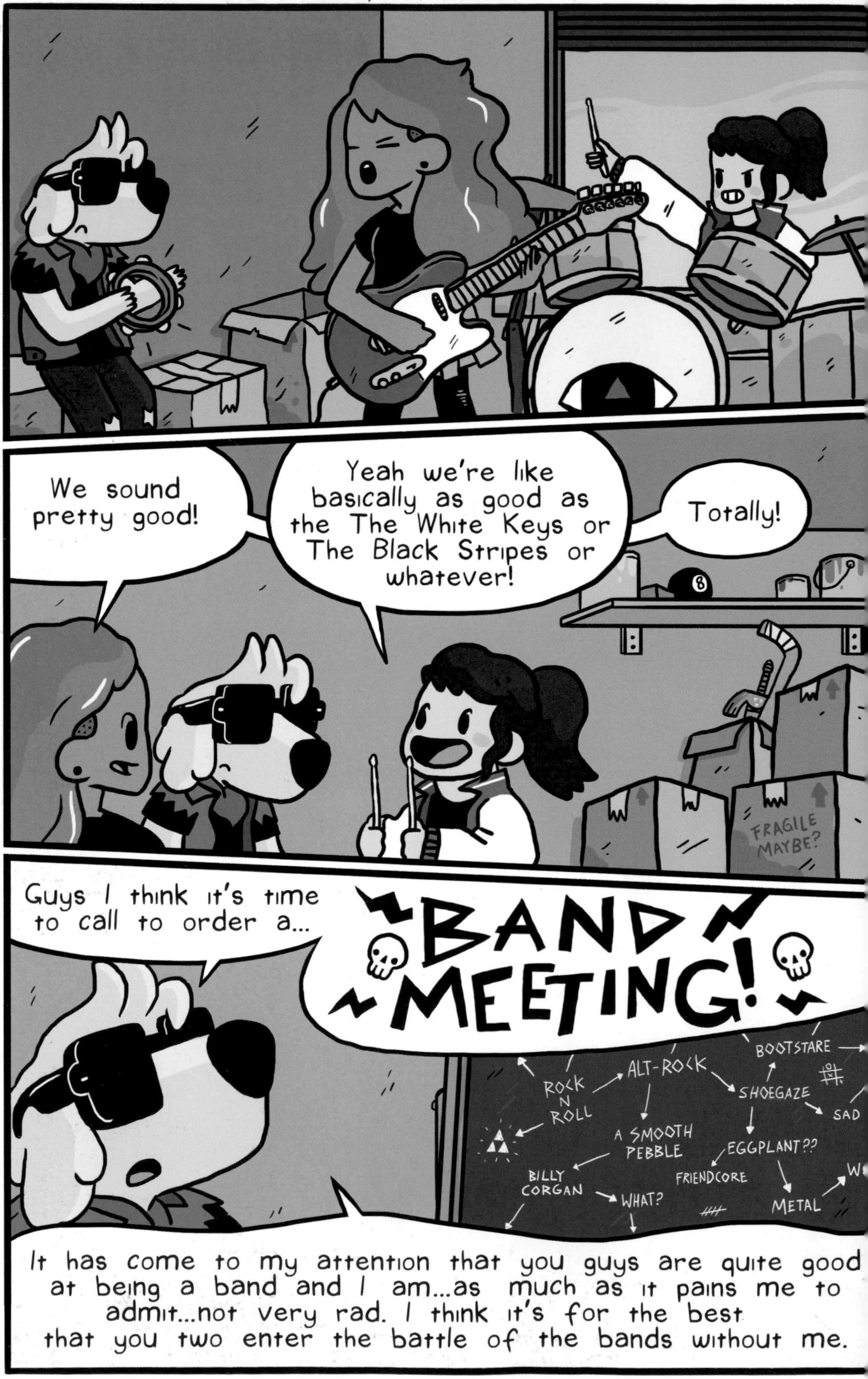
We sound pretty good!
Yeah we're like basically as good as the The White Keys or The Black Stripes or whatever!
Totally!
FRAGILE MAYBE?
Guys I think it's time to call to order a...
BAND MEETING!
ROCK N ROLL
ALT-ROCK
BOOTSTARE
SHOEGAZE
SAD
A SMOOTH PEBBLE
EGGPLANT??
BILLY CORGAN
FRIENDCORE
WHAT?
METAL
It has come to my attention that you guys are quite good at being a band and I am...as much as it pains me to admit...not very rad. I think it's for the best that you two enter the battle of the bands without me.

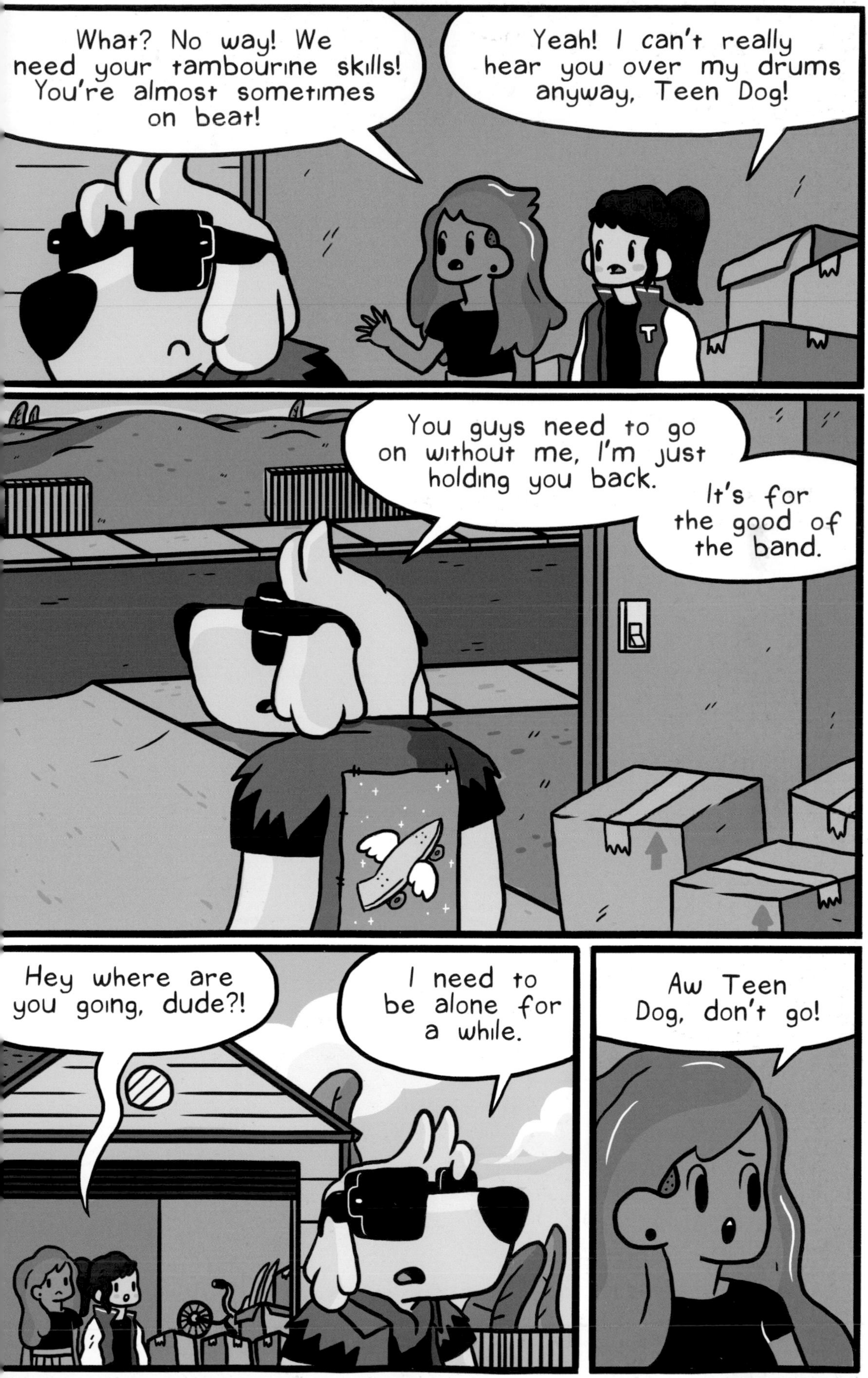
What? No way! We need your tambourine skills! You're almost sometimes on beat!
Yeah! I can't really hear you over my drums anyway, Teen Dog!
You guys need to go on without me, I'm just holding you back.
It's for the good of the band.
Hey where are you going, dude?!
I need to be alone for a while.
Aw Teen Dog, don't go!

HEAVEN KNOWS I'M MISERABLE NOW

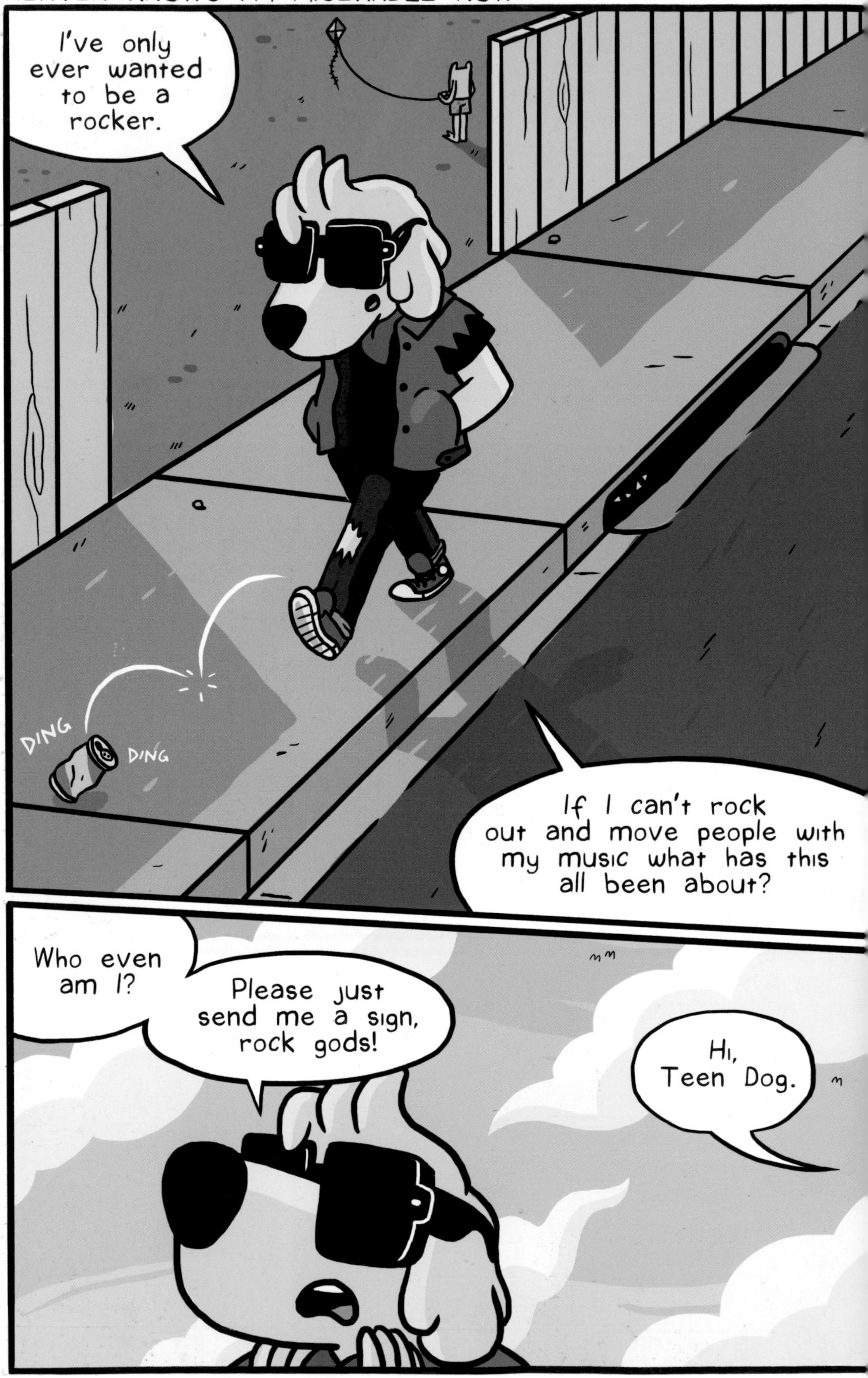

I've only ever wanted to be a rocker.
DING
DING
If I can't rock out and move people with my music what has this all been about?
Who even am I?
Please just send me a sign, rock gods!
Hi, Teen Dog.

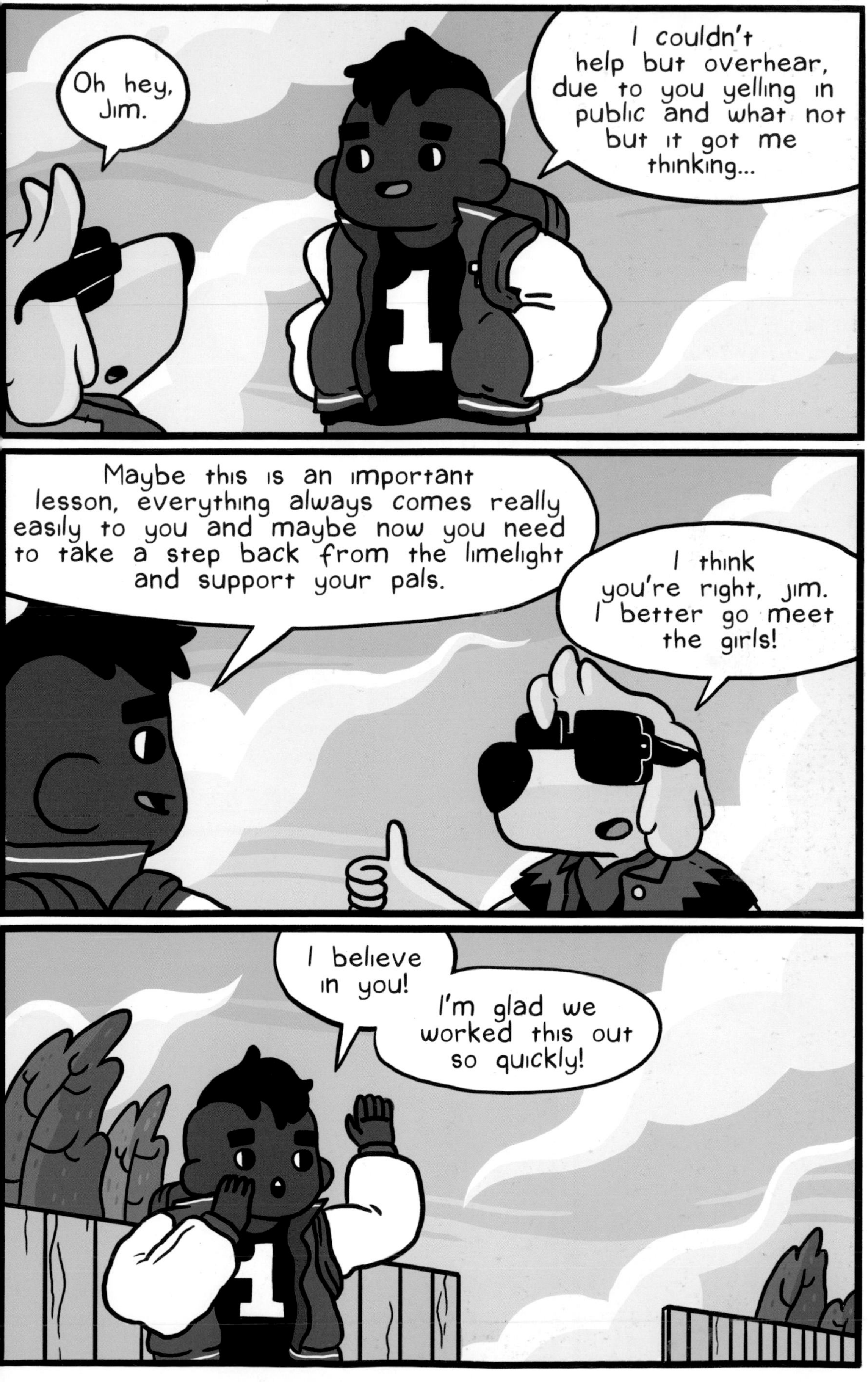
Oh hey, Jim.
I couldn't help but overhear, due to you yelling in public and what not but it got me thinking...
Maybe this is an important lesson, everything always comes really easily to you and maybe now you need to take a step back from the limelight and support your pals.
I think you're right, Jim. I better go meet the girls!
I believe in you!
I'm glad we worked this out so quickly!

UNDER COVER OF DARKNESS

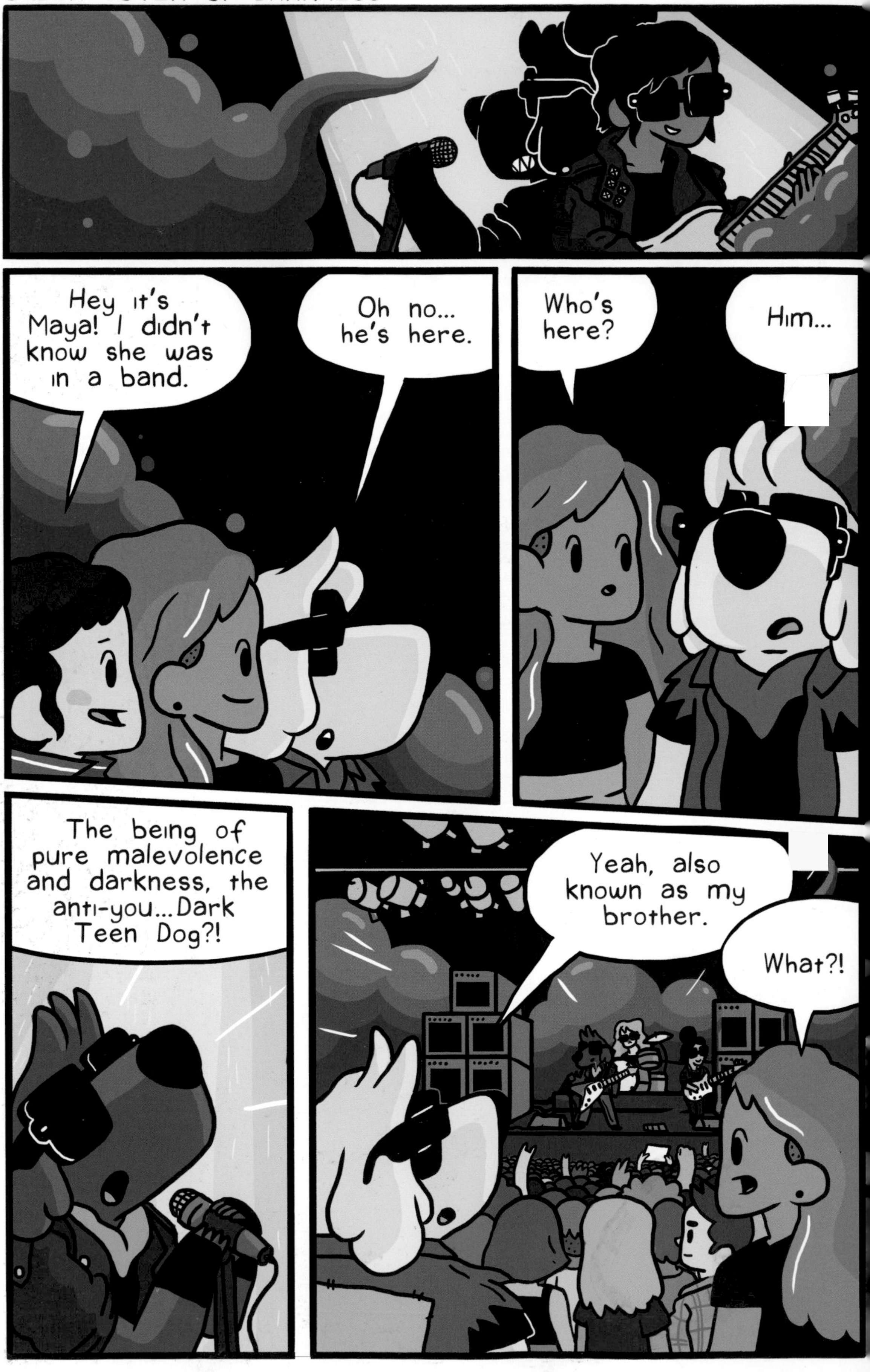

Hey it's Maya! I didn't know she was in a band.
Oh no... he's here.
Who's here?
Him...
The being of pure malevolence and darkness, the anti-you...Dark Teen Dog?!
Yeah, also known as my brother.
What?!

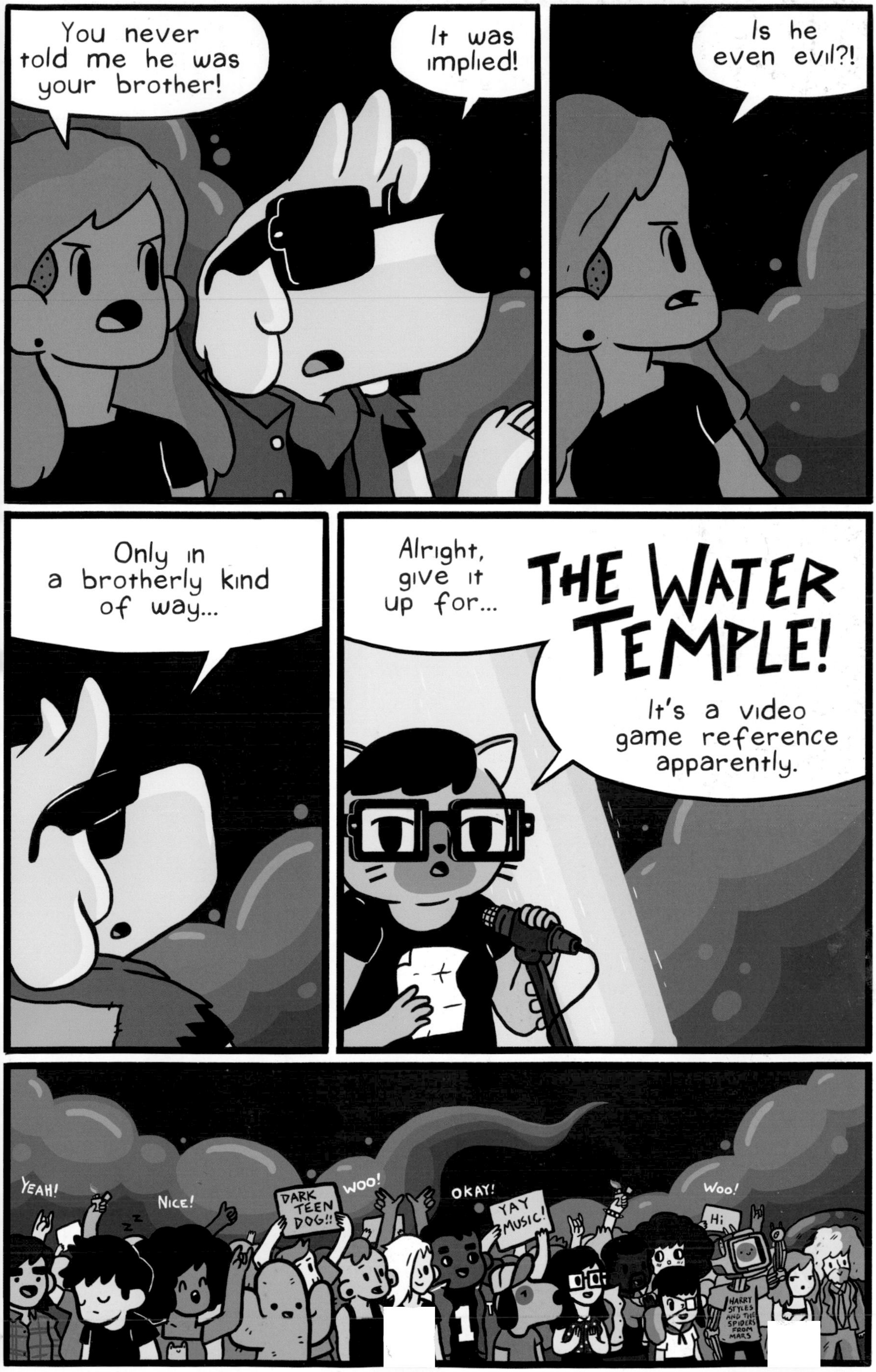

You never told me he was your brother!
It was implied!
Is he even evil?!
Only in a brotherly kind of way...
Alright, give it up for...
THE WATER TEMPLE!
It's a video game reference apparently.
YEAH!
NICE!
DARK TEEN DOG!!
WOO!
OKAY!
YAY MUSIC!
WOO!
HI
HARRY STYLES AND THE SPIDERS FROM MARS

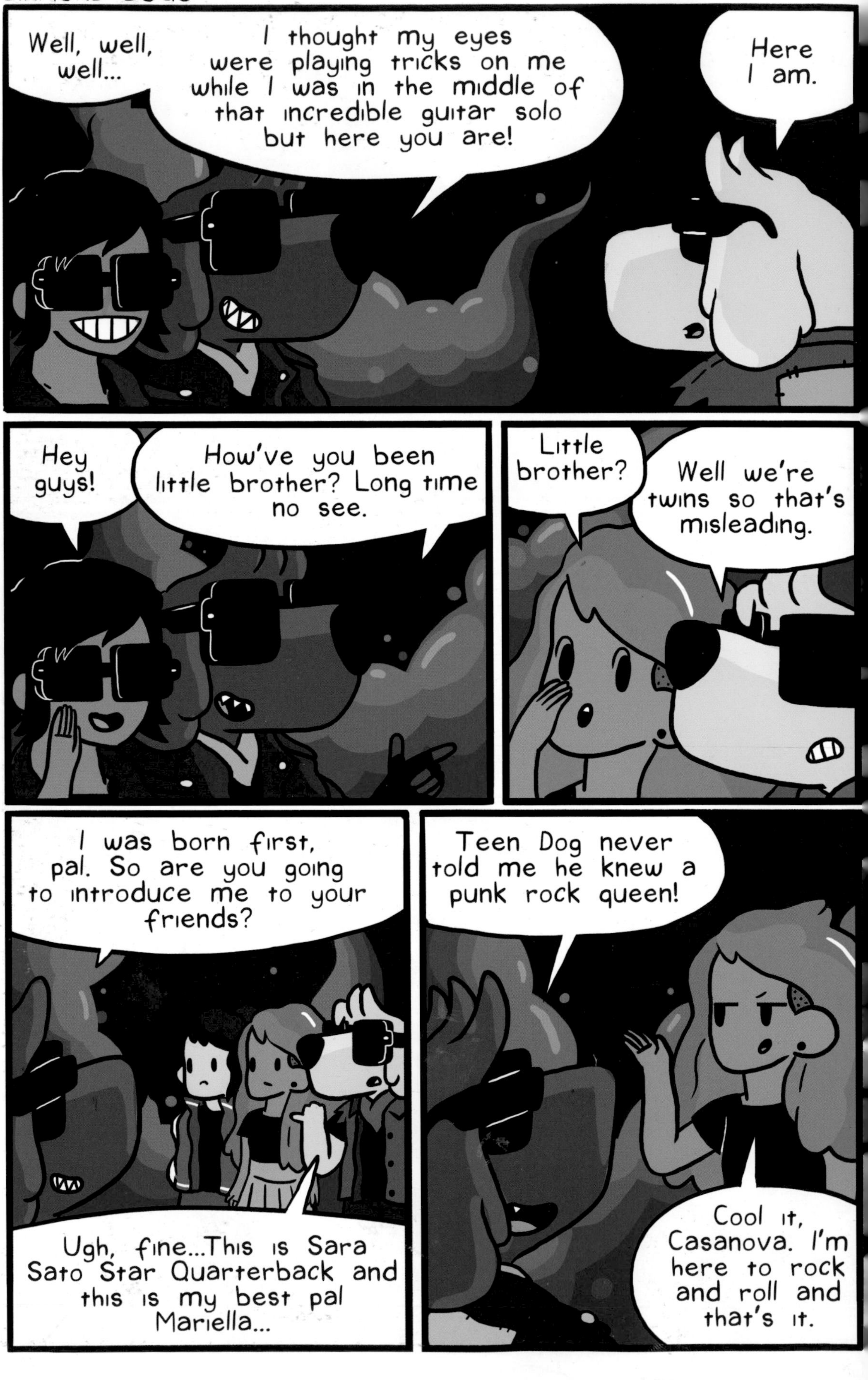
Well, well, well...
I thought my eyes were playing tricks on me while I was in the middle of that incredible guitar solo but here you are!
Here I am.
Hey guys!
How've you been little brother? Long time no see.
Little brother?
Well we're twins so that's misleading.
I was born first, pal. So are you going to introduce me to your friends?
Ugh, fine...This is Sara Sato Star Quarterback and this is my best pal Mariella...
Teen Dog never told me he knew a punk rock queen!
Cool it, Casanova. I'm here to rock and roll and that's it.

VEIN OF STARS

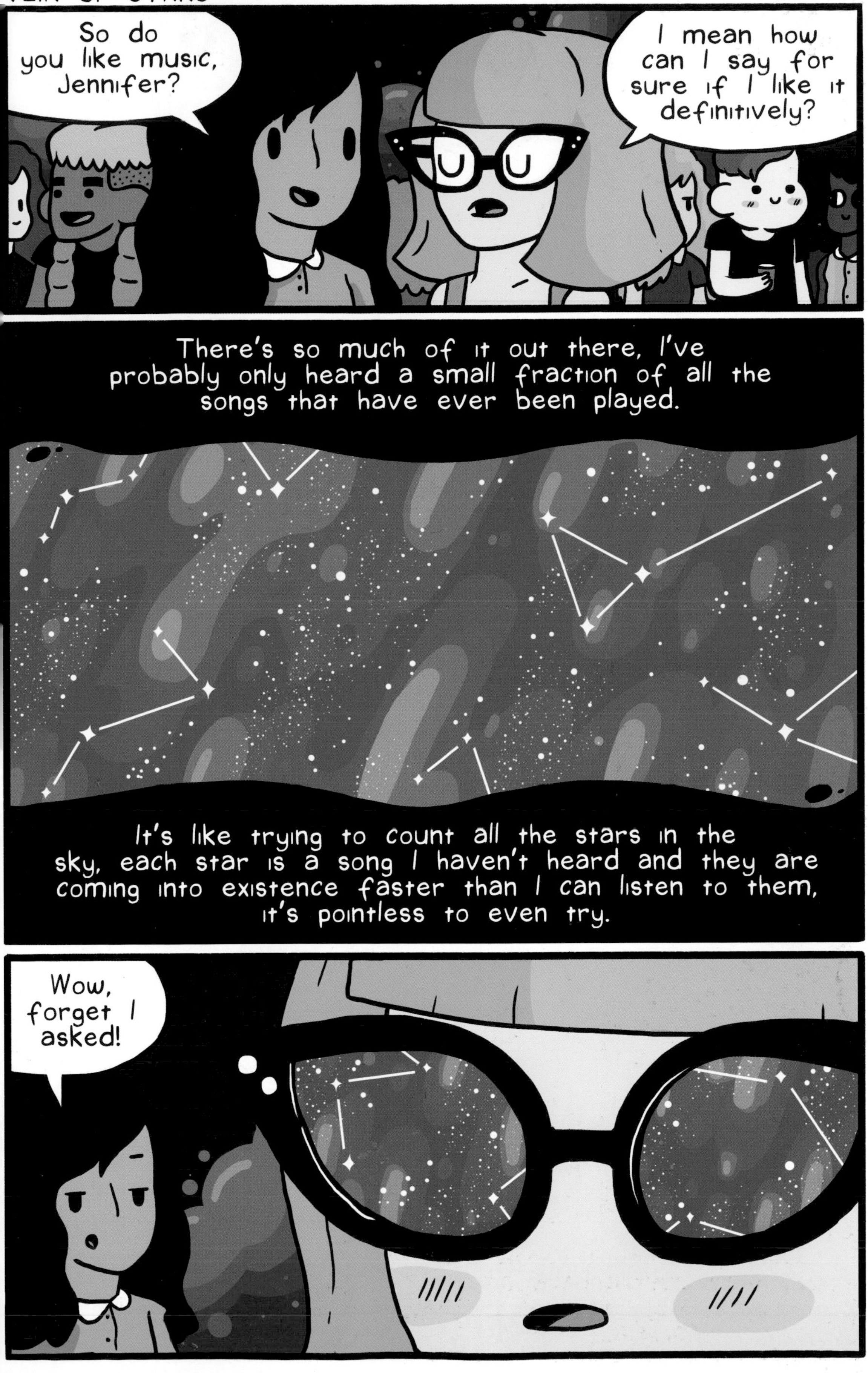
So do you like music, Jennifer?
I mean how can I say for sure if I like it definitively?
There's so much of it out there, I've probably only heard a small fraction of all the songs that have ever been played.
It's like trying to count all the stars in the sky, each star is a song I haven't heard and they are coming into existence faster than I can listen to them, it's pointless to even try.
Wow, forget I asked!

INACCESSIBLE MYSTERY

Up next we have the surliest pug in music, make some noise for...
THE THUG PUG EXPERIENCE!
OK
This song is dedicated to my biggest fan...
Me.
OH MY WOW

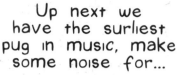

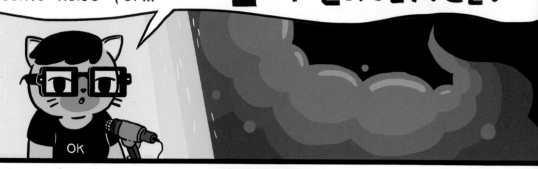

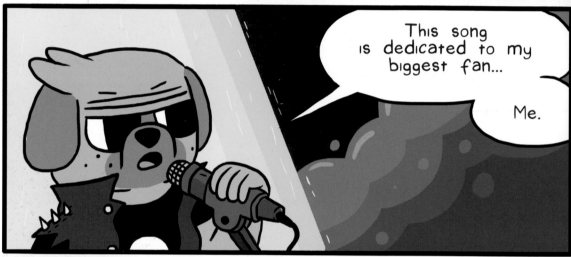

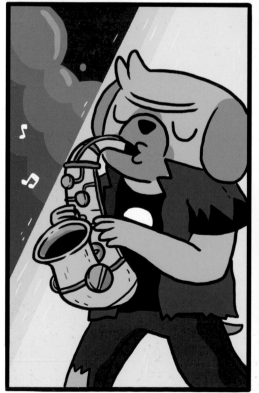

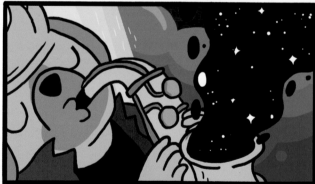

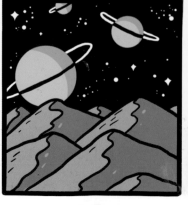

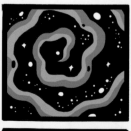

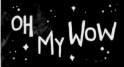

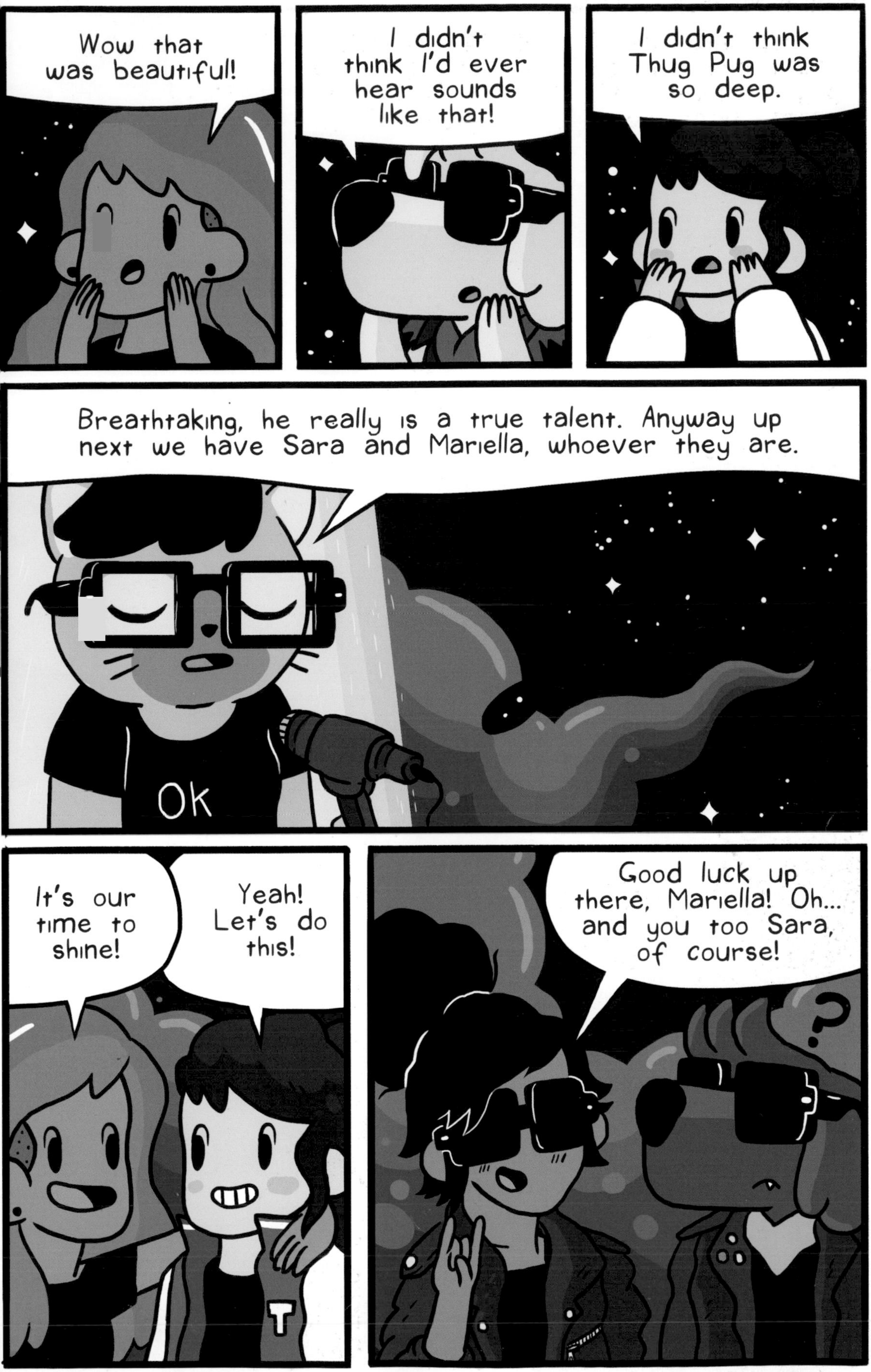
Wow that was beautiful!
I didn't think I'd ever hear sounds like that!
I didn't think Thug Pug was so deep.
Breathtaking, he really is a true talent. Anyway up next we have Sara and Mariella, whoever they are.
OK
It's our time to shine!
Yeah! Let's do this!
Good luck up there, Mariella! Oh... and you too Sara, of course!
?

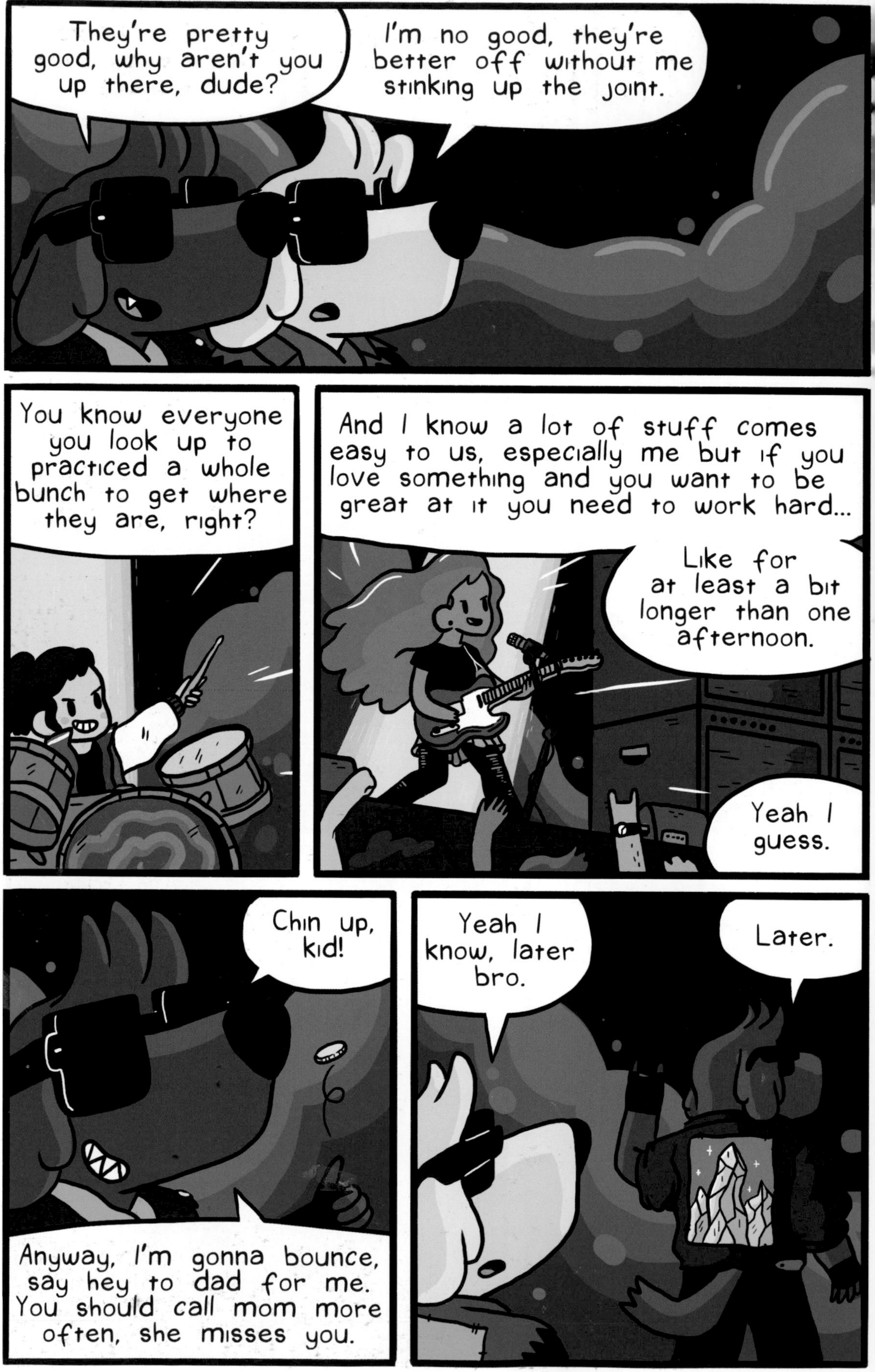
They're pretty good, why aren't you up there, dude?
I'm no good, they're better off without me stinking up the joint.
You know everyone you look up to practiced a whole bunch to get where they are, right?
And I know a lot of stuff comes easy to us, especially me but if you love something and you want to be great at it you need to work hard...
Like for at least a bit longer than one afternoon.
Yeah I guess.
Chin up, kid!
Anyway, I'm gonna bounce, say hey to dad for me. You should call mom more often, she misses you.
Yeah I know, later bro.
Later.

RACE FOR THE PRIZE

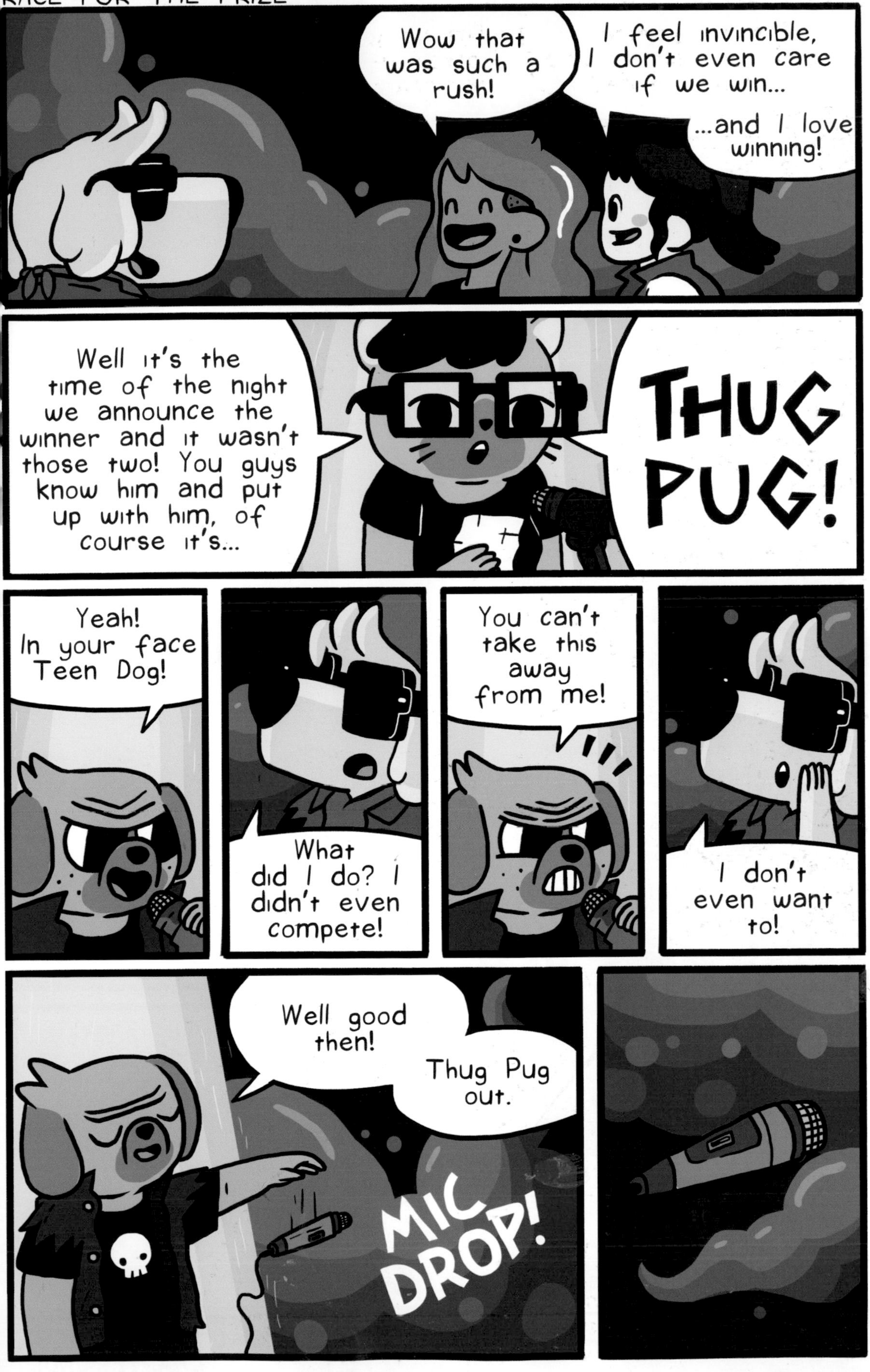
Wow that was such a rush!
I feel invincible, I don't even care if we win...
...and I love winning!
Well it's the time of the night we announce the winner and it wasn't those two! You guys know him and put up with him, of course it's...
THUG PUG!
Yeah! In your face Teen Dog!
What did I do? I didn't even compete!
You can't take this away from me!
I don't even want to!
Well good then!
Thug Pug out.
MIC DROP!

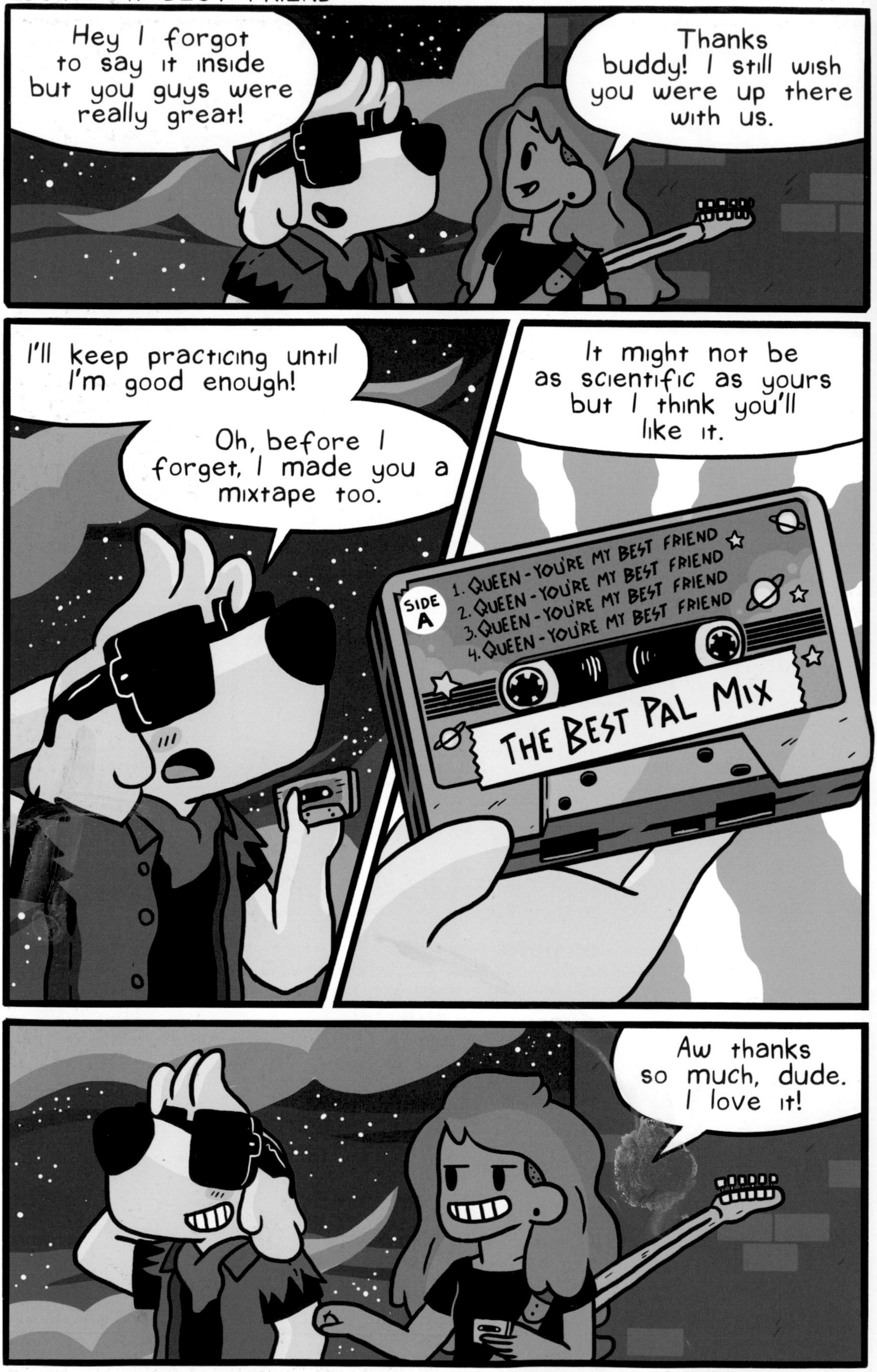
Hey I forgot to say it inside but you guys were really great!
Thanks buddy! I still wish you were up there with us.
I'll keep practicing until I'm good enough!
Oh, before I forget, I made you a mixtape too.
It might not be as scientific as yours but I think you'll like it.
SIDE A
1. QUEEN - YOU'RE MY BEST FRIEND
2. QUEEN - YOU'RE MY BEST FRIEND
3. QUEEN - YOU'RE MY BEST FRIEND
4. QUEEN - YOU'RE MY BEST FRIEND
THE BEST PAL MIX
Aw thanks so much, dude. I love it!

CHAPTER ENDS

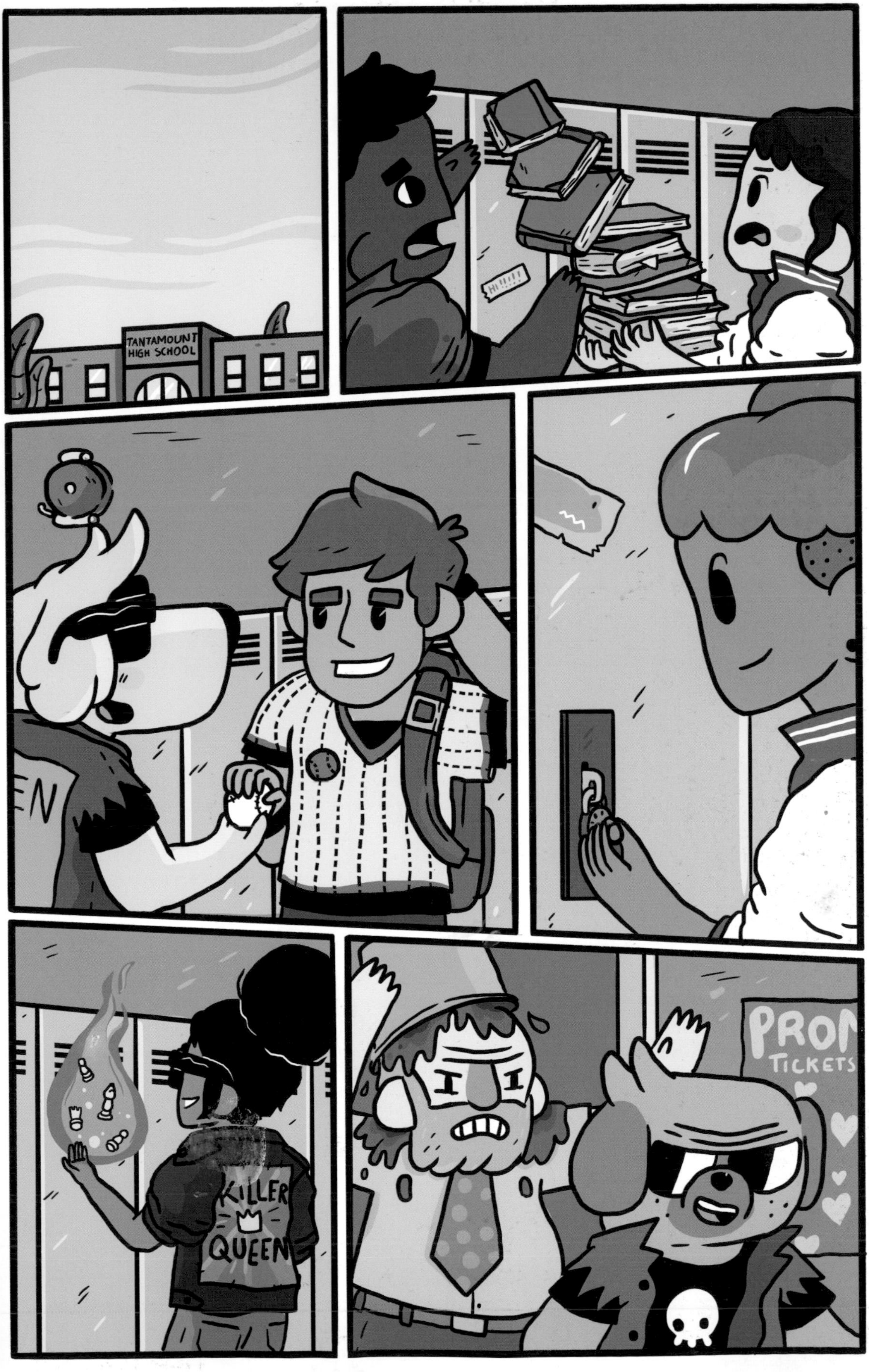
TANTAMOUNT HIGH SCHOOL
HI!!!!!
EN
KILLER
QUEEN
PROM
TICKETS

NINE TO FIVE

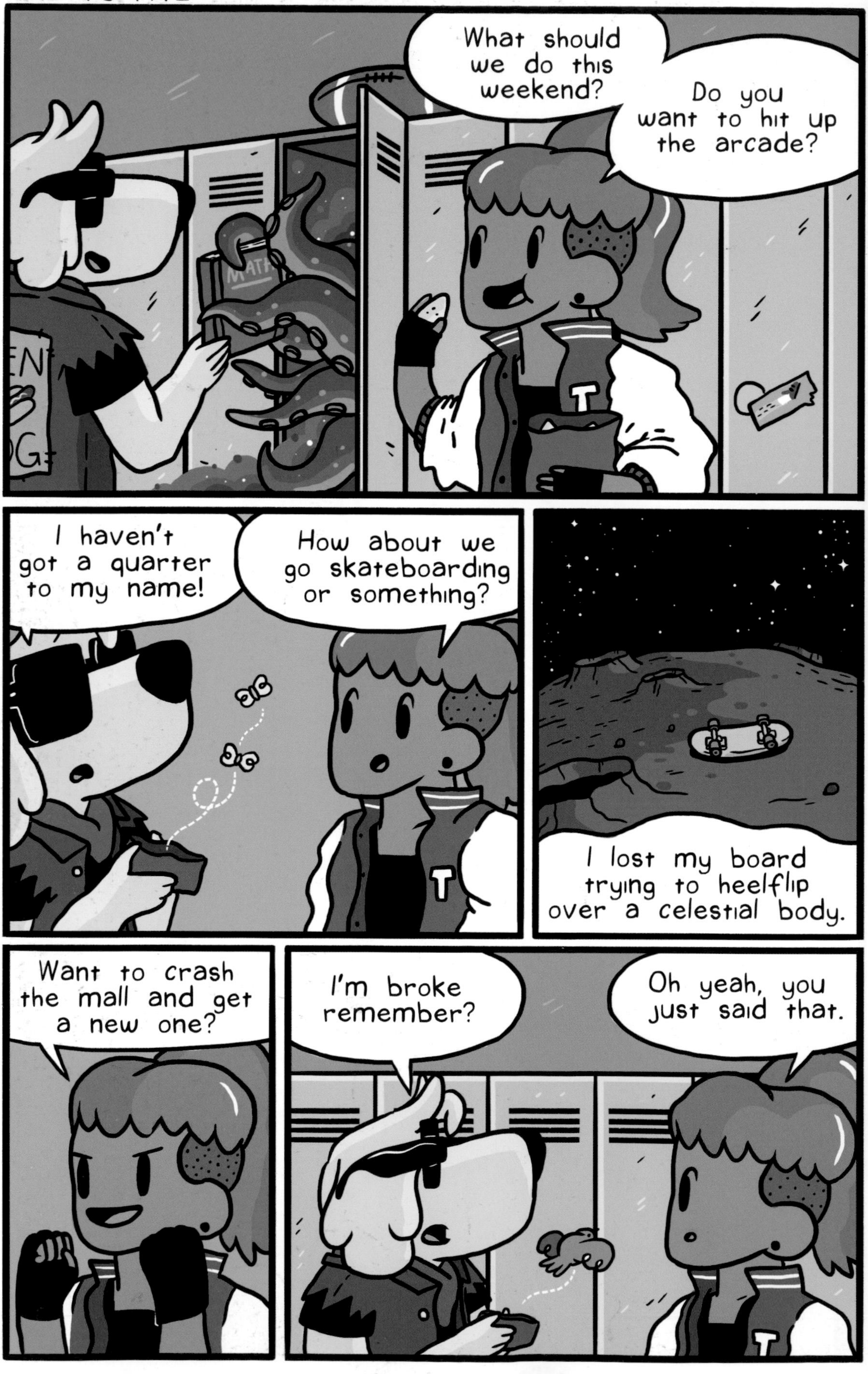

What should we do this weekend?
Do you want to hit up the arcade?
MATH
I haven't got a quarter to my name!
How about we go skateboarding or something?
I lost my board trying to heelflip over a celestial body.
Want to crash the mall and get a new one?
I'm broke remember?
Oh yeah, you just said that.

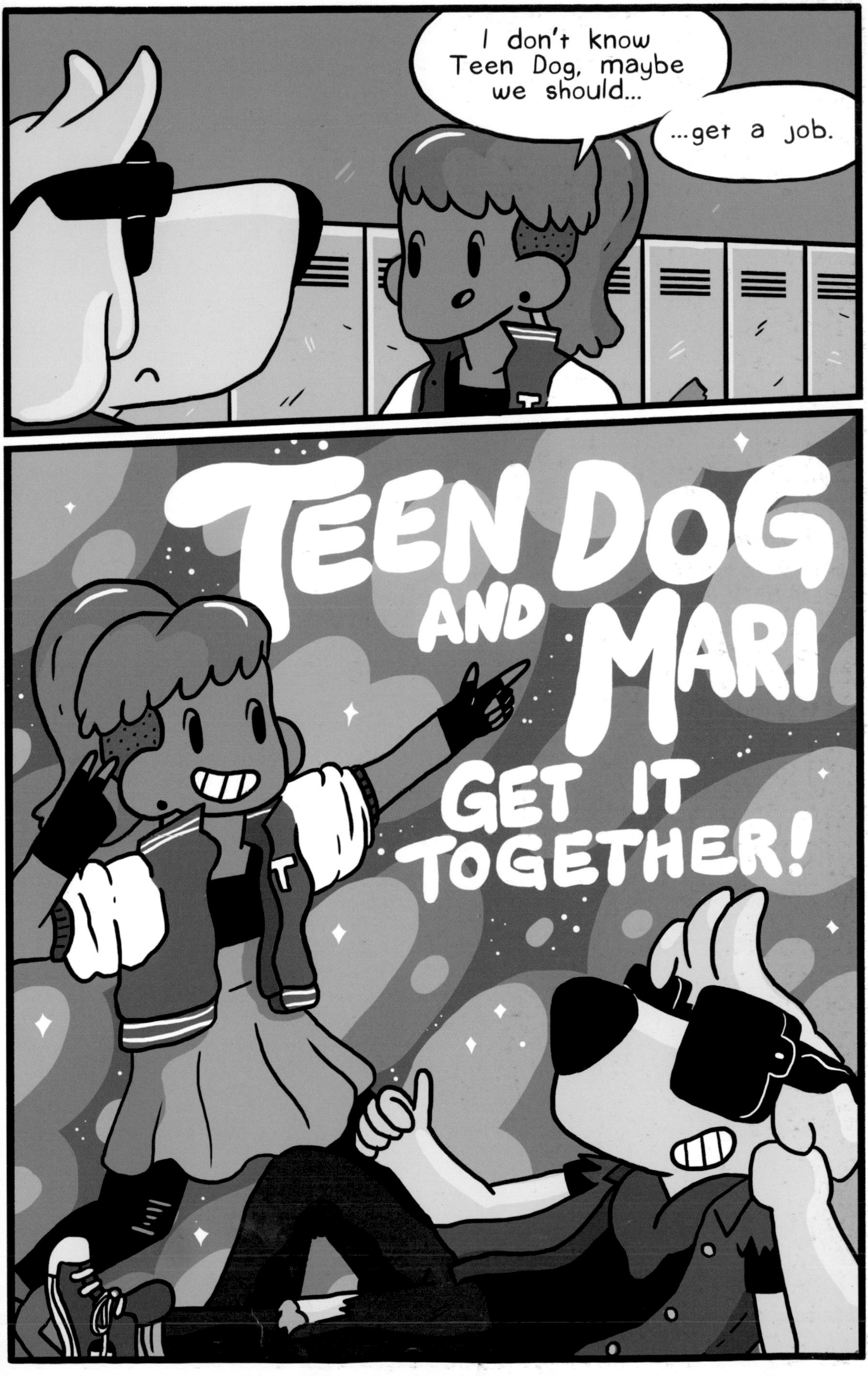
I don't know Teen Dog, maybe we should...
...get a job.
TEEN DOG AND MARI GET IT TOGETHER!

TAKING CARE OF BUSINESS

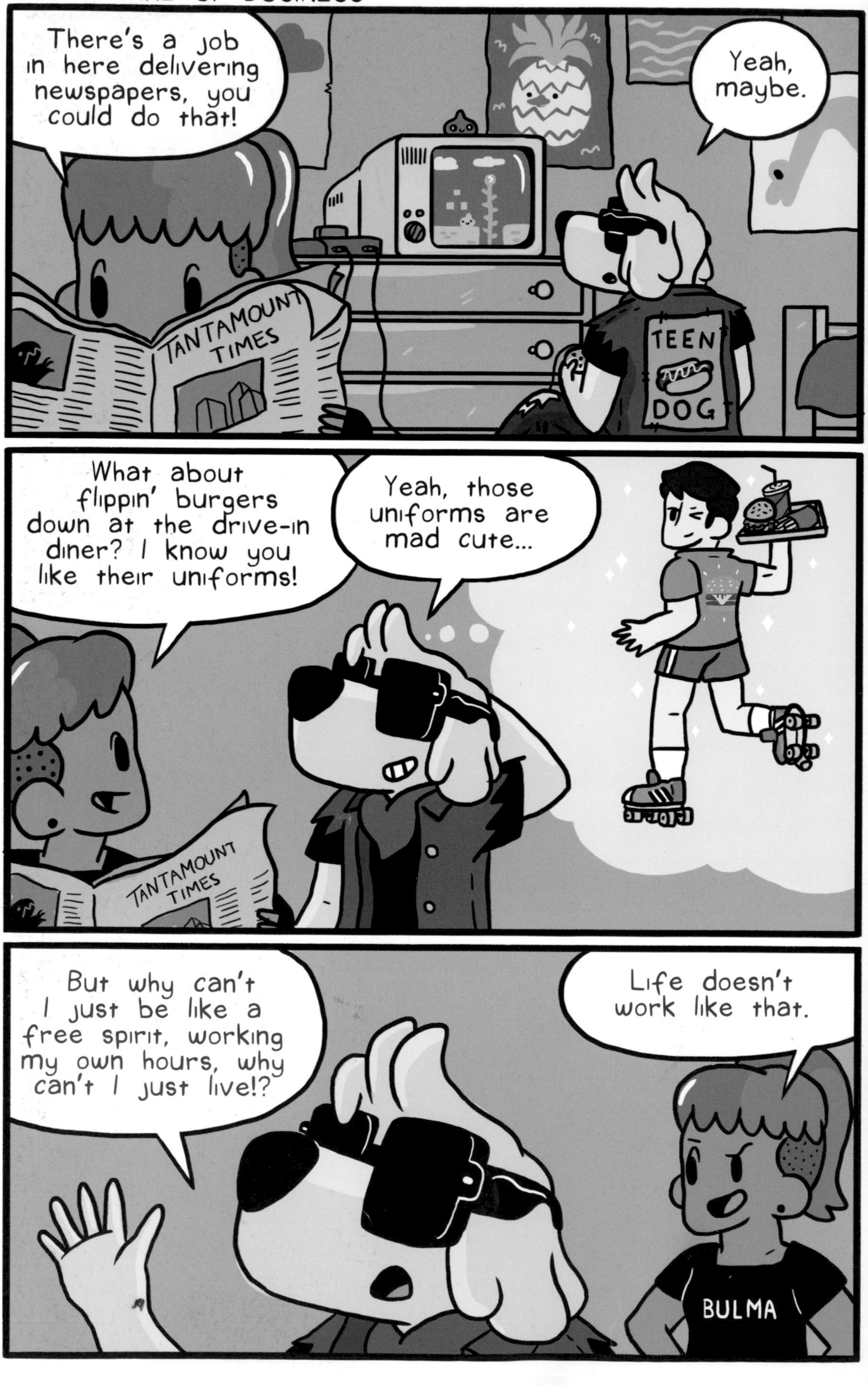

CHAPTER SIX

There's a job in here delivering newspapers, you could do that!
TANTAMOUNT TIMES
TEEN DOG
Yeah, maybe.
What about flippin' burgers down at the drive-in diner? I know you like their uniforms!
Yeah, those uniforms are mad cute...
TANTAMOUNT TIMES
But why can't I just be like a free spirit, working my own hours, why can't I just live!?
Life doesn't work like that.
BULMA

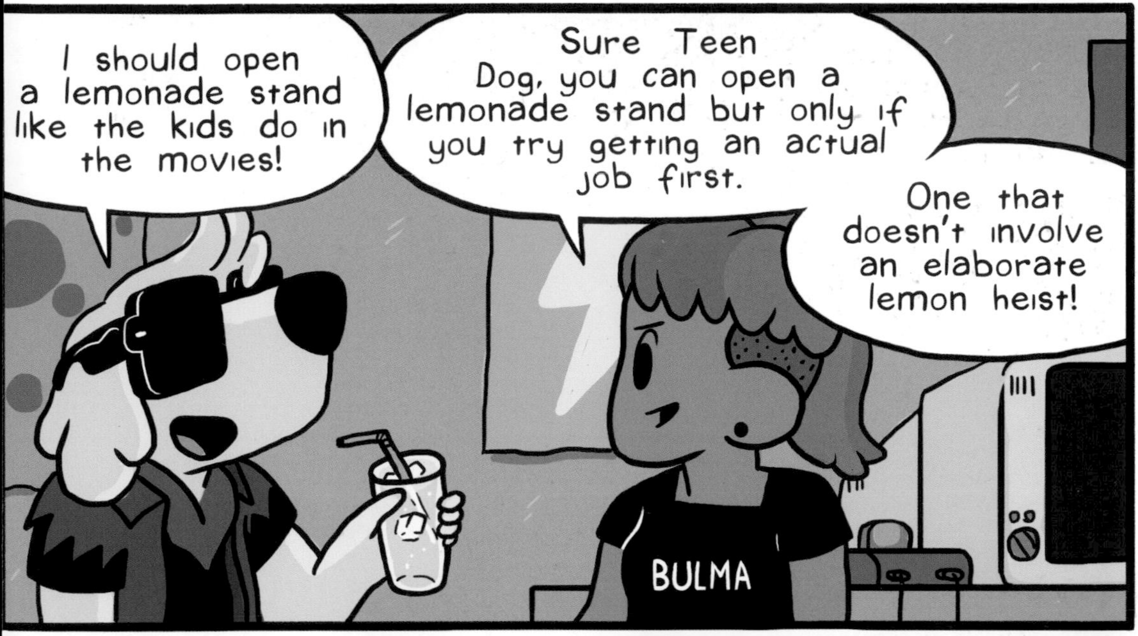
I should open a lemonade stand like the kids do in the movies!
Sure Teen Dog, you can open a lemonade stand but only if you try getting an actual job first.
One that doesn't involve an elaborate lemon heist!
BULMA

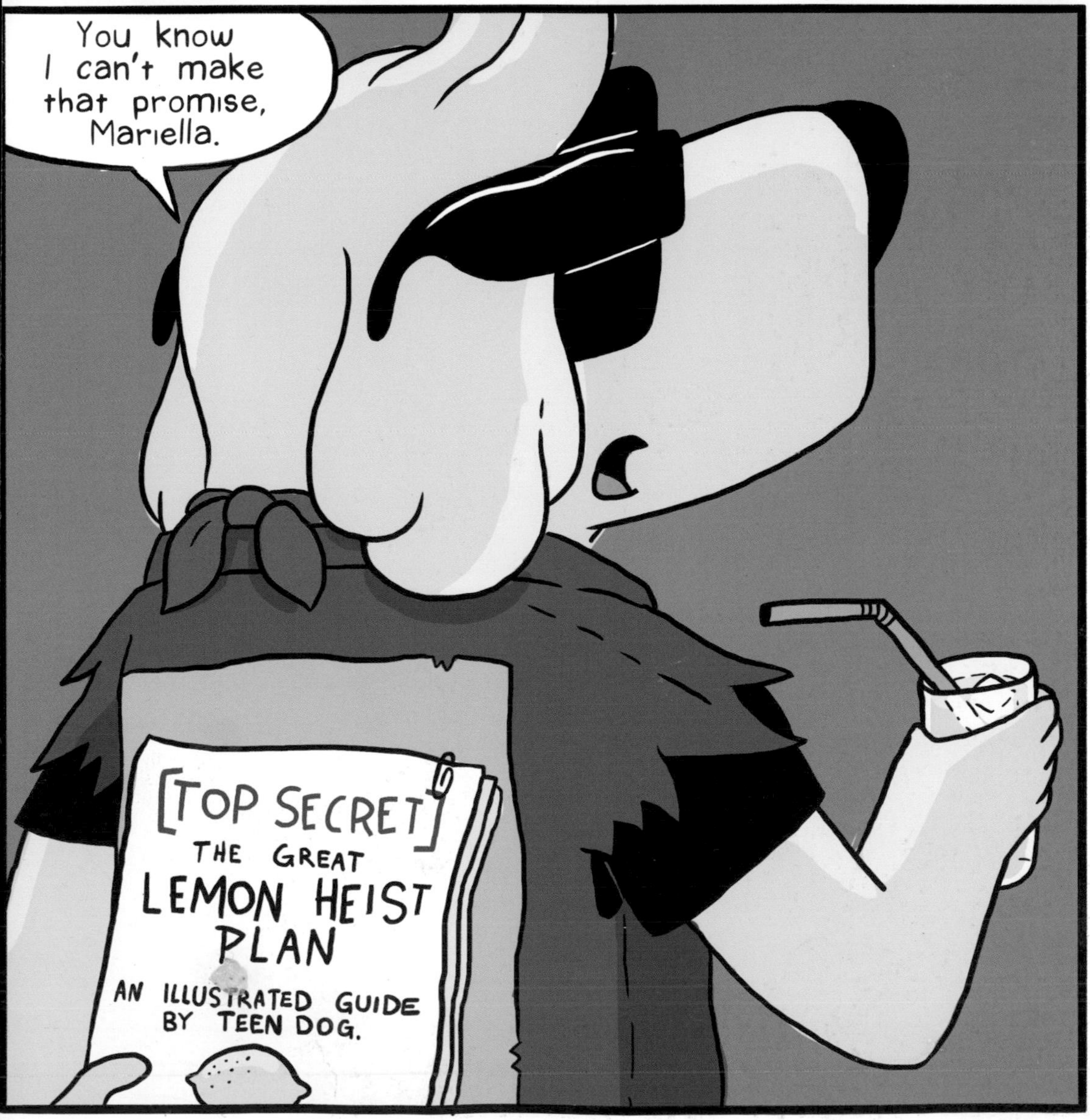
You know I can't make that promise, Mariella.
[TOP SECRET]
THE GREAT LEMON HEIST PLAN
AN ILLUSTRATED GUIDE BY TEEN DOG.

AMERICAN IDIOM

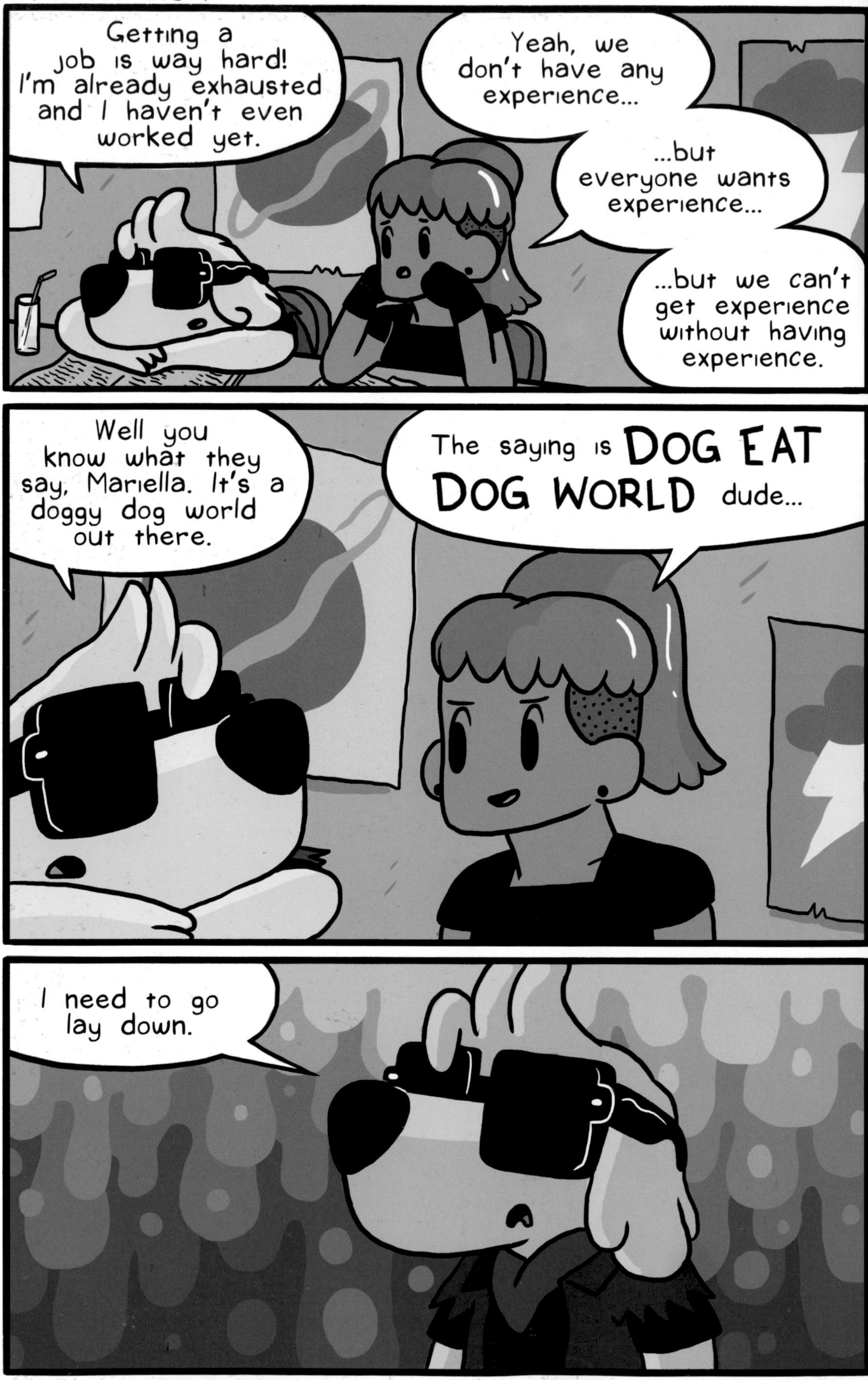

Getting a job is way hard! I'm already exhausted and I haven't even worked yet.
Yeah, we don't have any experience...
...but everyone wants experience...
...but we can't get experience without having experience.
Well you know what they say, Mariella. It's a doggy dog world out there.
The saying is DOG EAT DOG WORLD dude...
I need to go lay down.

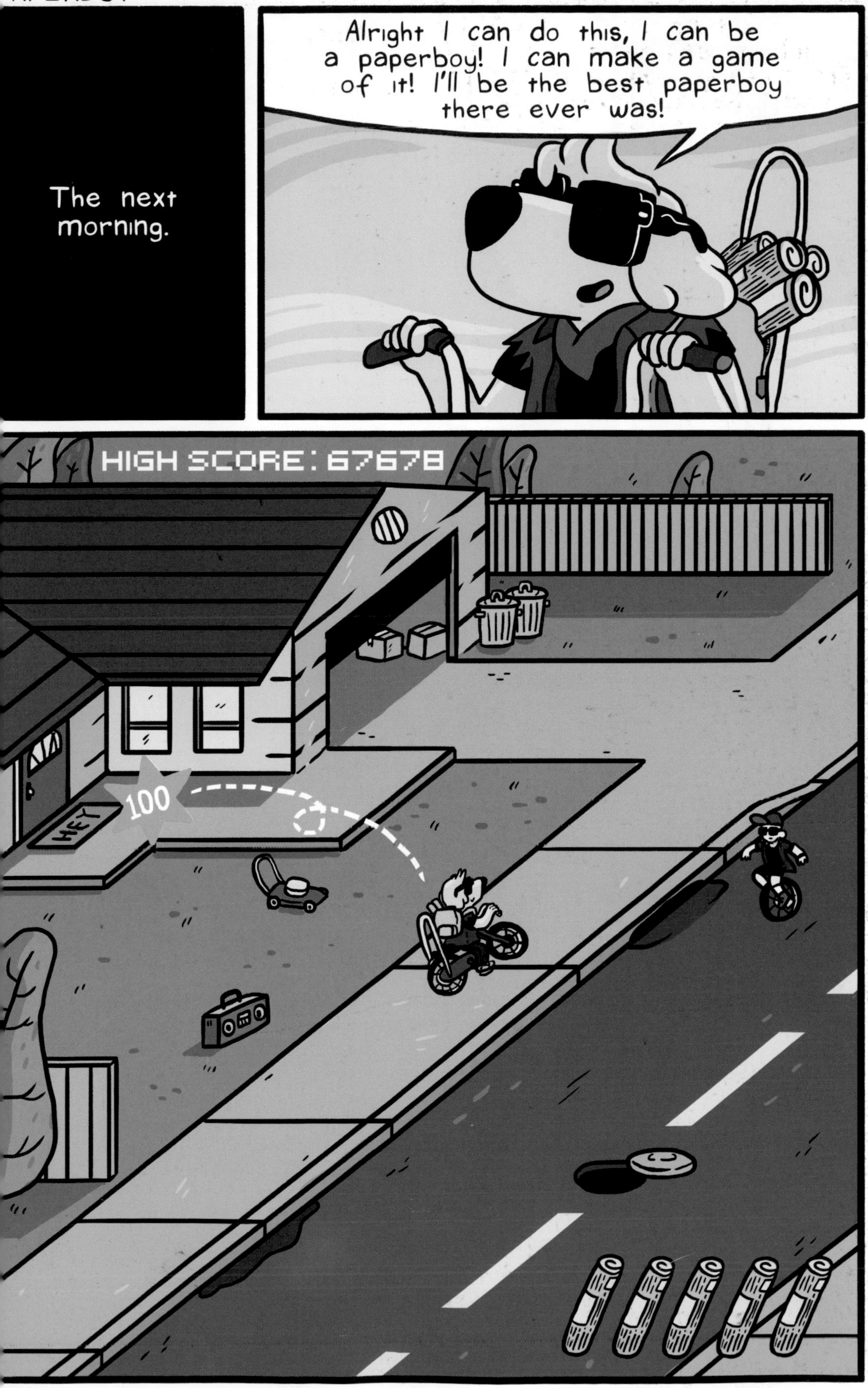
The next morning.
Alright I can do this, I can be a paperboy! I can make a game of it! I'll be the best paperboy there ever was!
HIGH SCORE: 67678
100
HEY

HIGHER FIDELITY

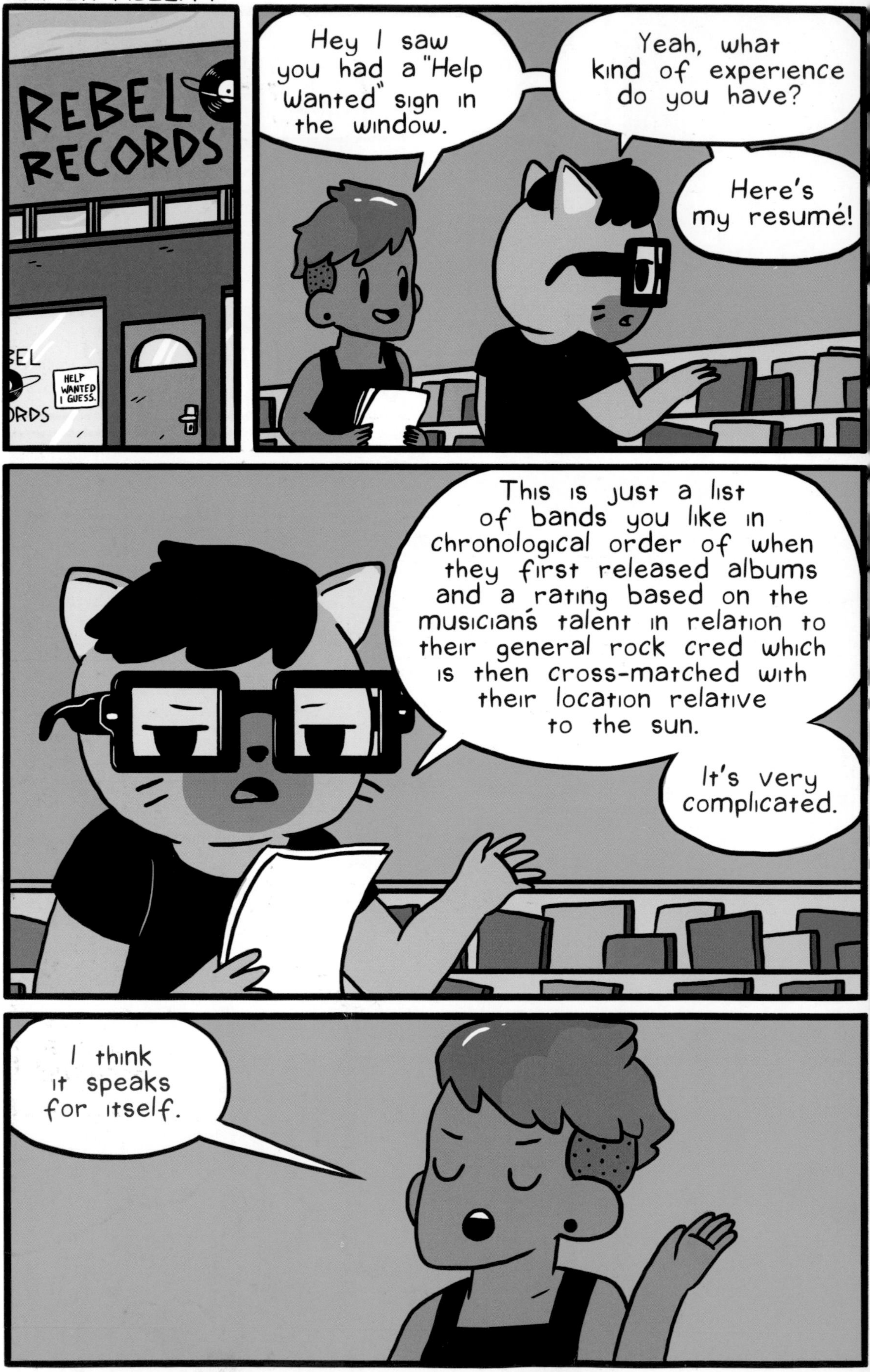
REBEL RECORDS
HELP WANTED I GUESS.
Hey I saw you had a "Help Wanted" sign in the window.
Yeah, what kind of experience do you have?
Here's my resumé!
This is just a list of bands you like in chronological order of when they first released albums and a rating based on the musician's talent in relation to their general rock cred which is then cross-matched with their location relative to the sun.
It's very complicated.
I think it speaks for itself.

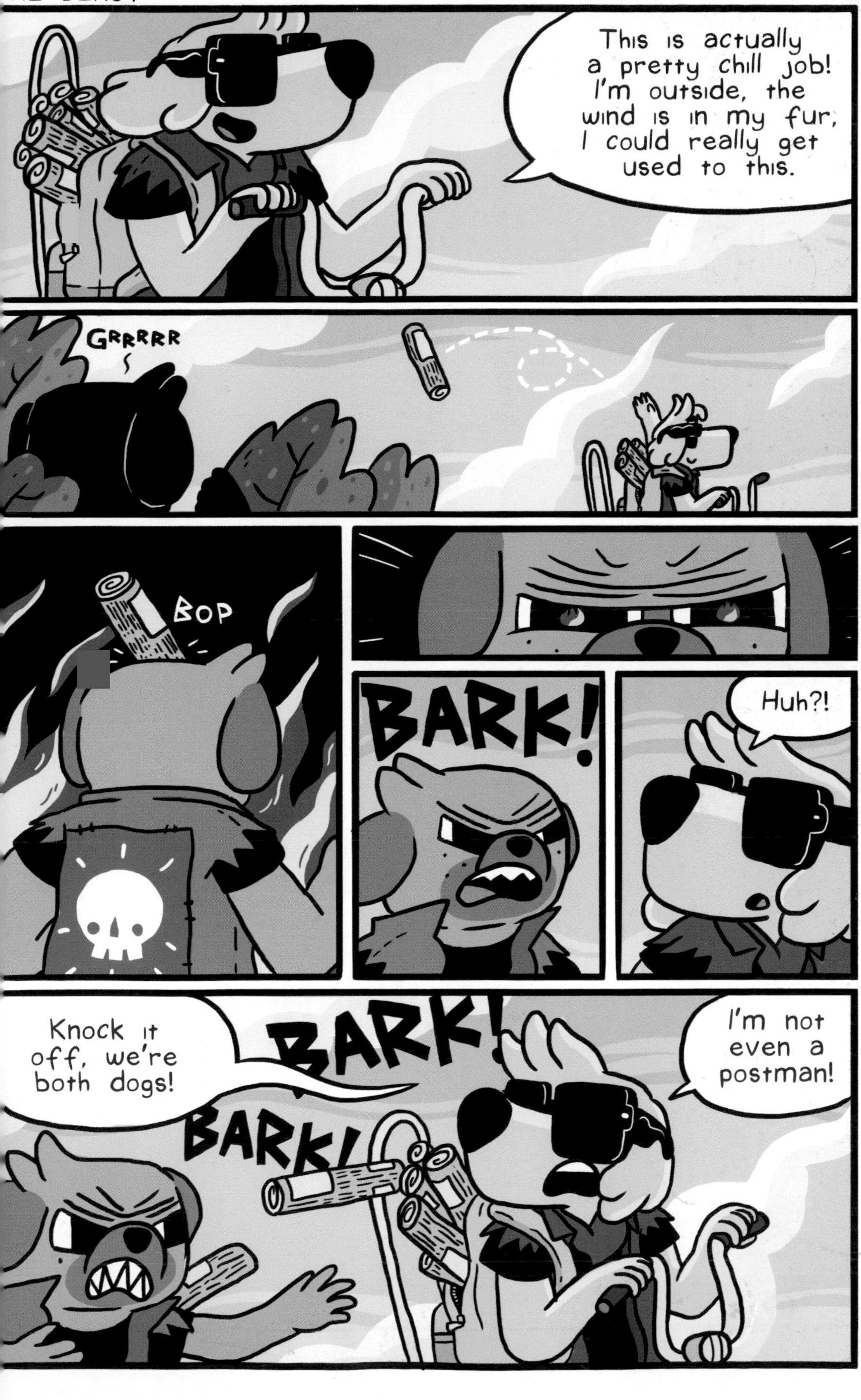
This is actually a pretty chill job! I'm outside, the wind is in my fur, I could really get used to this.
GRRRRR
BOP
BARK!
Huh?!
Knock it off, we're both dogs!
BARK!
BARK!
I'm not even a postman!

SHE WORKS HARD FOR THE MONEY

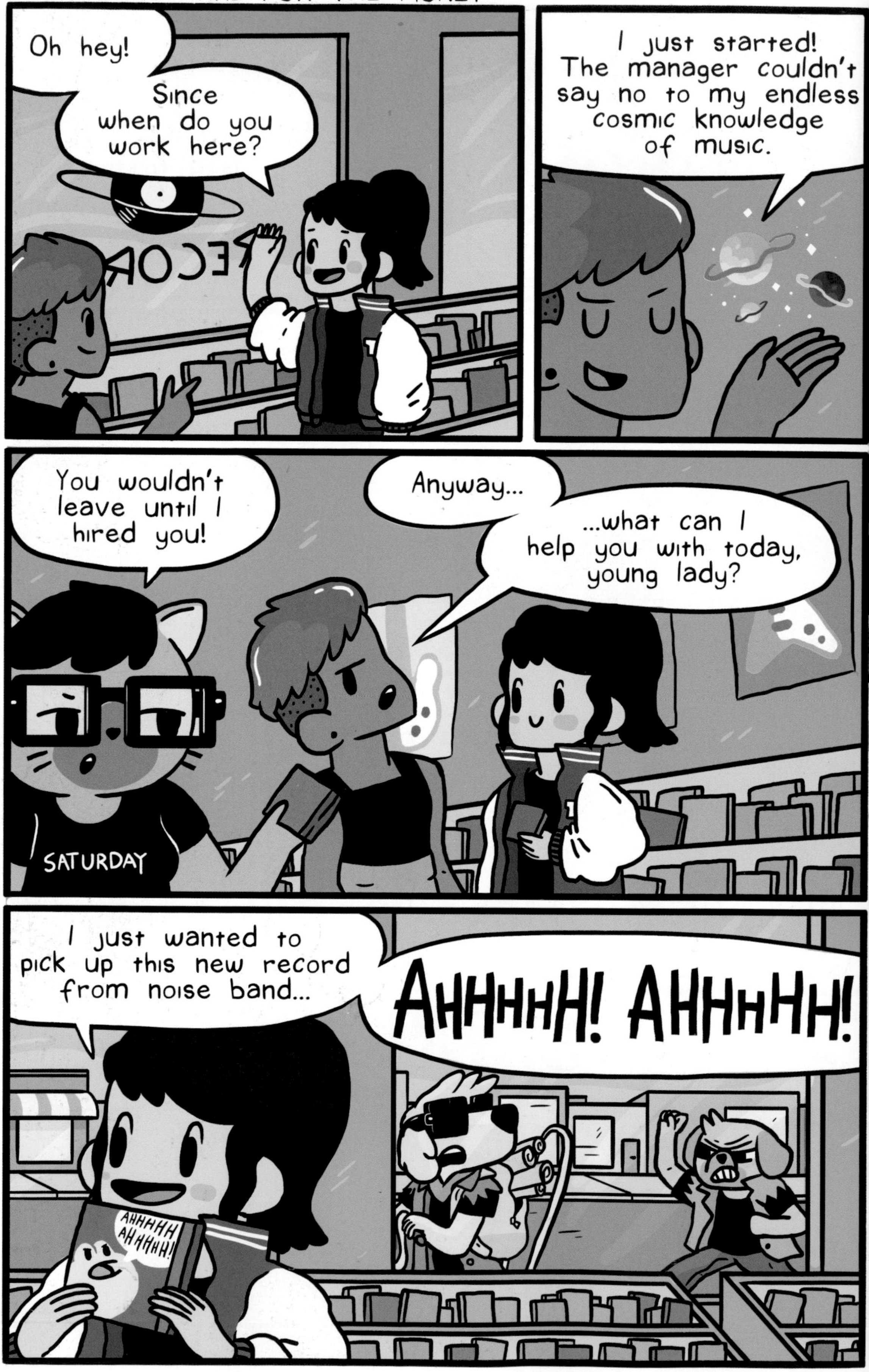
Oh hey!
Since when do you work here?
I just started! The manager couldn't say no to my endless cosmic knowledge of music.
You wouldn't leave until I hired you!
Anyway...
...what can I help you with today, young lady?
SATURDAY
I just wanted to pick up this new record from noise band...
AHHHHH! AHHHHH!
AHHHHH AHHHHH!

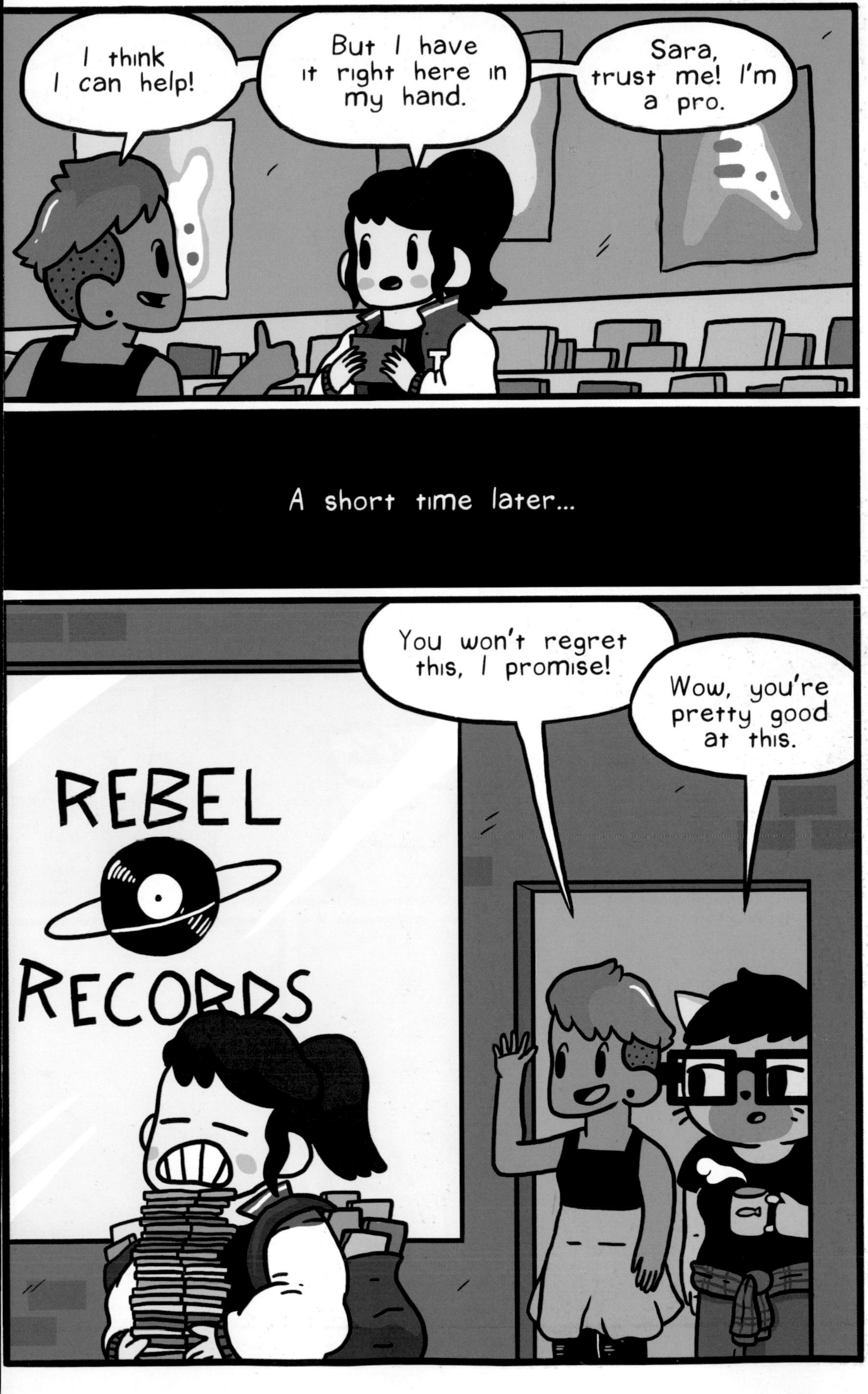
I think I can help!
But I have it right here in my hand.
Sara, trust me! I'm a pro.
A short time later...
REBEL RECORDS
You won't regret this, I promise!
Wow, you're pretty good at this.

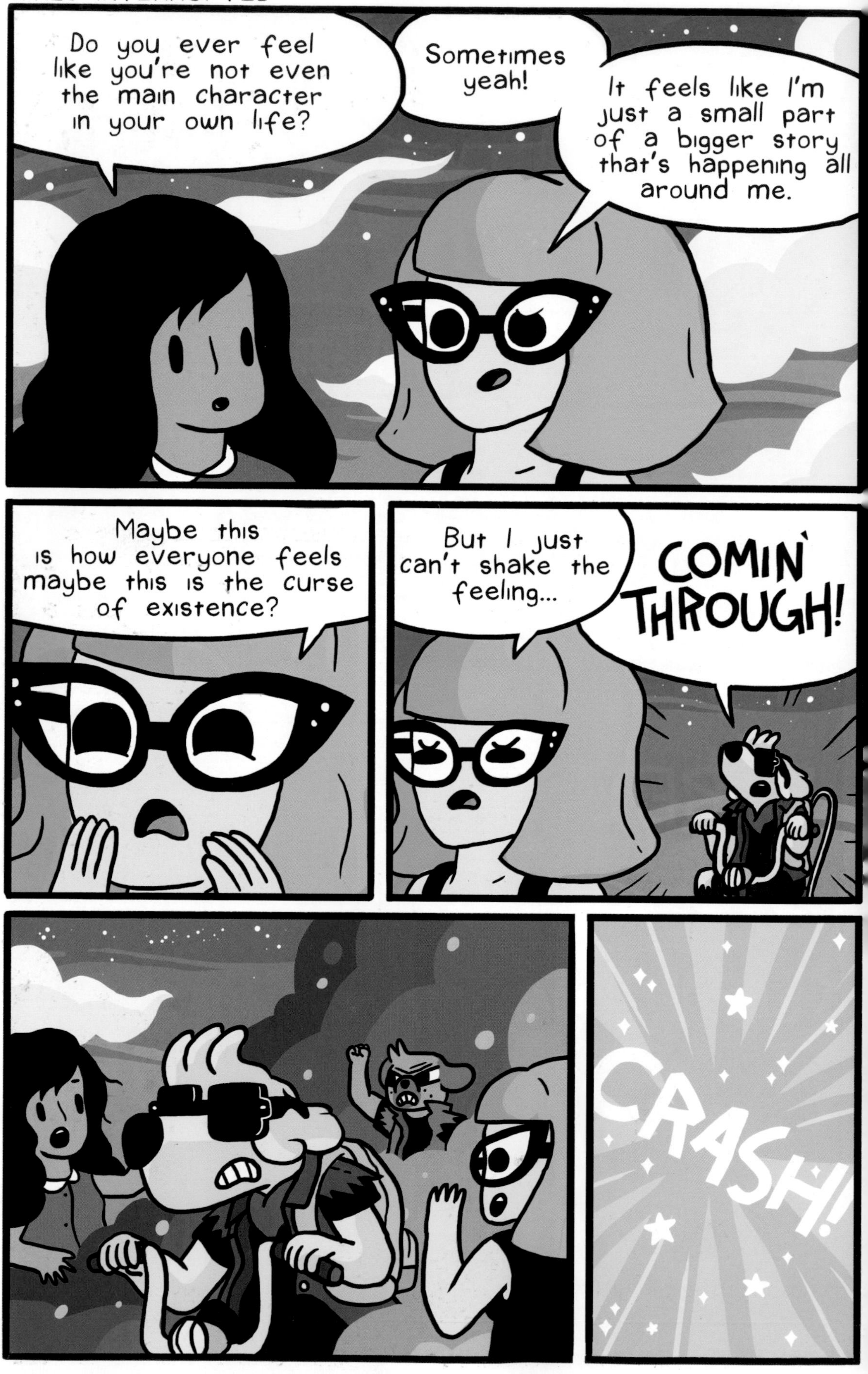
Do you ever feel like you're not even the main character in your own life?
Sometimes yeah!
It feels like I'm just a small part of a bigger story that's happening all around me.
Maybe this is how everyone feels maybe this is the curse of existence?
But I just can't shake the feeling...
COMIN` THROUGH!
CRASH!

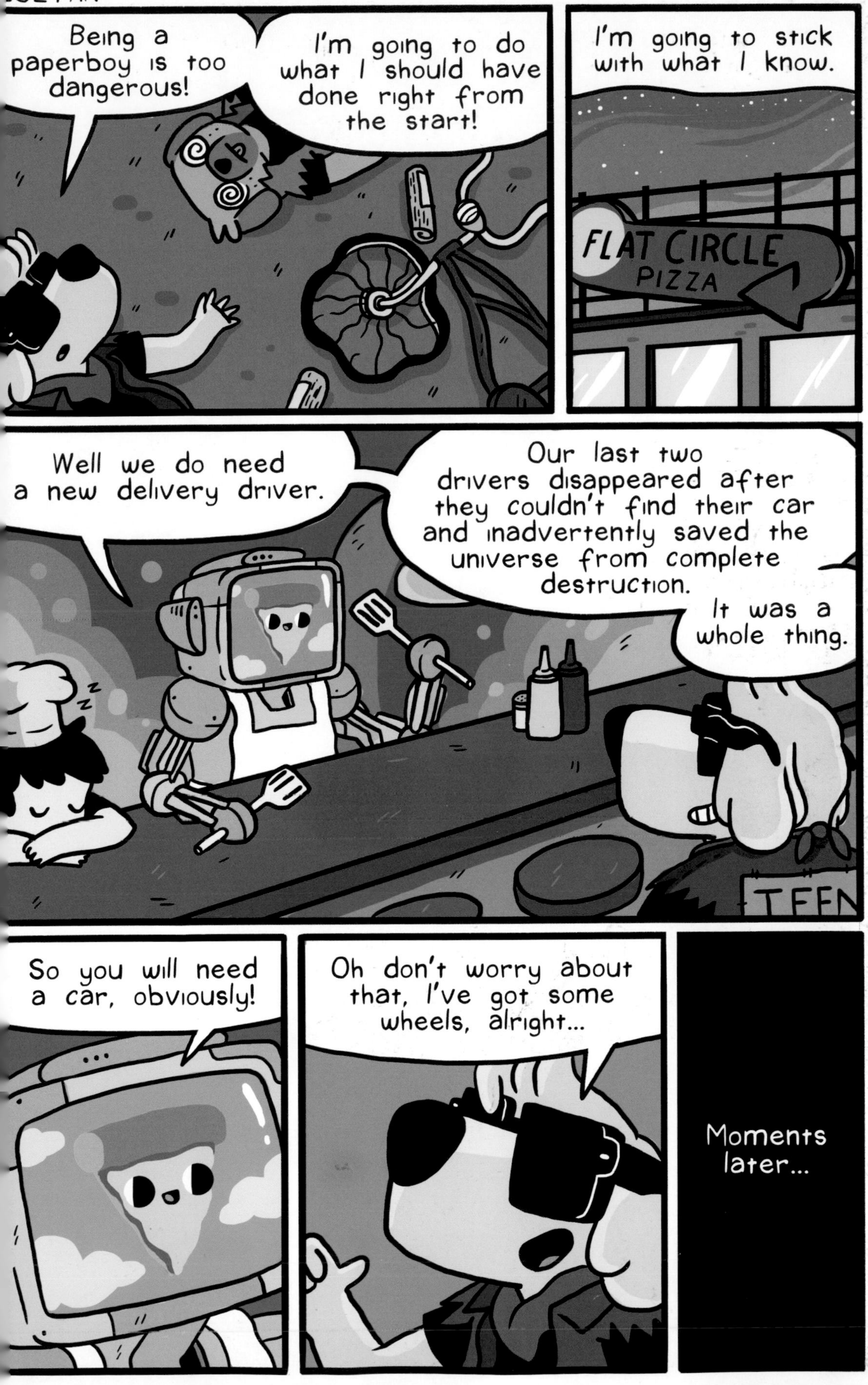
Being a paperboy is too dangerous!
I'm going to do what I should have done right from the start!
I'm going to stick with what I know.
FLAT CIRCLE PIZZA
Well we do need a new delivery driver.
Our last two drivers disappeared after they couldn't find their car and inadvertently saved the universe from complete destruction.
It was a whole thing.
So you will need a car, obviously!
Oh don't worry about that, I've got some wheels, alright...
Moments later...

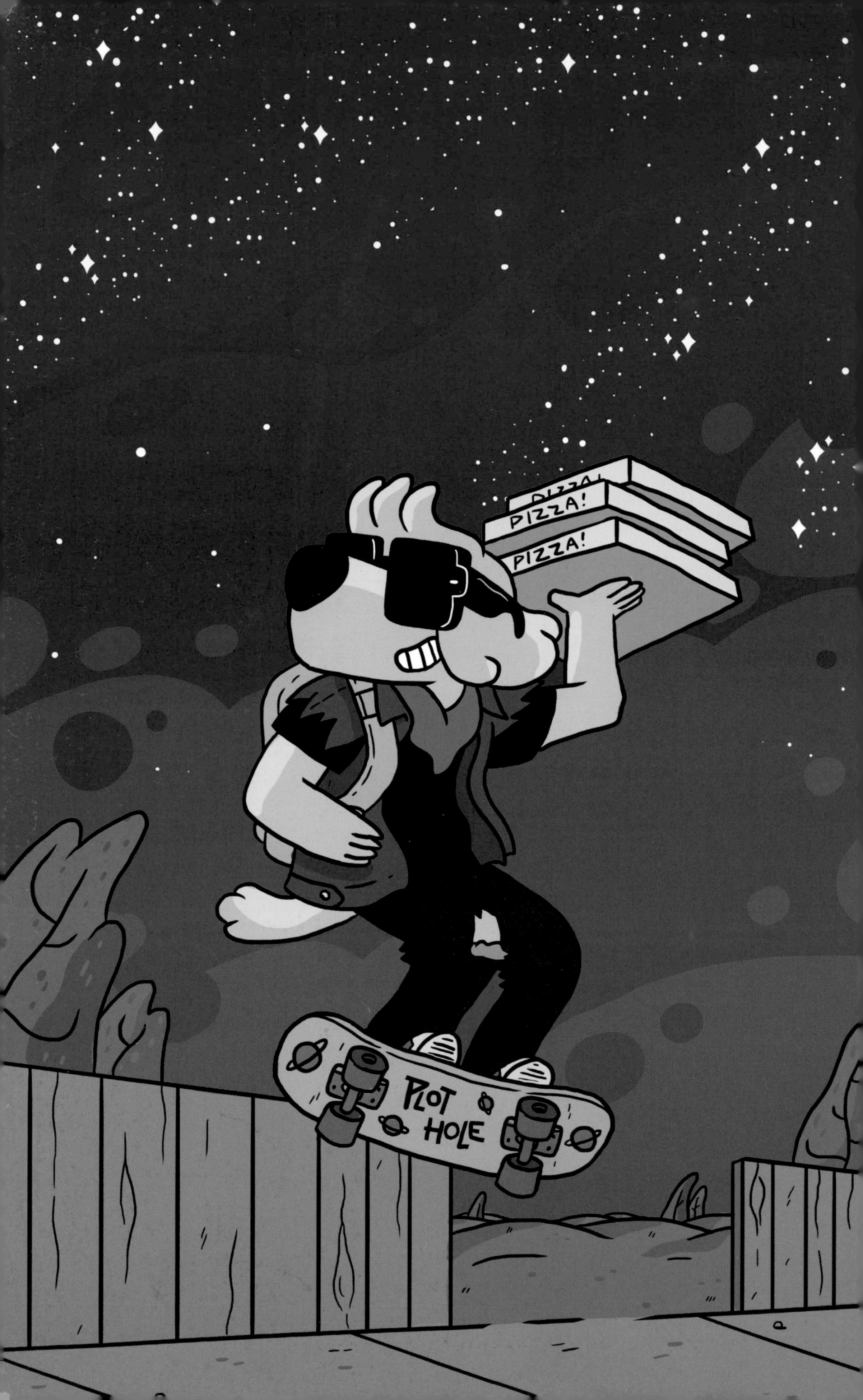
PIZZA!
PIZZA!
PLOT HOLE

THE LOOK

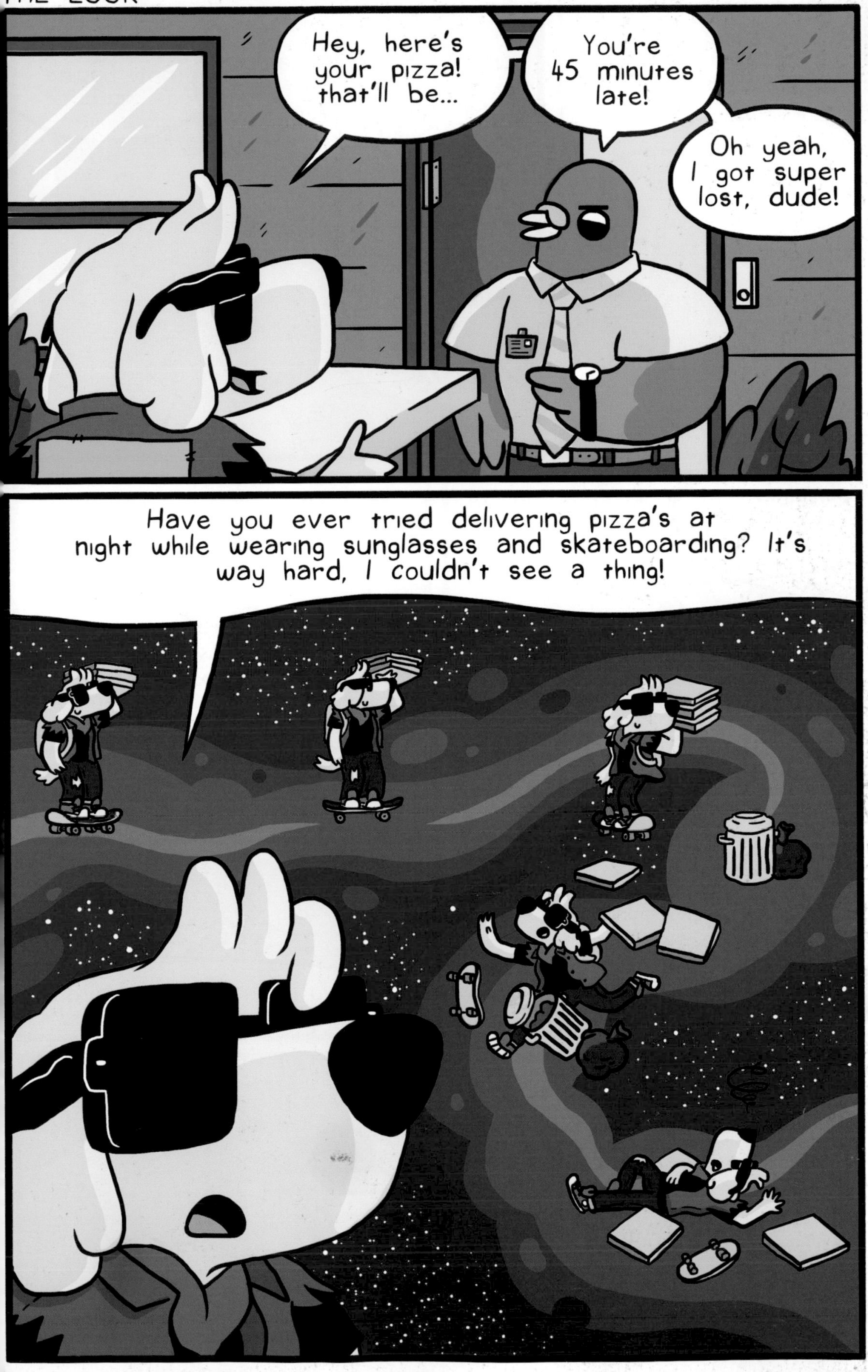
Hey, here's your pizza! that'll be...
You're 45 minutes late!
Oh yeah, I got super lost, dude!
Have you ever tried delivering pizza's at night while wearing sunglasses and skateboarding? It's way hard, I couldn't see a thing!

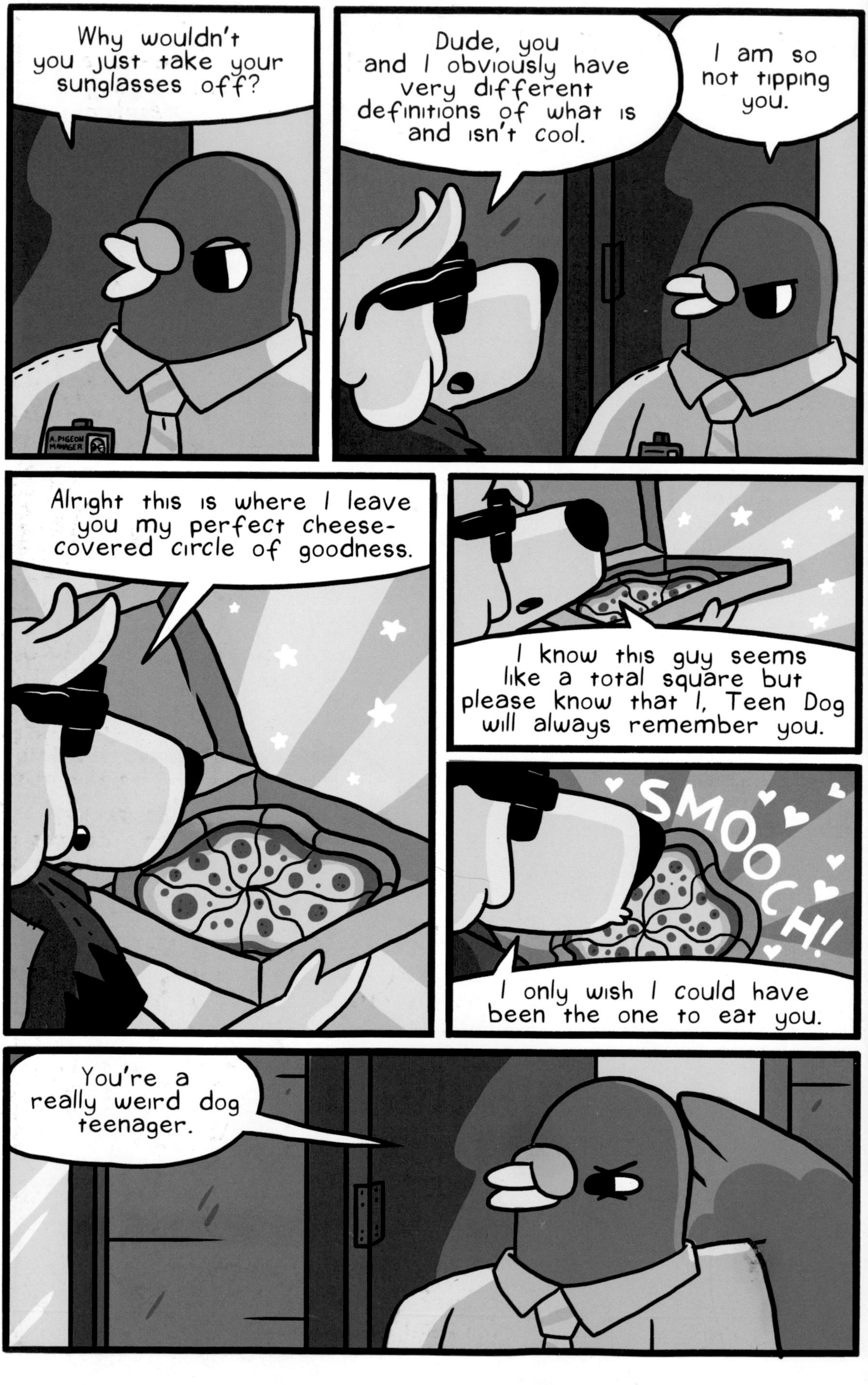
Why wouldn't you just take your sunglasses off?
A. PIGEON MANAGER
Dude, you and I obviously have very different definitions of what is and isn't cool.
I am so not tipping you.
Alright this is where I leave you my perfect cheese-covered circle of goodness.
I know this guy seems like a total square but please know that I, Teen Dog will always remember you.
SMOOCH!
I only wish I could have been the one to eat you.
You're a really weird dog teenager.

TOP FIVE RECORDS

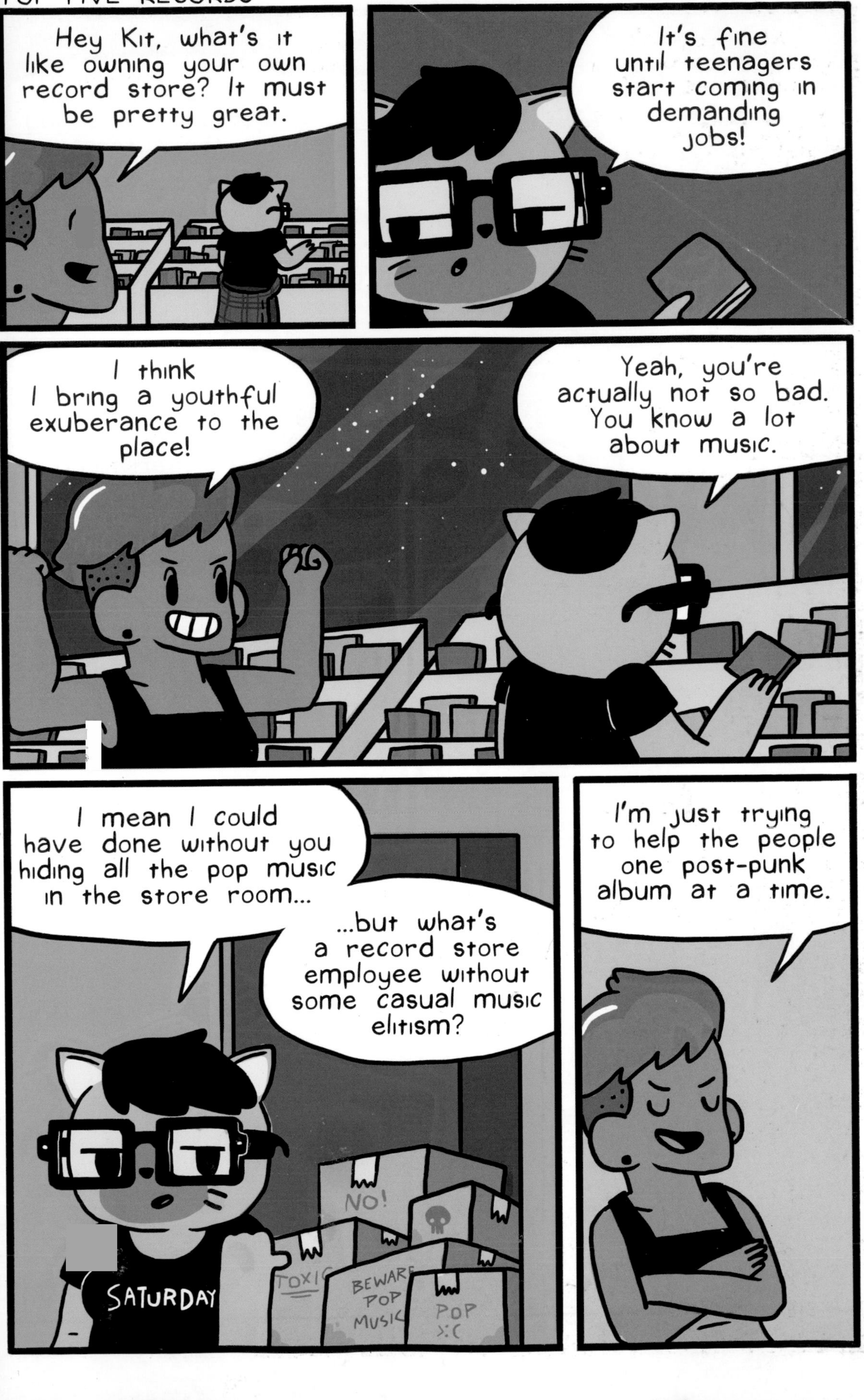
Hey Kit, what's it like owning your own record store? It must be pretty great.
It's fine until teenagers start coming in demanding jobs!
I think I bring a youthful exuberance to the place!
Yeah, you're actually not so bad. You know a lot about music.
I mean I could have done without you hiding all the pop music in the store room...
...but what's a record store employee without some casual music elitism?
I'm just trying to help the people one post-punk album at a time.
NO!
TOXIC
BEWARE POP MUSIC
POP >:(
SATURDAY

ECONOMICS 101

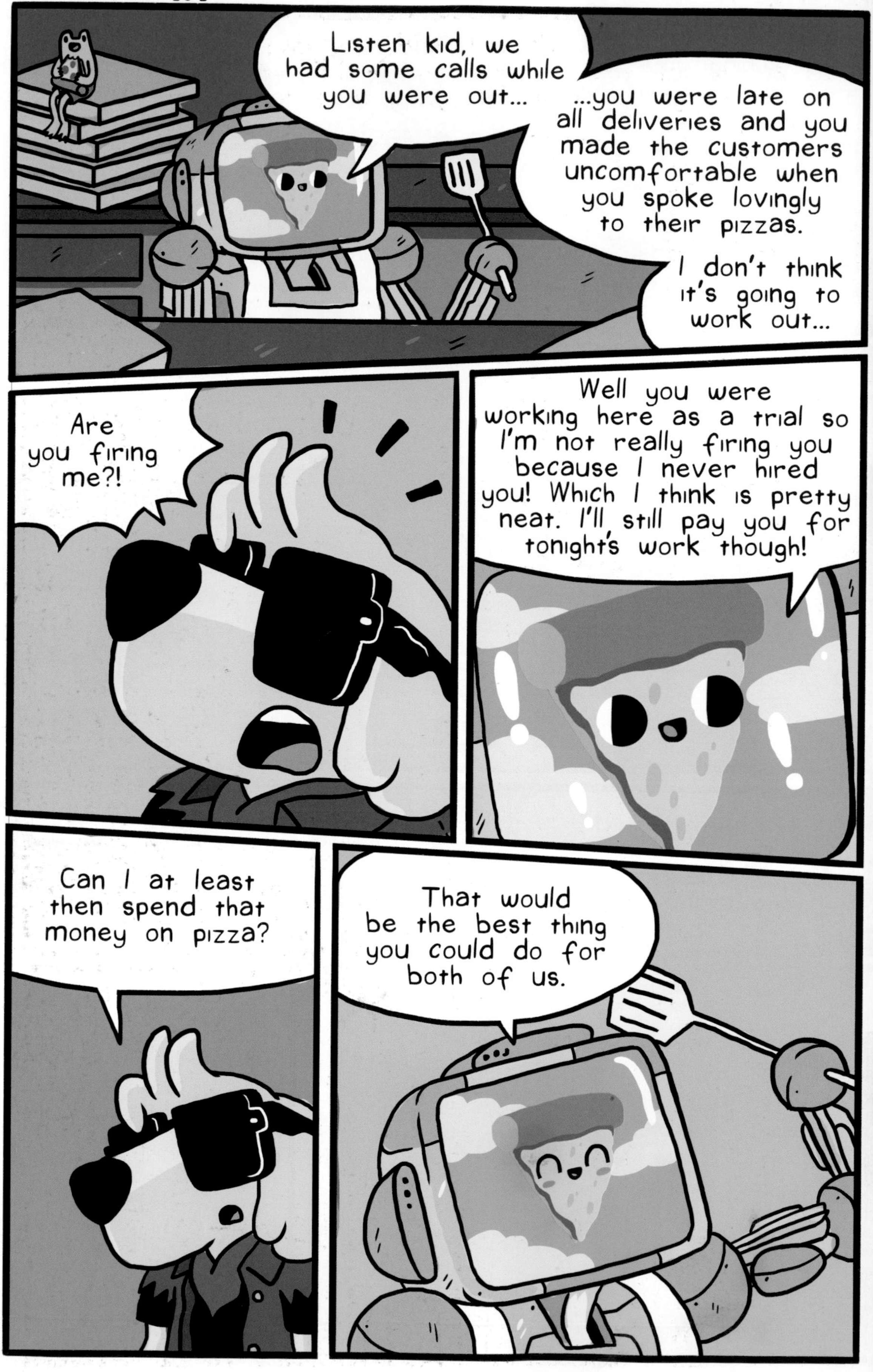
Listen kid, we had some calls while you were out...
...you were late on all deliveries and you made the customers uncomfortable when you spoke lovingly to their pizzas.
I don't think it's going to work out...
Are you firing me?!
Well you were working here as a trial so I'm not really firing you because I never hired you! Which I think is pretty neat. I'll still pay you for tonight's work though!
Can I at least then spend that money on pizza?
That would be the best thing you could do for both of us.

NDEPENDENT

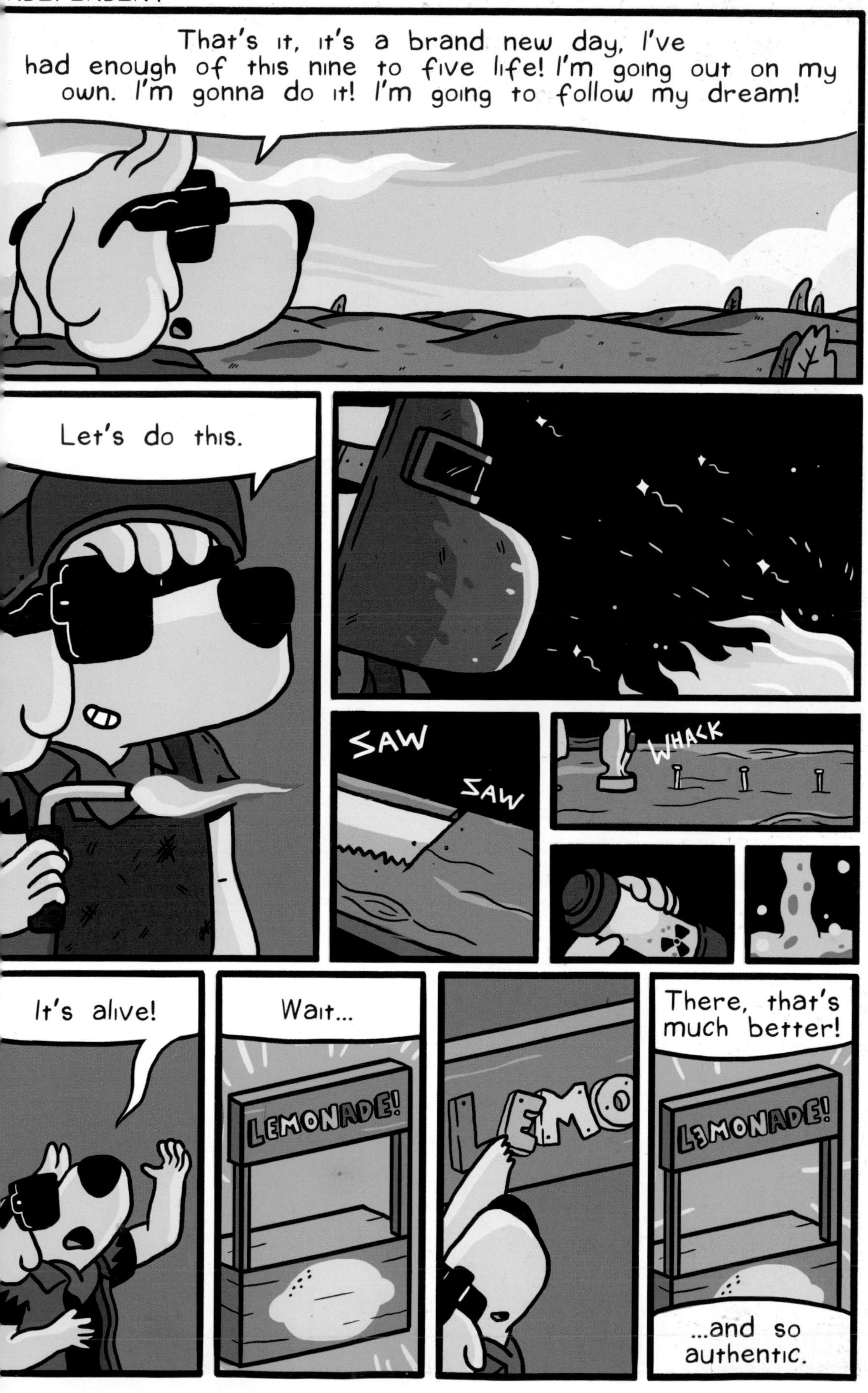
That's it, it's a brand new day, I've had enough of this nine to five life! I'm going out on my own. I'm gonna do it! I'm going to follow my dream!
Let's do this.
SAW
SAW
WHACK
It's alive!
Wait...
LEMONADE!
LEMO
There, that's much better!
LƎMONADE!
...and so authentic.

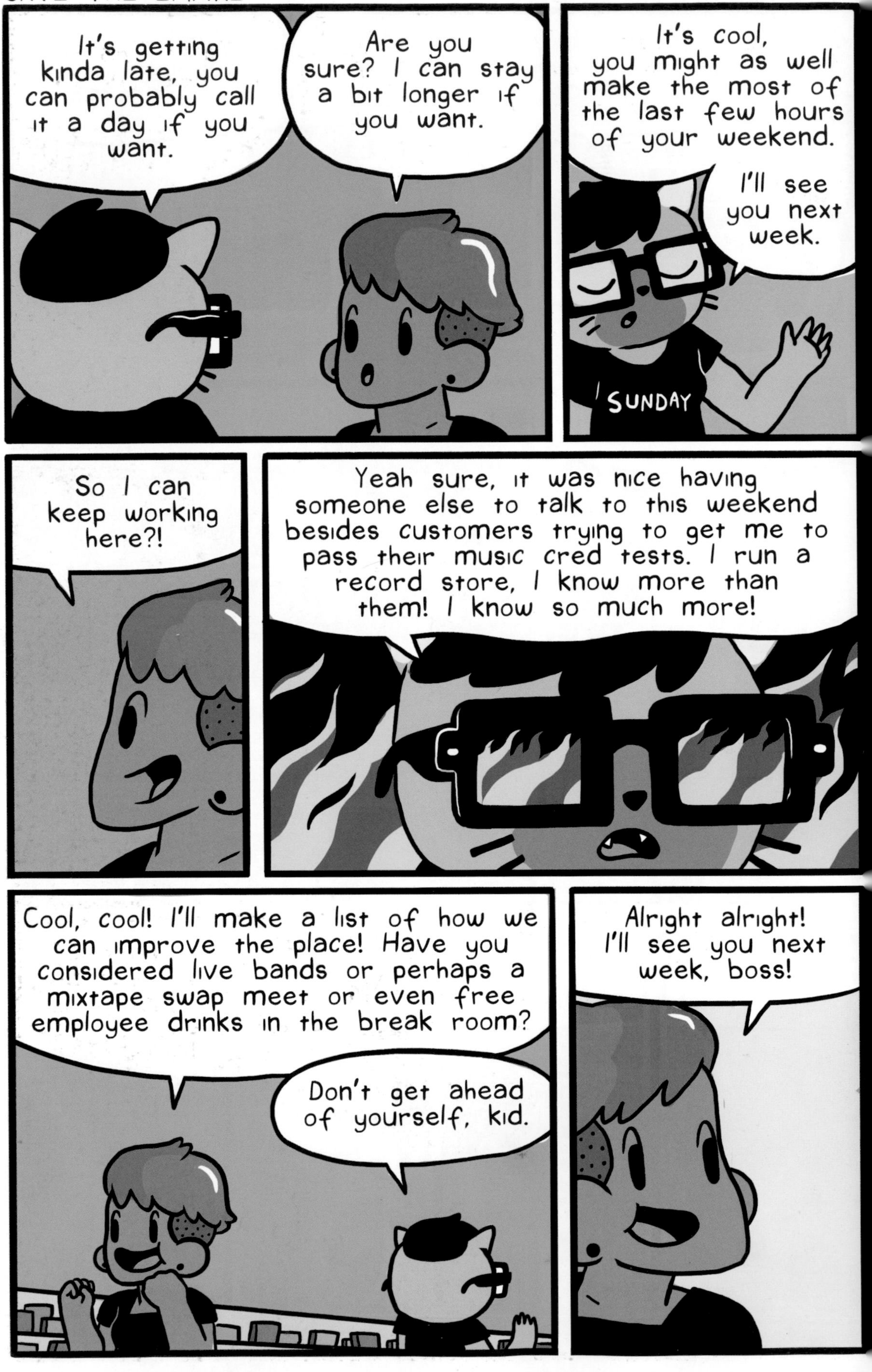
It's getting kinda late, you can probably call it a day if you want.
Are you sure? I can stay a bit longer if you want.
It's cool, you might as well make the most of the last few hours of your weekend.
I'll see you next week.
SUNDAY
So I can keep working here?!
Yeah sure, it was nice having someone else to talk to this weekend besides customers trying to get me to pass their music cred tests. I run a record store, I know more than them! I know so much more!
Cool, cool! I'll make a list of how we can improve the place! Have you considered live bands or perhaps a mixtape swap meet or even free employee drinks in the break room?
Don't get ahead of yourself, kid.
Alright alright! I'll see you next week, boss!

WORKING FOR THE WEEKEND

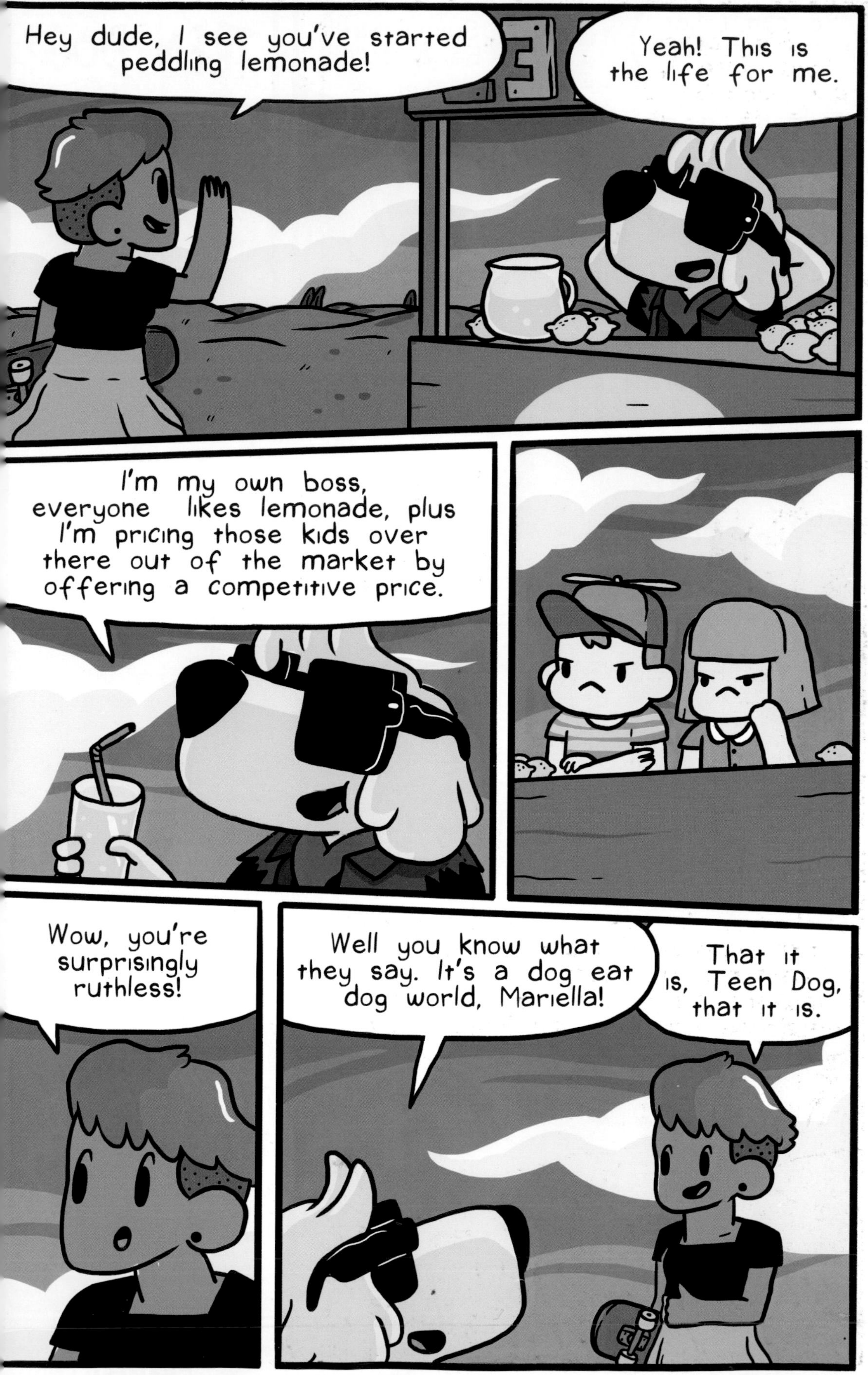
Hey dude, I see you've started peddling lemonade!
Yeah! This is the life for me.
I'm my own boss, everyone likes lemonade, plus I'm pricing those kids over there out of the market by offering a competitive price.
Wow, you're surprisingly ruthless!
Well you know what they say. It's a dog eat dog world, Mariella!
That it is, Teen Dog, that it is.

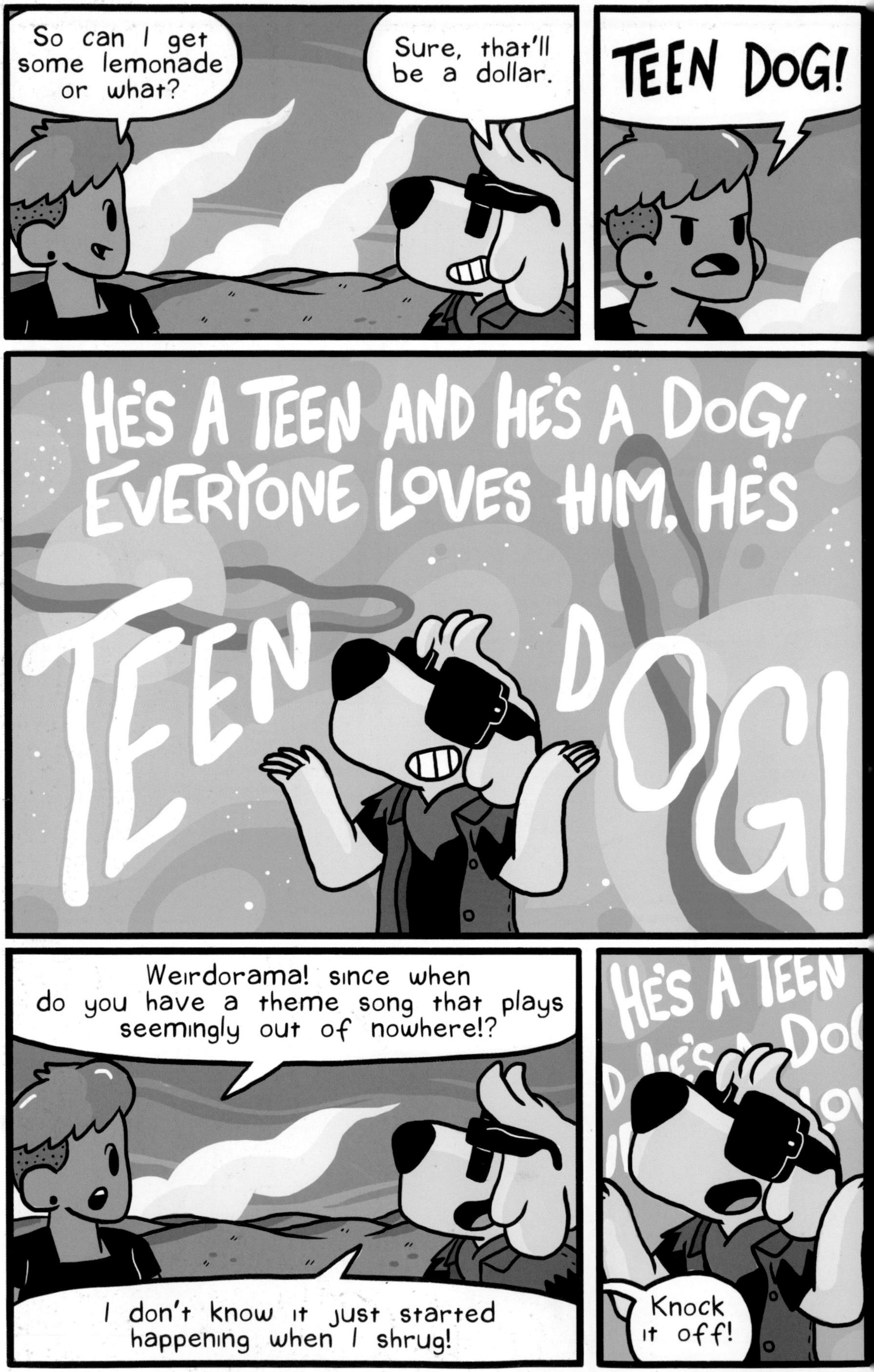
So can I get some lemonade or what?
Sure, that'll be a dollar.
TEEN DOG!
HE'S A TEEN AND HE'S A DOG! EVERYONE LOVES HIM, HE'S
TEEN DOG!
Weirdorama! since when do you have a theme song that plays seemingly out of nowhere!?
I don't know it just started happening when I shrug!
HE'S A TEEN
Knock it off!

CHAPTER ENDS

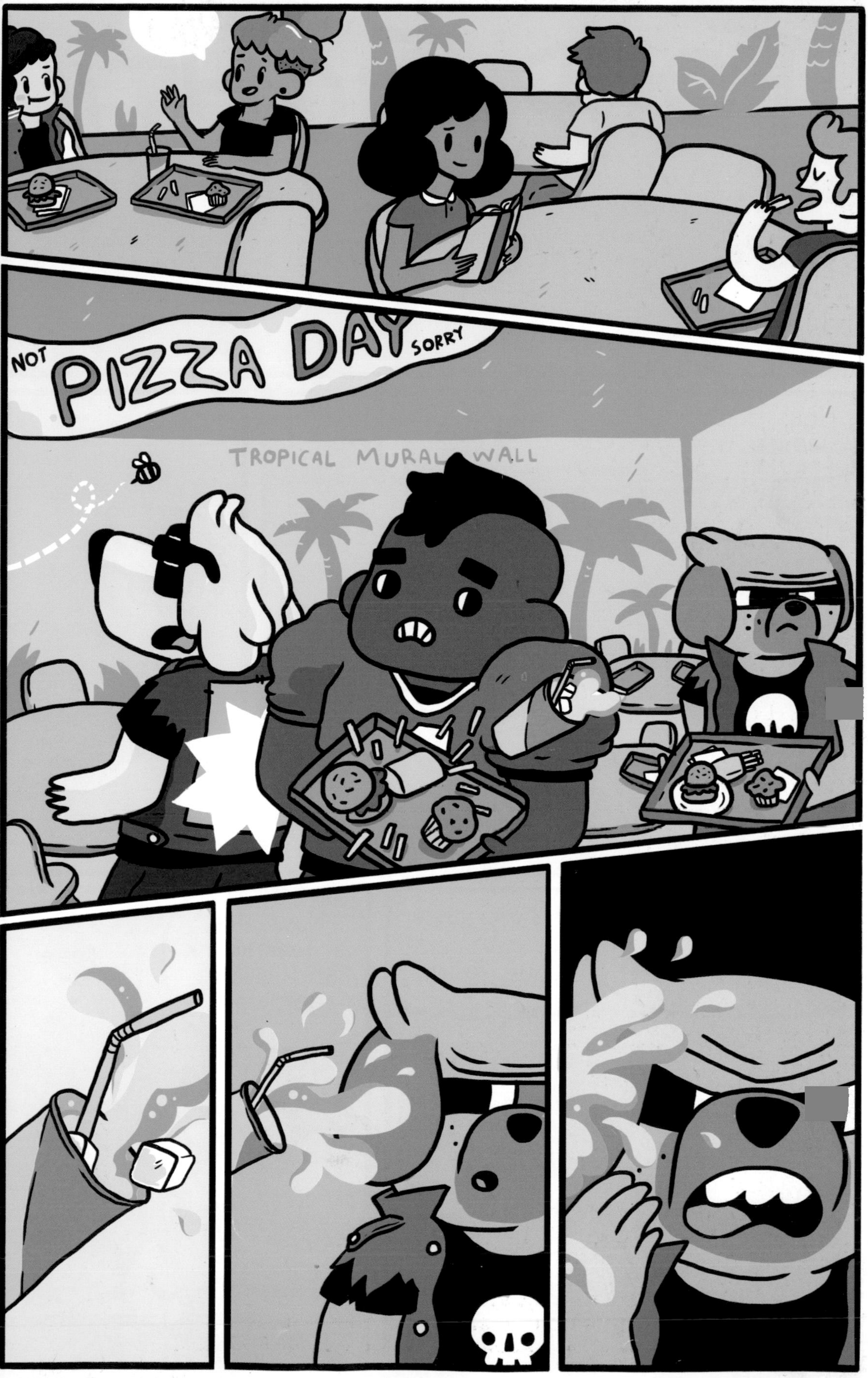
NOT PIZZA DAY SORRY
TROPICAL MURAL WALL

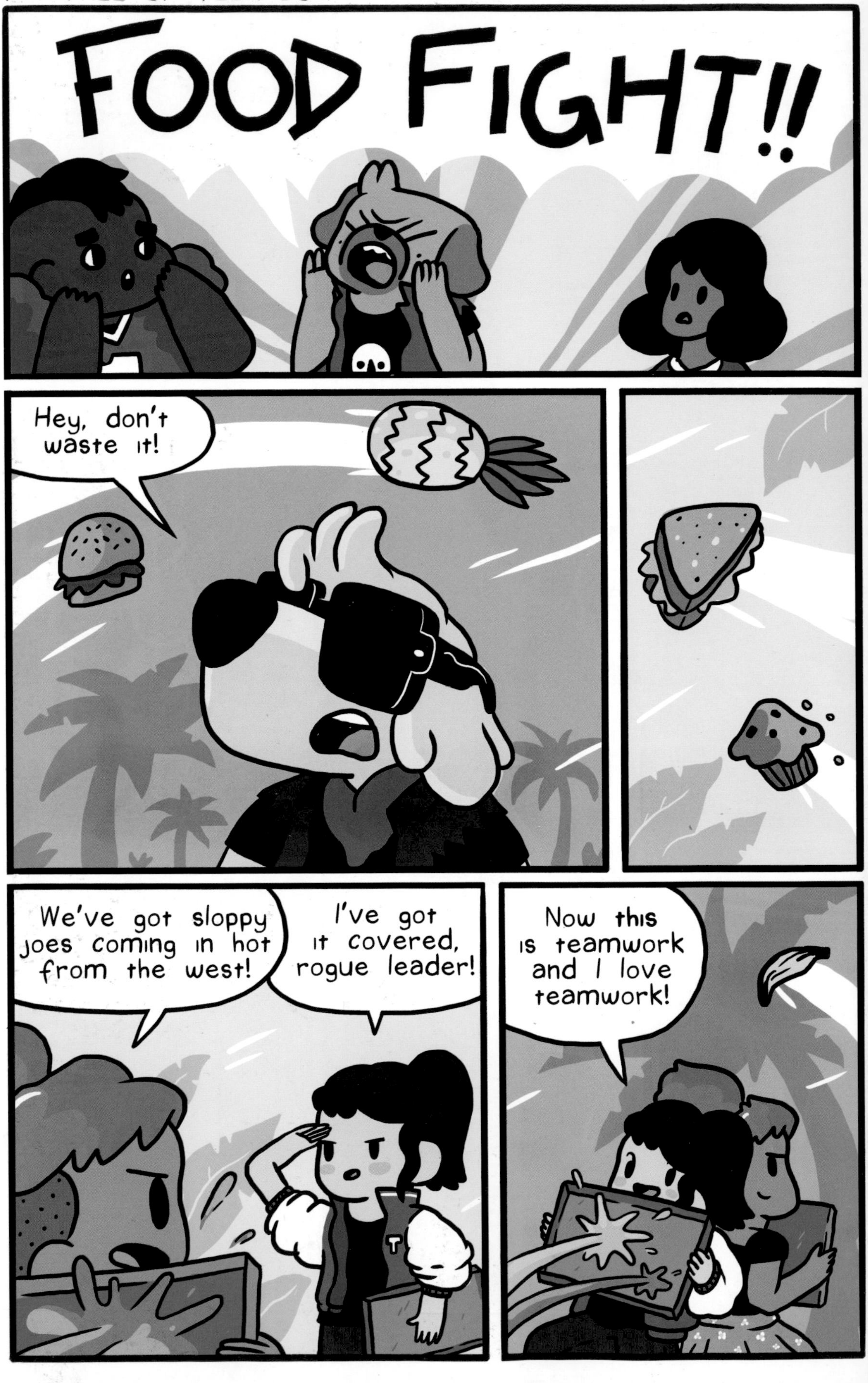
FOOD FIGHT!!
Hey, don't waste it!
We've got sloppy joes coming in hot from the west!
I've got it covered, rogue leader!
Now this is teamwork and I love teamwork!

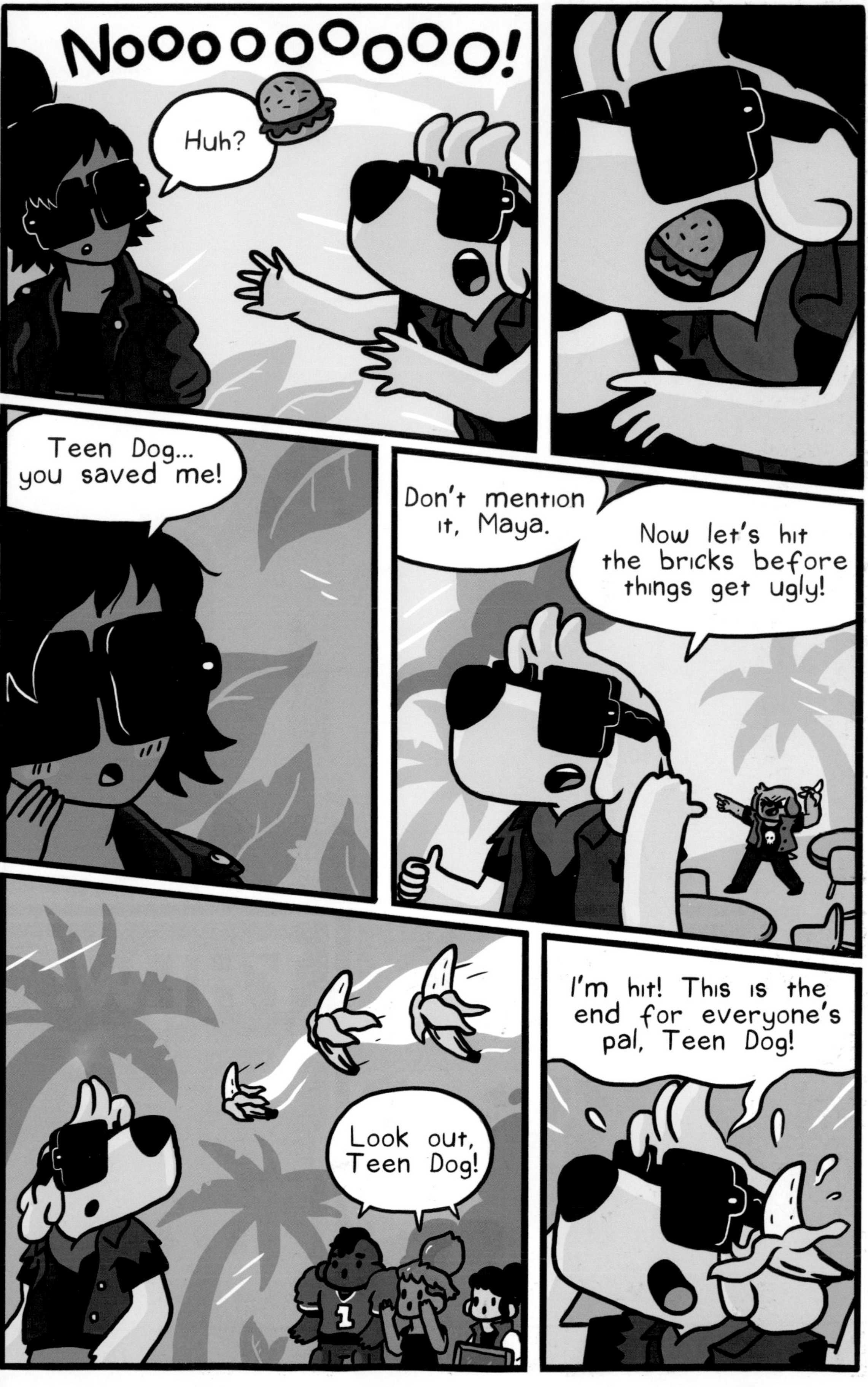
NOooOOOOOO!
Huh?
Teen Dog... you saved me!
Don't mention it, Maya.
Now let's hit the bricks before things get ugly!
Look out, Teen Dog!
I'm hit! This is the end for everyone's pal, Teen Dog!

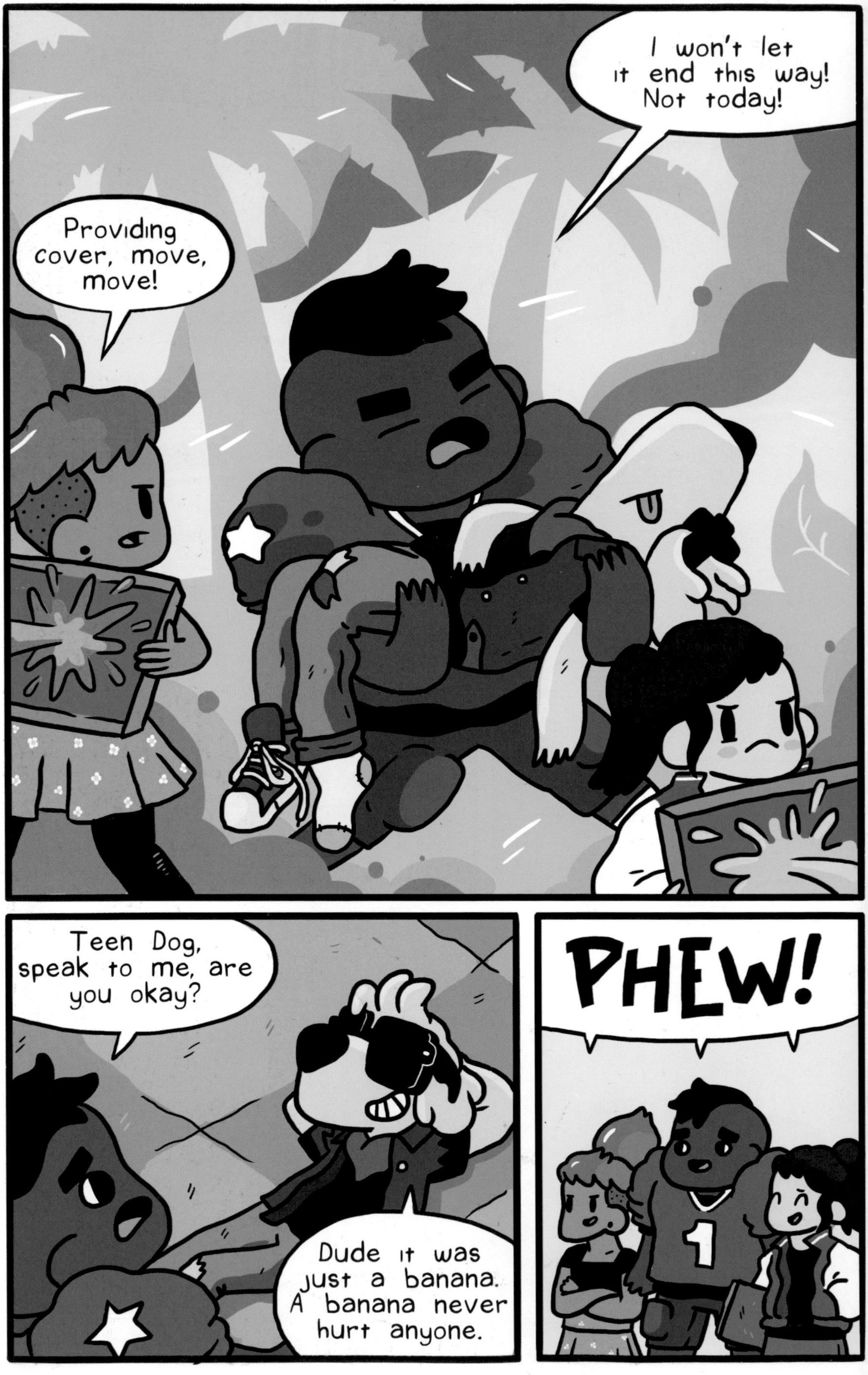
Providing cover, move, move!
I won't let it end this way! Not today!
Teen Dog, speak to me, are you okay?
Dude it was just a banana. A banana never hurt anyone.
PHEW!

THE MOST MAGICAL NIGHT OF THE YEAR

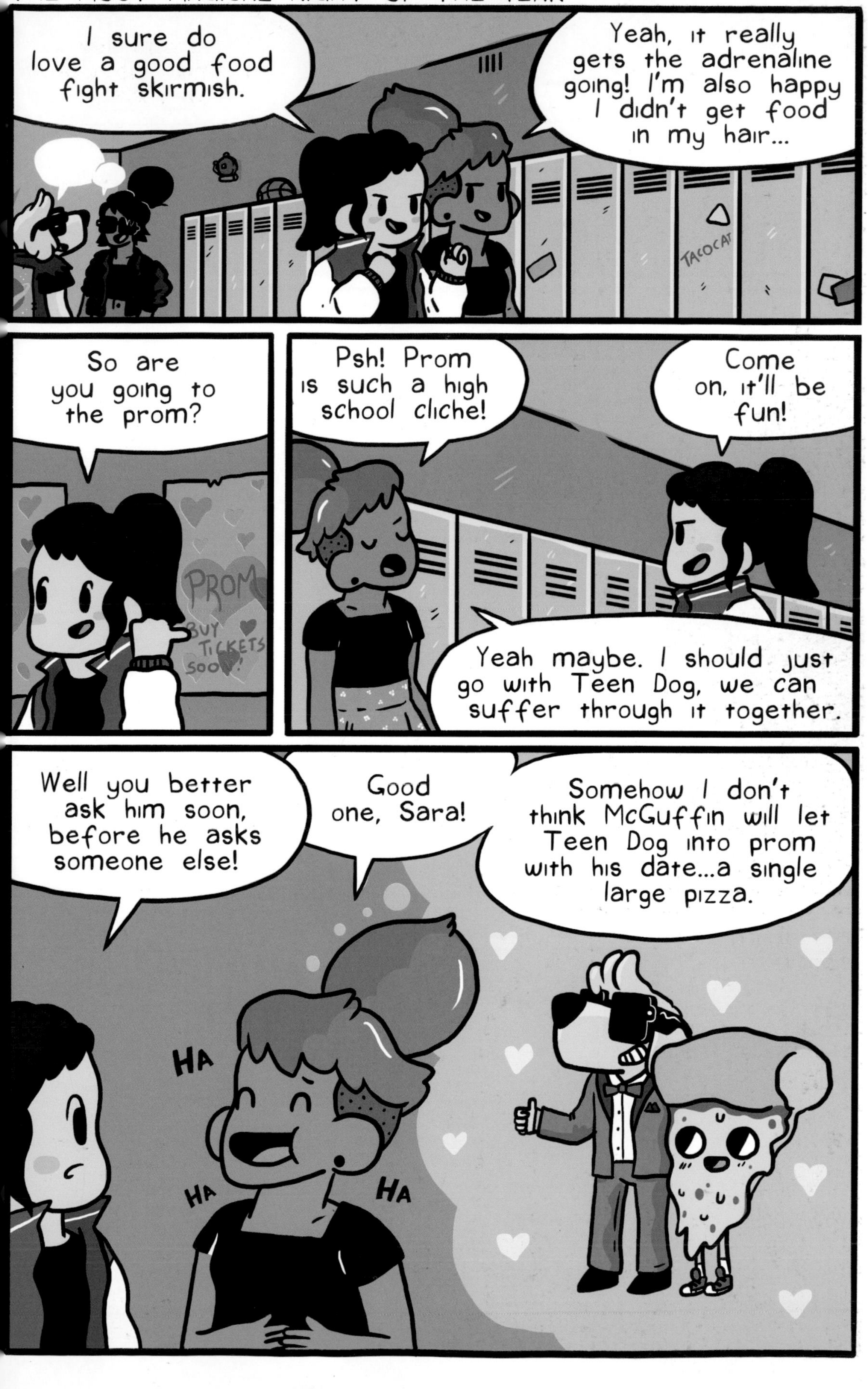
I sure do love a good food fight skirmish.
Yeah, it really gets the adrenaline going! I'm also happy I didn't get food in my hair...
TACOCAT
So are you going to the prom?
PROM
BUY TICKETS SOON!
Psh! Prom is such a high school cliche!
Come on, it'll be fun!
Yeah maybe. I should just go with Teen Dog, we can suffer through it together.
Well you better ask him soon, before he asks someone else!
Good one, Sara!
Somehow I don't think McGuffin will let Teen Dog into prom with his date...a single large pizza.
HA
HA
HA

AERODYNAMICS 101

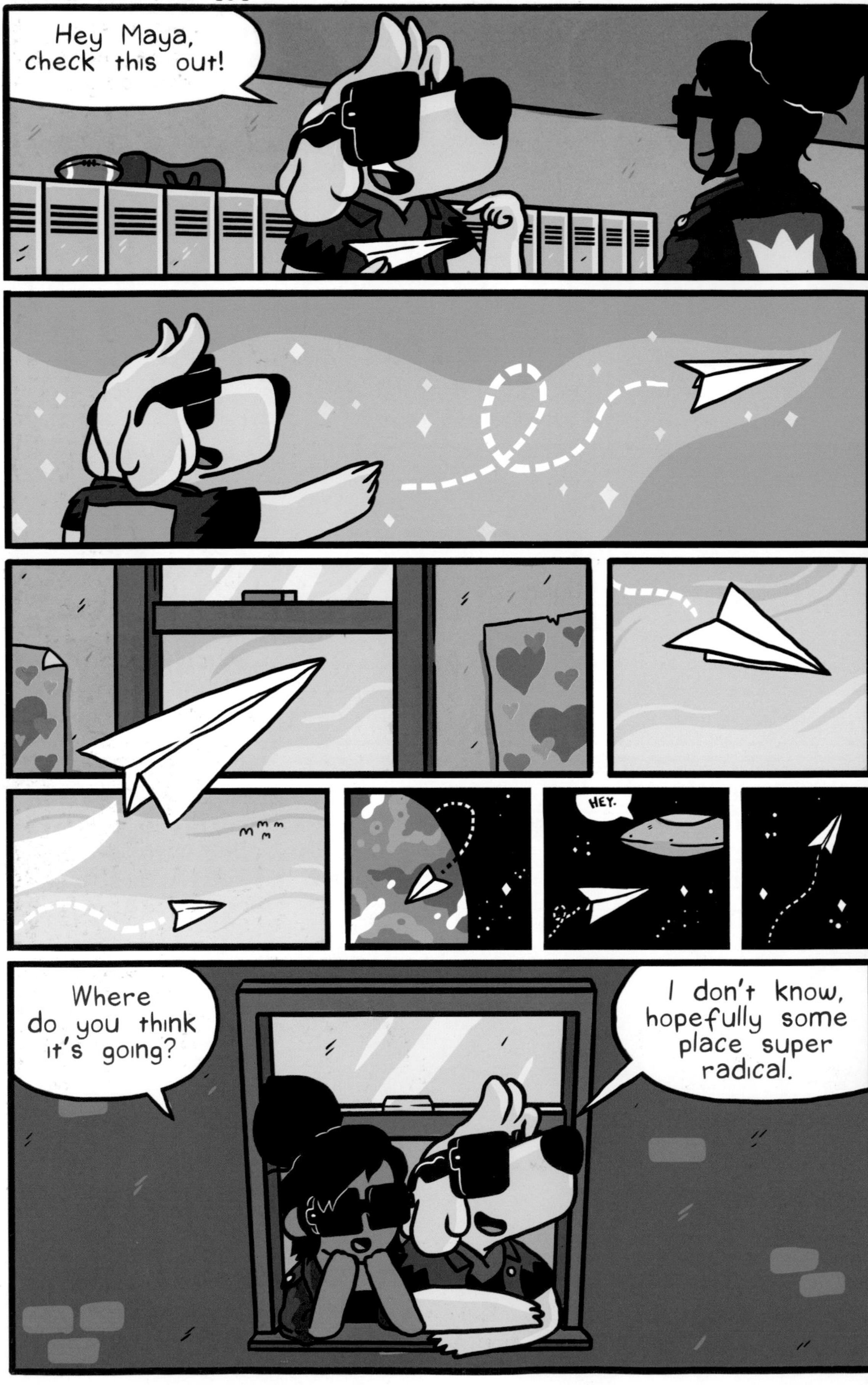

Hey Maya, check this out!
HEY.
Where do you think it's going?
I don't know, hopefully some place super radical.

GAME PLAN

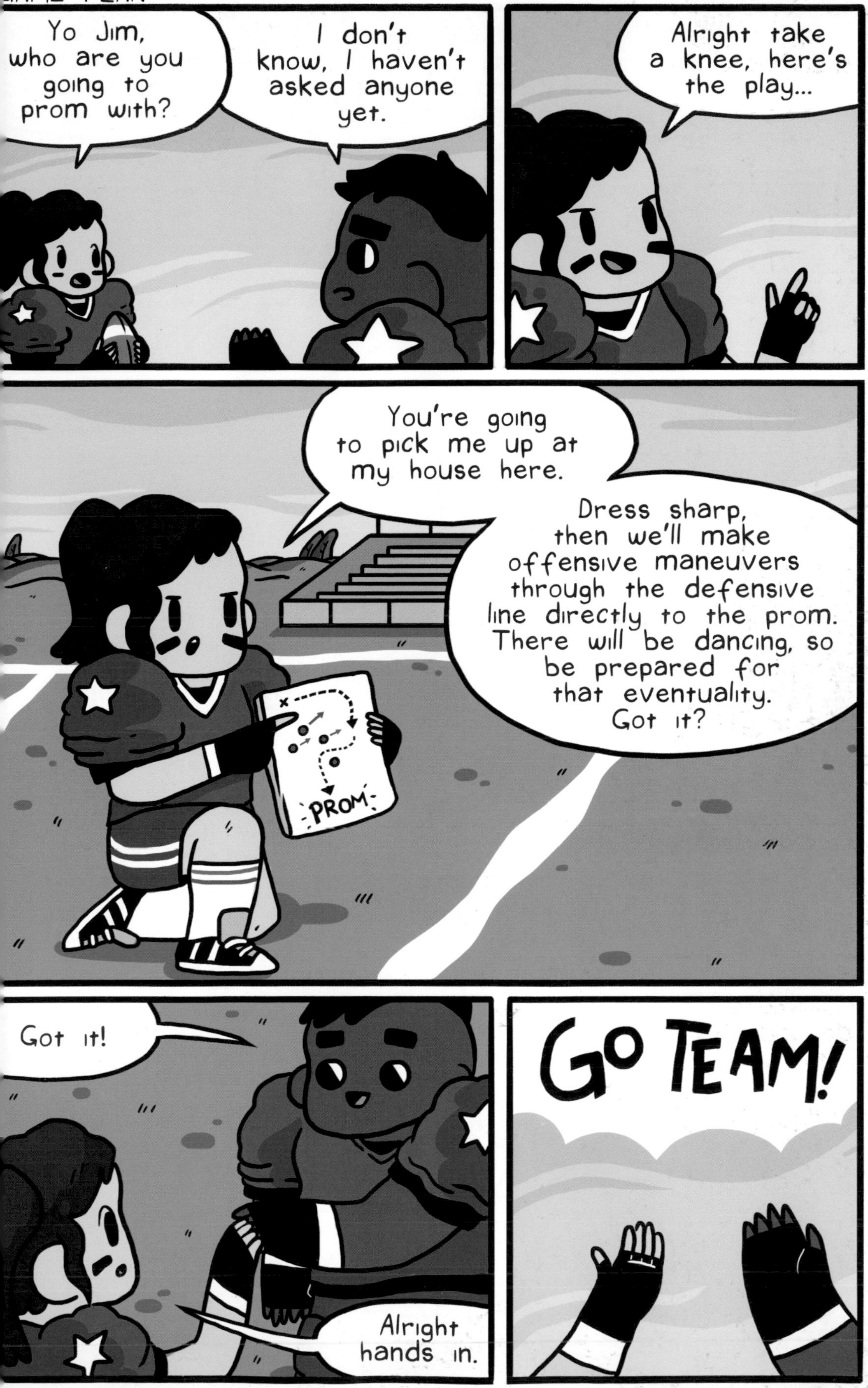

Yo Jim, who are you going to prom with?
I don't know, I haven't asked anyone yet.
Alright take a knee, here's the play...
You're going to pick me up at my house here.
Dress sharp, then we'll make offensive maneuvers through the defensive line directly to the prom. There will be dancing, so be prepared for that eventuality. Got it?
PROM
Got it!
Alright hands in.
GO TEAM!

ONE TRUE LOVE

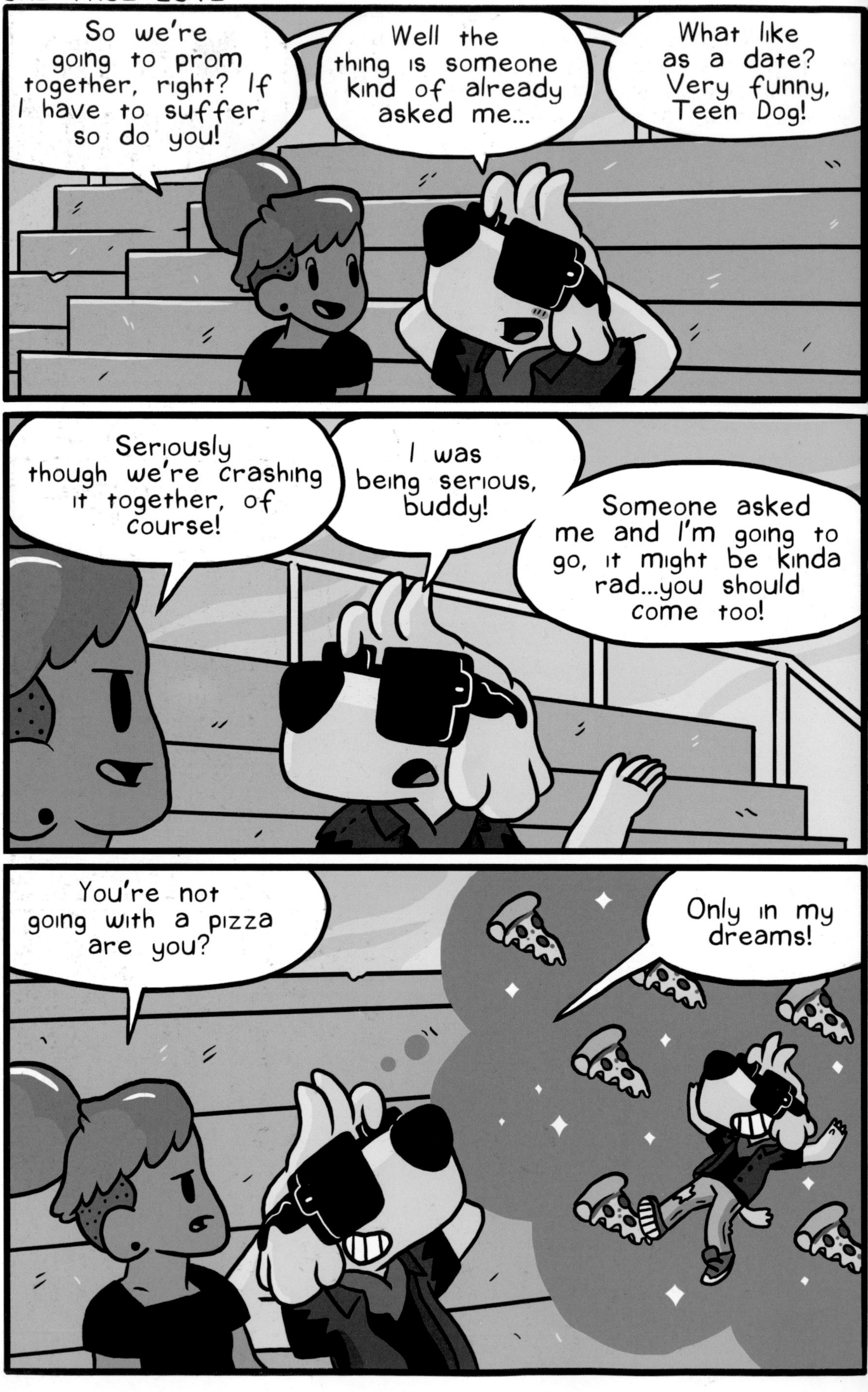

So we're going to prom together, right? If I have to suffer so do you!
Well the thing is someone kind of already asked me...
What like as a date? Very funny, Teen Dog!
Seriously though we're crashing it together, of course!
I was being serious, buddy!
Someone asked me and I'm going to go, it might be kinda rad...you should come too!
You're not going with a pizza are you?
Only in my dreams!

CHESS CLUB BLUES

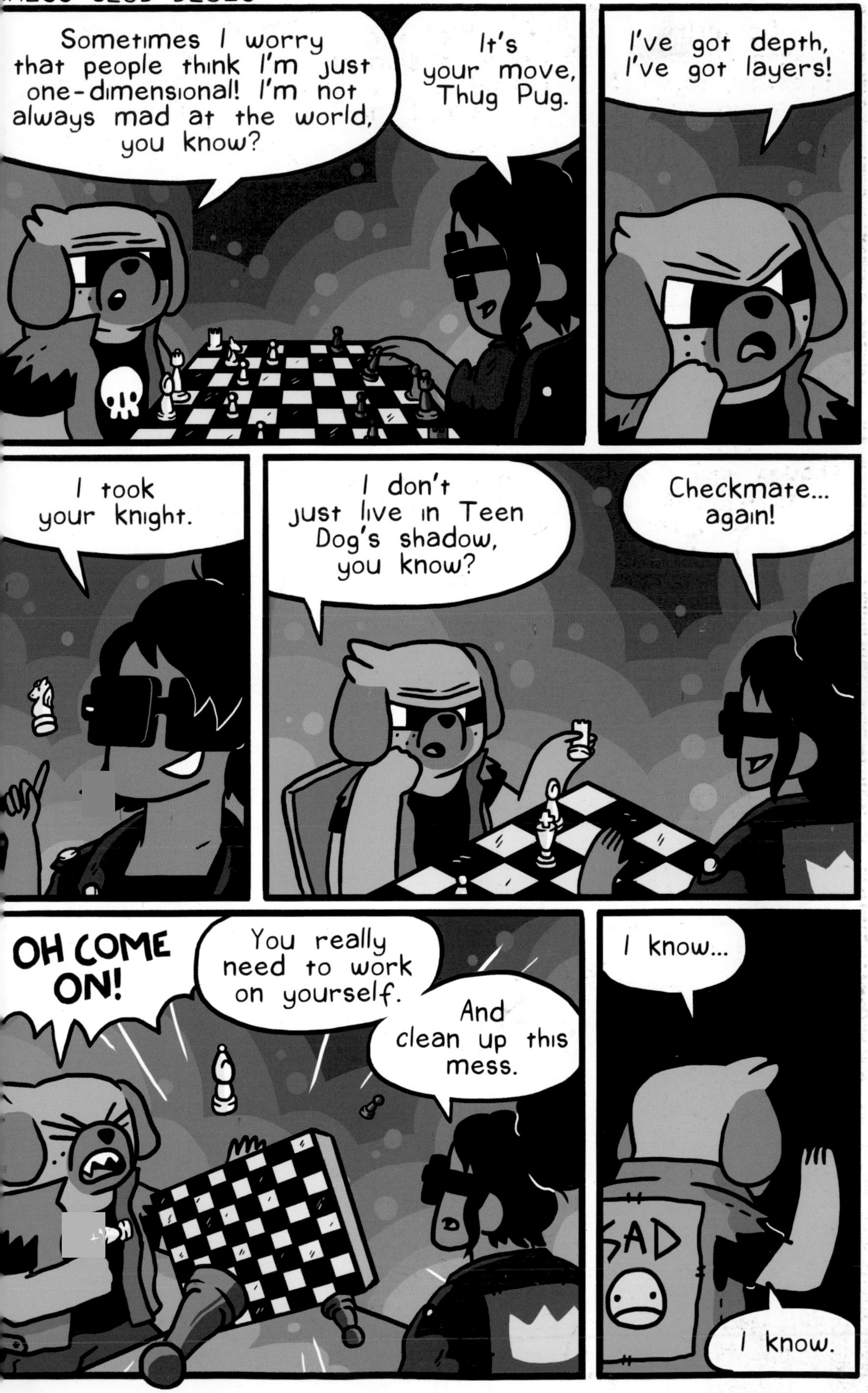

Sometimes I worry that people think I'm just one-dimensional! I'm not always mad at the world, you know?
It's your move, Thug Pug.
I've got depth, I've got layers!
I took your knight.
I don't just live in Teen Dog's shadow, you know?
Checkmate... again!
OH COME ON!
You really need to work on yourself.
And clean up this mess.
I know...
SAD
I know.

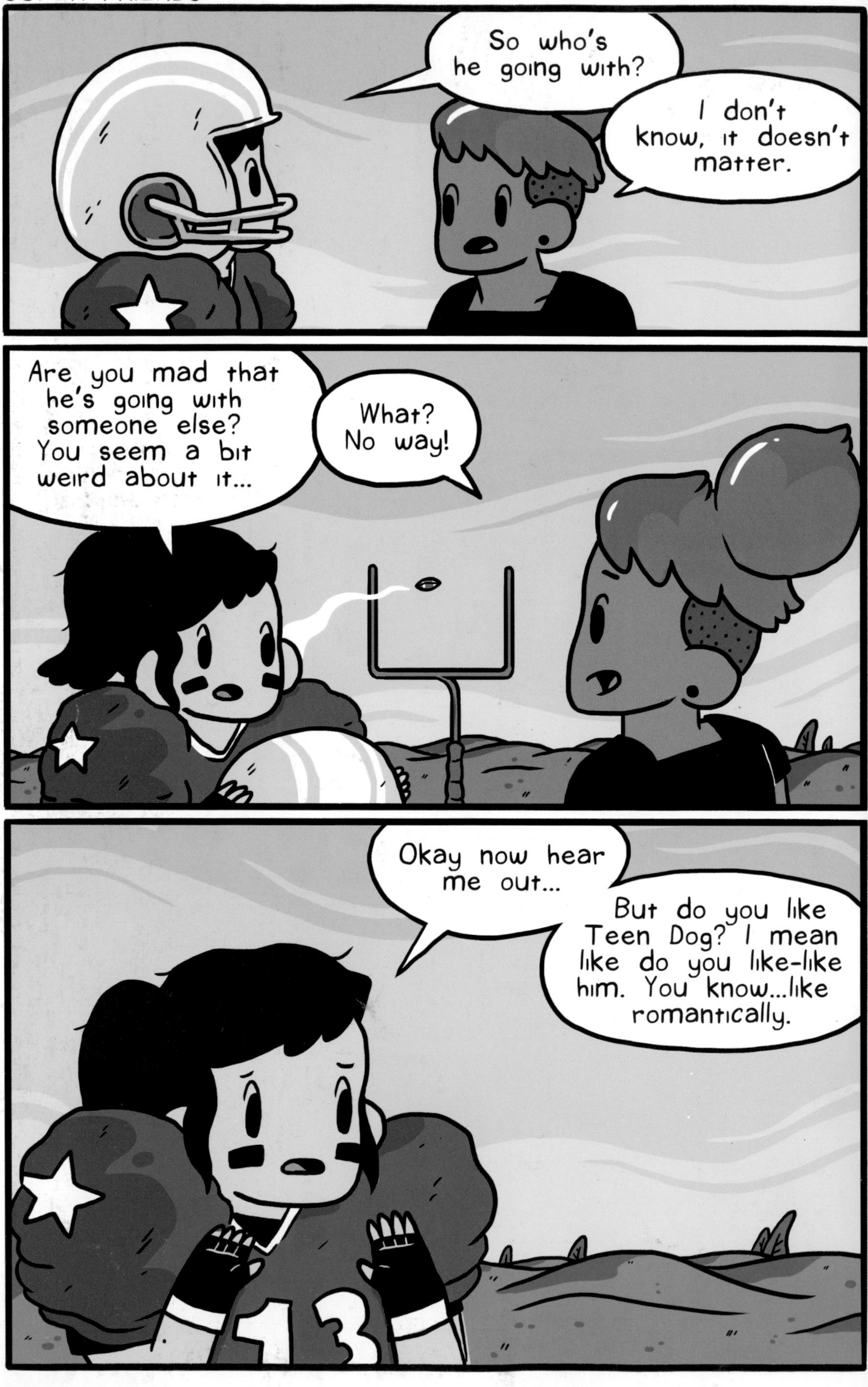
So who's he going with?
I don't know, it doesn't matter.
Are you mad that he's going with someone else? You seem a bit weird about it...
What? No way!
Okay now hear me out...
But do you like Teen Dog? I mean like do you like-like him. You know...like romantically.
13

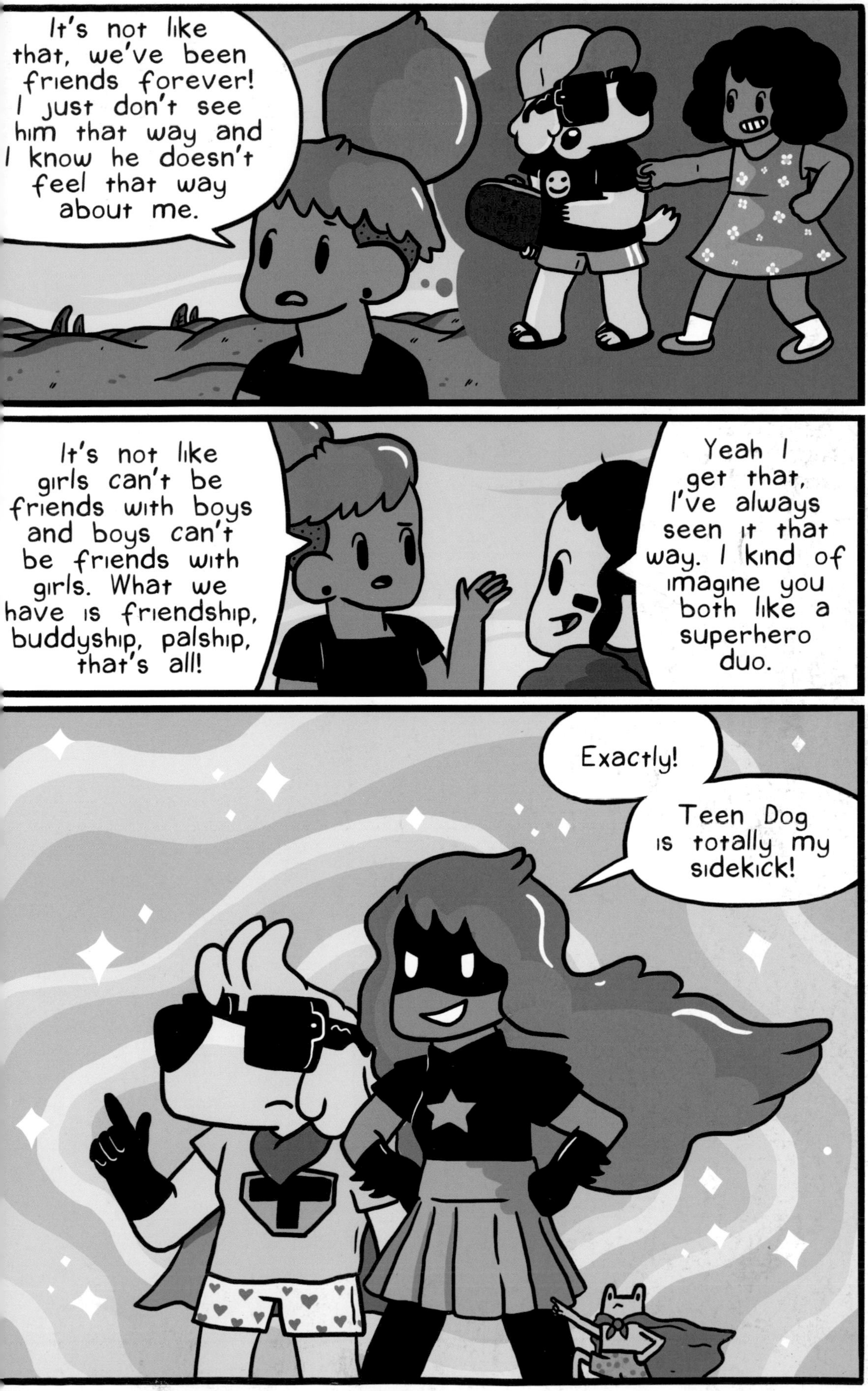
It's not like that, we've been friends forever! I just don't see him that way and I know he doesn't feel that way about me.
It's not like girls can't be friends with boys and boys can't be friends with girls. What we have is friendship, buddyship, palship, that's all!
Yeah I get that, I've always seen it that way. I kind of imagine you both like a superhero duo.
Exactly!
Teen Dog is totally my sidekick!

IMPORTANT PLANS

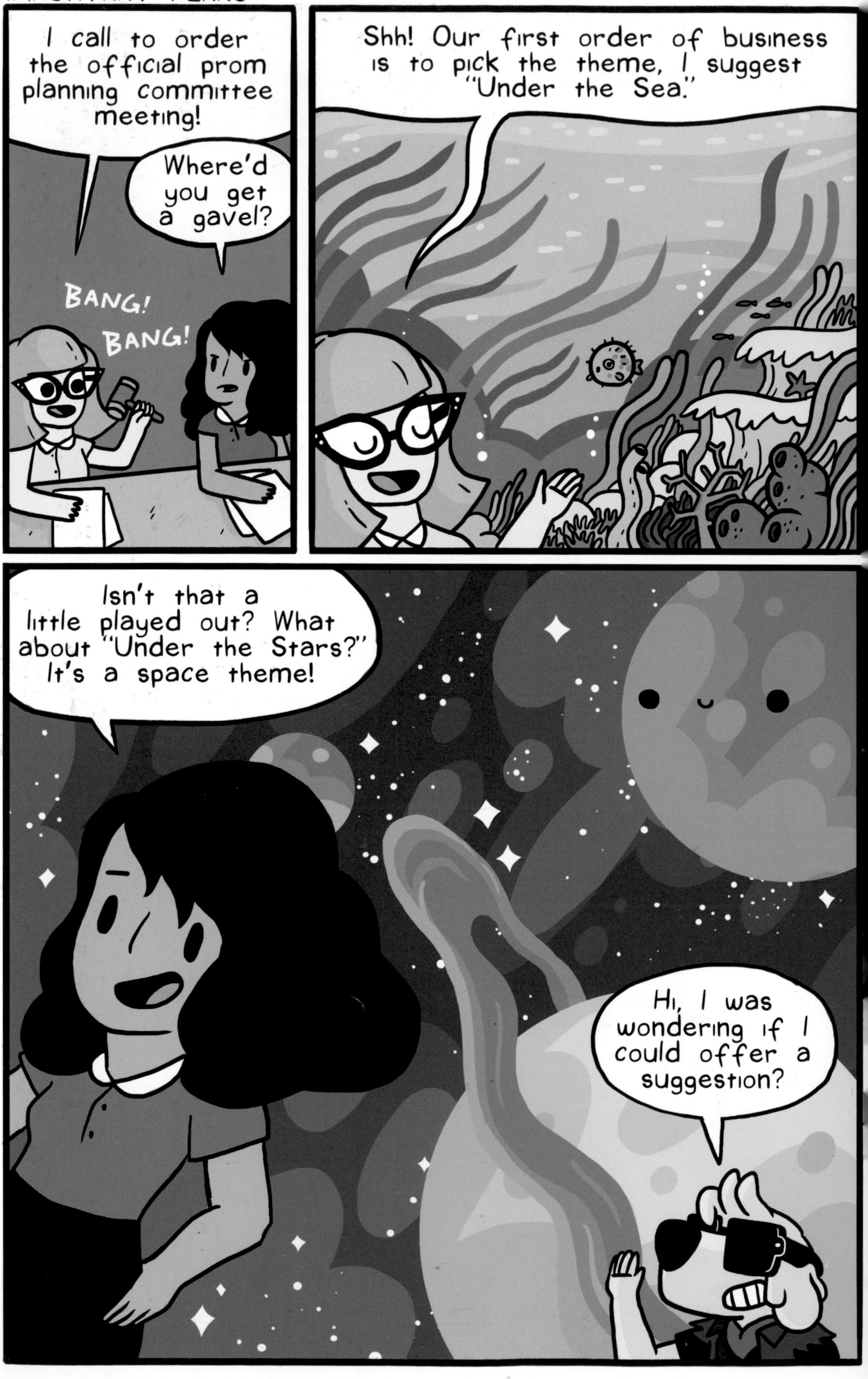
I call to order the official prom planning committee meeting!
Where'd you get a gavel?
BANG! BANG!
Shh! Our first order of business is to pick the theme, I suggest "Under the Sea."
Isn't that a little played out? What about "Under the Stars?" It's a space theme!
Hi, I was wondering if I could offer a suggestion?

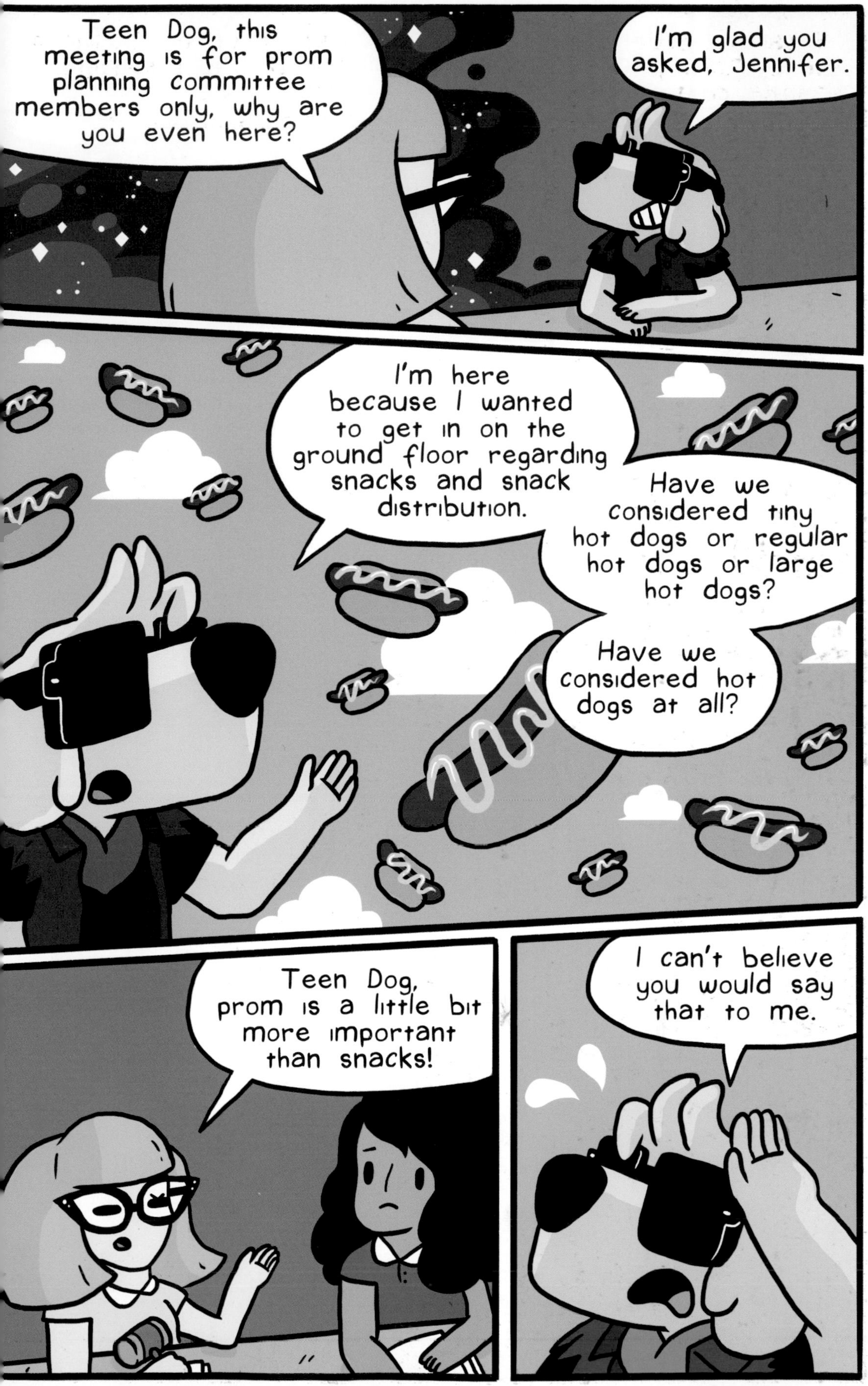
Teen Dog, this meeting is for prom planning committee members only, why are you even here?
I'm glad you asked, Jennifer.
I'm here because I wanted to get in on the ground floor regarding snacks and snack distribution.
Have we considered tiny hot dogs or regular hot dogs or large hot dogs?
Have we considered hot dogs at all?
Teen Dog, prom is a little bit more important than snacks!
I can't believe you would say that to me.

TEEN ANGST

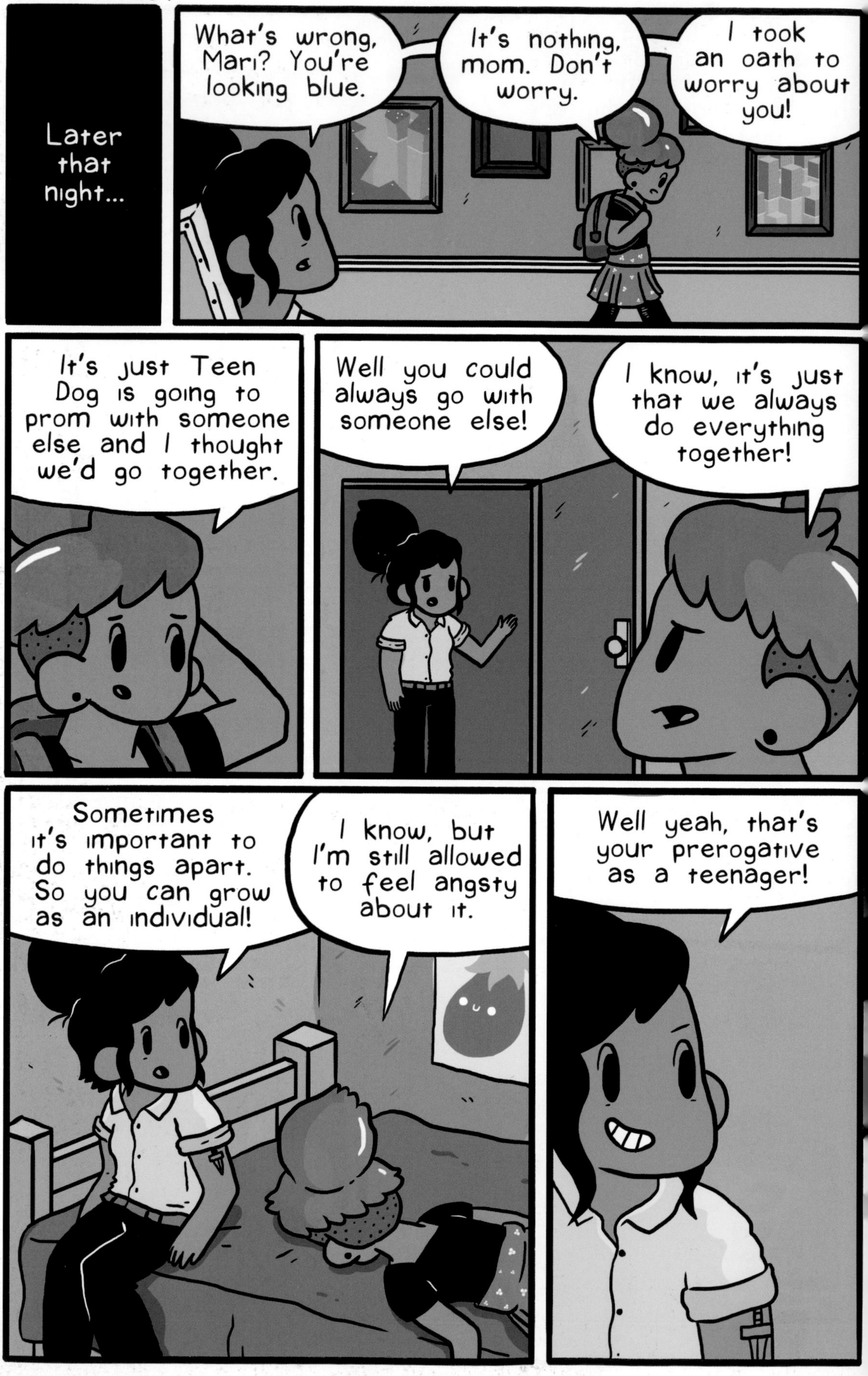

Later that night...
What's wrong, Mari? You're looking blue.
It's nothing, mom. Don't worry.
I took an oath to worry about you!
It's just Teen Dog is going to prom with someone else and I thought we'd go together.
Well you could always go with someone else!
I know, it's just that we always do everything together!
Sometimes it's important to do things apart. So you can grow as an individual!
I know, but I'm still allowed to feel angsty about it.
Well yeah, that's your prerogative as a teenager!

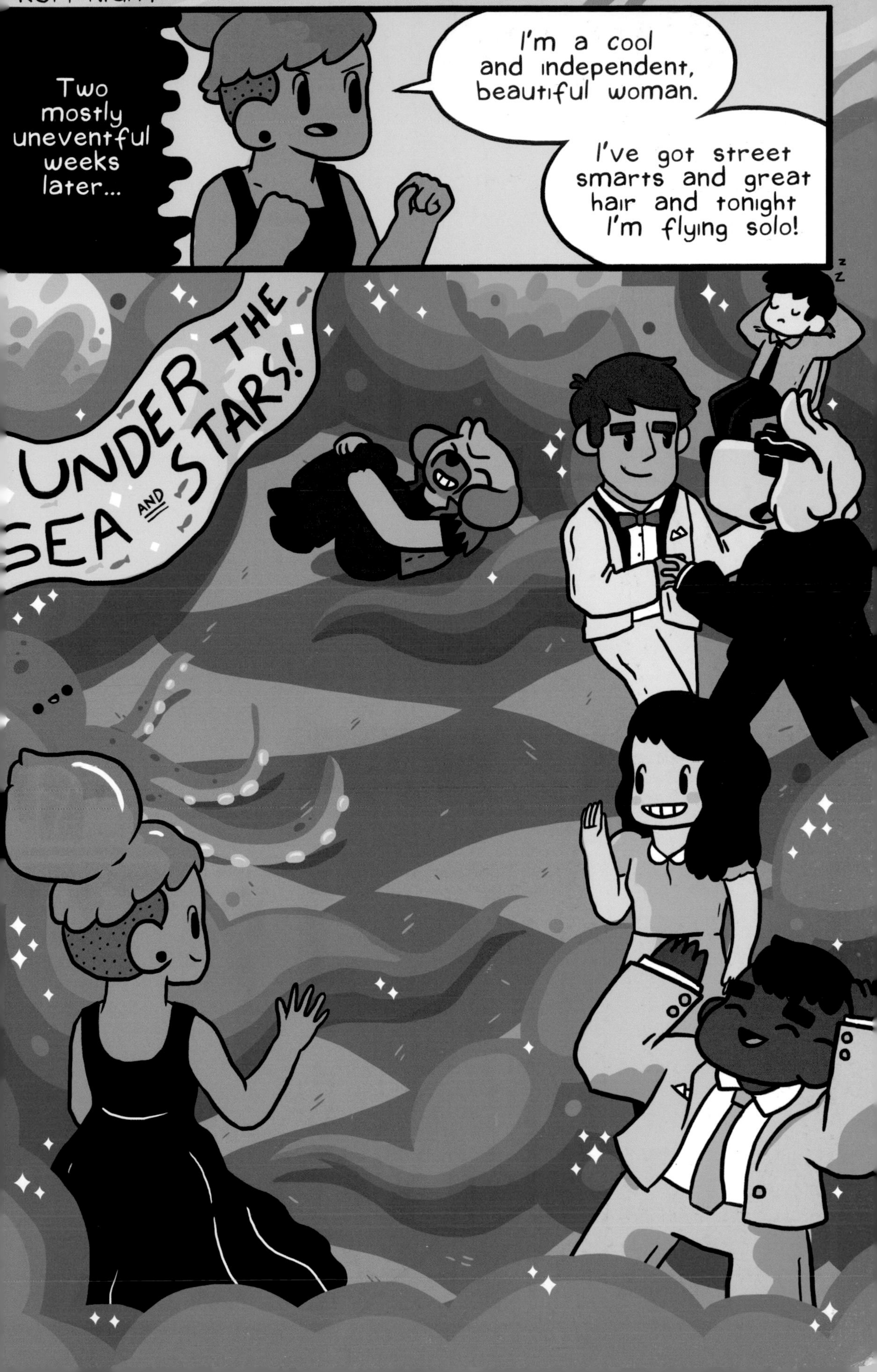
Two mostly uneventful weeks later...
I'm a cool and independent, beautiful woman.
I've got street smarts and great hair and tonight I'm flying solo!
Z Z
UNDER THE SEA AND STARS!

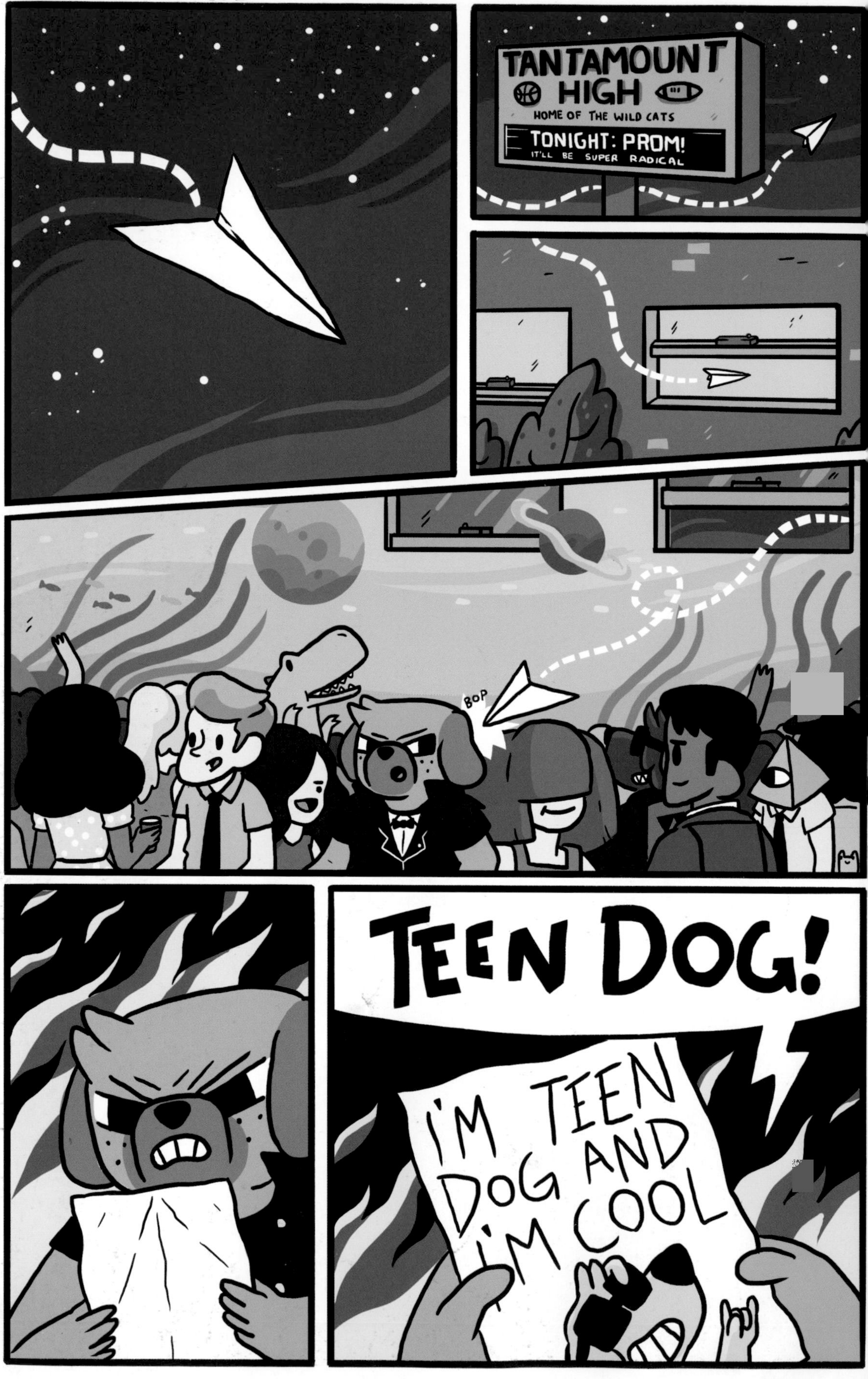
TANTAMOUNT
HIGH
HOME OF THE WILD CATS
TONIGHT: PROM!
IT'LL BE SUPER RADICAL
BOP
TEEN DOG!
I'M TEEN DOG AND I'M COOL

PUT ON YOUR DANCING SHOES

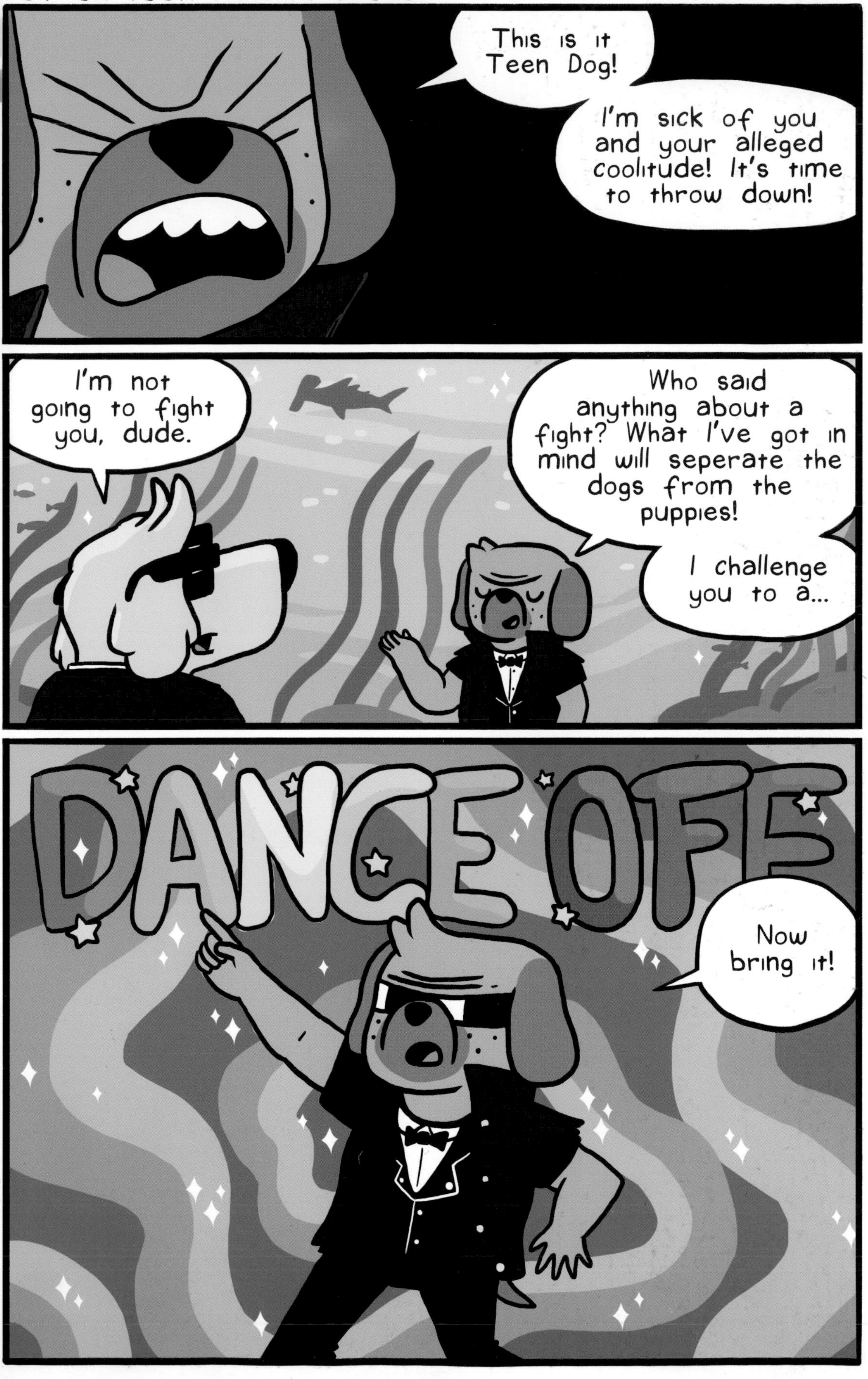
This is it Teen Dog!
I'm sick of you and your alleged coolitude! It's time to throw down!
I'm not going to fight you, dude.
Who said anything about a fight? What I've got in mind will seperate the dogs from the puppies!
I challenge you to a...
DANCE OFF
Now bring it!

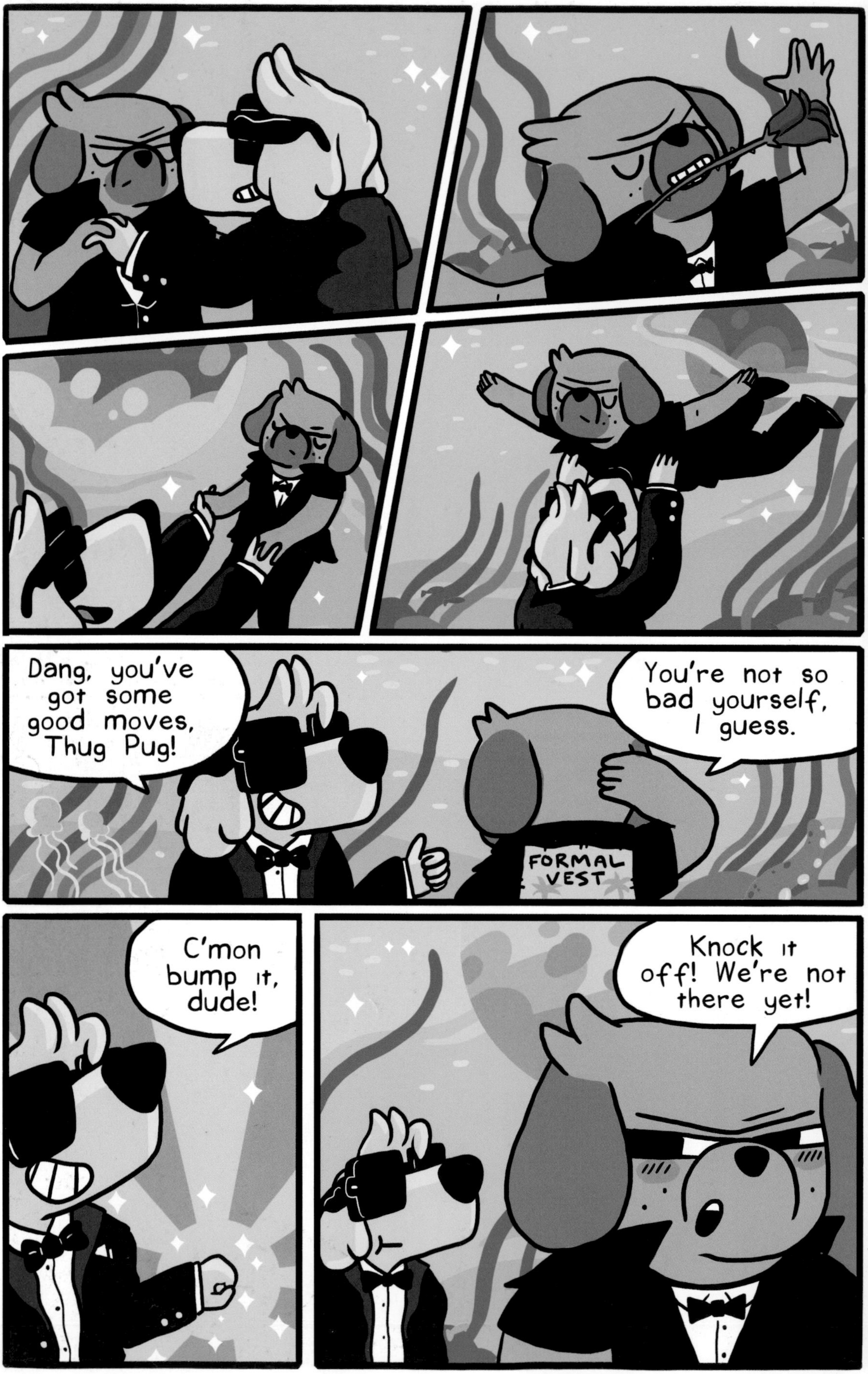
Dang, you've got some good moves, Thug Pug!
You're not so bad yourself, I guess.
FORMAL VEST
C'mon bump it, dude!
Knock it off! We're not there yet!

MONARCHY

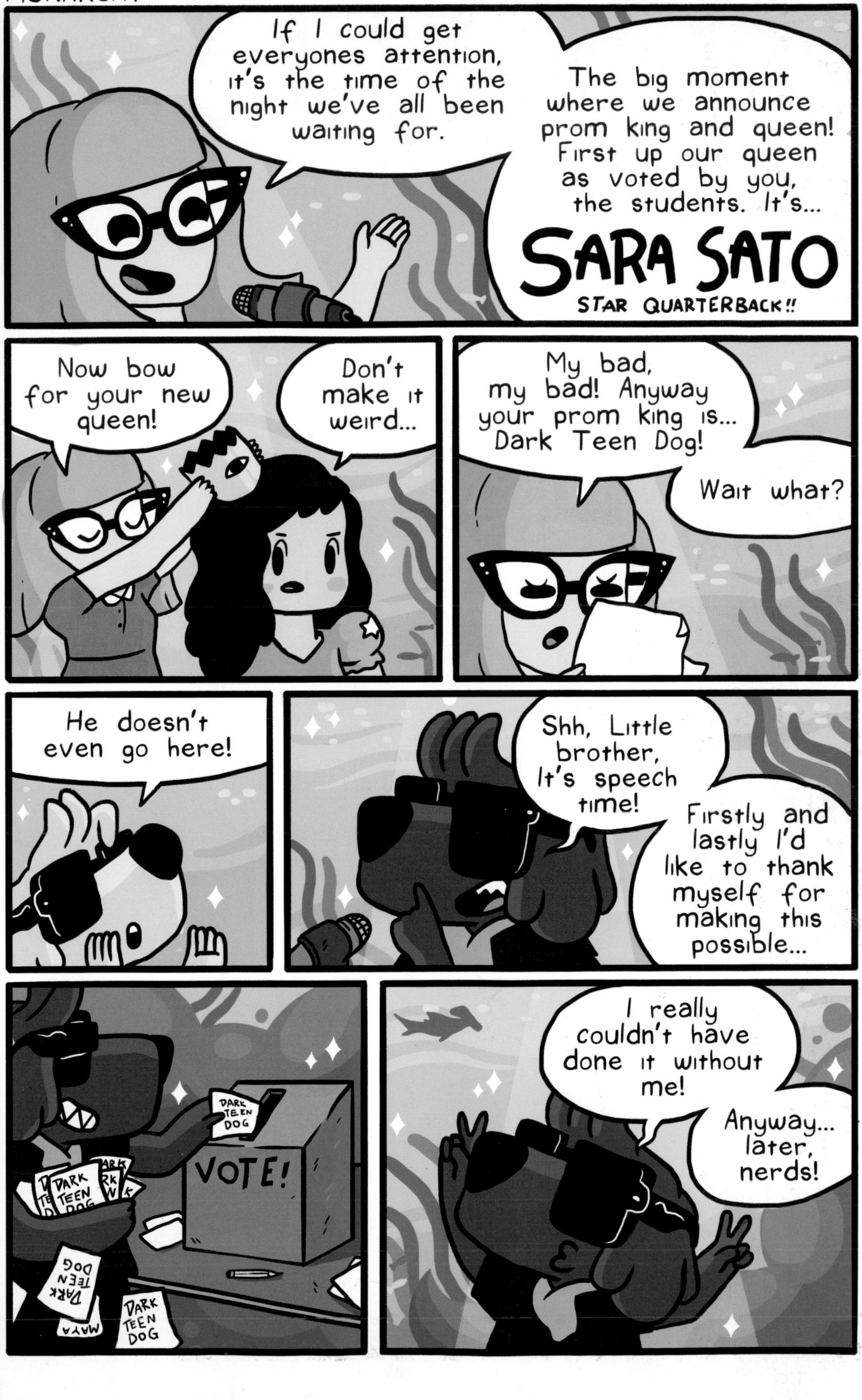
If I could get everyones attention, it's the time of the night we've all been waiting for.
The big moment where we announce prom king and queen! First up our queen as voted by you, the students. It's...
SARA SATO
STAR QUARTERBACK!!
Now bow for your new queen!
Don't make it weird...
My bad, my bad! Anyway your prom king is... Dark Teen Dog!
Wait what?
He doesn't even go here!
Shh, Little brother, It's speech time!
Firstly and lastly I'd like to thank myself for making this possible...
DARK TEEN DOG
VOTE!
DARK TEEN DOG
DARK TEEN DOG
MAYA
DARK TEEN DOG
I really couldn't have done it without me!
Anyway... later, nerds!

THE LAST DANCE

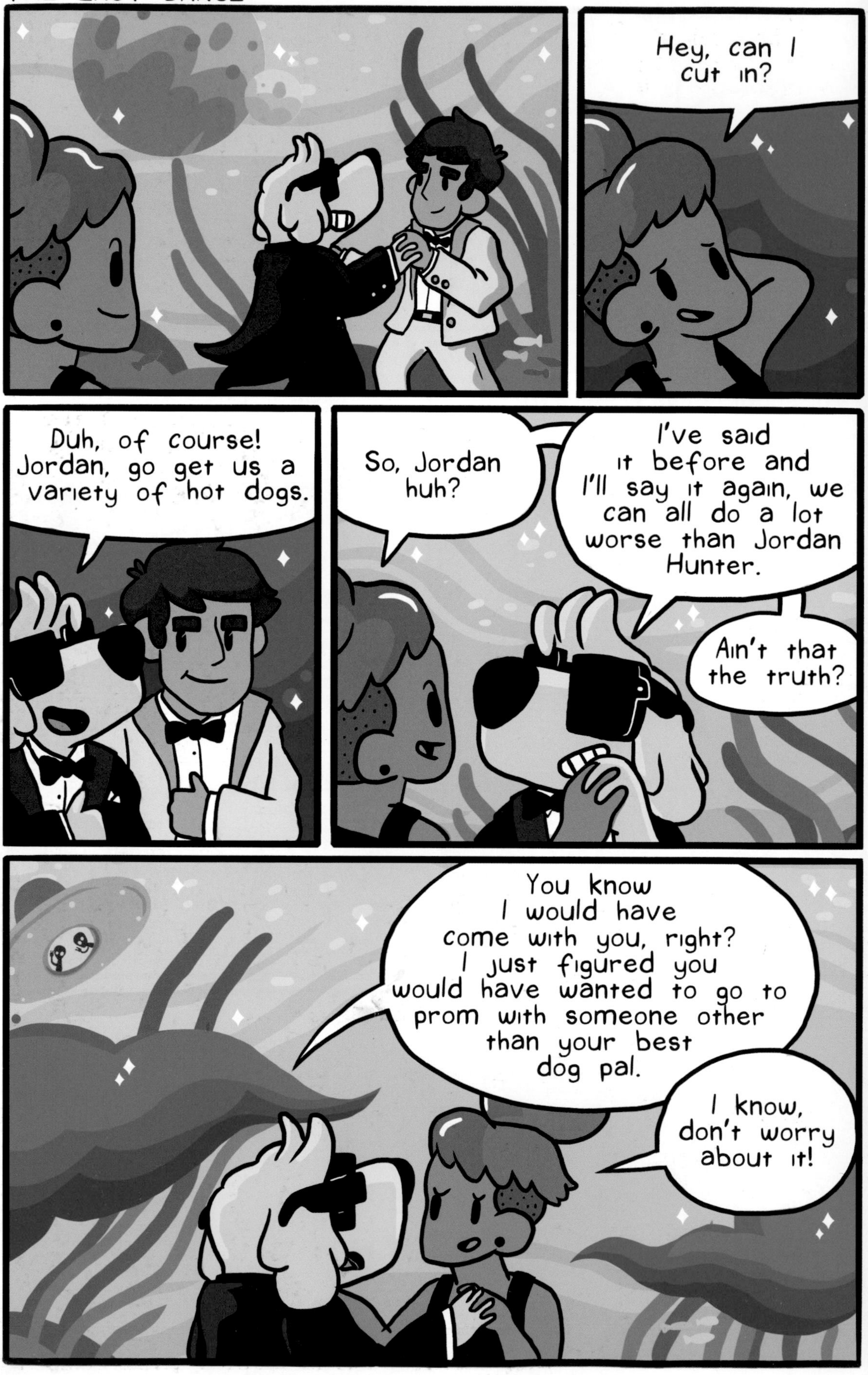
Hey, can I cut in?
Duh, of course! Jordan, go get us a variety of hot dogs.
So, Jordan huh?
I've said it before and I'll say it again, we can all do a lot worse than Jordan Hunter.
Ain't that the truth?
You know I would have come with you, right? I just figured you would have wanted to go to prom with someone other than your best dog pal.
I know, don't worry about it!

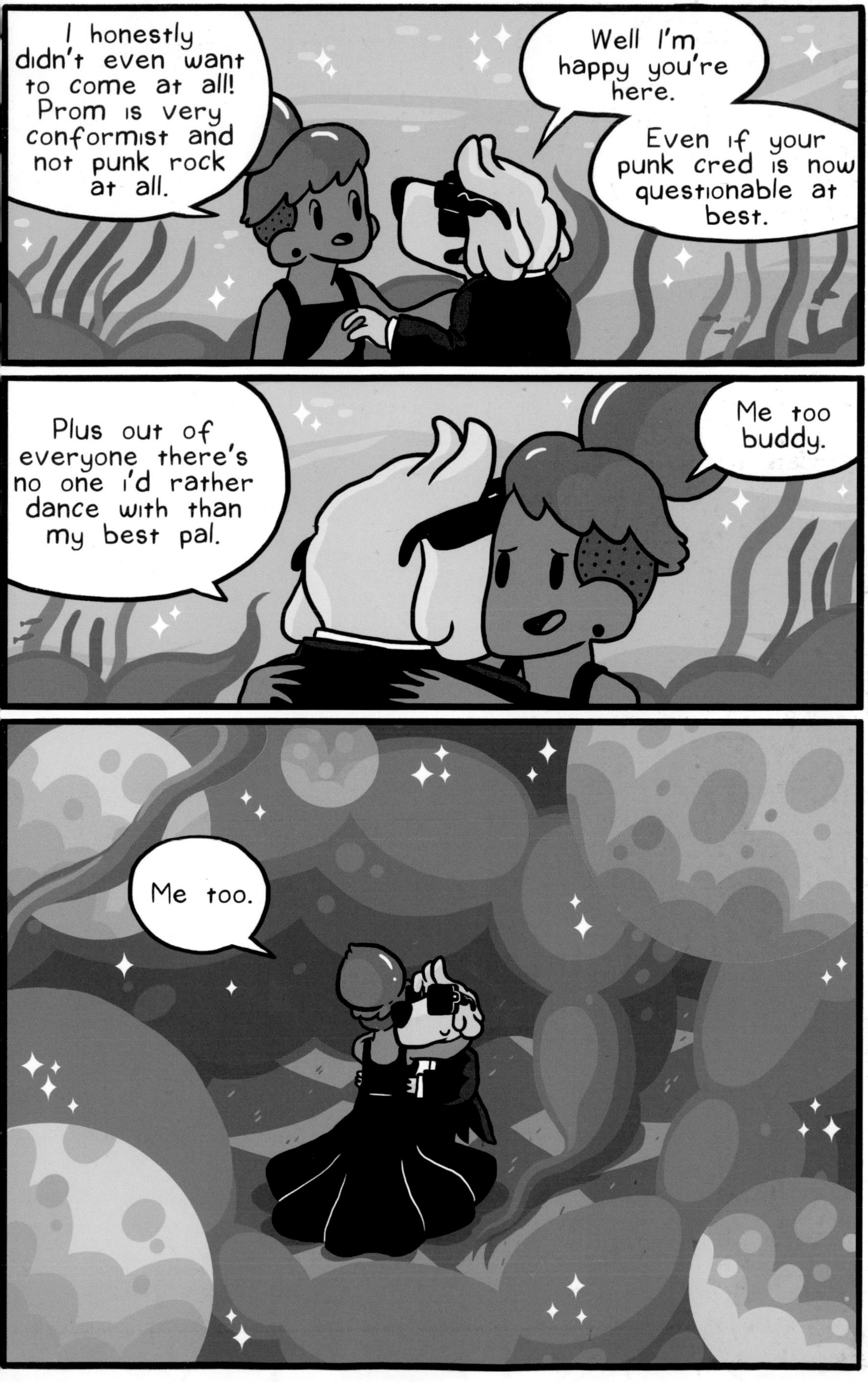
I honestly didn't even want to come at all! Prom is very conformist and not punk rock at all.
Well I'm happy you're here.
Even if your punk cred is now questionable at best.
Plus out of everyone there's no one I'd rather dance with than my best pal.
Me too buddy.
Me too.

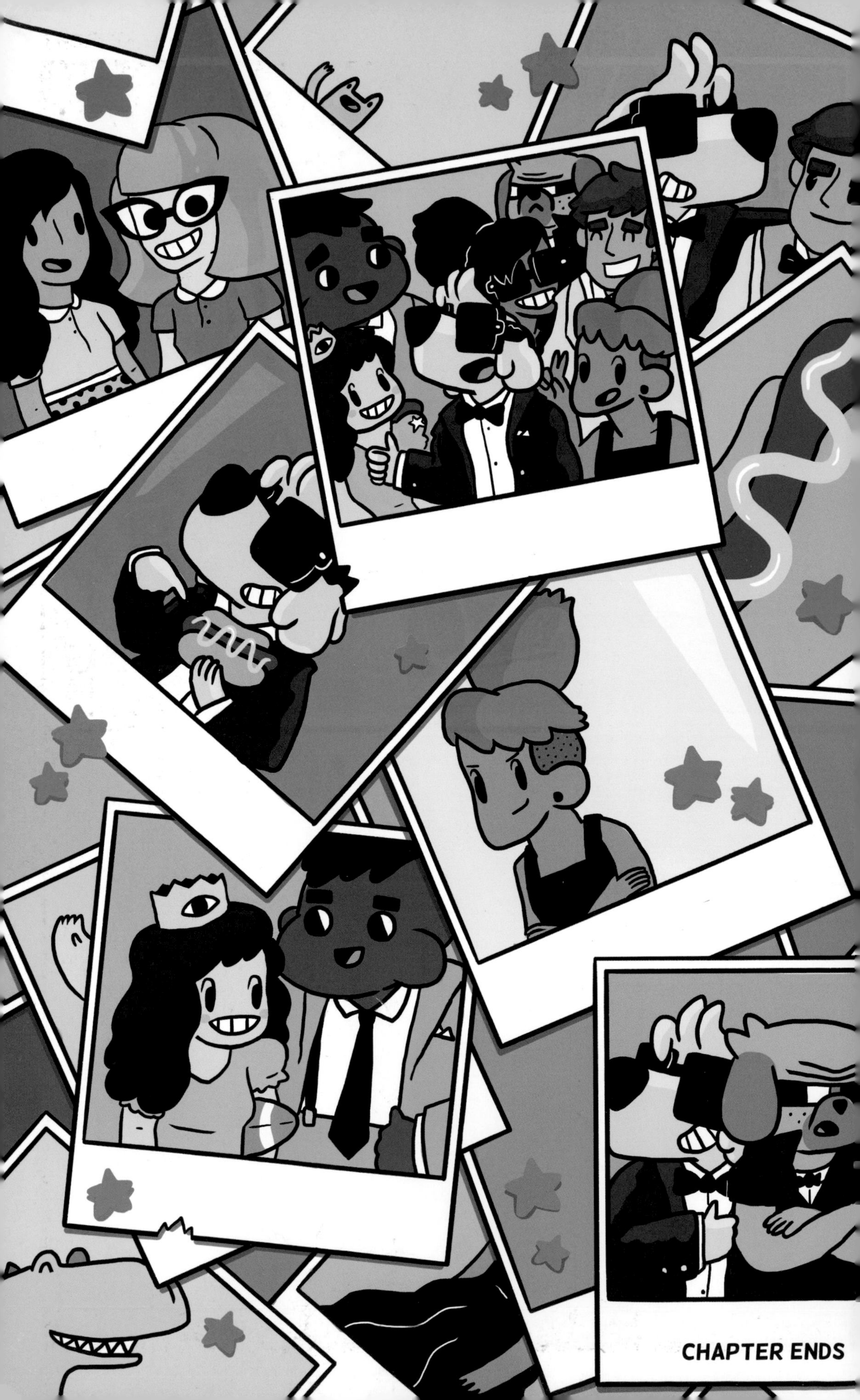
CHAPTER ENDS

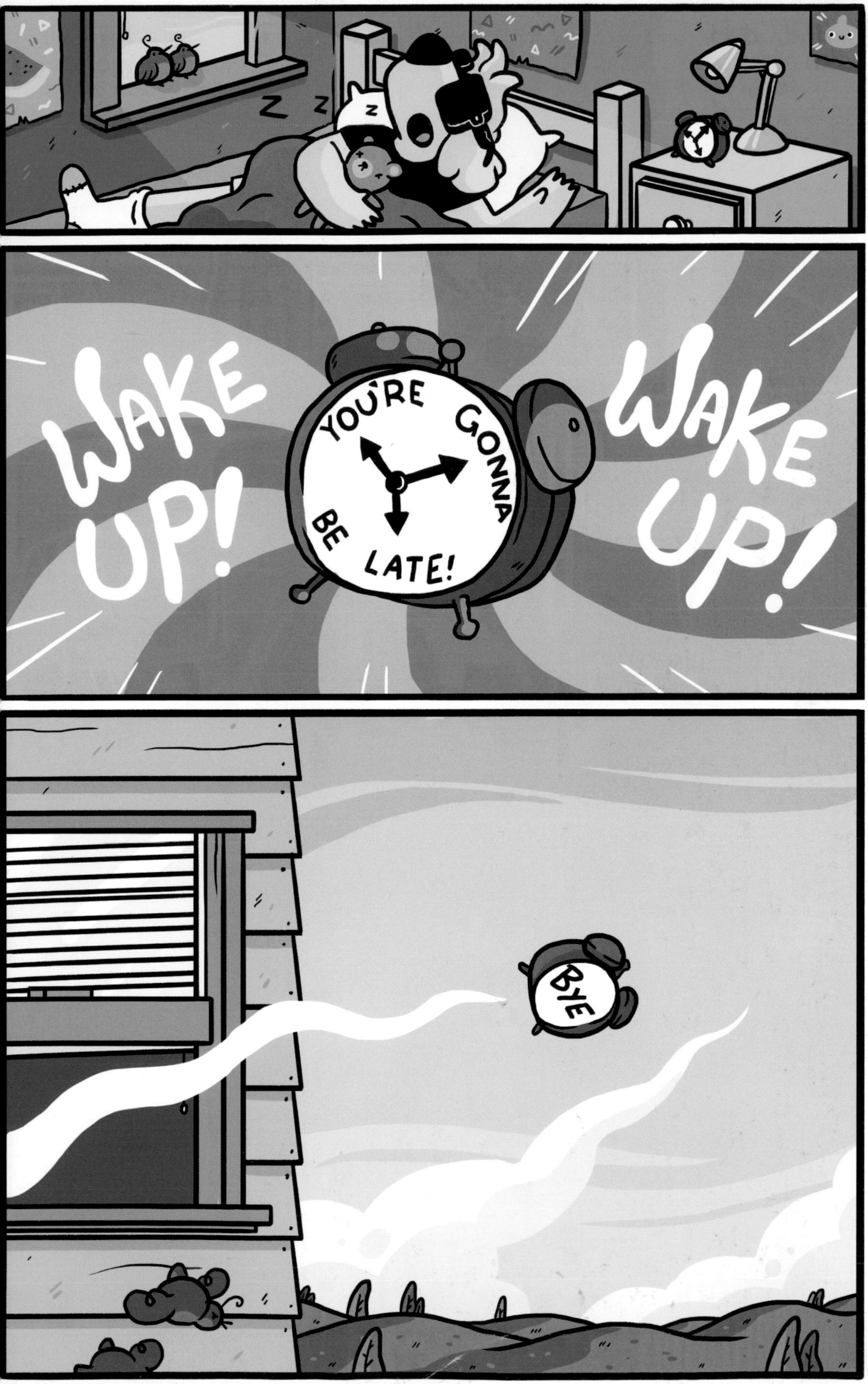
Z Z
z
WAKE UP!
YOU'RE GONNA BE LATE!
WAKE UP!
BYE

LATER SKATERS

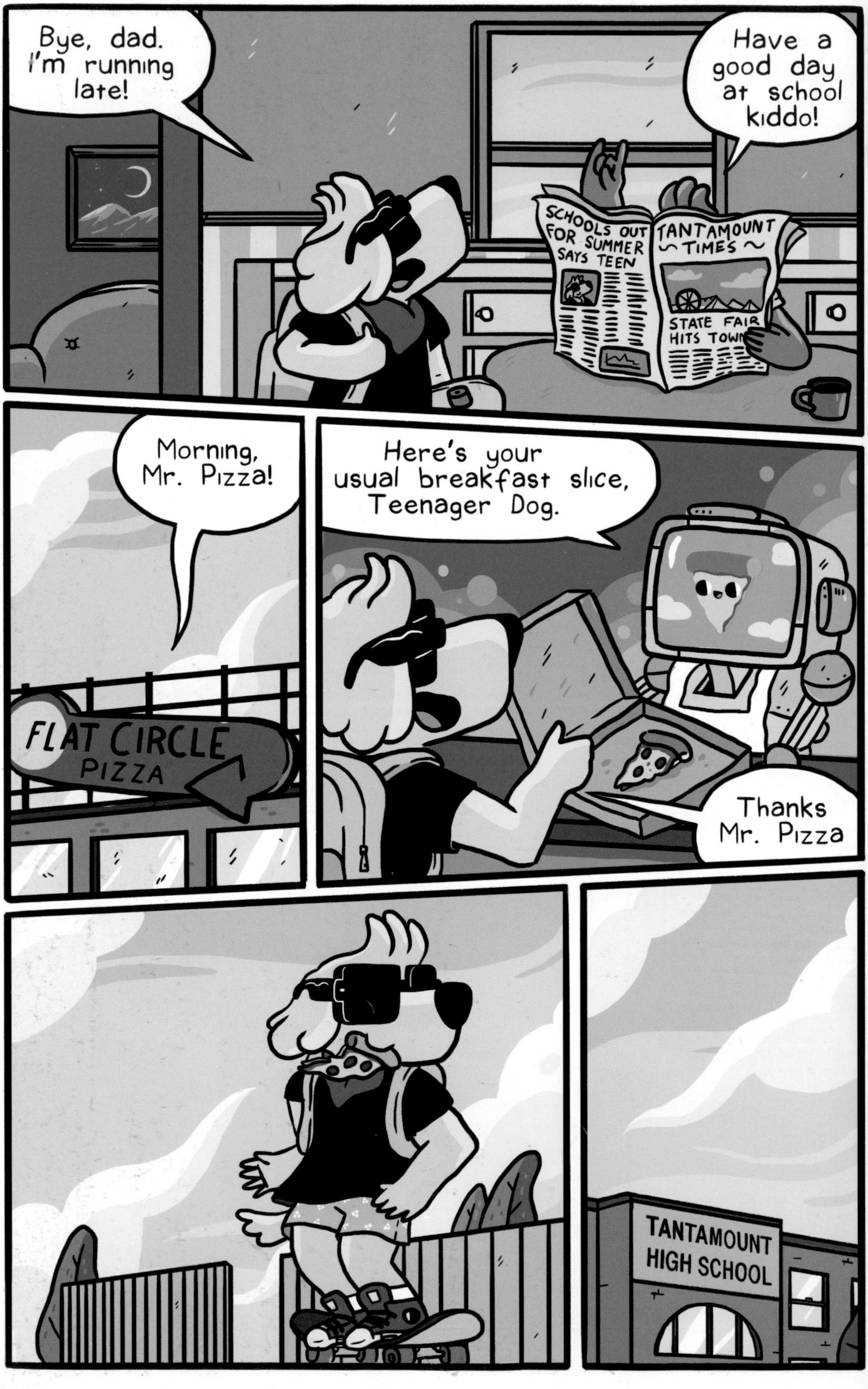
Bye, dad. I'm running late!
Have a good day at school kiddo!
SCHOOLS OUT FOR SUMMER SAYS TEEN
TANTAMOUNT ~TIMES~
STATE FAIR HITS TOWN
Morning, Mr. Pizza!
FLAT CIRCLE PIZZA
Here's your usual breakfast slice, Teenager Dog.
Thanks Mr. Pizza
TANTAMOUNT HIGH SCHOOL

THE TEEN DOG ZONE

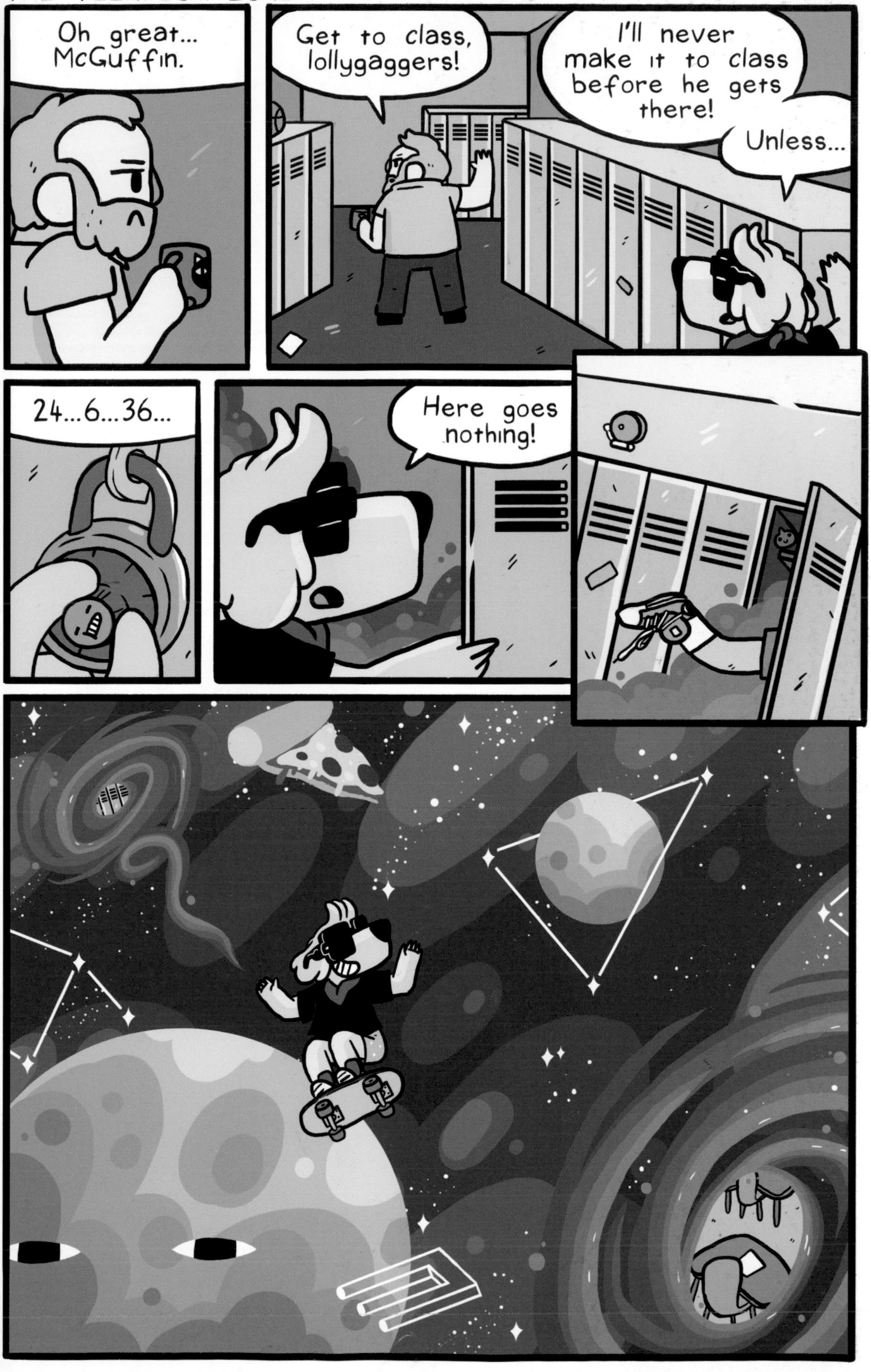
Oh great... McGuffin.
Get to class, lollygaggers!
I'll never make it to class before he gets there!
Unless...
24...6...36...
Here goes nothing!

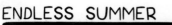

CHAPTER EIGHT

Sup.

I almost thought you weren't going to make it!

oof

Zzz

It's the last day of school before summer!

Our last day of monotony and homework and rules before we can go out and chase the sun and have adventures and live our lives, Mariella!

It's freedom. It's feeling the wind in our fur. It's everything.

I figured suffering through one last day will make summer all the sweeter.

So I plan on making the most of it.

SUMMER SCHOOL

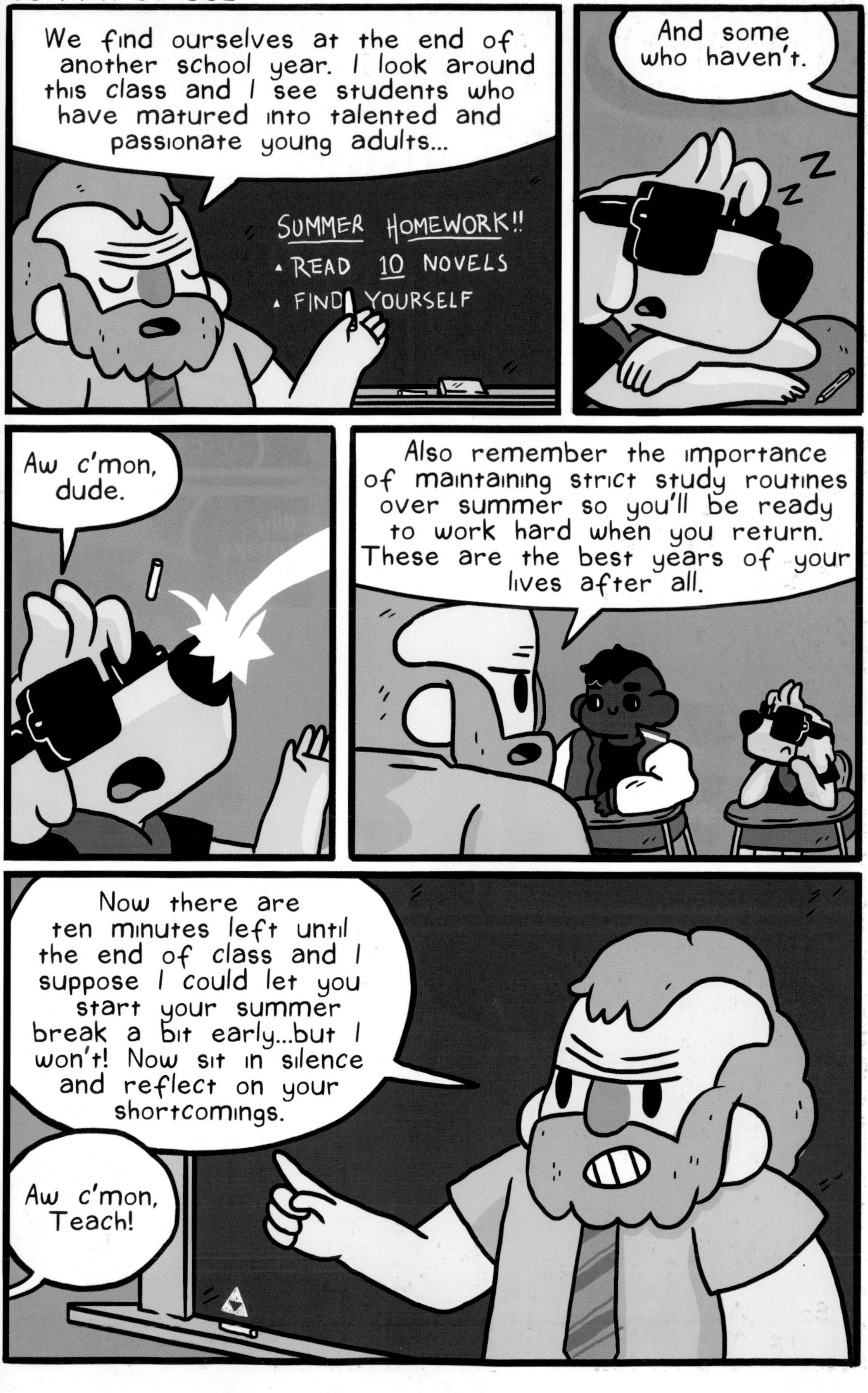
We find ourselves at the end of another school year. I look around this class and I see students who have matured into talented and passionate young adults...
SUMMER HOMEWORK!!
▲ READ 10 NOVELS
▲ FIND YOURSELF
And some who haven't.
Z Z
Aw c'mon, dude.
Also remember the importance of maintaining strict study routines over summer so you'll be ready to work hard when you return. These are the best years of your lives after all.
Now there are ten minutes left until the end of class and I suppose I could let you start your summer break a bit early...but I won't! Now sit in silence and reflect on your shortcomings.
Aw c'mon, Teach!

HE SAVED LATIN

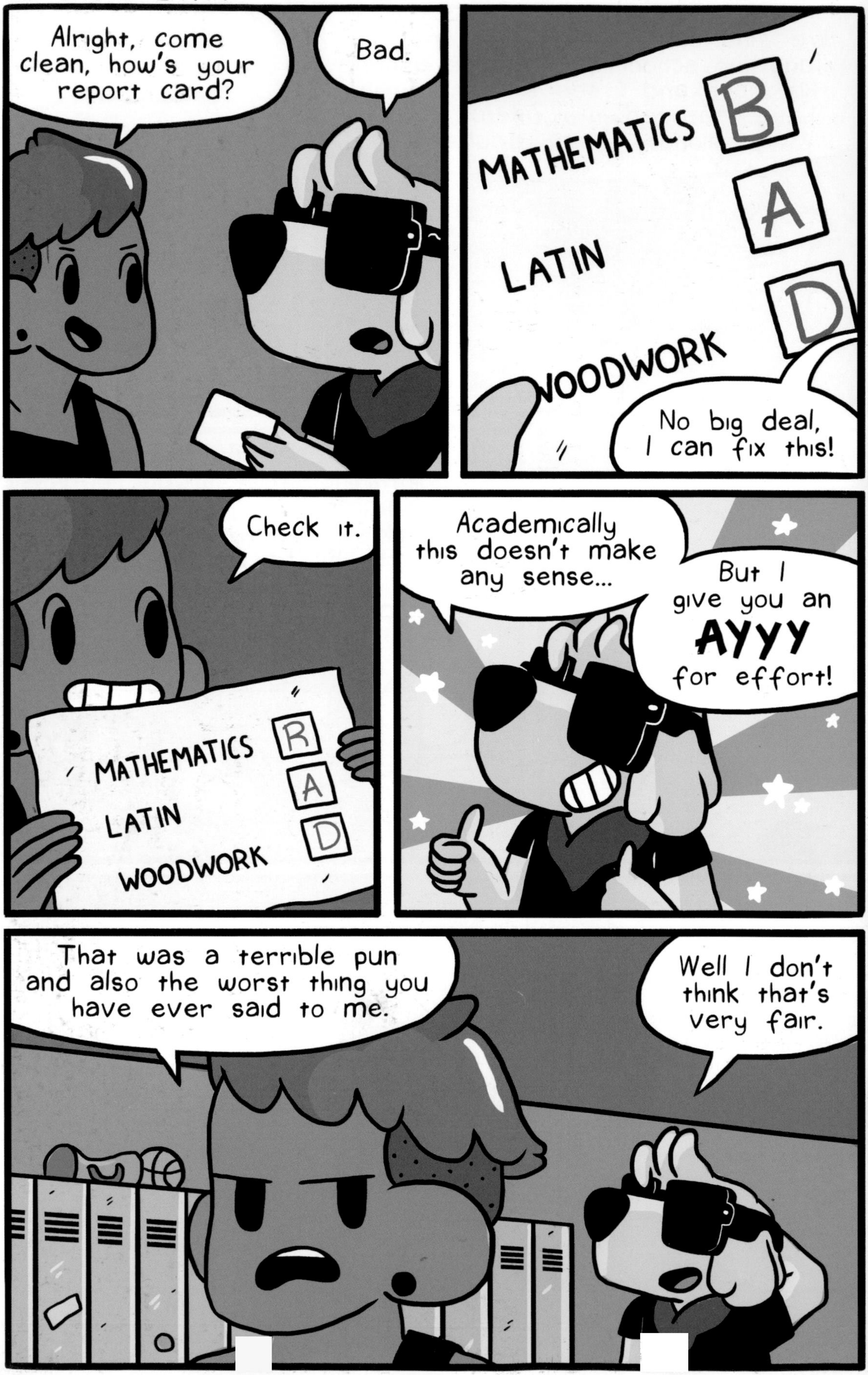
Alright, come clean, how's your report card?
Bad.
MATHEMATICS B
LATIN A
WOODWORK D
No big deal, I can fix this!
Check it.
MATHEMATICS R
LATIN A
WOODWORK D
Academically this doesn't make any sense...
But I give you an AYYY for effort!
That was a terrible pun and also the worst thing you have ever said to me.
Well I don't think that's very fair.

Hey, Teen Dog, will you sign our yearbooks?!

Of course! It would be my pleasure.

So cool

TEEN DOG
"WHAT'S COOLER THAN BEING COOL? TEEN DOG!"

MARIELLA BELL
"BEING NICE IS PUNK-ROCK!"

JENNIFER FINCH
"BE MORE LIKE ME!"

You just drew stuff on our faces!

JAMES KI...
"HI!"

FROG
"RIBBIT, RIBBIT"

SARA SATO
"TEAMWO...

MOLLY KATIL
...LLOW YOUR DREAMS
...F YOU WANT!"

THUG...
"NO..."

It's a sign of affection! Remember vandalism is the highest form of flattery.

I don't think that's how the saying, goes Teen Dog.

SENTIMENTAL

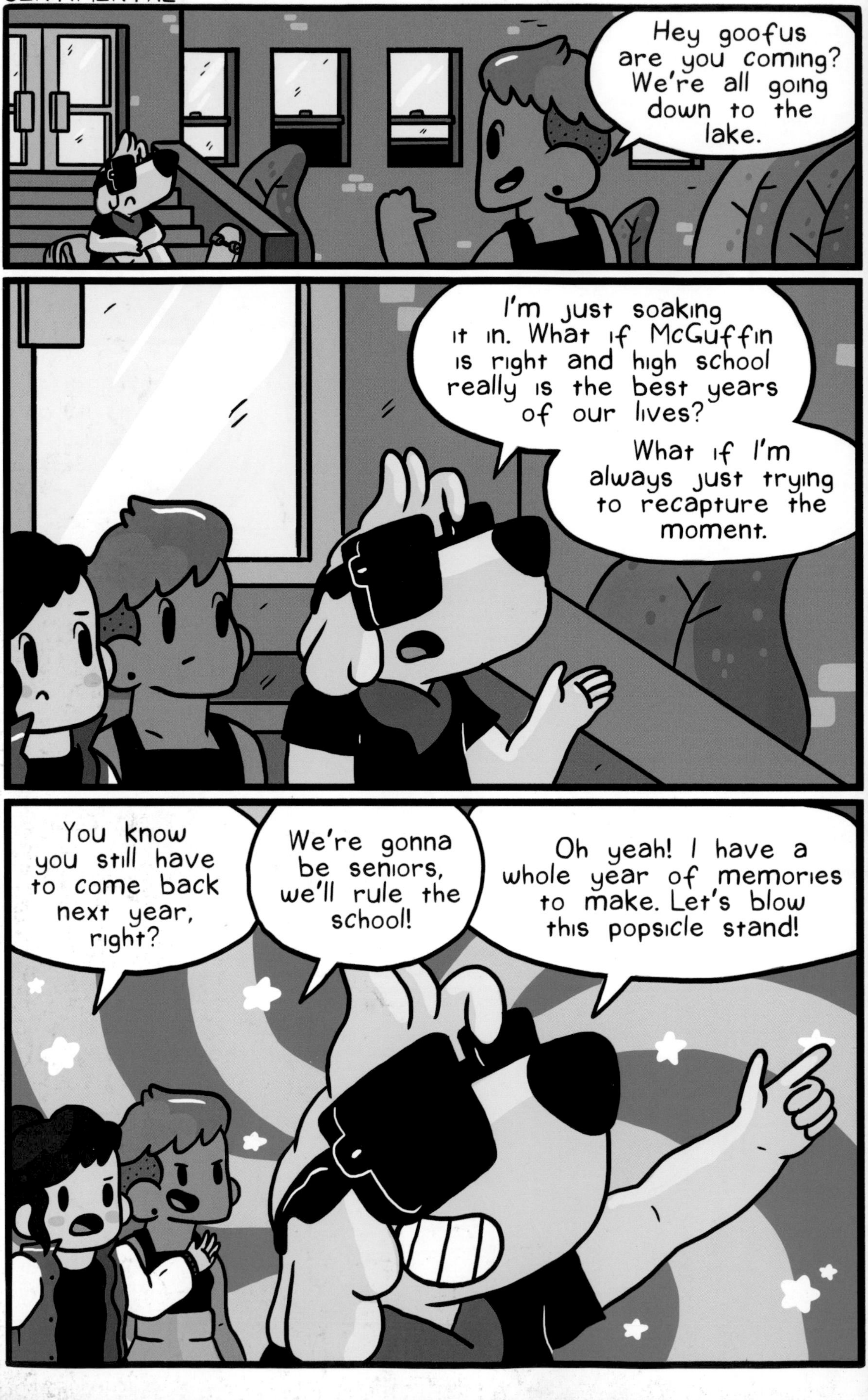
Hey goofus are you coming? We're all going down to the lake.
I'm just soaking it in. What if McGuffin is right and high school really is the best years of our lives?
What if I'm always just trying to recapture the moment.
You know you still have to come back next year, right?
We're gonna be seniors, we'll rule the school!
Oh yeah! I have a whole year of memories to make. Let's blow this popsicle stand!

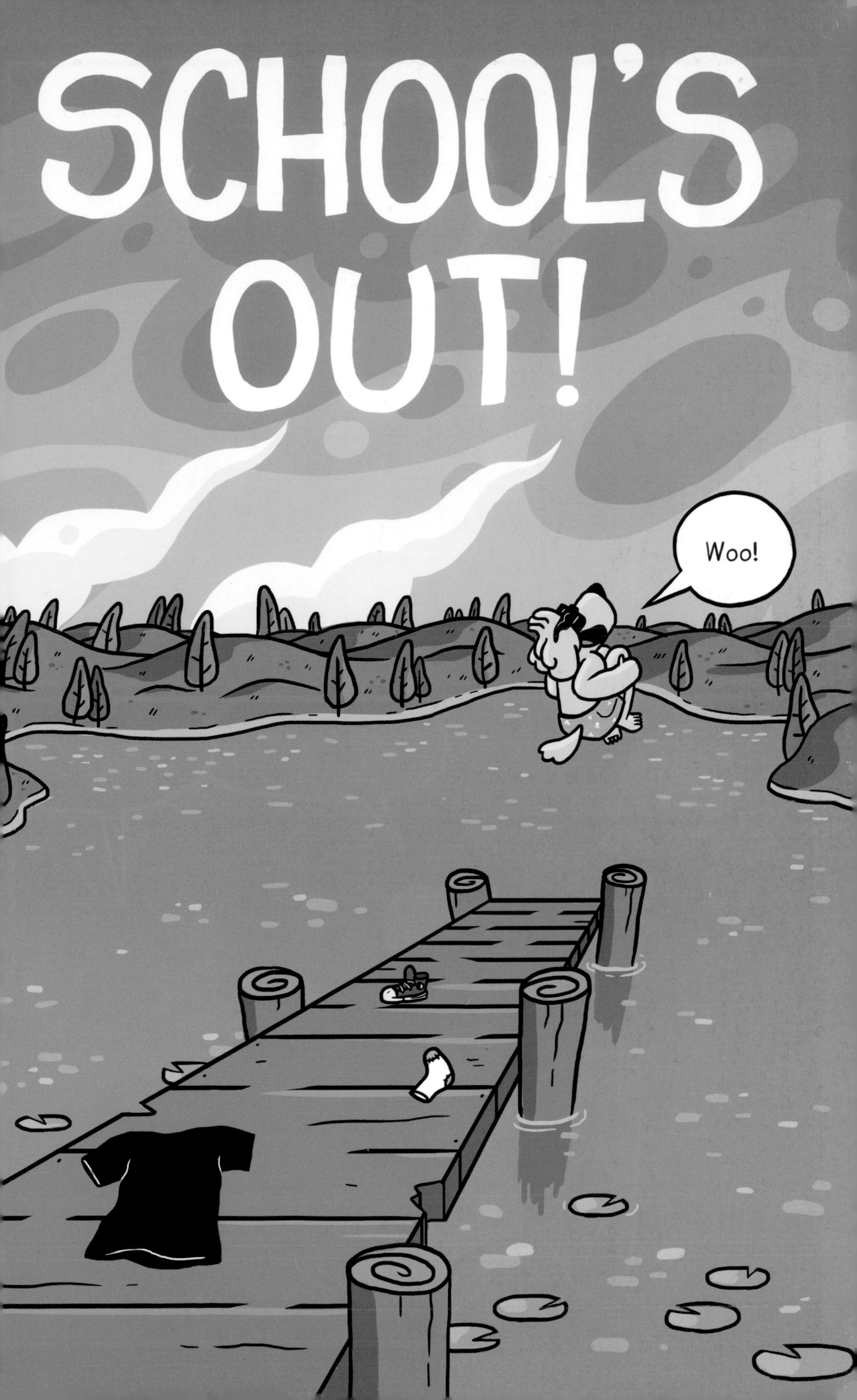
SCHOOL'S OUT!
Woo!

WET DOG

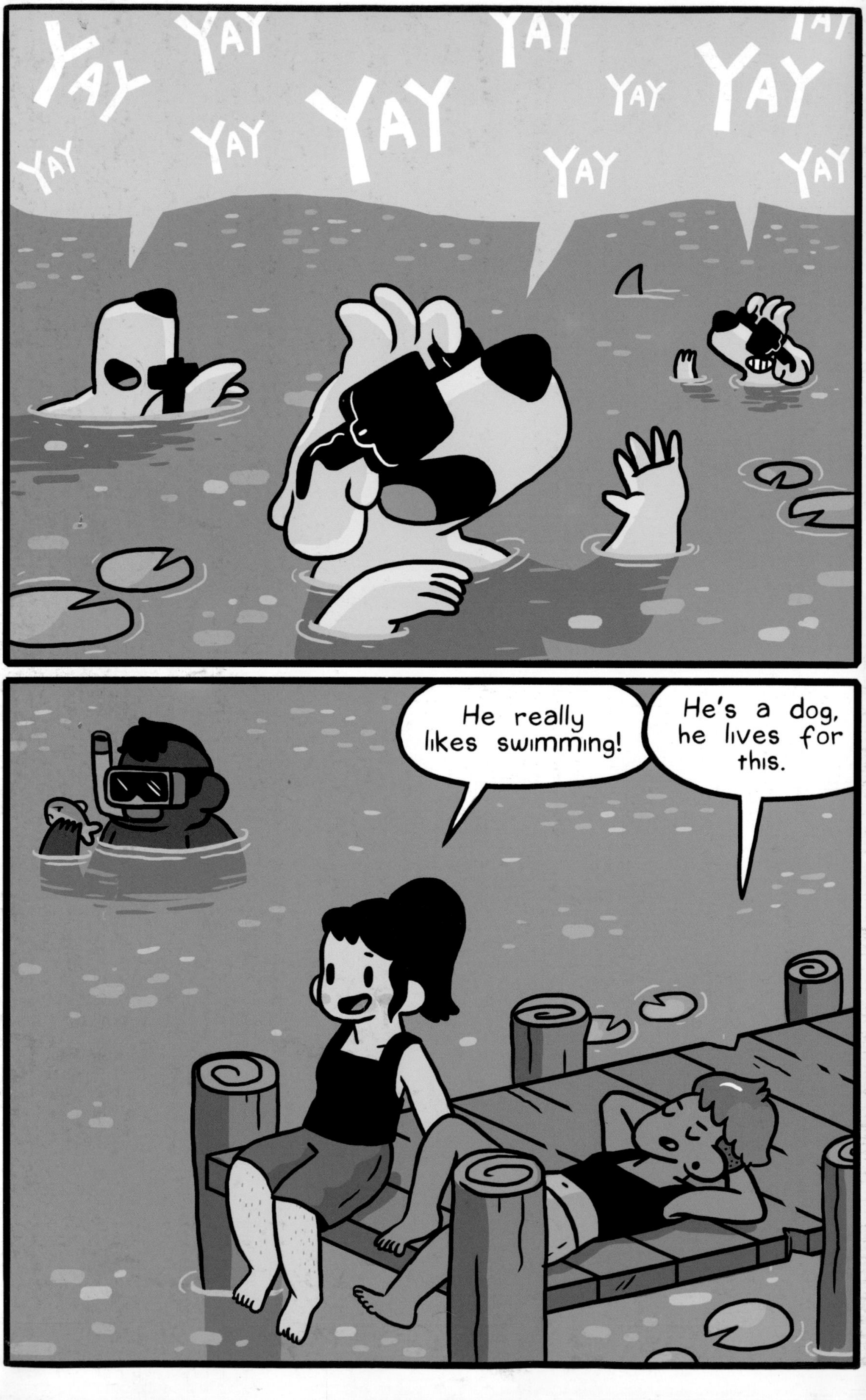
YAY YAY YAY YAY YAY YAY YAY YAY YAY YAY
He really likes swimming!
He's a dog, he lives for this.

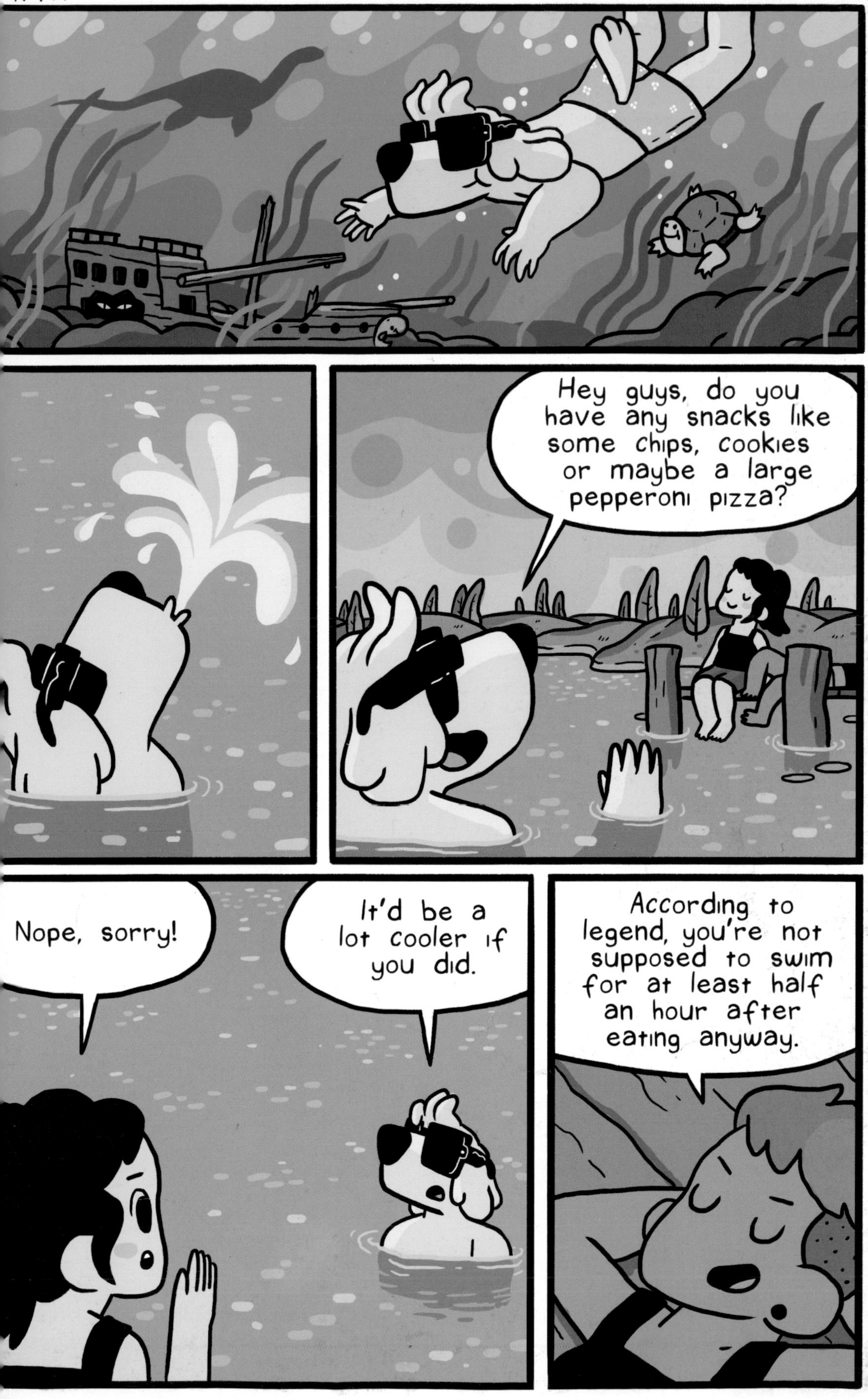
Hey guys, do you have any snacks like some chips, cookies or maybe a large pepperoni pizza?
Nope, sorry!
It'd be a lot cooler if you did.
According to legend, you're not supposed to swim for at least half an hour after eating anyway.

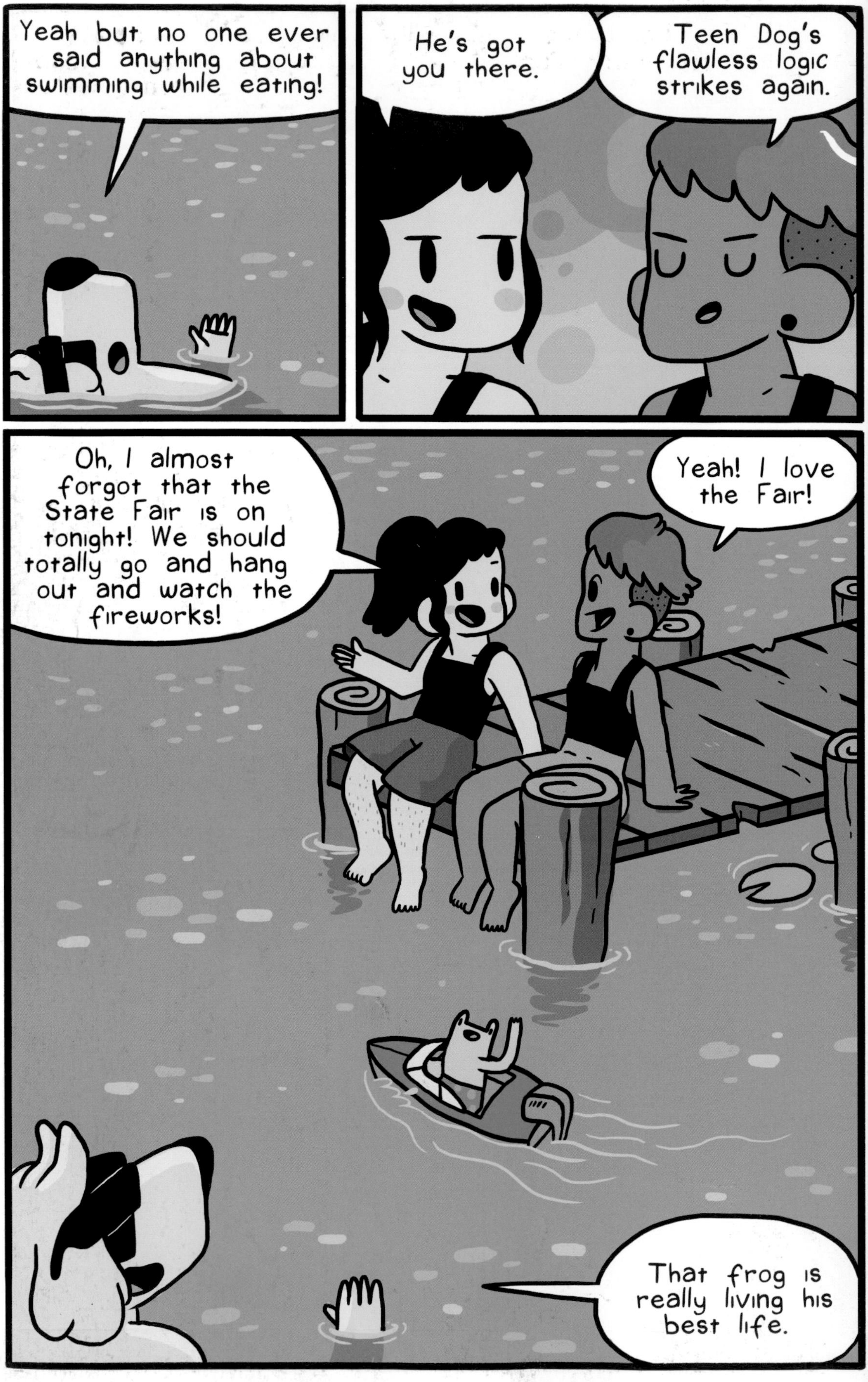
Yeah but no one ever said anything about swimming while eating!
He's got you there.
Teen Dog's flawless logic strikes again.
Oh, I almost forgot that the State Fair is on tonight! We should totally go and hang out and watch the fireworks!
Yeah! I love the Fair!
That frog is really living his best life.

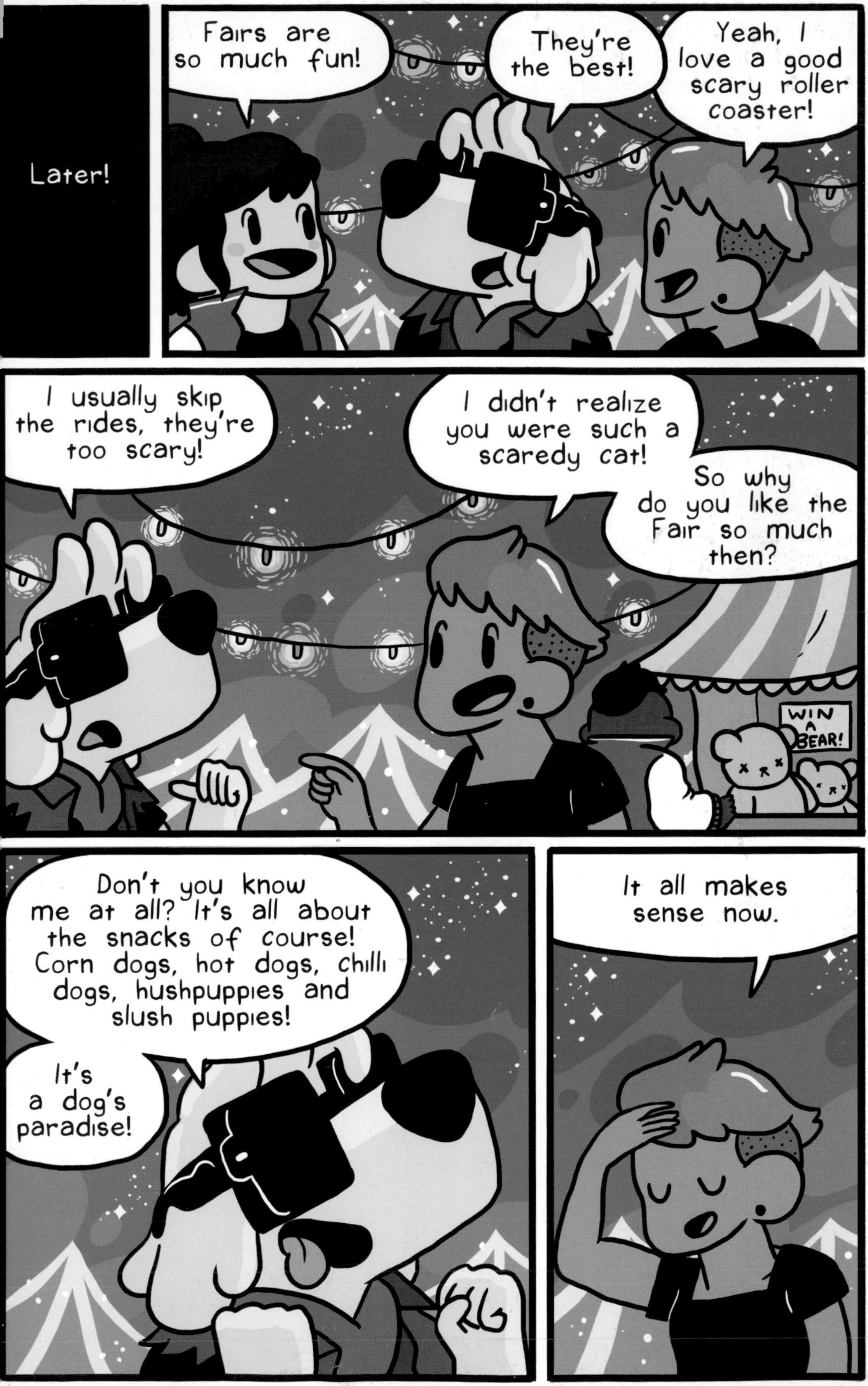
Later!
Fairs are so much fun!
They're the best!
Yeah, I love a good scary roller coaster!
I usually skip the rides, they're too scary!
I didn't realize you were such a scaredy cat!
So why do you like the Fair so much then?
WIN A BEAR!
Don't you know me at all? It's all about the snacks of course! Corn dogs, hot dogs, chilli dogs, hushpuppies and slush puppies!
It's a dog's paradise!
It all makes sense now.

SUGAR RUSH

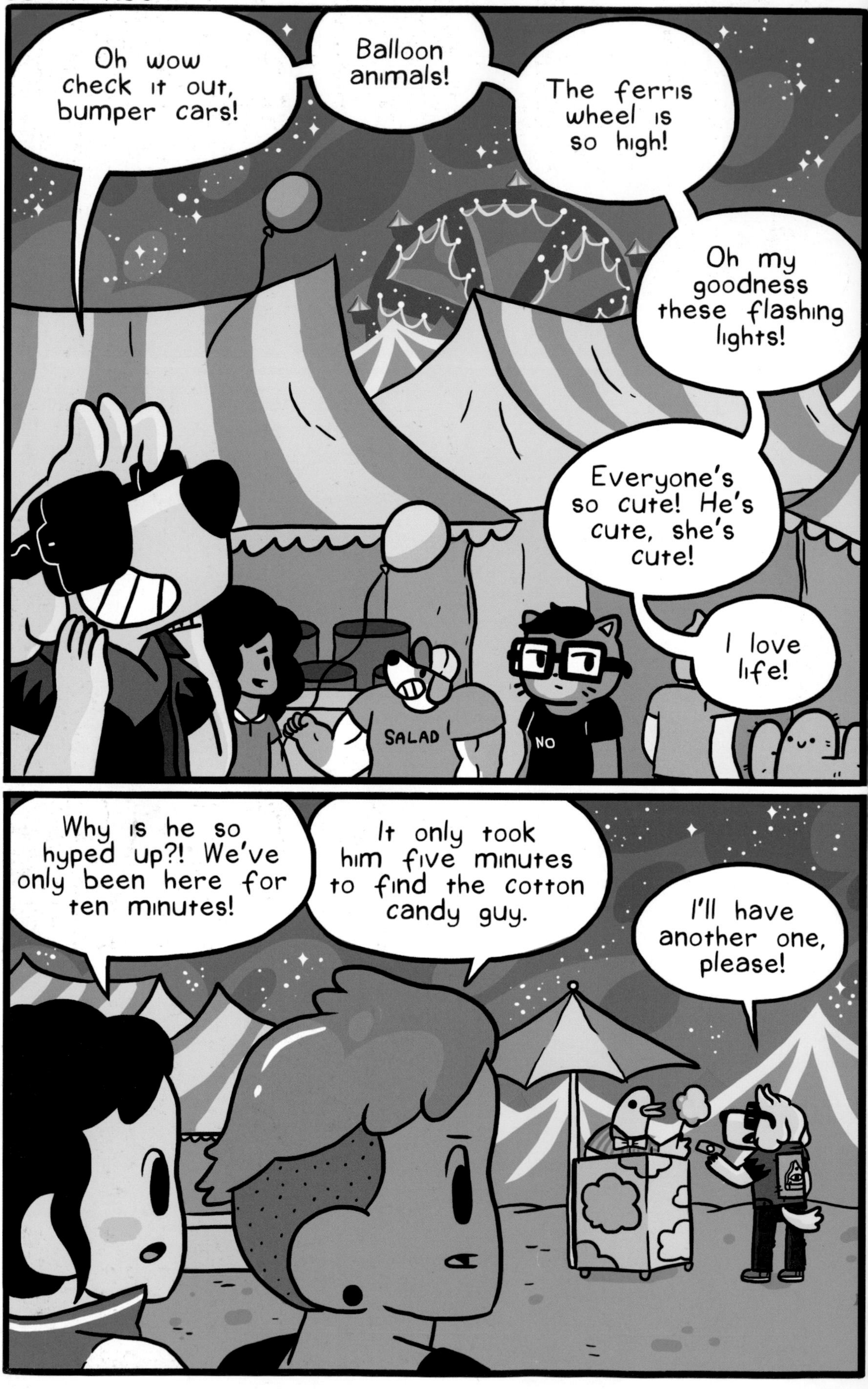
Oh wow check it out, bumper cars!
Balloon animals!
The ferris wheel is so high!
Oh my goodness these flashing lights!
Everyone's so cute! He's cute, she's cute!
I love life!
SALAD
NO
Why is he so hyped up?! We've only been here for ten minutes!
It only took him five minutes to find the cotton candy guy.
I'll have another one, please!

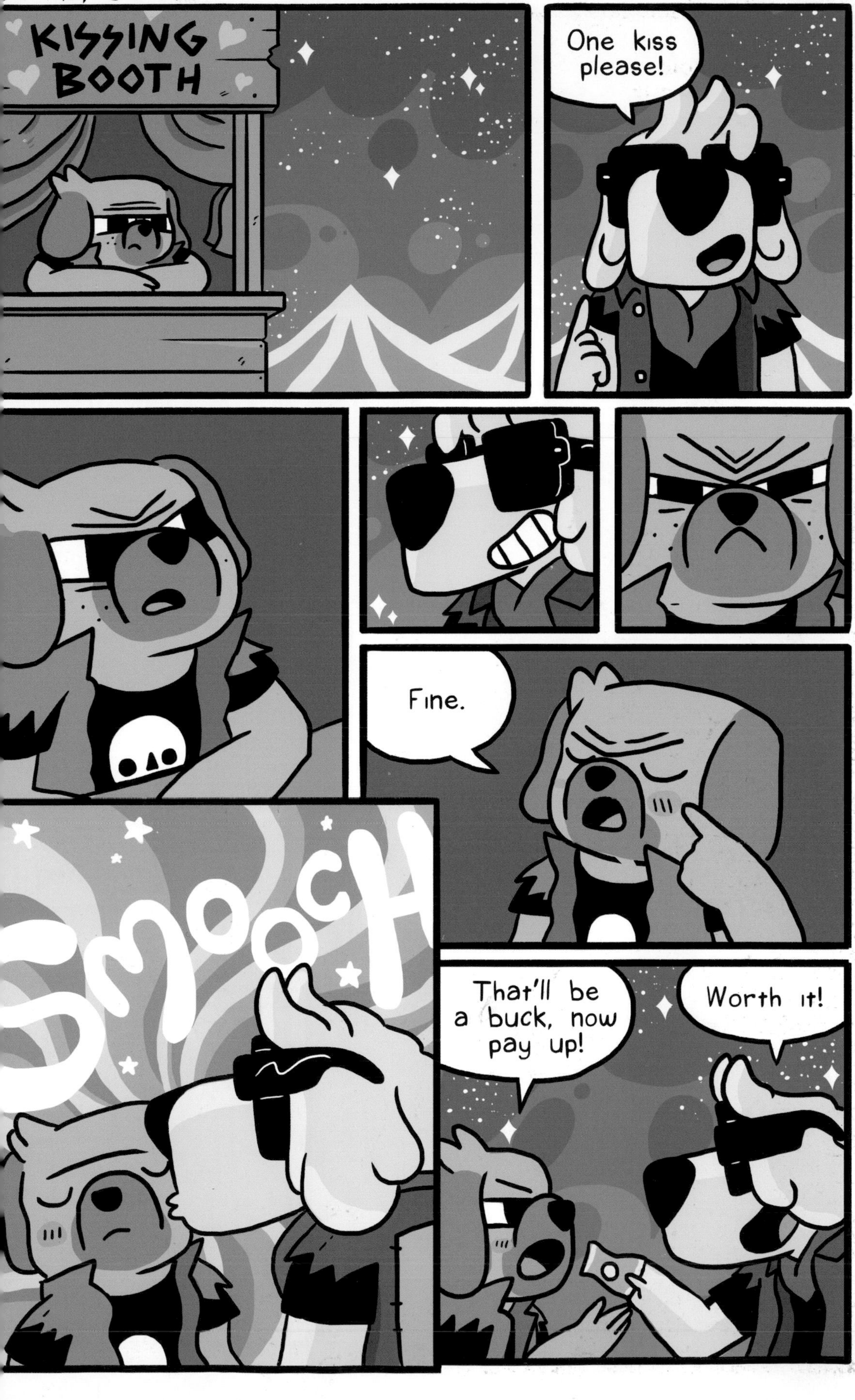
KISSING BOOTH
One kiss please!
Fine.
SMOOCH
That'll be a buck, now pay up!
Worth it!

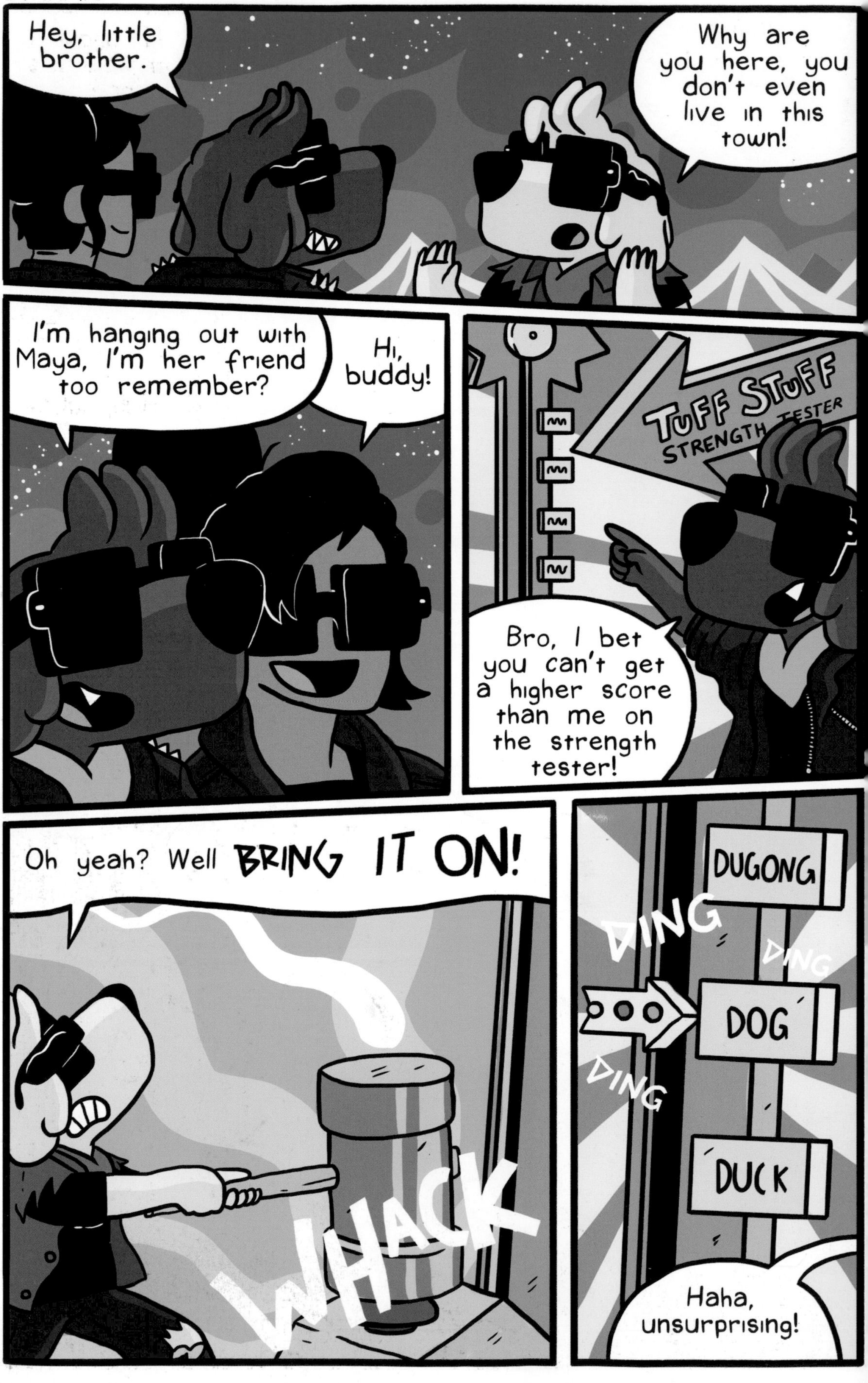
Hey, little brother.
Why are you here, you don't even live in this town!
I'm hanging out with Maya, I'm her friend too remember?
Hi, buddy!
TUFF STUFF
STRENGTH TESTER
Bro, I bet you can't get a higher score than me on the strength tester!
Oh yeah? Well BRING IT ON!
WHACK
DUGONG
DING
DING
DOG
DING
DUCK
Haha, unsurprising!

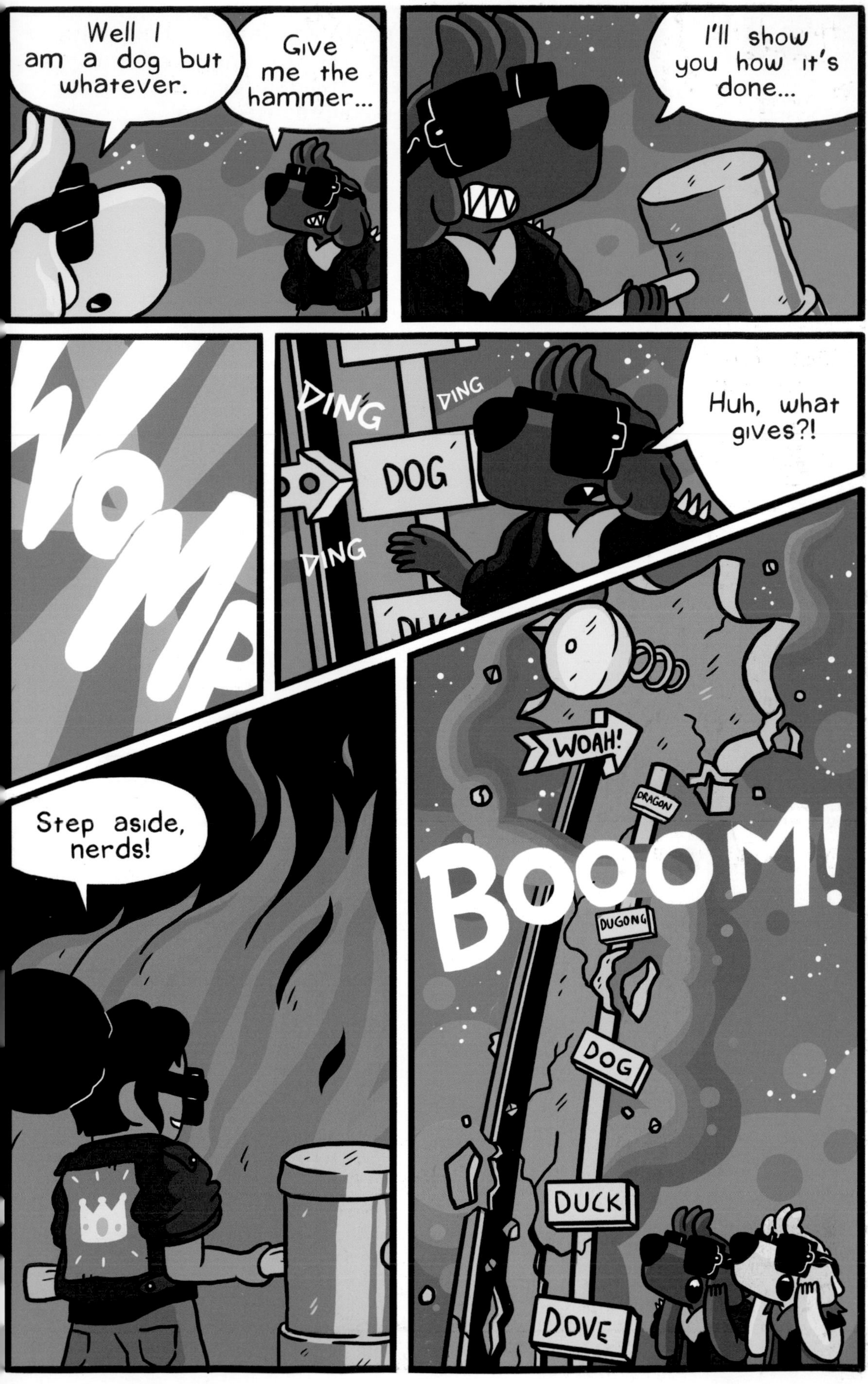

Well I am a dog but whatever.
Give me the hammer...
I'll show you how it's done...
WOMP
DING
DING
DING
DOG
Huh, what gives?!
Step aside, nerds!
WOAH!
DRAGON
BOOOM!
DUGONG
DOG
DUCK
DOVE

DOG DAYS ARE OVER

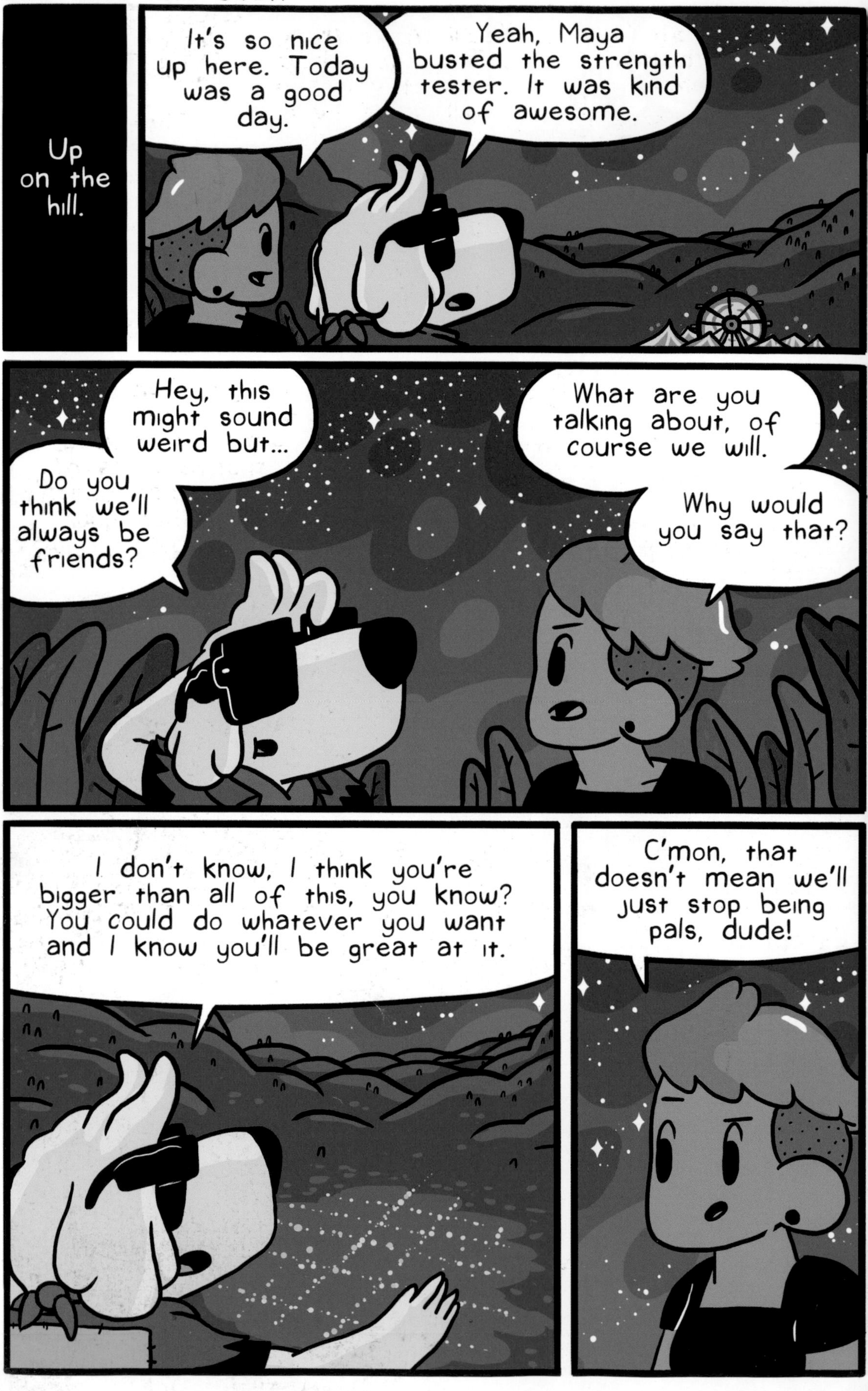
Up on the hill.
It's so nice up here. Today was a good day.
Yeah, Maya busted the strength tester. It was kind of awesome.
Hey, this might sound weird but...
Do you think we'll always be friends?
What are you talking about, of course we will.
Why would you say that?
I don't know, I think you're bigger than all of this, you know? You could do whatever you want and I know you'll be great at it.
C'mon, that doesn't mean we'll just stop being pals, dude!

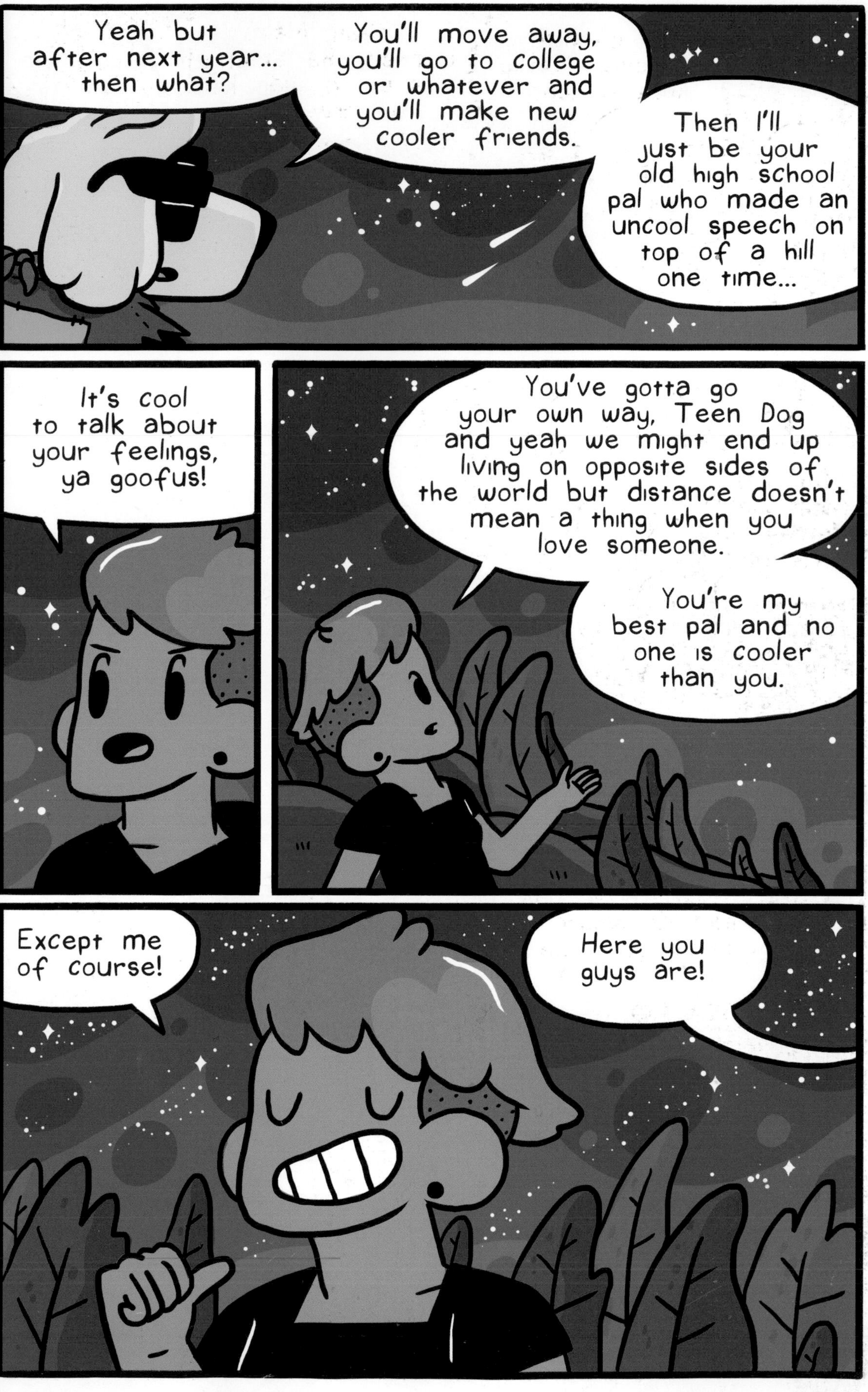
Yeah but after next year... then what?
You'll move away, you'll go to college or whatever and you'll make new cooler friends.
Then I'll just be your old high school pal who made an uncool speech on top of a hill one time...
It's cool to talk about your feelings, ya goofus!
You've gotta go your own way, Teen Dog and yeah we might end up living on opposite sides of the world but distance doesn't mean a thing when you love someone.
You're my best pal and no one is cooler than you.
Except me of course!
Here you guys are!

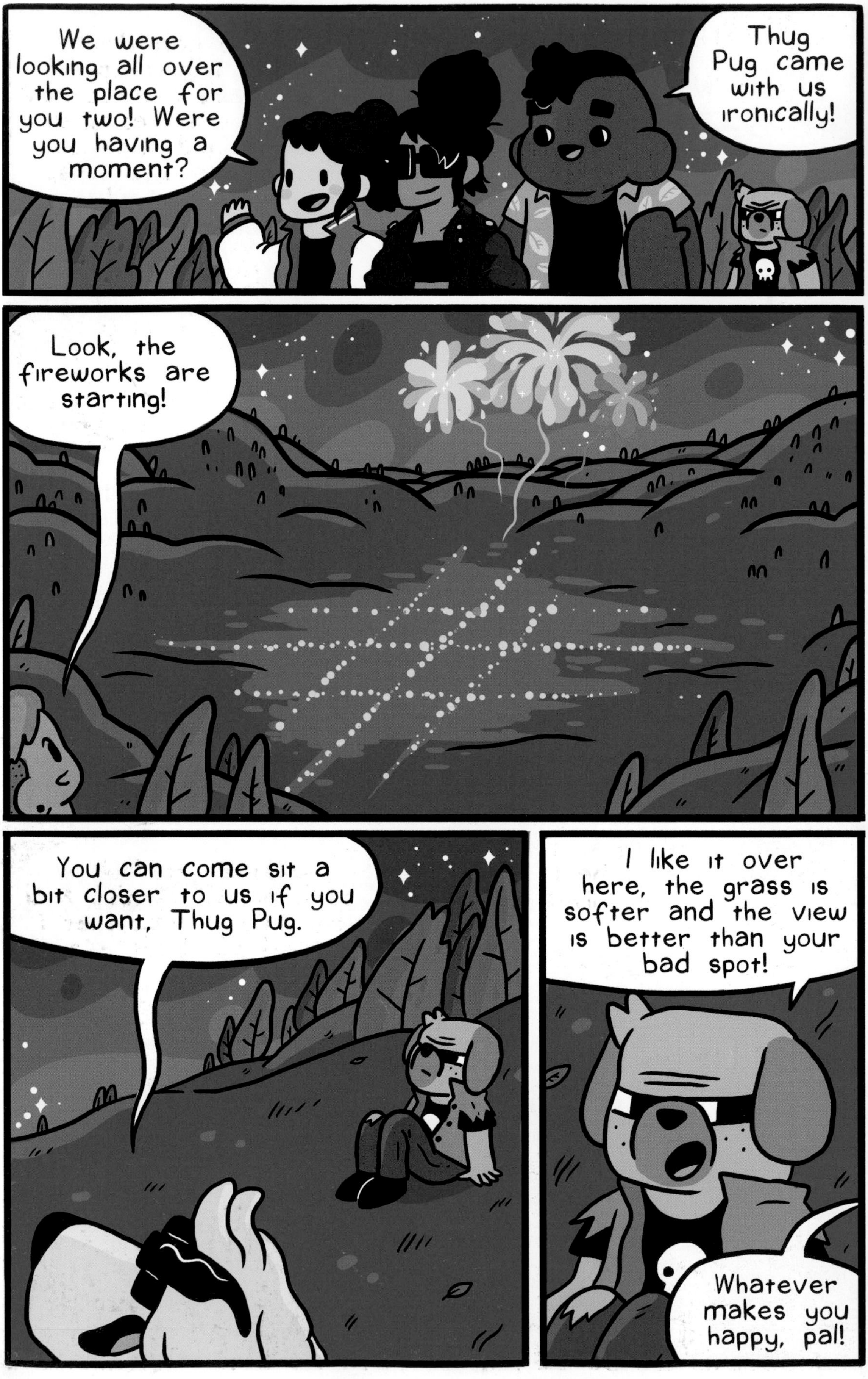
We were looking all over the place for you two! Were you having a moment?
Thug Pug came with us ironically!
Look, the fireworks are starting!
You can come sit a bit closer to us if you want, Thug Pug.
I like it over here, the grass is softer and the view is better than your bad spot!
Whatever makes you happy, pal!

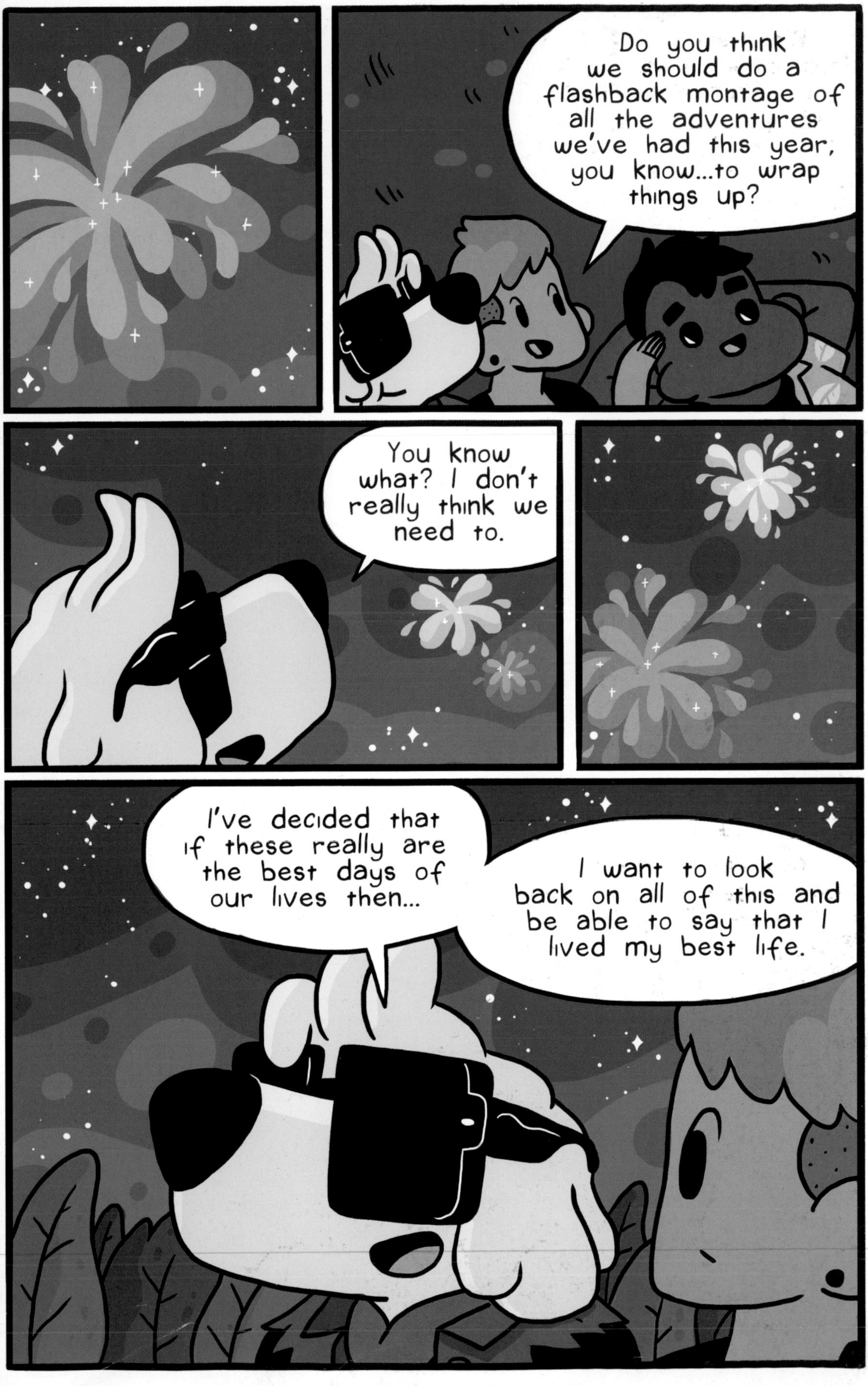
Do you think we should do a flashback montage of all the adventures we've had this year, you know...to wrap things up?
You know what? I don't really think we need to.
I've decided that if these really are the best days of our lives then...
I want to look back on all of this and be able to say that I lived my best life.

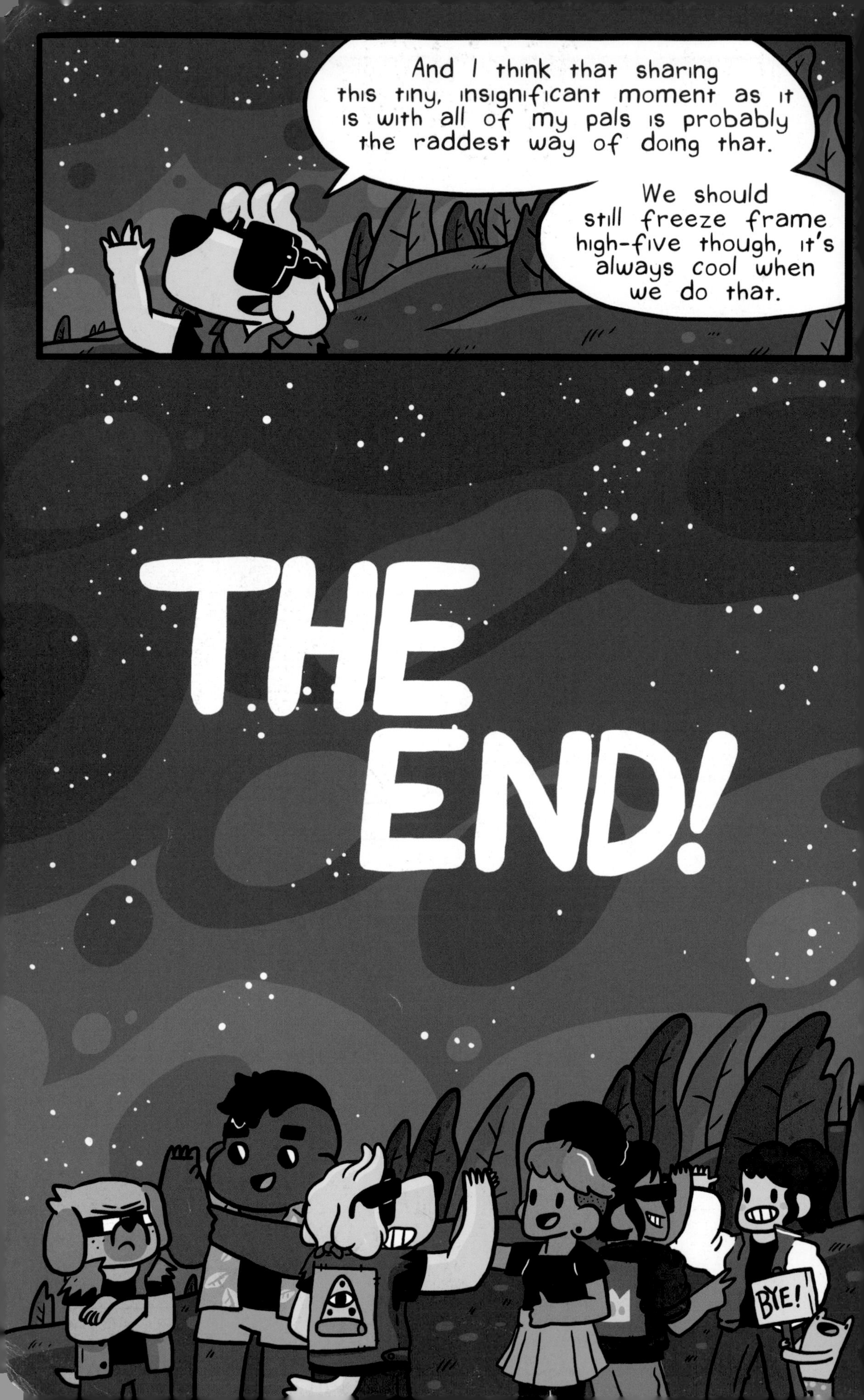
And I think that sharing this tiny, insignificant moment as it is with all of my pals is probably the raddest way of doing that.
We should still freeze frame high-five though, it's always cool when we do that.
THE END!
BYE!

COVER GALLERY

REBEL RECORDS

Cover Art by
JAKE LAWRENCE

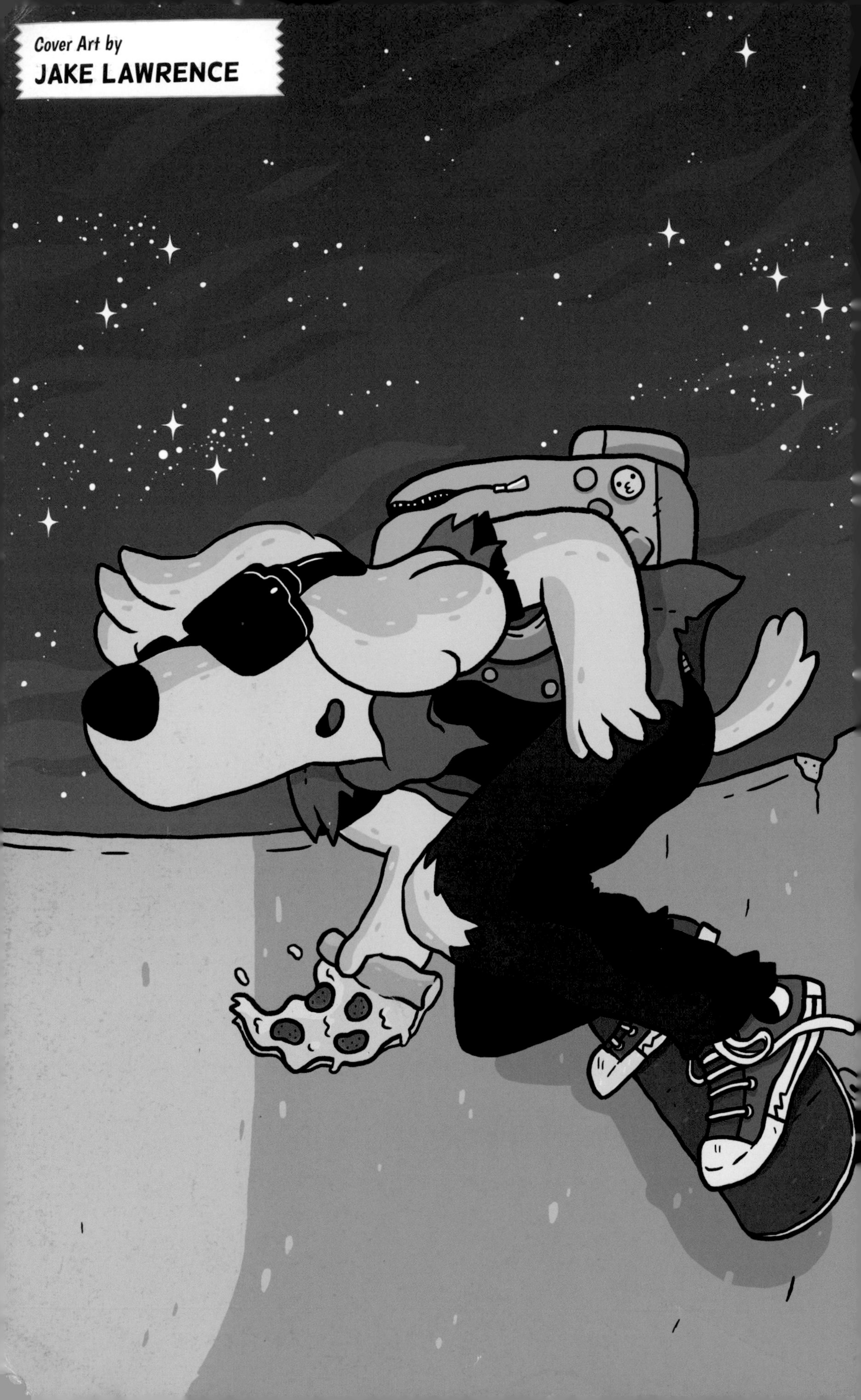

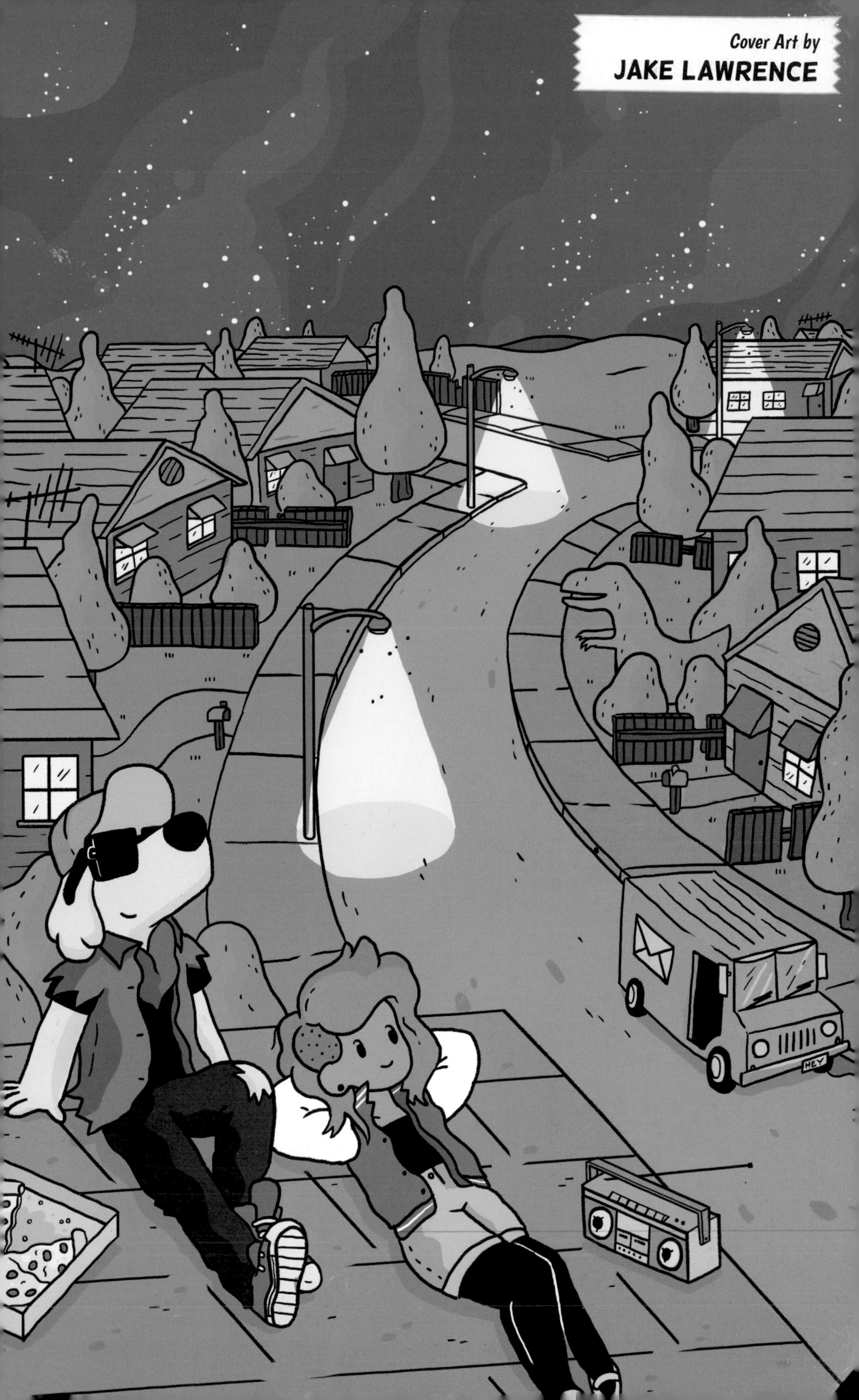

Cover Art by
JAKE LAWRENCE

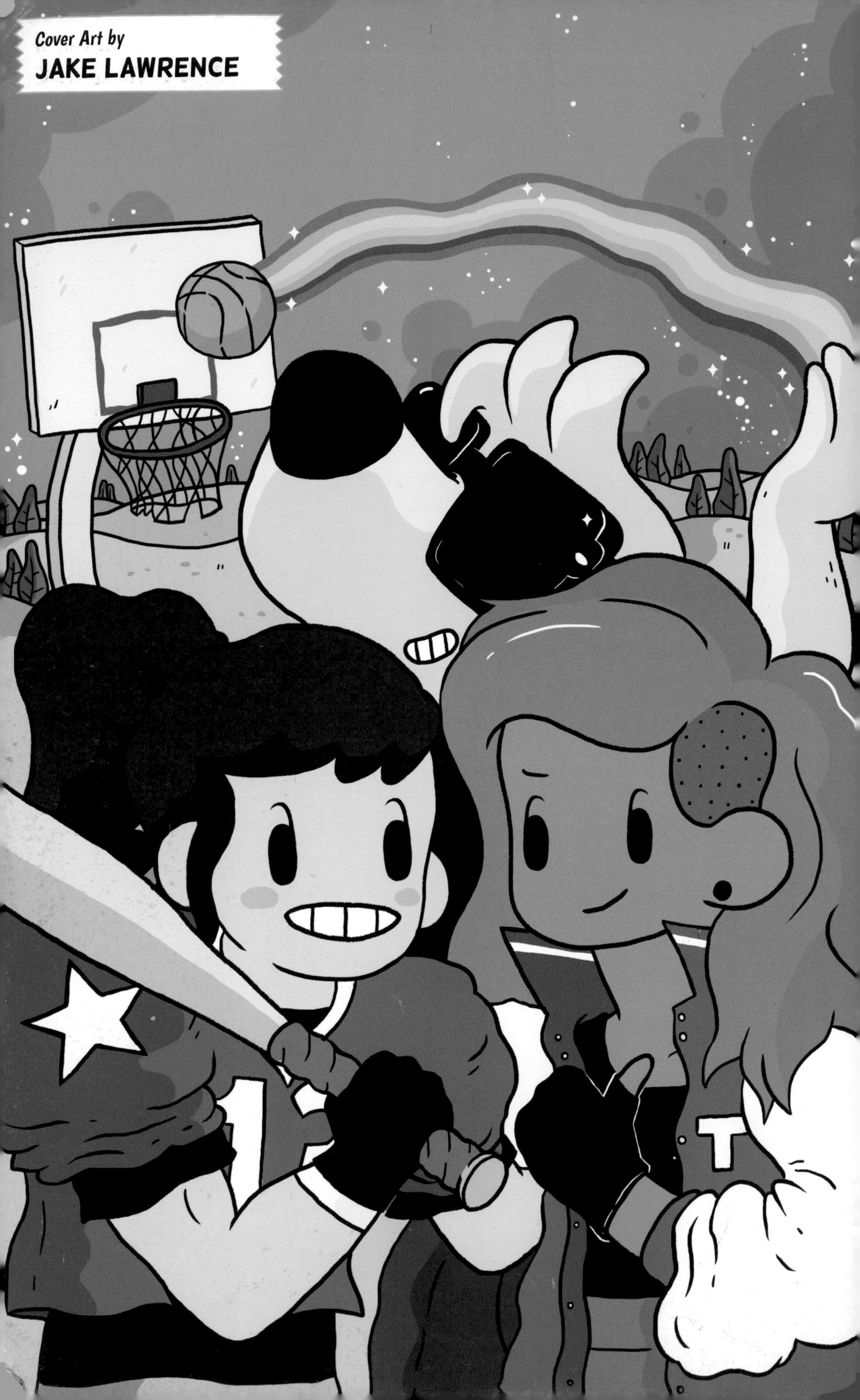
Cover Art by
JAKE LAWRENCE

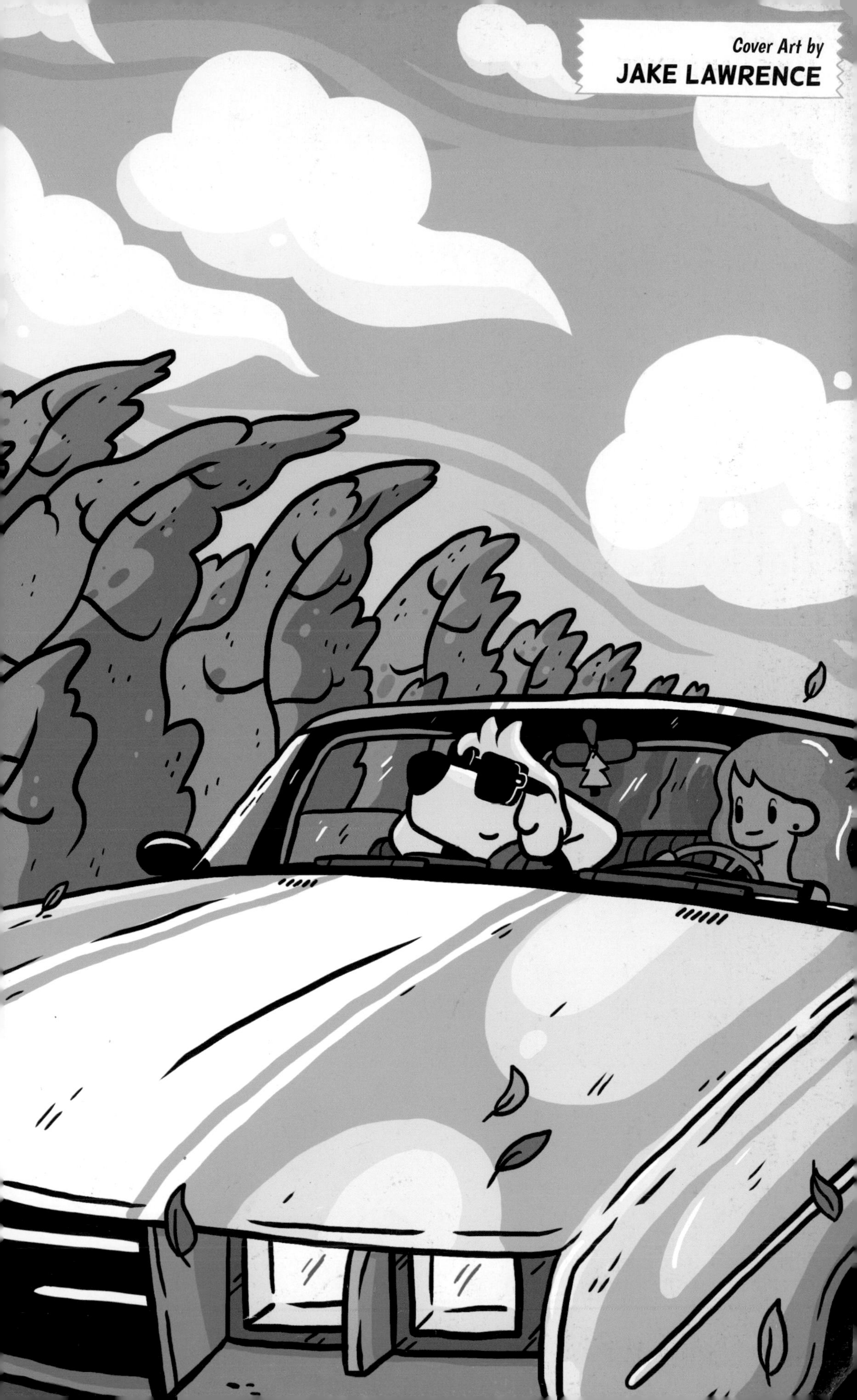

Cover Art by
JAKE LAWRENCE

Cover Art by
JAKE LAWRENCE

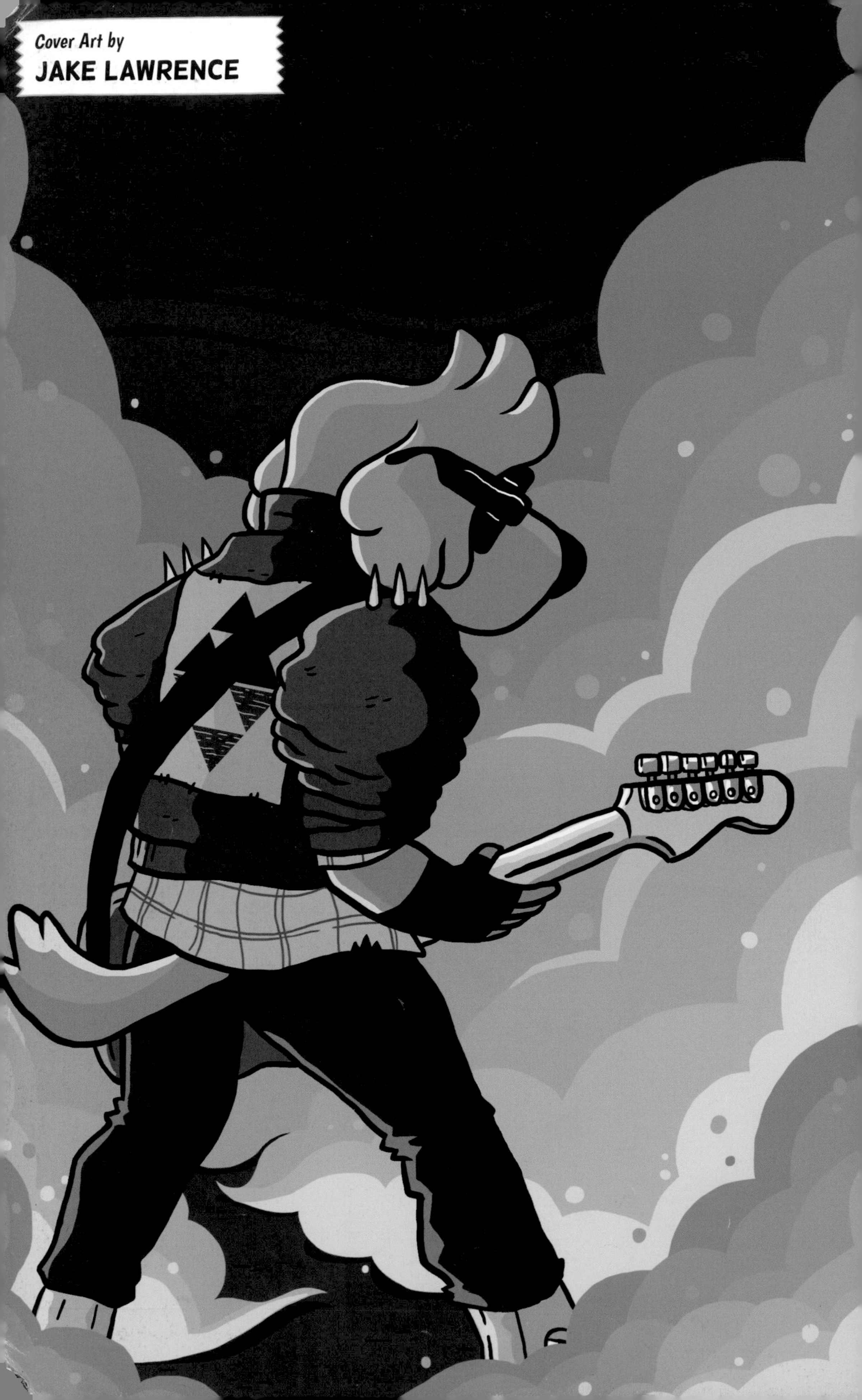

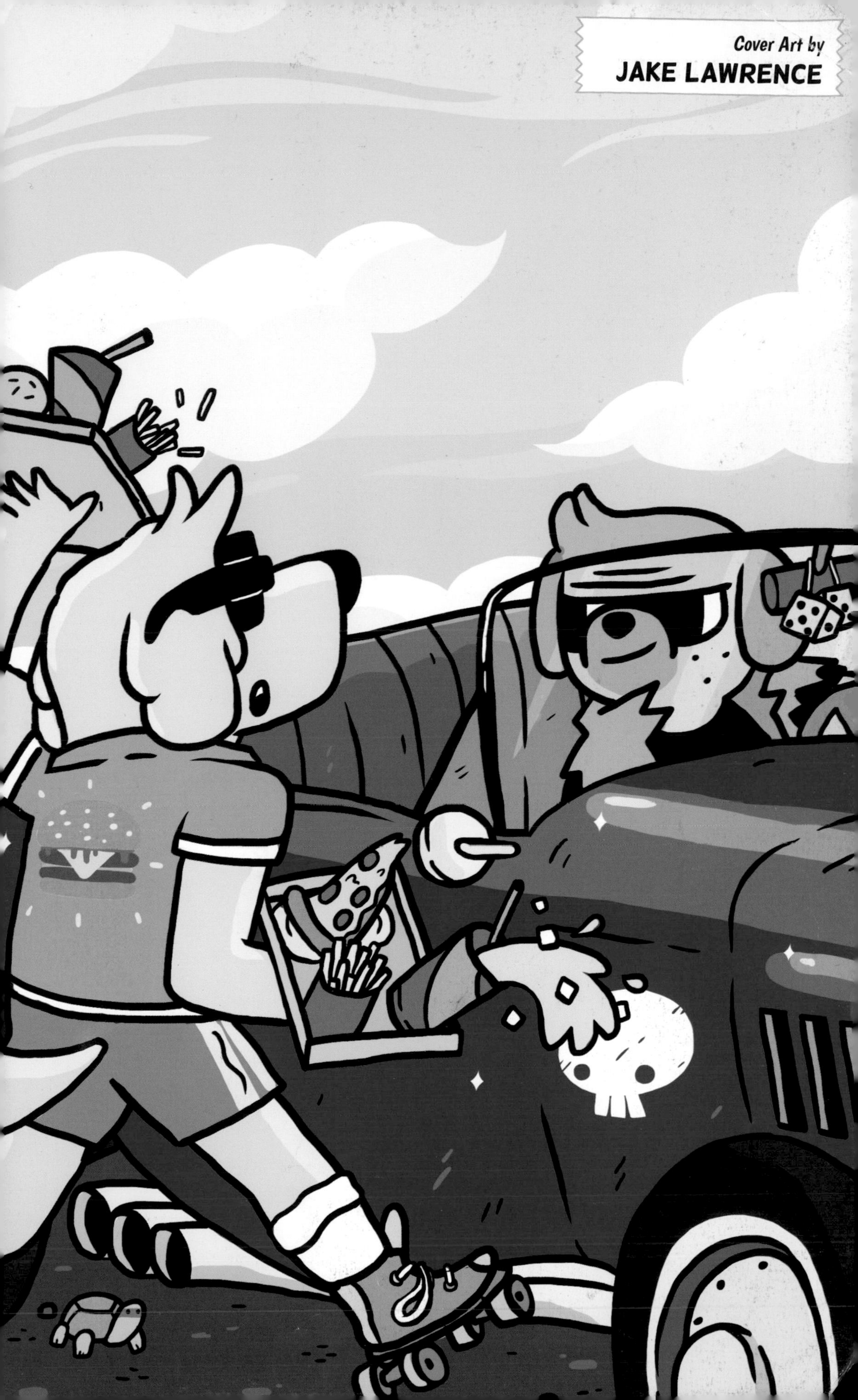
Cover Art by
JAKE LAWRENCE

Cover Art by
JAKE LAWRENCE

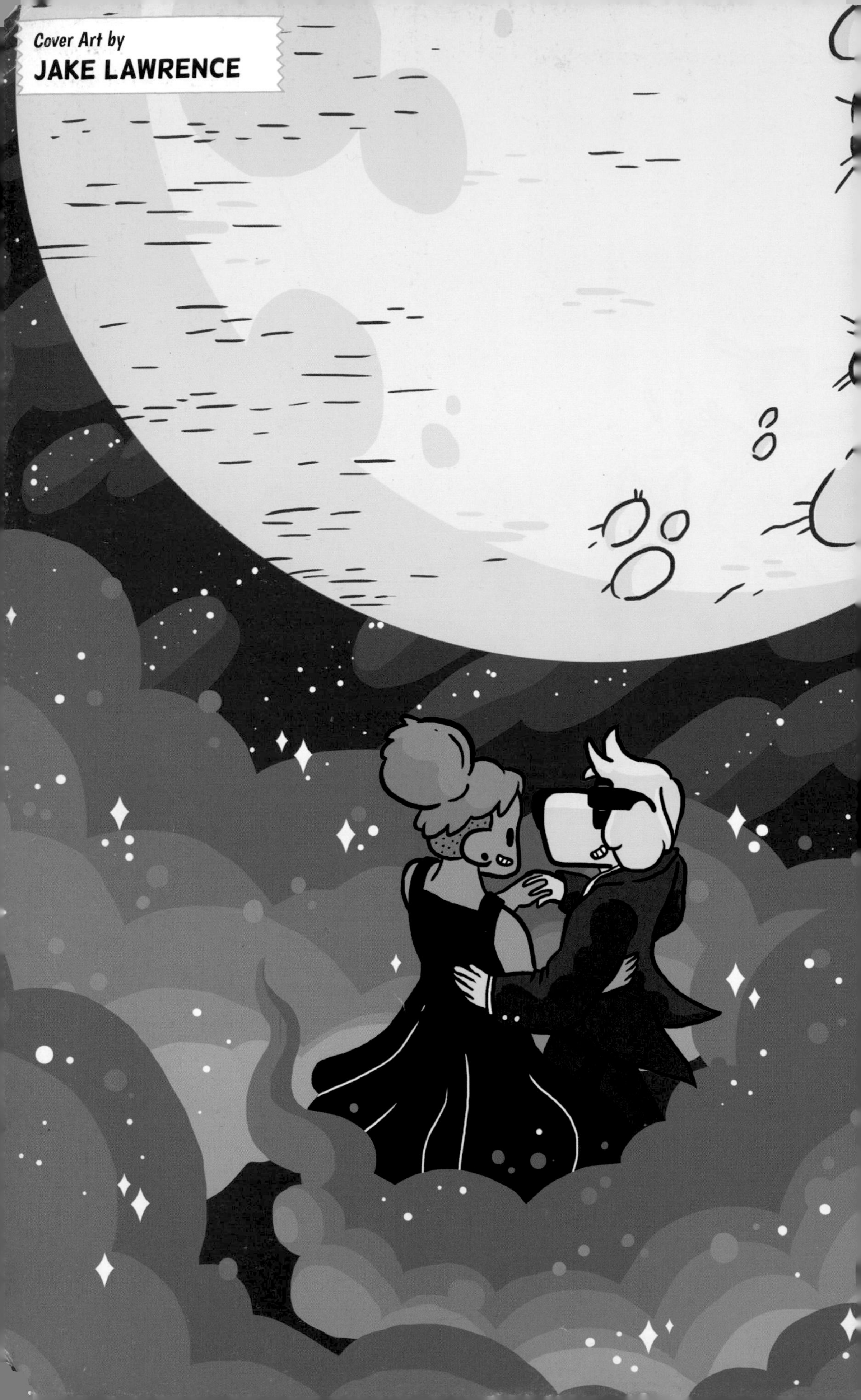

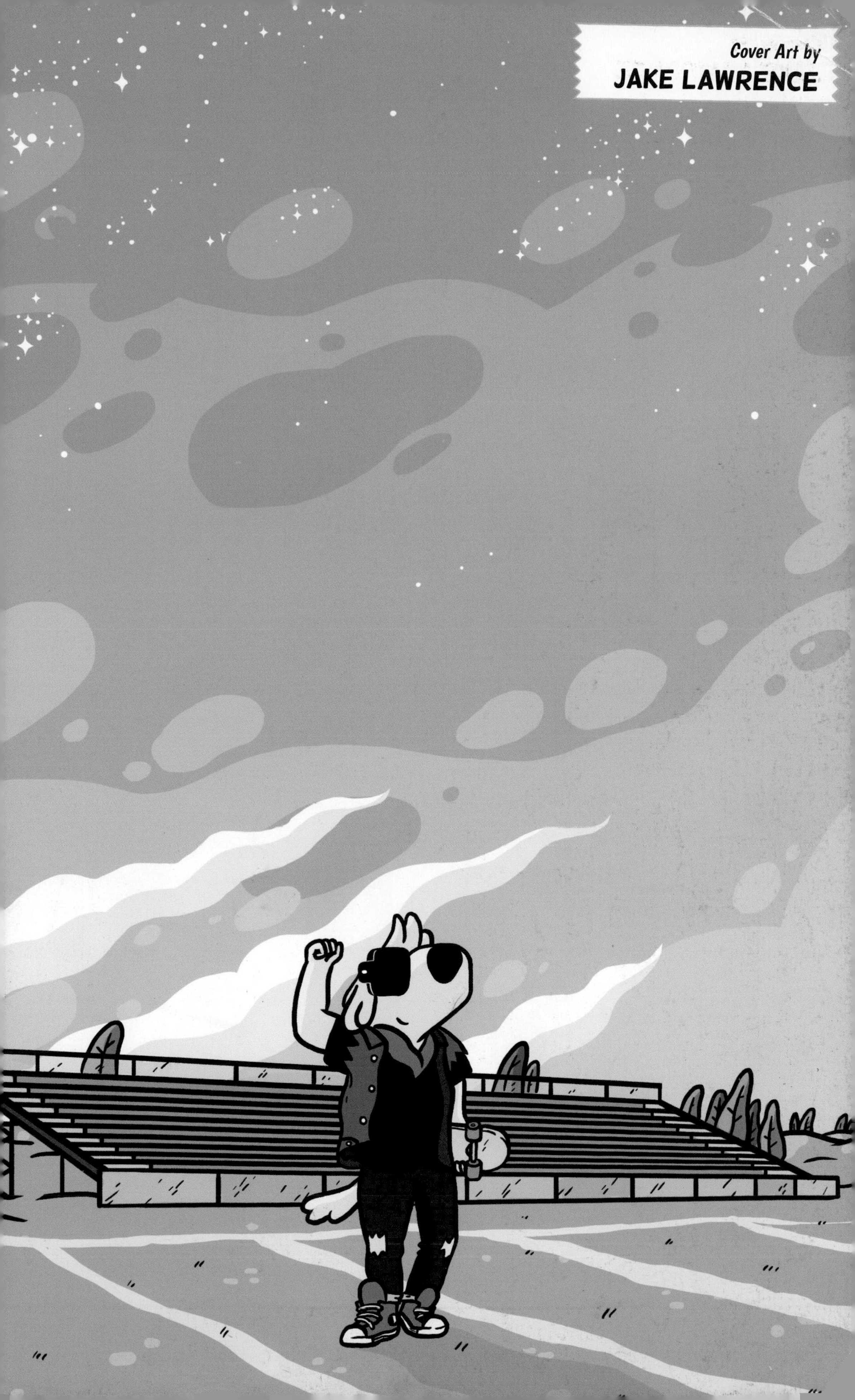

Cover Art by
JAKE LAWRENCE

Cover Art by
RIAN SYGH

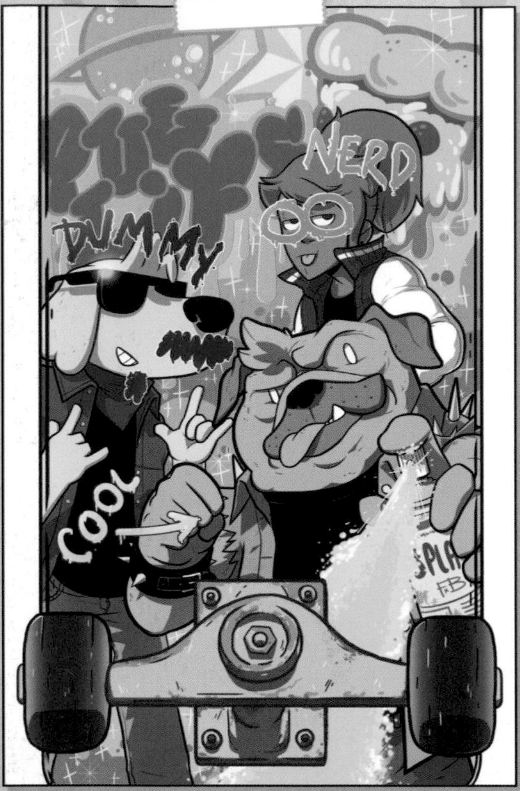
NERD
DUMMY
COOL

Cover Art by
ALEXIS ZIRITT

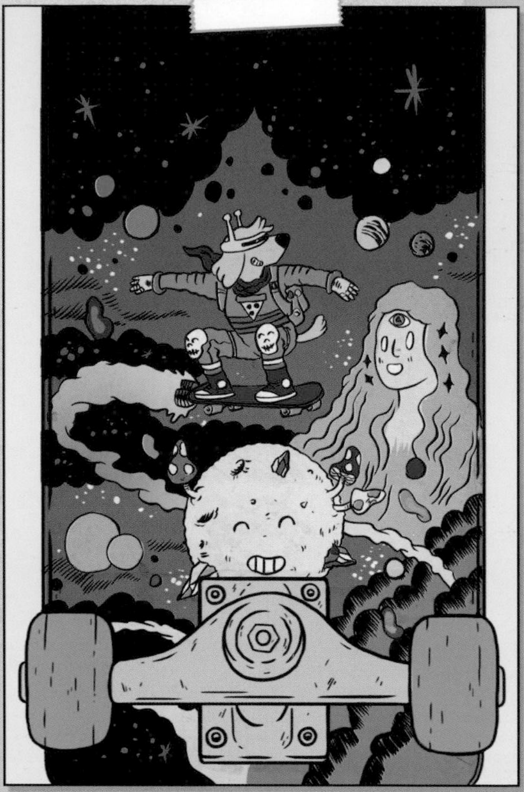

Cover Art by
ADAM X VASS

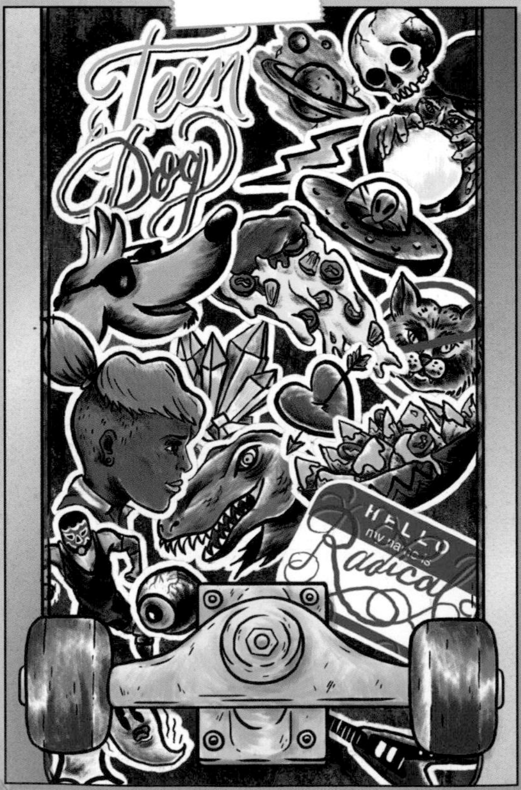
Teen Dog
HELLO
my name is
Radical

Cover Art by
W. SCOTT FORBES

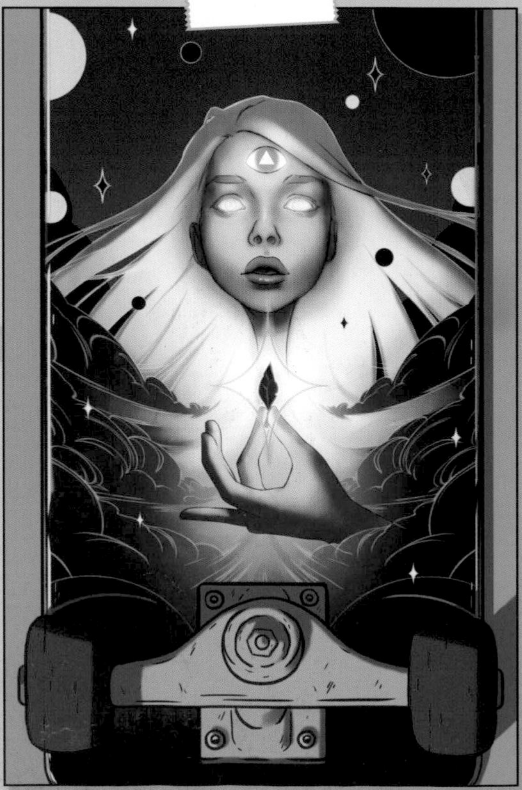

Cover Art by
JEN LEE

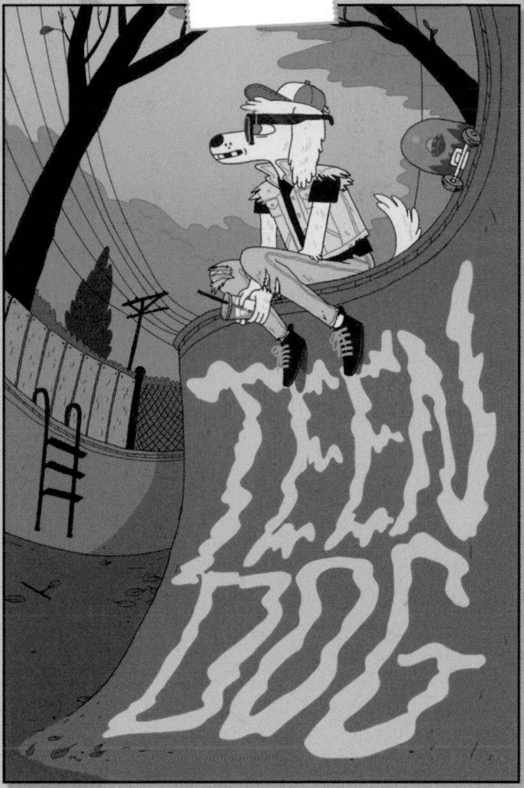
TEEN DOG

Cover Art by
JAKE LAWRENCE

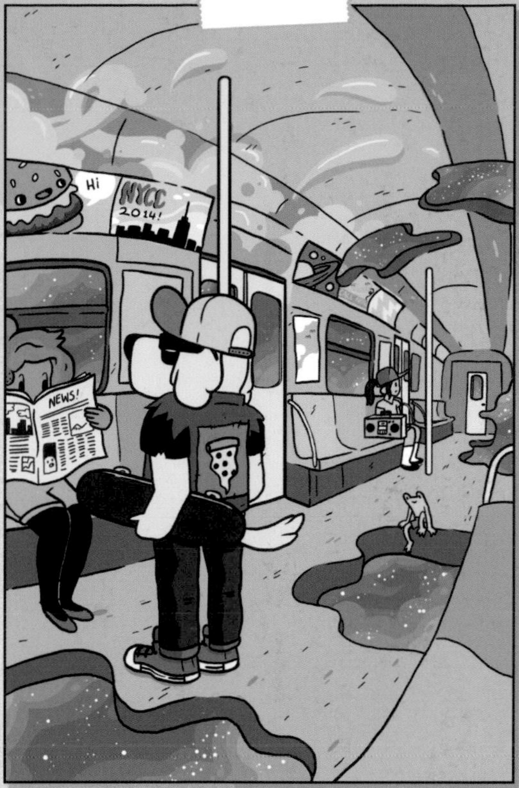
Hi
NYCC 2014!
NEWS!

Cover Art by
KRIS MUKAI

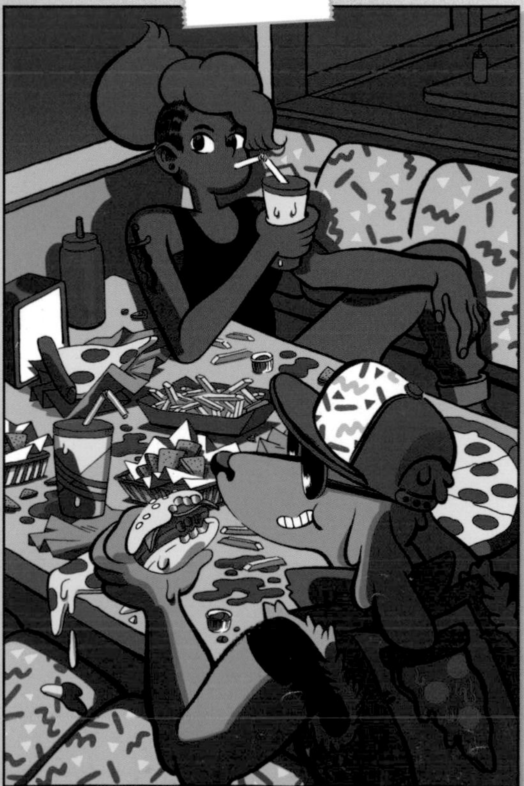

Cover Art by
JESS FINK

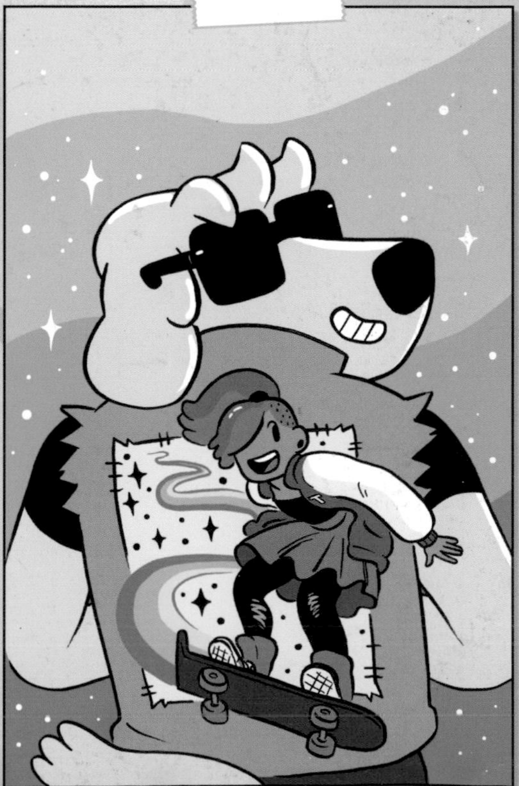

Cover Art by
BECCA TOBIN

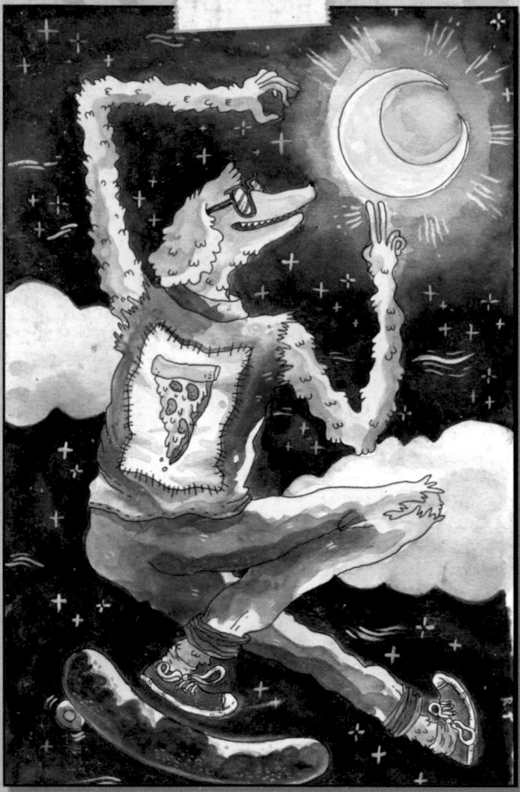

Cover Art by
TOM ECCLES

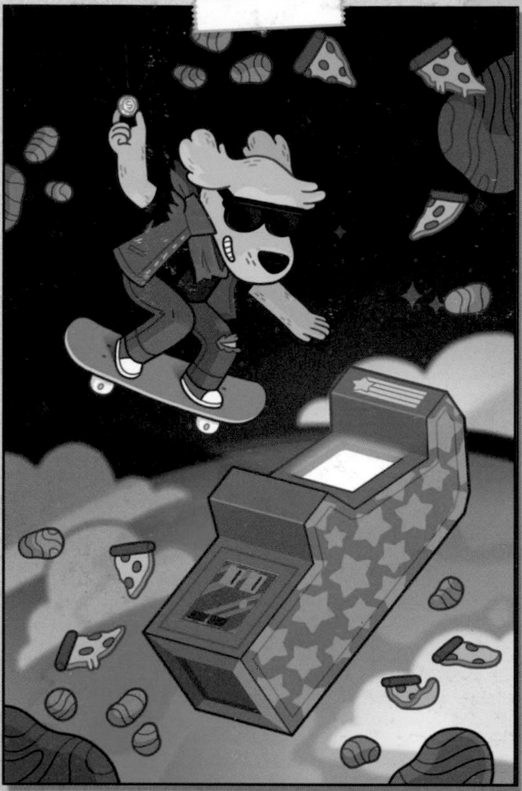

Cover Art by
TOM ECCLES

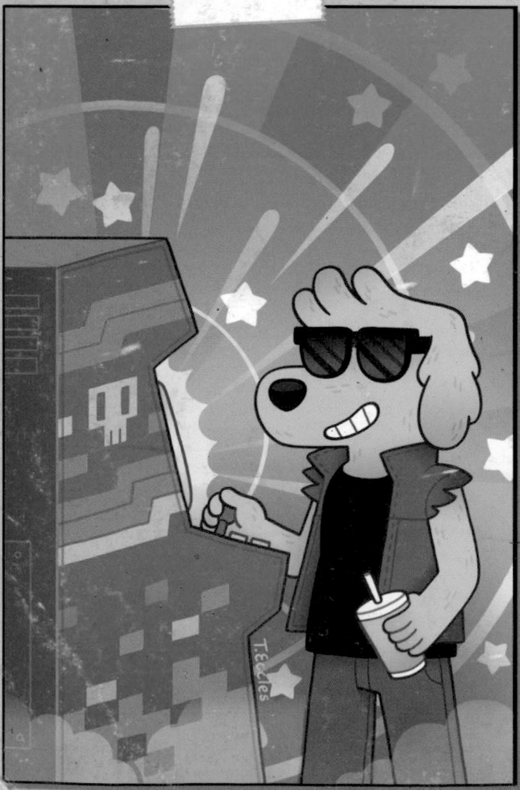

Cover Art by
ANNA STRAIN

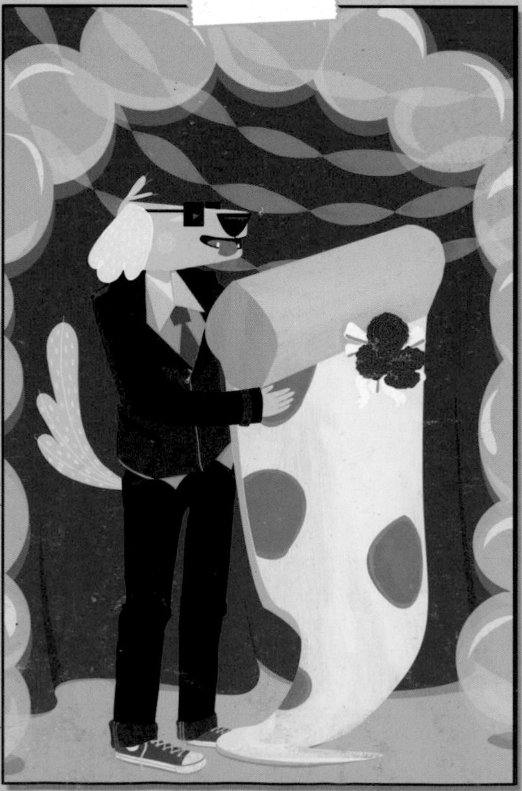